MYTHOLOGY FROM THE ROCK

A COLLECTION OF SHORT STORIES

MYTHOLOGY FROM THE ROCK

EDITED BY ELLEN CURTIS & ERIN VANCE

Library and Archives Canada Cataloguing in Publication

Title: Mythology from the Rock : a collection of short stories / edited by Ellen Curtis & Erin Vance.
Names: Curtis, Ellen, 1993- editor. | Vance, Erin, 1992- editor.
Description: Series statement: From the Rock ; 8
Identifiers: Canadiana (print) 20210181036 | Canadiana (ebook) 20210181060 | ISBN 9781774780305 (softcover) | ISBN 9781774780312 (PDF)
Subjects: CSH: Short stories, Canadian (English)—Newfoundland and Labrador | CSH: Canadian fiction (English)—21st century
Classification: LCC PS8329.5.N3 M98 2021 | DDC C813/.01089718—dc23

Distributed by:
Engen Books
www.engenbooks.com
submissions@engenbooks.com
First mass market paperback printing: April 2021
Cover Image: © 2021 Kit Sora Photography

Engen Books thanks Kit Sora Photography, Mae Dalton-Summers, and Sci-Fi on the Rock for helping make this collection possible.

CONTENTS

Introduction
Dr. Christopher Lockett

At first glance, the idea of *Mythology from the Rock* might seem, if not impertinent, than at least counter-intuitive. After all, the word "mythology" connotes ancient cultures and timeless stories that articulate universal truths—Gilgamesh, the Fall of Troy, Ra in his chariot soaring across the vault of the sky. What claim does a sparsely populated society scarcely a few centuries old, clinging to an island at the periphery of a continent, have to be in that august library?

Naw, b'y ... Folklore, mythology's rustic and parochial sibling, seems more the thing—as indeed the reams of pages filled by scholars about the tales told and shanties sung by generations of Newfoundlanders would seem to attest.

But is this really a fair distinction? Or does it aggrandize mythology—something abetted by such champions of the form as Carl Gustav Jung and Joseph Campbell—by eliding the fact that all stories start small? That all myths find their origins as a set of tropes laden with local accents and sensibilities? That, through the accidents of history and the rise and fall of civilizations, find themselves repeated and disseminated, with all the rough edges of local inflection we associate with folklore sanded off, until the stories take on the sheen of universality?

The late lamented Sir Terry Pratchett, recounting how as a child he tore through his local library "like a chainsaw," said so fast was his reading "that I read my way into the mythology and folklore section without realizing it." It was folklore, he said, that he found more amenable, as the gods of mythology were largely dull and stupid, "and in any case mythology just seemed like folklore of the winners."

It might seem odd to cast aspersions on mythology in an introduction to a collection of stories about or dealing with mythology, but rest assured that is not my intent here. I am, rather, interested to do what the stories in this volume themselves do to greater or lesser extents: trouble our understanding of "mythology" writ large. Mythology is better understood in the plural—not a singular or monolithic concept, but a collection of stories and narratives that, through repetition and retelling down through the years, come to define the way we understand the world. Mythology, suggested Roland Barthes, is not something ancient and timeless, but a function of language that occurs when we start mistaking history for nature. Which is to say: when we start assuming that products of human imagination and artifice—law, for example, or justice, mercy, good and evil, the hero's journey—are naturally occurring, extant *things,* as opposed to compelling concepts emerging from the stories we tell each other.

All mythology starts small. It becomes mythology writ large when, in our cultural imagination, it is taken as expressing something universal—or, conversely, when its fictionality fades away. And if mythology is the folklore of the winners, then, like history (which is written by the winners), it obliges us to be skeptical … and remember its humbler origins.

And, if one is so inclined, to write stories reminding us of that.

Yasmine Dalloul

Yasmine Dalloul is an astonishing fresh talent from Kuwait City, and currently residing in Montreal.

Her previous work includes articles such as "Za'atar Grows in Palestine" in *A Matter of Taste.*

Mythology from the Rock will be her first fiction credit, with her poem 'Old Wives.'

Old Wives

Old wives they sit and they tell tall tales
How many of them are true?

Legends and cautions to us they regale
And I shall tell them to you.

You, who has birthed a beautiful girl,
with rich chocolate hair and eyes,
But less lucky is she than a boy would be,
so for a mostly blessed life you should try

A lady when born as an infant still ensure
her arms to be bare
And this will not happen only until
you diminish her follicles of hair

"But babies their hair must wait to grow"
any old person might think
But ah, she may one day have hair on her toes,
so we bathe her over the sink

"Bathe her with what?" You begin to ask,
weary of what you might hear
You slaughter a bat and take his blood
to dab it behind her ear

"Which ear?" You wonder because as you know
there's always something to say
Such things must be done from the right-hand first
as it keeps the Devil away!

Baby then gets bathed in blood of bat
her body rubbed down and rinsed
"A foolproof method, in blood I once sat
and haven't had body hair since!"

And shall baby be cursed with envy
there are ways for her to get by
Keep whispers of malice at bay
and give her a protective evil eye

A glass blue eye or Fatima's hand
both charms shall do the trick
And after each praise you knock on wood
if you want all good luck to stick

And shall her beauty start to fade
or her fortune begin to hollow
Take her to the old mountain woman
who will give her an egg to swallow

"How come an egg?" a curious fact;
this egg has special powers
For the birth of the bird was taken to God
and thus prayed upon for hours

And if she is cursed then you will notice
she's taking much too long to be wed
Wrap a ring in a cloth placed under her pillow
for her to sleep with each night in her bed

And if she fails to attract a prince,
it could be from a heavier curse
Write a prayer on paper wrapped up in a cloth
and hide it in her purse

"But beware," you should tell her,
"keep it concealed, allowing no one to ever find
the secret prayer that sits by your side
meant to guide you at all times"

As for her house, be sure that she prays
the verses for them to bless
And refrain from hanging pictures with faces
for the *djinn* will be able to watch her undress

The *djinn* they are the sneakiest of creatures
hidden in objects and walls
They make themselves appear whenever they want,
or you might never see them at all

They come in different shapes and sizes
evil and good, fire, water and air they are too
But with a talisman here and a couple of spits there
you can keep them away from you

Beware, do not anger, scorn or tempt them
with satin, perfume and lace
For when least expected she may wake up
with drawings all over her face

Alas, for fair beauty and for life to be pleasant,
such good fortunes must be preserved
As the envious and jealous and the overzealous
may take what they do not deserve

And all around us in this life are tricks
that are waiting to scare
So. the ultimate protection against all jinxing
is for beauty to cover her hair

It is these tall tales all small girls are told between the
deserts, mountains and seas

And for such little myths we live our whole lives with all
the old wives to please.

Hannah Jenkins

Hannah Jenkins is an incredible up-and-coming author who is taking the Newfoundland writing community by storm. She has won the monthly Kit Sora Flash Fiction competition twice with her stories "Coming Out" (February 2020) and "Waiting" (July 2020). She has ranked highly in the competition many other months in addition, placing as a runner-up in March 2019 with "Flicker." She was published in the special COVID-19 issue of Word Magazine with her article "How to Succeed in Skip-Bo by Really, Really Trying."

In 2020 she was awarded the Moynes-Keshen John McCrae Poetry Award.

Pygmalion and Galatea

One

Today, God mumbles.

He does this often, muttering curses Galatea assumes lands in some other far-off shoreline to hit some other, far less fortunate woman.

With only half her mind constructed, Galatea does not know much about this world. But she knows of the sea, and the sky, and the grass. She knows of the air and its birds, who are also only half constructed. And she knows of the television set, which sits in the corner of God's living room. Often, the screen screams. It has shown her many things throughout her short life: violence, sex, races, art, plays.

Some days, if God is angry enough, if he slams his door hard enough, the television blinks, as though it were human.

Galatea learns much from the television. There are commercials, which God hates, but Galatea loves. They show her how to eat, drink, drive, and dance. They show her babies and old men, puppies and elephants; they show her hands entwined together, and blades skating across ice. Most of all, the television tells her of God. Often, the television plays a sermon or two and God listens to the men praise him. At least, Galatea assumes it is him they are praising. He must, of course, be God. What other creature could create life like he does? Who else could encompass an entire world in his canvas? Her God is an artist. She likes it that way.

Everyday he comes to work on her, promising that she will be as perfect as possible. That no woman alive could have eyes as blue as hers or skin as gleaming white. She would be kind, thoughtful, docile – not like the other women. The other women, Galatea learns, are whores. They also will not let Him touch them. This confuses Galatea, but her mouth has not yet been painted, her lips are unable to part, and even if she could question God, she would not want to. She has seen the other canvases, torn and brutalized with half drawn women on the flaps of white parchment. Did they displease him? Did they speak too quickly? Learn too slowly? Galatea did not intend to discover the cause of this wrath. So, Galatea did not question God.

Today, God finishes outlining himself. He is slimmer on the canvas, his beard fuller, but it is him. His eyes are the same gentle almond shape, the same nose adorns his face, his cheekbones sit exactly where they ought to and Galatea longs to reach out her hand to graze her fingertips along the soft grey line there. Soon, God draws his right hand, entwined with hers and Galatea breathes her first sigh. It is tiny, infinitesimal, and it aches to release, but she has a companion now; she is no longer alone, and this of all things, must be celebrated with breath.

Soon, God strokes her hair with the pad of his thumb, bids her goodnight and Galatea is left alone with her own smaller Paper God.

Suddenly Galatea becomes far too aware of her body, when before she struggled to notice it. What does she say to him, now that she thinks she can speak? Does she sing, like the people in the church do? Does she praise him? Does she kneel? Can she kneel?

Before she can decide what to do, The Paper God squeezes her fingers.

"My Lord?" she says timidly, her excitement and fear threatening to overthrow her.

"My Lord?" he replies, sounding confused.

"Of course," Galatea suddenly realizes. "You're only new, you don't know of yourself yet. You are God," she explains, eager to tell him of everything she knows, "or at least a drawing of him."

"A drawing?"

"Yes. One day, we will be painted, and it will be beautiful, you told me so. The other you, that is," she quickly corrected. "The bigger one, the one out there, that draws the world."

"The one that draws the world?" he asks slowly. "And what world are we in?"

"Ancient Greece, he tells me. It'll be lovely when it's done. And one day, he will give us life, proper life. We will be large, beautiful things. We will leave the painting and join him out there. And -" she falters, blushes, "... and we will be in love... or perhaps he and I will be in love. I do not quite understand God's will yet. But everyday he tells me more of his plans for me."

The Paper God is silent. Galatea worries for a moment that he has reverted to lead. But finally, slowly he speaks.

"What is your name?"

"Galatea."

"How do you know?"

"He calls me it. And it's the name of the painting. Pygmalion and Galatea."

The Paper God thinks. "So, Pygmalion, that must be me then?"

Galatea pauses. It makes sense. "I suppose so," she says.

There is another silence.

"It hurts to speak," Pygmalion says.

"It does," she agrees. The corners of their mouths are still stiff. "I think it will get easier, once the paint comes."

Another pause.

"We don't have to speak," Galatea offers.

"No," he assures her, his lips turning into a crinkled smile. "I want to speak with you."

And so, Pygmalion and Galatea speak the whole night through.

Two

"It's charming," she assures Pygmalion while the snores of their God drift in from his bedroom.

"Charming? I look demonic!" Pygmalion laughs.

God seemed less concerned with his own likeness then with Galatea's and so Pygmalion now had a smidgen of beige paint extending past the lines of his right ear, like sand drifting away from the shoreline of his face.

"It adds character," Galatea tells him

"What character is that?"

"You're rugged now. Adventurous, even. It's very handsome."

"It's messy."

"It's cute."

Pygmalion sighs and smiles, "Fine, it's cute."

"Besides, it'll be corrected soon enough. God promised."

"But you wish he'd leave it?"

Galatea examines her lover's face again. "I like the humanity of it," she says simply.

There is of course, nothing human about pigment floating past one's being. But there was something profoundly human about the error of it. And it was this trait that stirred the affection in Galatea's heart. Pygmalion was beautiful, far more beautiful than God, but when he sang to her at night, his voice horrendously off key, that was when Galatea fell in love.

It had been weeks since Pygmalion had first spoken to her, weeks of stretching limbs and exploring hands. They had learned of each other as thoroughly as possible. Everyday there was something new added to their beings. Skin, lips, toes, the shadow beneath their cheekbones in the setting sunlight. She had hoped that they would be painted into a bright, blue day, but she had come to love the purples and pinks of her horizon. It wasn't a bad sight to look at for forever.

Forever. It was something that hung between them. *Forever*. They knew somewhere that this was true. That they would be here forever. Here. In this tiny stretch of beach with only the gulls and each other to love. Perhaps God would cut the painting up, but even then, would they really die? Or would they survive somehow, ripped in two, not quite alive, not quite dead. Both options were horrendous to imagine.

What if they outlived Him? What if they watched their creator die and were carried off to some storage room, to stare at each other for eternity. Would she still love him in a thousand years? In a hundred? Tomorrow? Already their loneliness weighed them down. They watched the TV when they could and spoke about what they had seen. And then they made love. That was all. She had no other life, no other opinions, she had no stories to tell. Neither did he. But this did not seem to bother him.

"We have today," he told her once. "All we have is today, and tomorrow we may have another today, maybe not. Just focus on this one."

She imagined one day, when their God was gone, and they had recounted every television program they had ever seen, repeated every film they had ever watched, regurgitated every second-hand account they had ever witnessed, one day, they would finally run out of things to say or things to think and they would be too tired to hold each other any longer. So, they would lie down on the sand instead and look up at the stagnant sunset and finally die.

It was her best-case scenario, to die beneath the ever-falling sun, with all their words spoken, all their love made, all the world explored. It would be peaceful, she hoped. But today they had watched a new show and theorized about a sketch on God's windowsill; today she had been tickled, and kissed, and asked her universe all of her questions as though it would answer, and she had basked in the silence as though it was the ever-elusive ocean.

Today was no day to die.

Three

"Looks like another today, Gal," he tells her as she sleepily opens her eyes. It was time to prepare herself for God to enter the room. She hated standing still for him. But she hated the idea of being ripped up more.

"We have another today," he repeated.

"We do."

"What shall we do when he leaves?"

An idea had been creeping into her mind recently. Could they paint? Could they create something else, someone else? If they took the still wet brown from a nearby tree, could they make a dog? Could they paint themselves a roasted chicken and finally know of food? Could they feast? If they painted more water, could they finally bathe in it?

"Have you ever thought about… later?" she poses hesitantly.

His hand halted slightly in her hair before resuming its measured strokes. "What do you mean by later?"

"The future. Years from now."

God's snores filled the silence.

"No."

"Why?"

"I like now," he tells her with a smile.

"I do too. But it could be better, couldn't it? More sea, more plants – "

"And how do you propose to get them?"

Galatea took in a shaky breath. Her voice was barely a whisper. "We keep the paint. Store it. Save it up while its wet. Then we draw our own creations. In the corner where he wouldn't notice."

Pygmalion grabbed her arms which had started shaking in excitement. "You really believe he won't notice?"

"So, what if he does? He made us, didn't he? How do we know he doesn't want us to come alive for him, to make our own world?"

"Moving paintings would likely only serve to scare him."

"Scare God? We can't scare him! He's –"

"He isn't God," Pygmalion interrupted her sharply.

Silence again.

"What do you mean?"

"He isn't God. He's just a man. A lonely, pathetic, slightly artistic man. If there is a God, it isn't the man sleeping with a bag of Doritos in the next room over."

Gal paused for a moment. Tried to process what he was saying.

"We're here by fluke," Pygmalion told her. Then, gently, his face softening, he took her hands. "Let's enjoy the miracle. Don't push it, love."

He reached up to tuck a strand of hair behind her ear, but she jerked violently away. "Of course, he's God. And he would want us to be happy."

Desperately, she turned toward the living room and called out to him.

Pygmalion's hand wrapped around her mouth, the other pulled at her waist, bringing her into him. "Shhh! What are you doing? You'll wake him. Do you wish to be ripped in two? Like the others?"

He forcefully moved her face toward the torn, discarded drawings in the corner of the room. "Is that what you want?" he whispered in her ear.

She bit down on his hand, breaking the skin until red paint ran coldly down her chin. He grunted but did not release her

"Calm down, Gal, please. Calm down."

The heat in her belly was suddenly diminished. She felt shaky, hot, and tired. She leaned against Pygmalion tears in her eyes.

"I can cry," she says.

"What?"

"I can cry. Why would a God make us capable of pain if we were not also capable of joy?"

"We have joy," he assured her. "With each other. I'm only trying to keep you safe."

"No, no there has to be more." Gal's voice hitched and broke.

"Don't you understand yet?" Pygmalion bursts out, shoving her away from him. "There is no 'more'. There is no 'after', there is no 'future', no 'decisions', no 'choice', not even an 'us'. We are whatever he wants us to be."

"No," Galatea interjects, tears streaming down her face, running streaks through Pygmalion's blood. "No, we have a choice. We always have a choice."

"What is it then? What choice is it that you see? He controls everything! We aren't even human, Gal. We don't even exist."

"We don't exist?" Galatea asks incredulously, taking a small step back. "Am I not alive? Do I not have hands, and skin, and hair? Do I not breathe and think? I must exist!" she screams, balling her hands into her ivory garment. "I must exist for I know of myself, for I can think, and, and dream, and hope. If I were nothing, truly nothing, I would think of nothing, I would know of nothing. I exist!" her voice cracks. "I exist! I exist, I exist… I exist...I exist…"

Four

Galatea stares across the storage unit, the graveyard where she always knew they would end up. The edges of the cardboard box in front of her had started to sag and grow mold.

They did not age exactly. But they faded and chipped. The crack in Pygmalion's face acted like a wrinkle in her mind, a smile line across his left cheek. They had had a long life together. A good one, she thinks. All things considered. Their God had died. Galatea supposed, then, that he was not a god and Pygmalion had been right all those years ago.

She remembers breaking like it was a dream. *I exist... I exist...*

They did not speak for days afterwards. She hoarded paint when she could. Pygmalion always turned a blind eye.

She painted a child one day, behind a bush where she thought God would not see her. She waited for the baby to cry or move or breathe, but it never did. Soon they painted over it. Pygmalion had taken her stained hand delicately in his. He told her, "That's enough now."

She never painted again.

But she did laugh. And she did cry. And she did scream when God went grocery shopping, just so she could hear herself. She did watch the television, until one day their canvas was moved and all they could hear were the sounds. They made a game of it then. They collected hypotheses in their minds, then, late at night, when God was snoring, they would trade them in secret.

"The man opened a bakery," Galatea would guess.

"It was a hotel," Pygmalion would rebuttal.

"He sounds handsome," she would say another time.

He would laugh and ask her what handsome sounded like.

"Like you of course," she would reply.

She thinks of her best-case scenario again, to die beneath the sunset, with all their words spoken, all their love made, all the world explored. It would be like falling asleep, she hoped.

She closed her eyes and waited for it.

Bronwynn Erskine

An Ontario native currently residing in Newfoundland, Erskine is an avid steampunk enthusiast and acrylic landscape painter.

Erskine made her publishing debut in 2018's *Chillers from the Rock* with her chilling tale: 'Scarlett Ribbons' and returned in 2019's *Flights from the Rock* with: 'Feather and Bone.'

She returns with her new story 'The Lindwyrm's Bride.'

The Lindwyrm's Bride

The sky was still a dull pewter grey when Margaret rose from the enormous feather bed she'd been given at the royal palace. Her newly assigned servants were unaccustomed to having a charge who rose before the sun, so she was alone in the enormous suite of rooms. The bedroom alone was bigger than the cottage where she'd lived with her parents and her older sisters.

She shook away the thoughts of her old life before they could distract her. There was much to do, and little time to do it. Soon enough, she'd be swarmed by a bevy of lady's maids to dress her for her wedding. Her own preparations would need to be completed before they arrived.

She pulled on a robe of wool velvet over her nightgown of fine imported cotton, allowing herself one brief moment to savour the delicious fabrics. They were softer and finer than anything she could have dreamed of mere weeks ago, and their textures still stole her breath at times.

That moment over, she slipped out the door and padded barefoot down the hall. Anyone who saw her would have been scandalised, she knew. Even the lowest servants here in the palace had shoes to wear. As a future princess she had so many pairs she could hardly fathom the expense, and the servants kept apologising for the scarcity of the wardrobe they had to dress her from. It boggled the mind.

She reined her thoughts back in again with a firm hand. If she wanted to live long enough to become accustomed to this life, she must have everything prepared for her wedding night. A chill crept through her that even the soft wool could not keep out. There was so much that could go wrong.

Twice she had to hide from royal guards on patrol. She'd almost convinced herself, after living here for nearly a month, that they wouldn't harm her, that they wouldn't throw her out of the palace as an intruder. But they might think she was trying to sneak away before the wedding, as the third bride had done, and she had too little time to waste any in arguing with them.

She reached the door to the privy garden at last. Reserved for the exclusive use of the royal family, the garden was lushly blooming and damp with morning dew. She breathed in the scents of a hundred different flowers she'd never seen before coming here and felt a kernel of hope. As a farmer's daughter she knew and understood plants, and she trusted them to aid her.

The paths of turf were soft and welcoming under her bare feet as she hurried through the garden. In a sheltered corner, cradled among the roots of a solemn birch tree, she found what she was looking for: a tiny rose bush, completely without bud or blossom amidst the riotous flowers around it. Just as she'd been told.

This rose had bloomed only once in twenty years. On

the day the seed had been planted, its branches had grown swift and hearty and it had sprouted two lovely, perfect blossoms. One was white as new fallen snow, the other red as fresh spilled blood.

The young queen, heartsick with longing for a child she'd been unable to conceive, had been told to pick and eat one rose. The white if she wished to bear her royal husband a son and the red if she wished a daughter. On no account was she to eat both.

This story was, of course, the deepest of royal secrets. Margaret had heard it by the light of a single candle, from the wise woman who sang the forest into sleep for fall and trained the midwives for all the villages thereabouts. The wise woman could not tell her what had happened next, but they both knew that the queen had taken to her bed and in due course a lovely baby with hair like the moon on ripened corn silk had been presented as the new crown prince.

And they both knew that not too long afterward, stories began to circulate about a wyrm prowling the forest to the north. It was said to have scales like the sun on bloody copper and eyes like coals.

The wise woman had long since surmised that the young queen had eaten both blossoms despite the dire warnings she'd been given. Margaret could not imagine what must have possessed her to do so, but it mattered little now. It was the present that she must deal with.

She took out the little knife the wise woman had gifted her, with its curved silver blade and an intricate swirling pattern carved into its bone handle. With it she cut two sections of rose vine, each as long as her hand, and a single section of birch branch as long as her forearm. Then she buried the knife in the soft dirt.

At once the rose bush began to wither with astonishing speed. By the time Margaret had stepped back onto the turf path, there was nothing left of the bush save a few brown leaves and dried out vines. Even these crumbled before her eyes until it was as if the rose bush had never been. She half expected the rose leaves in her hand to shrivel as well, but they remained supple and green.

She turned away quickly and retraced her steps. Back to the garden door, then up through the halls to the suite of rooms she could scarcely fathom as being hers.

There, she tucked the birch branch out of sight beneath her pillow and then made the bed. It flustered the servants when she did this, but she had not been raised to leave a mess for someone else to tend to. And today it served a second purpose as well. She straightened the coverlet and plumped the pillows carefully, making sure everything was in perfect order so that no one would have any need to touch the bed before she returned to it for her wedding night; so that no one might chance to notice the birch branch beneath the pillow.

She was just straightening up from this task when the bedroom door opened to admit her chief lady's maid.

"Madam, you've servants to tend to that for you," Lena half chided, her expression a mix of exasperation and bemusement.

Margaret smiled at her. "I couldn't sleep this morning, and wanted something to do with myself," she replied, moving over to the dressing table where Lena was already busy laying out freshly cut flowers that would be braided into her hair. It was easy enough to slip the two sections of rose vine in among the rest.

Lena tutted quietly. "You should have rung for one of us, madam, to fetch your breakfast and warm your robe. You'll catch a chill if you're not careful. And not even slippers on your feet."

"I know," Margaret agreed. It was hard not to duck her head like a scolded child, but she managed it somehow. "I'll do that next time, Lena. I just wanted a little time alone this morning."

The maid's brisk expression softened. "A wedding's a big day, and it can feel overwhelming even without..." she trailed off with a swift, superstitious glance towards the window and the forest beyond.

"I'm sure the day will be very busy," Margaret said with a glance of her own towards the window but also the head of the bed which rested beside it.

"Very busy indeed," Lena agreed, pulling out the little chair before the dressing table and gesturing Margaret into it. "Liz will be up with your breakfast in a few minutes. I know you might not feel hungry, the nerves often do that to a bride, but you must try and eat something."

Margaret made an agreeable sound and tried to will herself to relax. The maid took up a hairbrush and began to unwind the braid with which Margaret had slept. Her hair was thick and tangled readily, but the motion of the brush was soothing all the same. It reminded her of being a little girl and struggling to sit still long enough for her mother to brush out the grass and twigs she'd managed to get lodged in her hair while she played.

There hadn't been a mirror to sit in front of then. Her family had been far too poor to afford anything nearly so grand as the oval of smooth, silver-backed glass from which her face stared back at her now. In its reflection,

Margaret searched for some hint of the wild haired girl who'd roamed fearlessly through the woods and meadows around her family's farm.

After weeks of pampering by what seemed a small army of maids, she looked softer and more ladylike than she could have imagined. Lena, with her stiffly proper bearing and tightly styled hair, no longer looked more like a princess than she did.

Breakfast arrived, as it always did here, on a gleaming silver tray. Dainty egg tarts, summer melon cut and arranged into the shape of a swan, and a flakey pastry whose name Margaret still could not pronounce that dripped with butter and honey.

Liz set the tray before her, careful not to disturb the flowers already on the table and stepped back with a curtsey. She was a shy girl who never spoke above a whisper so far as Margaret knew, but she offered an encouraging smile before slipping away to ensure everything was in order in the dressing room.

Margaret watched her departing back in the mirror. She wondered suddenly if Lena and Liz and the others had tended to the other brides before her. If they had, how must it feel to dress a string of girls, each more frightened and hopeless than the last, in the same white gown and send them to wed the monster. Perhaps that was what sharpened Lena's tongue, and drained the strength from Liz's voice.

The savour faded from the delicacies on her breakfast tray at that thought, but she forced herself to eat them anyway. Lena was right that she would need something in her stomach to face this day.

When Lena was finished brushing out her hair, she

moved on to curling tongs and mother-of-pearl combs. She wove the flowers expertly in place among strings of pearls and stitched tiny braids in place with white silk thread.

Then came the clothing. The undergarments were of cotton so fine it was translucent. On account of this, the seamstress had told her, at least three shifts were necessary to protect a lady's modesty. It had seemed absurd to a girl accustomed to making do with a single shift that served as both her sole undergarment and her nightgown, but evidently this was another area where royalty had quite different expectations.

No one had batted an eye when she'd asked for seven shifts. It was a lucky number after all, a magical number even, and she would need any luck and magic she could get.

She donned them now one after another, each more elaborately decorated than the last with embroidery, lace, and ribbons. In spite of the near-weightless fabric, she felt bulky and silly wearing so many layers. The wise woman had been insistent that this was necessary, however. And they'd been made especially for her, as nothing else in the wardrobe had been. She would feel ungrateful not to wear them now, even if she'd dare to ignore the wise woman's instructions on the matter.

After the shifts came the corset, then the underdress of silk velvet. Then, at long last, the gown. It was as heavy and stiff as the shifts were light. The brocade was weighty on its own, but much of the fabric was completely hidden by intricate embroidery that made it nearly as stiff as the corset. Across her chest there was even a panel where some of the embroidery was worked in thread of spun gold. It was a good thing there would be no dancing for this wedding, as Margaret was sure she couldn't move enough to manage it.

Her reflection peered back from the mirror as Liz fastened an elaborate necklace of pearls and diamonds. It might have been a stranger. Her mother and father would not have recognised their own daughter in the noble lady decked out with fine jewels and exquisite fabrics.

That was just as well. Margaret was grateful they weren't here, though it felt strange to go to the alter with none of her family there to see her wed. It would be better if her parents took the money they'd been given in exchange for her and bought a larger plot of farmland or used it for her sisters' dowries. Let them not think of their youngest daughter anymore.

"It's time, madam," Lena announced. In the mirror Margaret saw the maid's lips thin and pale, and her throat work as if the words pained her.

Margaret turned away from the mirror and surveyed the women who'd cared for her since her arrival at the palace. "Thank you all for your help getting ready," she told them, trying to smile though her face felt rigid as if her cheeks had been dipped in wax.

Several of the younger girls burst into tears at her words. Liz raised both hands to her mouth in a vain attempt to cover her stricken look. Even Lena drew a heavy, shuddering breath that made her whole frame shake. They all stared at her, but no one had anything to say.

Margaret supposed there really wasn't anything. She took a deep breath, squared her shoulders, and headed for the door.

An honour guard of a dozen royal guardsmen awaited

her outside the suite's door, every inch of their uniforms polished and brushed until they gleamed. Six of them walked ahead of her and six behind, as much to stop her if she attempted to run as for her protection. The only threat she faced was the one she went towards.

The walk was interminable. Between the tiny steps she had to take to avoid becoming tangled in her heavy gown, and the incessant rattle of her guards' armour, she wondered if she might go mad before she reached the great hall. It was almost a surprise when the huge double doors loomed ahead.

By tradition, a royal wedding should have taken place in the great cathedral of St Mary the Mother in the capital city of Seaford on the banks of the river Veld. If it was entirely necessary to hold it in the northern provinces near Lindly Wood, it should at least have been in the old and venerable church of St John the Divine in Wildefell. Failing even that, the palace chapel might have been moderately acceptable.

Margaret had been told why it was being held in the great hall instead, but she had not fully understood until the moment she stepped through the doors. An altar had been built and consecrated at the front of the hall for the occasion, and before it waited her bridegroom.

The Red Wyrm of Lindly Wood, or the Lindwyrm as the locals had come to call the beast, had grown significantly since the earliest sightings and rumours. It was impossible to guess its length, coiled as it was about itself, but it certainly would never have fit into the chapel.

Its head turned on a long, sinuous neck at the sound of the door opening. The head alone was as large as an ox, a squat arrowhead shape that seemed to be almost entirely composed of jaws. Its scales toyed with the candlelight like a heap of bloody rubies, glistening almost wet or oily in their sheen. When the jaws parted, they revealed teeth like a row of longswords and a massive tongue forked like an adder's.

Margaret couldn't move. It was not that she didn't want to. She could not, not for any reason. Her muscles had frozen solid under the wyrm's unblinking gaze, and she suddenly felt a great kinship with the mouse paralysed by the cat's regard. In the back of her mind, some primal part of her gibbered with unreasoning terror.

A hand coming to rest on her elbow finally distracted her enough to break the trance. Her gaze flinched sideways to the man who'd stepped up next to her.

Prince Fionntan was much lauded in song and gossip as the handsomest man in the kingdom. 'Fair as moonlight on still water,' a travelling minstrel had called him in the village inn, and Margaret had listened with as much interest as any other girl. Looking up at him now, she was struck less by his height and strength than by his eyes, which were pale grey and softened by sorrow.

"I'll walk with you," he murmured, quiet enough that only she would hear. "Since your father isn't here to give you away."

Margaret drew a shuddering breath and inclined her head a little. "Thank you," she managed to whisper.

The prince's lips twitched as if attempting a smile, but the expression wilted as quickly as it had come. He tucked her hand into his elbow, covered it with his own, and eased her forward a step. All the while, he continued to speak. "I feel as if this is partly my fault. I agreed to it. He's my twin brother, you see, my *older* twin brother, and he said it was his right to marry before I did. And of course, I agreed; I didn't know then what he had in mind."

The prince's voice was hurried, almost frantic, as if he must get all this out before they reached the alter. Margaret wondered, in a distant sort of way, if he'd said the same thing to the other brides. Not the first, perhaps, but the other five.

Then they were beneath the Lindwyrm's great shadow and there was no more time to wonder.

Margaret heard little of the ceremony above the roaring of blood in her ears. When the Lindwyrm spoke its vows, its voice washed over her like thunder and made her chest ring like a bell. Prince Fionntan prompted her gently when it was time to speak hers. She sipped wine from the wedding cup without tasting it, numb through from watching the wyrm's long tongue dart out to the same cup.

Then it was over. Margaret, Princess Margaret now, walked arm in arm with her new mother-in-law back to the royal suite. It occurred to her that perhaps she'd been given a suite with such enormous rooms to ensure that her bridegroom could fit in them.

The queen's expression was haunted, and she made no effort to speak as they walked. Finally, just as they reached the door, she took Margaret's face between hands that seemed nothing but bone and kissed her brow. "I always wanted a daughter, but not like this," she whispered. "I'm sorry, child. I'm sorry for everything."

Margaret thought back to the wise woman's story. She thought of asking the queen why she'd eaten both blossoms, instead of only one. She looked into the queen's eyes, a grey almost as pale as her son's, and thought only of how much this woman had already suffered for her ill-fated choice.

She kissed her mother-in-law's cheek and held her peace.

The maids were silent and tearful as they helped Margaret back out of her wedding gown. Even Lena's eyes looked a trifle dewy. They removed the underdress and the corset, but when they reached for the first of the shifts Margaret waved them away.

"Pray, let me keep them on," she murmured. "I don't want to be cold while I wait."

Likewise, she waved away the hairbrush, saying, "You worked so hard on it. It would be a shame to take it down again so soon."

With nothing else left to do, the maids left her alone in the cavernously empty bedchamber to wait. She hurried across the room as soon as the door was shut behind them to check that the birch switch was still where she'd left it. She sighed gratefully when her fingers brushed its smooth bark.

Her heart beat like a drum and the minutes dragged by like years, but all too soon she heard the door being opened again. Scales rasped at the doorframe as the Lindwyrm eased its immense bulk into the room.

Margaret remained facing the curtained window, struggling to master her terror. She breathed slow and deep until her heart hammered a little less fiercely.

Behind her she could hear the beast shifting and settling itself, but it didn't speak. She was grateful for that.

When she was as calm as she thought she could make herself, she turned to face her bridegroom. The wyrm took up most of the room. Its head rested on the floor, which put its eyes only a little higher than her own. They were dark, less like coals than pools of ink, and their focus was so intent that she felt it like a weight against her skin.

"You're a brave little thing, I'll give you that," it whispered. The sound was so quiet it only just carried across the scant distance between them, but Margaret still felt it in her bones. Its tongue flicked out towards her, almost touching her cheek. "I can taste your fear, but I like that you can still stand there and face me."

Margaret's throat was so dry she could not have spoken even if she'd known what to say. Standing there and facing it was all she could do.

It chuckled and the sound rasped her nerves like the scrape of an axe on the grindstone. "Well, my brave little wife, will you not take off your shift? You promised you would obey me, after all." Its tongue darted out again, this time touching the fabric of her outermost shift and making it rustle in the quiet room.

Margaret flinched back instinctively, but then firmed her resolve and held her ground. Lifting her chin so she could look it in the eyes, she replied, "I did promise to love, honour, and obey you, husband, just as you promised the same. I will take off my shift if you will first shed your skin for me."

The wyrm chuckled again. "Brave words, my little wife. You amuse me, so I will do as you ask," it said.

Its ink-pool eyes grew milky and it twitched the end of its massive snout, then began to wriggle and twitch all down the length of its massive body. The blood-ruby scales peeled back almost like a garment being removed. Beneath them it revealed a second layer of scales, red as rowan leaves in the fall.

Margaret bent to lift the hem of her shift and peeled it off, revealing the next one beneath.

The wyrm hissed and reared back, nostrils flaring wide and tongue flicking rapidly in and out of its mouth. "Now that is unfair," it said, lips pulling back in a snarl.

Margaret quailed inside, but she crossed her arms before her. With what she hoped was a suitably haughty tone she said, "I may have been born a poor peasant girl, but I am a princess now. And a princess does not wear just one shift. See how thin this fabric is? It would be indecent."

It slithered close again. That awful tongue darted out to touch the next shift, then grew bolder and rasping across her cheek, swift as an arrow. "I will allow that may be true. Will you take off this shift as well, little wife?" it asked, breath hot against her face.

"I will remove the shift if you will first remove your skin for me," she replied again.

The wyrm hissed again, but it chuckled as well. "As you wish," it replied.

It wriggled free of the rowan-leaf scales, revealing another set beneath that were red as the clouds of a bloody sunset. Margaret lifted away her second shift to reveal another. By now she could see that the wyrm was appreciably smaller than it had been at first. Its head seemed shorter and there was a slight broadening visible a little way down its body.

"This game cannot last forever, little wife," the wyrm said with a huff of breath that flattened her remaining shifts against her body. Baring a mouthful of teeth like shorts words, it added, "You will run out of shifts before I run out of skins."

Margaret shrugged and lifted the hem of the next a trifle, just far enough to show there was still another beneath. "Shall we test that theory?" she asked.

It threw back its head and roared with laughter so loud it shook the walls. "Oh, you think yourself clever, do you? Let us see."

The shedding took longer this time. The wyrm wriggled and writhed and peeled away the sunset scales. Its sides heaved with the force of its breathing by the time it had revealed another set, red as the finest wine.

Margaret shed another shift, then waited while the beast caught its breath. She watched it shake itself all over, from its head all the way down the length of the body which had grown lumpier than ever.

It lifted its head to peer at her again with eyes that were no longer ink but the brown of dark, imported coffee. Its tongue dipped out, lingering over her cheek this time and flicking down along the curve of her throat. "I admire your bravery to play this game, little wife, but our wedding night draws on. Will you not put it aside?"

"Some say it is the waiting, the anticipation, which makes a thing worthwhile," Margaret replied, daring to reach up and touch the scales of her bridegroom's muzzle though her fingers trembled. "Will you not play a little longer?"

"A little longer," the wyrm allowed. Its scaled face moved enough to show a hint of expression now, eyes crinkling at the corners in what might have been tolerant amusement.

When it had shed the wine-dark scales, it lay a while panting with exertion. Its new coat of scales was as red as a cardinal's breast, and the faintest wingbeat swift tremors shuddered along its still formidable length.

"Are you quite well?" Margaret asked, concern beginning to creep in around the edges of her fear at the state the creature had been reduced to.

It hissed angrily and raised itself up to glare at her. "I'm growing peckish with the effort of all this chit chat," it replied sharply, baring teeth like knives.

Margaret nodded. "Conversation can feel wearisome indeed when you've grown unused to company. If you don't feel up to continuing, I will quite understand."

"Of course I'm up to it!" the wyrm snarled, beginning to wriggle its lumpy, distorted body out of the cardinal scales.

The skin did not come off smoothly in one long piece, as it had before. Instead, the wyrm had to squirm and tear the patchy thing off, revealing wide swaths of scales red as sweet summer cherries and awkward, bony looking protrusions at its sides long before it was finished shedding.

When it saw that Margaret had merely revealed yet another shift beneath the last she'd removed, it growled low in the back of its throat and went right on squirming. The cherry bright skin came away in pieces as well. The one beneath was red as rust, patchy and dull, and the wyrm could not seem to catch its breath now.

Margaret poured a cup of water from the ewer on the bedside table and came to kneel beside the shivering wyrm. It was scarcely longer than the height of a tall man now and seemed hardly deserving of the fearsome moniker.

"Here, drink this and rest a little," she told it gently, lifting its short, blunt head to the water.

Its tongue lapped twice, then flicked out to trace her cheek once more. This time it flicked up towards her temple, and the wyrm gave a startled yelp as its tongue was pierced by the thorns of the rose vines woven into her hair. She saw bright blood on the tongue as it snapped back behind rows of teeth that were merely like teeth, sharp and curved but no longer than the width of Margaret's thumb.

"You still have shifts left," the wyrm grumbled sullenly. It gave a desultory squirm that made the protrusions on its sides wobble like awkward flippers.

Margaret smiled down at it. "This is the last," she admitted. "Have you one more skin to shed?"

It regarded her for a long moment with eyes that had faded to the colour of strong tea. At length it nodded.

This final shedding was the most difficult yet, and Margaret had to help peel the rust red scales away. In the end, what was left was not a wyrm at all. Its skin was red as apple blossoms and the first pink light of dawn, and it had no scales at all to cover its sad, misshapen body. It groaned softly and rolled golden hazel eyes to look up at Margaret as she stepped away from it.

"What have you done to me?" it whispered.

Margaret retrieved the birch switch she'd cut that morning from under the pillows and approached the creature that was no longer a wyrm. "I have done nothing but ask. You did all this yourself," she said gently, gesturing to the heaps of shed skins and scales that filled much of the room.

The former wyrm craned its head about, but it looked mostly at its own body. "Like a lump of unbaked dough," it muttered sullenly.

"Yes, very like," Margaret agreed. She raised the birch switch and brought it down hard, leaving a stripe as red as holly berries across the former wyrm's pale back.

It let out an undignified squeal and tried to squirm away from her. "What was that for?" it demanded as she walked calmly after it and delivered a second stripe. Though it had once been fast and clever enough to evade the most persistent knights sent to slay it, now it wriggled like a worm and to about as much effect.

Margaret struck it with the switch a third time, noting as she did so that the blobby protrusions were starting to shape themselves into something that might be limbs. They looked more like the wings of a plucked chicken than anything else so far, but it was a start.

"You've eaten six brides in as many months," she pointed out sternly, punctuating the words with two blows in swift succession.

It squealed again and writhed its whole body like it was trying to shed another skin. "It's my nature!" it cried piteously, completely failing to evade the next swipe of the switch.

"You would have happily eaten me as well," Margaret continued. She watched the lumpy limbs elongate as she continued to strike it. "And you have tormented the people living around Lindly Wood for years."

"I can't help what I am!" the former wyrm whined, flailing at her uselessly with a tail that had begun to separate into legs.

Margaret frowned ferociously and struck it again. "You have not tried to be anything better than your basest instincts, and for that I am ashamed to call you my husband," she said.

It lay still, panting and trembling with its form halfway between the wyrm it had been and the man it might become. It raised pleading eyes to her face. "I don't know how," it whispered, voice shivering along with its half-formed body.

Margaret hesitated then. She crossed her arms and asked, "oh really?"

"I was cast out of the palace as a monster when I was only hours old and have lived all my life alone in the wood," it told her, looking away from the intensity of her gaze. "I only wanted a companion, to make my life less lonely, but all the girls feared and hated me. I did what I have always done when faced with fear and hatred for what I am. I do not know another way."

Margaret settled to her knees beside the former wyrm and laid a hand on its quivering back. Its skin was surprisingly soft. "If I show you what to do, will you be better than you have?" she asked.

It raised damp eyes to stare at her. "You would do that? But don't you hate me as well?" it asked. A tongue red as pomegranate seeds lapped across plump lips, long but no longer forked.

"I was afraid of you," Margaret said slowly, feeling for the right words carefully as she said them. "And I'm still very angry with you. You've done terrible things, and ignorance doesn't excuse them."

She saw the former wyrm's throat work as it swallowed. "I can't undo them, but I could do better," it whispered thickly.

"It will be very hard. Are you willing to do the work of changing your ways?" Margaret asked.

"I..." The former wyrm ducked its head and squeezed

its eyes shut. Its voice was muffled against Margaret's knee as it said, "If you will show me how, then I will try my best."

She moved her hand up to the back of its head and cradled it there for a moment before speaking again. "I promised to honour you, and I can think of no better way than by helping you to do and be better."

"How should we begin?" the former wyrm asked, peeking up at Margaret from behind damp lashes red as harvest apples.

"I think we already have," she replied. "We've peeled away the layers of your armour and arrogance. Now you're soft and malleable as dough and must be shaped into something new."

It huffed with a trace of its former pique and said, "beaten into shape with your switch, you mean."

Margaret shrugged. "This is what the wise woman in my village told me I must do, when I was chosen by lot to come and be your bride," she told it.

"Isn't there some less painful way?" it whined, baring teeth that were straight and flat and hardly threatening at all now.

"Change is painful no matter how it's accomplished," she admonished sternly. "And it isn't as if you haven't been a very naughty wyrm and earned some punishment, is it?"

The former wyrm gulped audibly and looked away. "I suppose so," it whispered.

"Shall we continue then?" Margaret asked.

She waited patiently while the former wyrm squirmed and grumbled under its breath. At length it nodded and said meekly, "Yes please, oh wise wife."

It took a great deal of time to beat the half-formed creature into the shape of a proper person. The lumpy wing-like stubs lengthened into arms, the tail split into legs, and the red stripes across its back became a fall of luscious hair as red sunlight on polished copper. At length there were no more changes forthcoming. They both were panting and damp with sweat.

The former wyrm looked up, cheeks damp with tears as well and eyes like wide, still pools of honey. "Am I a man now?" it asked in a voice gone horse from weeping.

"Not, exactly," Margaret replied slowly. Unexpected heat crept up her cheeks as she looked at the form sprawled on the floor in front of her.

"What more must I do?" the former wyrm asked, exhaustion making it wilt piteously. "Only tell me, and I will do whatever you ask."

Margaret shook her head, at a loss for words. "Come look in the mirror," she finally said.

She had to help the former wyrm up and support it while it struggled to master clumsy new legs. They made their slow way to the mirror, the former wyrm's arms clinging tight and awkward to the last shift that Margaret still wore and stared in silence for a long while at their reflections.

"But I'm..." The former wyrm trailed off and looked to Margaret in confusion. "Does this mean I can't be your husband?"

Margaret nodded. "You're a woman. My wife."

"Your wife," the former wyrm repeated in an awed tone. With lips as soft and red as the rose that had brought her into being, Princess Raudeilin shaped her first, shy smile. "I like the sound of that."

Ainsley Hawthorn

Ainsley Hawthorn, Ph.D., is a cultural historian, author, and multidisciplinary artist. Raised in Steady Brook, Newfoundland & Labrador, and now based in St. John's, she earned her doctorate in Near Eastern Languages and Civilizations at Yale University.

Hawthorn is passionate about using her academic knowledge to bring new ideas about culture, history, and religion to a general audience.

As a public scholar, she blogs for *Psychology Today*, writes for CBC, and has contributed to various other publications, including *The Globe and Mail*, the *National Post*, and the *Newfoundland Quarterly*.

She edited the anthology *Land of Many Shores: Stories from a Diverse Newfoundland and Labrador*, and is currently completing her first solo-authored non-fiction book, *The Other Five Senses*.

She brings with her her story, 'The Patchwork Skin.'

The Patchwork Skin

Adeline found the hat at a kiosk in the mall, the kind that bloom like algae in the months leading up to Christmas, dotting the stark, coral-tiled plazas with skerries of colour. Normally, she enjoyed shopping – or browsing, at least. She liked to meander up and down aisles stacked with baubles, one arm outstretched so her hand could skim from rough to smooth, over angles and curves. Rarely did she bring anything home with her, not only because her budget weighed on her mind but because it was the abundance that dazzled her, soothed her. Anything she bought was a disappointment. Back in her little house, it lost its magic, lifted out of the sea of treasures where she had found it.

Shopping at this time of year, however, she found nearly unbearable. She couldn't bear the press of the crowds, the anxiety of the staff, the tinny music that battered her slender ears like icicles. Once-leisurely outings became strategic, the luxe of languor sold dearly for pace, for love of family and love of novelty and love of goods. So she was rushing that day and might have easily missed it. Yet, as she bustled towards Victoria's Secret to buy a pajama set for her step-daughter Marley, a flash of scarlet in motion caught her eye, like a flare in the dimness of her daytime – signal and spectre, question and answer at once. It cut through the fog of her, revealing too briefly a depth within herself, entombed under earthly thoughts and earthly dreams, salt reclaimed for soil.

Adeline paused, pivoted. The flare was a fiery-hued fur hat in the hand of a kiosk clerk. He was repositioning it on a grate-metal ledge as a prospective buyer turned away, mounting it on a stand like a hunter's trophy, falsely full and cocked sidelong with simulated life, as though it listened, prey-shy, to the throng surging past it. The crowd streamed around Adeline like a shoal in a current. Swaddled in layers of cloth – cotton and fleece and wool against the cold – she sweltered in the dense indoor air, sweating from the unnatural heat, the unexpected discovery. Transfixed, she edged up to the stall.

"How may I help you?" beamed the clerk. Noticing Adeline's approach, he had turned the breadth of his polo-shirted chest towards her in a movement that was surely meant as welcome but felt like warning. She sensed him waiting for her to close the gap between them, by foot or by voice. The space that separated them, that separated whole and part, drew out dizzyingly in the uncertain moment.

"That hat…." The rest caught in her sand-parched throat.

"This one?" he said, plucking it nimbly from its stand. Instinctively, Adeline spread her palms to keep it from falling, this precious fragment that had no place on the earth, that ungrounded and unmoored her, a shard of gemstone no less brilliant for its breakage. The clerk dropped it lightly into her hands. The ease of the exchange took her aback. It felt more like a gift than a theft, the clerk made incautious by the heft of himself, by the gravity of trade and counter-trade, by the pressure of his soles on sod.

"Perfect for the holiday season!" he chirped.

Adeline smoothed her fingers over the short, cat-sleek fur, stroking with the grain so it felt slick as oil. The hat was domed and edged with a wide cuff. It had been sewn from a seal pelt dyed red, turning the spots a deep crimson so they nearly vanished into their scarlet surroundings. Mistaking her silence for the reticence of a woman tempted to buy for herself in the giving season, the clerk urged her on with practised courtesy.

"It's discounted as part of our Black Friday Week special. 15% off. You'll save yourself the tax."

Adeline barely heard him, drunk as she was on the aromas of salty hide and acrid dye. There was an oval mirror fixed by its frame to the loam-black countertop of the kiosk, and he swivelled it towards her.

"Why not try it on?" he coaxed, his razor smile at her shoulder bounded by the looking-glass. Was that all she had feared, all she had coveted? The almond eyes, the teeth, the bare skin stretched on lank-framed bone? Obediently, Adeline lifted the scarlet fur and slipped it over fine, dew-dark hair flecked with steel.

The hat's unnatural hue made a stranger of her reflection. It was an unsettling contrast that made her scalp itch. Adeline had no great savings and afforded herself few luxuries, but there should still be a little kitty left over in the shared account from her last teaching contract, assuming Kurt hadn't spent it. While her husband had his virtues, thrift and forethought were not among them. The easy contentment that had baffled and intrigued her when they met, she later realized, was the product of a certain amiable self-absorption that led him to treat all but his own immediate needs with benign neglect. So the oversight of their small holdings fell to her, the housekeeping, the finances, even the gift shopping, and with it the profound weight of unfulfilled expectations.

"I'll take it."

"Do you do donation receipts?" she asked.

"I think so, my love," answered the blue-vested volunteer on the other side of the counter. Frothy grey hair crested on the margins of her gauzy face. She glanced into Adeline's trash bag of used clothes, nudging rimless glasses up the bridge of her nose with the back of her wrist. Shelves behind the counter were stacked pell-mell with donations yet to be sorted, boxes and bags, flotsam and jetsam to be found and lost and found again. "Let me go check with Linda. I'll be back in a jiffy. You just have yourself a look around in the meantime."

At loose ends in the spring semester, without a contract and floundering for purpose, Adeline had put what fire she had into purging the house of its detritus, clearing out Kurt's old band shirts, her unworn cocktail dresses, and Marley's outgrown school clothes. If not meaningful, the work was at least measurable, and the tangibility of her progress anchored her lightly in the world. So long she'd been a resident of the realm of thought, her existence expressed in writing, research, teaching, and she had begun to crave a return to the flesh.

She drifted toward Housewares, thinking to find a replacement for a teapot she had broken, that was dragged from her graceless fingers by its own water-weight, the fluid bursting outwards from its porcelain shell. She brushed her hand along a rack of winter coats as she floated past.

Thick duffle, coarse tweed... smooth fur. Adeline curled her fingers reflexively into the low nap, stiff strands pricking at her fingertips, and looked down in surprise. Her palm rested on a pewter shoulder seam. Stooping eagerly, she leafed through jackets and parkas on either side until she was able to fish the garment out by its hooked hanger.

It was a sealskin car coat, cut slim to mid-thigh. Though the coat's tan lining was discoloured at the neck and chafed at the wrists, the fur still glistened under the thrift shop's fluorescent lights. Adeline felt her throat swell, and, when she was sated with looking, she pressed the coat against her breast, feeling it curl to her body like a twin in the womb. She eased it over her shoulders and slid her arms into the sleeves, propelling the scent of mothballs into the air. Sundered and transmuted, the pelt was tight on her – the buttons wouldn't fasten over her bust. She slipped it off but brought it with her to the till, draped over her forearm like a maniple, a swab to soak up all her tears.

The foam-haired volunteer was back, hunched over a yellow notepad whose pages were crisscrossed by vein-blue lines, segmented and subdivided, every point to its place. With a last flourish of her ballpoint pen, the volunteer finishing writing, snapped the top page off the pad, and passed the slip of paper to Adeline.

"There's your receipt, my dear," she said crisply. "Thank you very much. You can fill your name and address in when you get home."

Pocketing the paper, Adeline gingerly spread the coat over the countertop. "I'd like to buy this, please."

"Ooh, now isn't that lovely?" cooed the volunteer.

"Must have just come in. If I'd have seen it, I'd be after buying it for my granddaughter. She's slender like that.

"Is this for your girl?" She gestured to a purple sweatshirt embellished with glitter that had half tumbled out of Adeline's bag of donations.

"No," answered Adeline. She pressed both hands into the fur; it rose like liquid mercury at the edges of her palms. Her upper body loosened, and she inclined her head forward, eyes heavy-lidded, speaking as much to hear her own words as to share them. "No, it's for me."

"Ah. Well." The volunteer cleared her throat awkwardly, then smiled. "I suppose you could have it dyed to match your hat."

The day was twelve degrees and blustery with a mackerel sky, clouds scalloped horizon to horizon like scales. *Mackerel sky, mackerel sky – never long wet, never long dry.* There would be rain in the evening. The solstice was hardly midsummer in Newfoundland, the wheel of the European year poorly fitted to this piecemeal island stitched together from the remnants of three continents. Arms folded like a prayer, Adeline watched the weather from the lee of the arena's side entrance before making her way back indoors, past caterers' trolleys and a docile dapple-grey mare. The horse huffed at the air, scenting the storm. *Mackerel scales and mare's tails make tall ships carry low sails.* If Adeline unlatched her corral, loosed her halter, would she gallop away? Would she remember how?

Inside the Techniplex was a mawi'omi for Indigenous Peoples Day, a gathering of all the nations that overlapped this ancient place. The floodlights and AstroTurf gave the illusion of fair skies and fertile earth despite the capelin weather beyond the walls. At the centre of the stadium was the circle for dancing, bounded on one side by a low crescent of bleachers and on the other by the musicians' tents. Between the two, along the edge nearest Adeline and marked simply on the ground by yellow tape, was the circle's eastern gate, its only entrance or exit, the way in the same as the way out. Against the far wall were activities for children – art supplies and a wigwam for play – while community groups lined the back.

To Adeline's left were the vendor tables, arrayed with handiworks of all kinds. She made her way from one stall to the next, from spiralling sweetgrass baskets to sere foraged teas, the land reshaped by human hands. She stopped at the kamiks, broad and sturdy boots with calves so thick they dwarfed the toes beneath. Beside them there were sealskin mittens. An Inuk woman, in her twenties or early thirties, sat beside the winter wear. Her serpentine-black hair was bobbed and streaked with purple near her face. The violet arced to her jaw like a lighthouse beam, illuminating three black lines that swept from lower lip to chin, ink that wrote her ancestry into her skin.

"This is gorgeous work," said Adeline, tracing the fine braided trim on a pair of caribou-skin kamiks with a fingertip. "Do you do all of this yourself?"

"Yes, I do," the craftswoman replied. "Cutting, sewing, beadwork – start to finish. All me." She laughed as though amazed by her own skill, not in arrogance but in appreciation, gratitude for all her gifts. The corners of her eyes creased with tiny grooves like rivulets, making an engraving of her joy. When erosion someday wiped her from the world, her lines and furrows would spell out the story of her life.

Adeline had sensed the mittens there before she saw them, their conch-call luring her with songs above her range of hearing. Each slate-dark seal fur mitt dissolved at the wrist into a flared black felt cuff beaded with a five-petaled flower, orange with green vines like springtime. They were edged in fox fur white as the mackerel clouds today, white as the sea-breakers in the storm tonight. Adeline slipped the mittens over her hands, fumbling with the second as though she were caught mid-transformation, one limb still human and the other already beast. Once she had them on, her fingers swam inside them, shrouded and strangely free. She folded her palm and the paw of the mitt curled with it, as if it were the flesh and she the bones.

"How much for these?" she asked

"Two-fifty."

Adeline swallowed. "Can I put them on credit?"

She eased the mitts into her tote, covering them with her wallet like a little black book, then returned to the circle where Marley danced with her friends. Kurt watched from the bleachers, sitting with his ex Ali, Marley's mother. Adeline kept her distance, giving them space to love their daughter together. Marley spun in the fancy shawl she had made for herself over the winter, its blue and green ribbons eddying brightly around her. She wore it with her cousin's hand-me-down moccasins, a matching dress and leggings Kurt and Adeline had ordered for her, and her mother's beaded earrings. She was piecing together her heritage into the whole of herself. She was growing up. When the song finished, Marley ran to her parents, and Adeline turned away.

The furrier's was empty of people, save Adeline, who was sitting at a bench, and a clerk. It was the kind of enviro-chic boutique that rebranded fur as sustainable fashion, turning conservationist critiques inside-out. The stark white walls were lined with carefully curated items, which were displayed in singles or pairs on modernist, boxy shelves of walnut-stained wood. These were interspersed with willowy houseplants that softened the severity of the place, but the plants, like the products, were decidedly artificial, natural in substance but synthetic in form. The clerk, a middle-aged man, knelt at Adeline's feet over a long, wide shoebox, and she idly watched his bald spot, how the greying hair swirled around it like a whirlpool, drawn always to the centre and the source.

"Now, these boots use European sizing, so you normally need to go one size up," he was explaining. "In your case, since you wear a half size, we're going to try a size-and-a-half up."

He pulled a sealskin boot from the box, tilting it before her at an accessible angle. The boot was trendy and streamlined. Dusky-spotted silver fur spilled down to black rubber wedge heels and a shapely, feminine foot. Dark piping ringed the calf and swooped about the ankle. Adeline pointed her toes like a servant in a fairy tale so the clerk could ease the boot up her leg, but it was no proposal, not to him or to anyone. Not a making, but an unmaking. He glided the boot closed, sealing its long zipper tooth by implacable tooth.

"Looks good," he said, eyeing the fit. He tugged at the waistline of his khakis before settling back onto his haunches. "Let's pop the second one on so you can have a little walk around in them and see how they feel."

He helped her on with the second boot, and she stood. The wool lining nestled into her calves like a pet or a witch's familiar, and the heels buoyed her off the ground, their height making her feel untethered from the earth. As she walked the length of the store, the boots seemed to adhere to her. Shutting out the air, they left no room for anything else, like crystal slippers or red shoes, compelling her to embrace her birthright or dance her doom.

"How's the fit?" the clerk asked.

"Perfect," replied Adeline, sinking into her more substantial self. A phone rang in a back room.

"Excuse me – I have to grab that. I'll be right back." Heaving himself back to his feet, the clerk rounded the blurred-glass checkout and disappeared into the office behind it.

Adeline watched him go, then, bowing, laid her purse down between the shoebox and the ballet flats she had worn into the shop, furling the shoulder strap over it like a winding sheet. From the bench above, she retrieved her thrifted sealskin coat, which smelled no longer of strangers' closets. She drew the sleeves over her arms and tugged the front as near to closed as she could. She picked up the scarlet hat, settling it low on her head, and slid the mittens onto her hands.

Covered in this second skin, she made her way out the door. An alarm sounded behind her. In the twilight, the autumn air was sienna-tinted and salty, and Adeline's breath rose from her mouth like smoke, as though she burned inside. She had sometimes felt like she were gasping for air, drowning on land, but now she inhaled deeply and didn't exhale. She set her feet towards the harbour. In water what was heavy becomes light.

Melissa Bishop

Born and raised in the Mount Pearl area, Bishop is a newcomer to the genre fiction scene in Atlantic Canada whose fantastic prose has taken the provinces community by storm. Her work won three Kit Sora awards: July 2019 'Cycles,' September 2019 'Huntress of the Woods,' and May 2020 'Brightest and Best.' In addition she has placed numerous other times.

Writing about her story 'The Photograph' in *Pulp Science-Fiction from the Rock,* R. Graeme Cameron of Amazing Stories wrote: "This is a classic SF tale... Possibly a reminder that things aren't always what they seem."

Bishop describes herself as a loyal Tolkien fan who enjoyed reading about different mythologies as a child. She currently works as a high school teacher, teaching at the same high school she attended in her youth. She started writing when she was very young and honed her skills in high school, when she started a pen pal friendship that has lasted for over 17 years, writing stories back and forth to each other.

She brings with her two short stories, 'Polaris' and 'The River that Runs.'

Polaris

At first there was the world, born from the great smithy's fire which resides in the heart of the earth. Apart from this was the un-life, the land where humans first dwelt — separate from the trees, seas, and sky. Between them was a bridge of darkness none dare cross, lest they be lost to its shadows.

A man named Polaris, seeing the bright world beyond, knew that life lay before them on this strange, distant shore. Gathering his people together, he dared to traverse the treacherous crossing to Earth.

As they descended into the shadows, a chill ran through the brave folk, for the darkness held dark things. Misery, pain, anger, and fear crept like creatures from this void, seeping slowly into the wary travellers. So brave was their leader that he bore the brunt of this malice, urging the others ever onward. These shadowy beasts latched onto him, tearing into him. Piece by piece they pulled at Polaris, yet still he moved forward, guiding those that followed him. A glimmering hope in the overwhelming gloom, he was.

When the people finally reached the world's shore

and felt the sun warm upon their cheeks, they rejoiced. Though the shades still lingered in their thoughts, joy, thankfulness, and peace filled their hearts. They were alive and here they would thrive. The people searched for their hero Polaris, to praise his valiant march through the dark. But the one who led them was gone, the shadows having consumed all but his small, indomitable spirit.

Una, the great smith goddess, maker of the world, sought to honour the guide that had brought his people to life. She carried his little spirit to her smithy within the earth, and there she laboured long with hammer and anvil. The sparks flew as she worked, scattering about the black ocean of night. From this the stars were born, so that none would walk the path of darkness hopeless and alone. But Polaris' soul shone brighter as she toiled. His spark became a flicker, then a flame, then a brilliant blaze that made the great smith shield her eyes from his dazzling light. His brilliance was the brightest of all her creations, save for the sun alone.

She hung his spirit in the northern sky, and still he shines today: a guide to all those lost in the dark, looking to find their way home.

The River that Runs

When the Earth was young and new, long before mankind's memories, rivers did not run. They sat still — silent, statuesque slips of silvery glass spread out over the lands. They never trickled over mossy groves or down through mountain valleys. The wind may break their stoic surface with a gust or bluster, but the watery forms made no movements of their own accord. The wide ocean lay still and sorrowful, with no arms outstretched into the land — for no tributaries searched for their mighty shores. The great lakes were lonely, imprisoned in isolation by the earth that encircled them. But none were so miserable as the little river that lay sheltered in a black forest.

Shadows were long in these woods, with the grounds seeing little light save for the few golden rays that filtered down through the green leaves. When such wisps of sun settled on the river, it delighted in the warmth, longing to know what being produced such a wondrous glow. The river could not see the sky, only small scattered blue fragments when the wind sent the trees softly swaying. The world above was a million little puzzle pieces to an image the young river would never see. So it wept for the land unknown, and the sorrow seemed to echo through the dense and lonely forest – where it was heard by another.

Danu, mother goddess of all, heard the lament of the little river. Pity filled her heart. She moved as graceful as a ghost through the grove, silent feet treading lightly upon grey moss. When she came to the weeping river, she knelt down beside it.

"Little River," she said softly to stay the water's sorrow. "What makes you weep so?"

"Oh Mother Danu," the river sobbed, its water still and sombre. "I long to see the world outside — the glowing gold and the ever blue above. But I have no way of walking, as you do, and so must stay forever here in darkness."

Danu's blue-green eyes shifted from the river, staring far off through the woods to a land she knew lay beyond. She let a finger glide upon the water's surface, leaving a trail of ripples in its wake.

"Well, little river," the goddess replied. "I shall teach you how to run."

Her pale hands, white as a full moon, dipped slowly into the still waters, scooping it gently into her cupped palms and bringing it to the grass at the river's edge. She spilled it out upon the earth, and the little droplets dripped down, rejoining the larger body. In doing so, the river gained an inch. It moved.

With the patience of a parent watching their child take its first steps, Danu guided the river with each slow, uncertain inch. It moved timidly at first, meandering its way through moss and grass. As courage filled it, the river became more daring, gurgling against little rocks and tiny roots. Under Danu's guidance the river began to run, soon chasing the goddess out of the woodland and through the valley. Down hills and mountains, they moved. Danu sang, and her song fell in tune with the river's rushing waters.

Countless miles they travelled, and the river saw many things it had longed to see. The sun's glittering glory shined above, rising high into the great blue sky. The river passed tall grasses and great trees laden low with ripened fruit. As time drew on, the colours of the world moved and shifted. The green leaves lost their lustre, descending to the earth in bright shades of orange and red and yellow. And at evening time, a silver face would grace the black night, and glittering stars would dance about her head. All the while Danu sang, and her song became the river's song — bringing the world alive with new music.

Little creatures came to their sound. Foxes splashed in the river and birds bathed themselves. Wild horses drank from its shores and ran along its edges beside the goddess. Their adventure went along merrily enough, until they reached the land's end. Now a world of water lay at the goddess' feet — they had finally found the sea.

Danu turned to the little river then.

"Now I must leave you to journey on your own," she said with her nurturing smile. "There are many things that the ocean can show you, and you can teach it our song."

So the river parted from Danu, goddess of all. For many years it travelled on the vast ocean. The deep waters began to dance to the river's song, making mighty waves against ragged shorelines. The sea still sways to that same sweet melody.

The little river saw much of the world. Shorelines of sands, of ice and snow were all things it came to know. It wore down rocks with its crashing waves and felt creatures move within its form, swollen now to greater weight in the immense ocean. The river was happy, having finally reached its journey's end.

Then one day, upon seeing a grove of trees across some distant shore, the little river remembered the woodland where it had lived in shadows. It remembered Danu, and the journey they had taken together. Having finally reached a world where the sky was ever above and the sun always bright, it began to miss the quiet forest, and its adventure to the sea.

"Oh mother Danu," the river said in reminiscence, "I miss the days when we would wander. What I would give to ramble the woods as we once did."

"And so you shall," a gentle voice seemed to whisper on the wind.

The sun shone bright that day and warmed the cool waters that made up the river's being. It began to feel as if made of air, rising from the dark waters of the deep sea. It ascended to the sky, shifting in form from vapour to cloud. High above the land, the little river glided in its fluffy countenance, moving past the shorelines that fenced in the ocean.

The cloud was carried by the wind, drifting along like a little boat loosed from its dock. It soared over mountains and valleys until once more the floating figure gazed upon its home. The little cloud had grown colder on its travels, the weariness of miles weighing heavily upon it now. It began to feel itself slip from the sky, falling back to the world in tiny little water drops.

And so the first rain fell upon the earth. The little river had come home.

Even to this day, the river makes its cyclic journey from its homeland into the sea, exploring the beauty of the natural world on its path. It has grown greater as the years have passed, no longer a creeping stream but a grand and flourishing form. It is known and praised throughout the wide world, flowing through many cities and many countries. Its name is Danube, after the goddess who taught it to run.

Kellee Kranendonk

Kranendonk is the New Brunswick author with over one hundred published short stories, poems, and articles to her credit.

She brings with her her story, 'Galwain of Cork.'

Galwain of Cork

Galwain leapt off his horse and kicked a patch of grass. The chance to be a MacCool warrior was going to slip right through his crooked fingers. Snatching up the horse's reins, he stalked to the stable. Inside, he pulled his gauntlets off then struggled to take the halter off the horse.

"Galwain, what's wrong?"

He turned around to see Iseult, his half-sister, standing in the doorway. "Nothing," he grumbled.

"I can see you are trying to hide something from me. What is it?"

"Go away, Iseult. Let me take care of Charger."

Iseult obediently turned to leave, but as Galwain hooked his fingers around the halter again, she spoke once more. "I saw your afflicted fingers yesterday, when you first arrived home. What bothers you so?"

Galwain took the halter off Charger, hung it on a peg, then affectionately swatted the horse's flank.

"Do you not find happiness being with your family after being away for so many years in training?" asked Iseult.

"'Tis not that."

"Please. Maybe I can help you."

Galwain looked at the young woman standing before him. He had not seen her since she was a child of three. But he'd heard the tales – they said his half-sister was a sorceress. A sorceress could take away his pain with a simple spell. "Are the tales true?"

"Tales?"

"The ones that tell of your powers."

Iseult smiled. "Do you believe everything you hear, Galwain?"

Galwain flung his misshapen hand out in front of her. "Can you help these?"

She leaned closer to him, her long hair falling over her shoulders. "I know someone who can help."

"Why did you not tell me when you saw my pain? Merlin says because of these fingers I cannot be knighted in three years. I must remain a squire."

"I am sorry, brother. I did not know these things."

"Merlin says I cannot even go to the Fair."

"The Knight's Fair?"

"Aye."

"Why do you wish to go there? Drunkenness, harlots, and brawling abound."

"I do not wish to do those things. I go because the squires are able show off their talents. Those who show exceptional ability may be chosen to be knighted early and may choose to become a knight in the King's Service or become a MacCool warrior."

"Which do you choose, Galwain?"

"I choose the help you spoke of."

"Of course." She took his hands in hers. "But you must pass many dangerous gates."

"I am not afraid."

"Not afraid of what, brother?" a voice came from the stable door. Galwain glanced past Iseult to see his younger brother, Ronan

"Peril," said Iseult, twisting her head around to look at Ronan. "Galwain wishes to seek aid for his affliction. 'Tis the only way he can become a King's knight, or a MacCool warrior."

Ronan frowned. "Father will not be happy if you choose to become part of MacCool's band."

"And what of you, Ronan?" asked Galwain. "What do you think?"

"A MacCool warrior fights for the people," said Ronan. "I believe that is more noble than fighting the King's battles as Merlin's knights do."

Galwain looked at Iseult again. "What must I do? Where must I go?"

"You must go to the Lu Chorpan Mountains."

Ronan gasped. He, like Galwain, knew the legends. They told of the danger within the black mountains. But Galwain would face the risk to be a warrior with MacCool's band.

"And what of Father?" asked Ronan.

"If I do not go, I'll never be more than a squire. Father will have to see that becoming a warrior is much more honourable."

Standing in the middle of a wooden barge, crossing

the river in the rain with his horse, Charger, nibbling the hair hanging down his back was not Galwain of Cork's idea of a good beginning. He hoped this wasn't a sign of things to come.

"And how might your father be, Galwain?" Maeldun's old, lined face gleamed with rain. His eyes, circled with dark rings, peered out from under the hood of a heavy cloak.

"My father is well," said Galwain offering nothing more. He suspected Maeldun asked about more than just Mark of Cork and he preferred to keep his concerns, his concerns. If the old ferrier knew, then all of Cork would know what an oaf Galwain was.

"Your stepmother and half-sister are well?" The old man pushed the barge away from shore with a heavy stick.

"The ladies are fine, as is my younger brother."

Maeldun nodded but narrowed his eyes as he looked at the young squire.

Galwain sighed and looked toward the opposite riverbank. Maeldun always seemed to know everything, even without one telling him. The younger man felt the eyes of the older boring into his back. "I seek help," he said when he could ignore the feeling no longer.

Maeldun placed his old, wrinkled hand over Galwain's gauntleted one. "For this, young squire?" he murmured.

Galwain looked into Maeldun's blue eyes. "Am I to forever be a squire, as Merlin says?"

Maeldun showed no surprise as he turned his gaze toward the black Lu Chorpan Mountains. "Some say there is magic in those mountains. Some say old Finn MacCool lives there yet with the fairies and wee bodies. They say when he dies all of Erin's land will hear the banshees scream his name." The rain slowed as he strained against the thick wooden stick, pushing the raft further across the river. With his other hand he reached deep into a pocket of his cloak, then shoved his hand into one of Charger's satchels. "You'll be needing that."

Both horse and rider well knew the way up the narrow path along the riverbank. Leading away from the river, it wound through the woods to the top of a small hill. Here, Galwain stared down across the open moor to the mountains on the other side. The rain had changed to mist and the sun peeked through the breaking cloud cover, shining on the purple heath below.

He'd played there in the meadow as a child. Some considered him still a child at eighteen. But he had finished his training and had returned home to carry out his duties as squire. The children were the knights-in-training.

If the magic of the mountains was powerful enough to heal his afflicted fingers, he could become a knight in three years. Sooner if he could prove worthy enough for MacCool's band of warriors.

Although Galwain had been down this path and across the moor many times, none of those times had led to the mountains. No one had ever dared get close.

He pulled the gauntlets off his hands and stared at the crooked fingers that had become worse with each injury he'd sustained in training. Even as his fingers ached, his wrist began throbbing as though the ailment were alive.

Would the mountain's magic be powerful enough to cure it? He could find out only one way.

Down the hill to the meadow, he rode. There at the edge of the green and purple, the horse began to gallop. Wind rushed through Galwain's hair, the hood of his cloak snapping as he raced across the heath.

Halfway across the lea, Galwain halted Charger. The ominous Lu Chorpan Mountains loomed before him as the sun reached its zenith. Shading his eyes with his gauntleted hand, he scanned the sky. A lone raven flew high above him then circled around, screeching as if calling out to him.

Ignoring the bird, Galwain kicked his horse's flanks and snapped the reins. Charger tossed his head then ran.

With stiff and weary arms and legs, he reached the base of the mountains, the sinking sun hidden behind them. After Galwain dismounted Charger, the horse wandered away, doubtless in search of drink and rest. But Galwain didn't worry. The horse never ventured too far from his master.

The young squire turned his gaze from horse to mountainside. He pulled off one of his gauntlets and ran his crooked fingers over the smooth stone. Iseult had told him to go through the mountains – that meant there should be either a long dark passageway right here under the mountains or a path leading somewhere else. But he saw neither. "Iseult, is there a secret you forgot to tell me of?" he muttered.

Suddenly part of the mountain wall opened up, revealing a dark cave beyond. Galwain peered into the gloom wondering if that were the way through.

At once unicorns began rushing out – two dozen or more, all pure white except for two who were the colour of a blacksmith's dead coals. One of the two stopped before him. "What is your task here, human?" The unicorn's voice, though husky, was distinctly female.

"I seek help," answered Galwain.

The black unicorn nodded her head. "Then you must prove you are strong enough to travel through the mountains."

"I am a squire in the King's service."

She snorted. "A squire means nothing to me, human. A duel is in order."

"Who must I fight?"

The unicorn lowered her head and pointed her coiled ebony horn. Galwain turned to find the white unicorns in a semicircle behind him. In the centre stood the other black.

Galwain reached for the sword on his back and forced his fingers to curl around the hilt. He held it out before him as the unicorn dashed at him, head down, horn pointed at his breastplate.

The squire swung his blade, slicing into the unicorn's horn. As half of it dropped to the ground, Galwain laughed. "You cannot hurt me," he shouted.

"Oh, can't I?" asked the unicorn in a male voice. He tossed his head and his coat twinkled like a thousand falling stars.

The other unicorns began making a strange noise that sounded to Galwain like all the people of Cork screaming at once. The black male's half horn started to grow and twist, longer and thicker than the one before it.

Galwain raised his sword. The unicorn swung his head, knocking the weapon to the ground. He pulled his great horn back and pushed forward, driving the horn into Galwain's leg. Then he lifted his head, Galwain dangling from the horn, and drew it down so swiftly it flung Galwain into the dark cave. He landed on the hard ground on his stomach and gasped for air.

As he tried to bring air into his lungs, get to his feet and watch for unicorns all at once, Galwain understood this was the first of the many gates Iseult had warned him about.

Once on his feet, the air flowing smoothly into his chest, he saw the unicorns had disappeared and the opening was closing, leaving him in the darkness. The puncture on his leg began to ache. He touched it with his bare hand. His fingers came away wet. But Galwain had many battle wounds. This didn't worry him. He fretted more about Charger. He could survive with a bloody wound in his leg, but he doubted he could survive without his horse.

A hushed laughing, along with a rustling and scuttling began. Galwain knew the legends of these mountains told of the Lu Chorpan – the wee bodies – that inhabited them. They also told of magic and fairies and Morrigan the goddess who could change her form at will. These stories were as much a part of Galwain's life as breathing. Could the magic that had kept Finn MacCool alive, as Maeldun had said, also—

Something hard hit his head and the darkness began to spin. He reached out for something to hold on to but there was only the darkness.

Galwain opened his eyes to an emerald glow. He smelled earth, green pastures, and heather. Sitting up to search his surroundings, he saw a little boy and girl, sitting in rocking chairs, watching him. Pushing his hair away from his face, he studied them. They looked like no children he'd seen before. Long green tendrils curled out of the girl's blonde hair and dangled around her ears. The boy's hair shot up in jagged green spikes. The glow seemed to come from them. Galwain wondered if they were fairies. He'd always thought fairies would be smaller, perhaps the size of sparrows, not his young nieces and nephews.

The boy rose from his chair and held his arms out in front of him. Galwain's sword lay across his palms.

"This belongs to you, sir," he said.

"Yes." Galwain said. "Who are you? Who is your father?"

"We have no father," the boy told him. "We are the fairies that live in this mountain."

"What happened to me?"

"The Lu Chorpan," said the little girl, as if that explained everything.

"The wee bodies?" asked Galwain.

"Yes. They do not like humans and try to turn them away," said the girl fairy. "But they can be helpful if there is something to be gained by it."

"They dropped a stone on your head," said the boy fairy and laughed, one spike falling over his eye. To Galwain, it looked like a giant blade of grass.

"'Tis not clever, Partholon," said the girl to the boy, then turned to Galwain. "He thinks everything the Lu Chorpan do is clever."

"It did not feel clever to me," said Galwain. "But I must continue my journey. Would either of you know where my steed is?"

The girl nodded then said something to Partholon which Galwain could not understand. Partholon left the room and the girl moved closer to Galwain's bed. "We dressed your wound," she said, pushing a thick woollen blanket away from his legs. "It will heal quickly."

Galwain looked down and saw a cloth that looked like woven vines tied around his leg.

"Here," said the girl. "Drink this and remember it."

She gave him a stone cup containing milk, which seemed to have appeared out of thin air, but Galwain drank thirstily. Fairies were magical after all.

As he finished, Partholon came back, leading Charger. Galwain got out of his bed and took the reins from the boy who held up a small brown skin bag. "Does this belong to you as well, sir? I found it near the steed."

Galwain took the skin bag from him. He'd never seen it before, but could it have been what Maeldun had given him? He opened the bag and emptied the contents into his hand. "A stone?" he said, looking at the small black stone lying in his palm. "'Tis all?"

"Things are not always what they seem," said the girl.

"Be on your way now," said Partholon and then both of them disappeared, leaving Galwain once again in the dark.

Charger whinnied softly as the stone began to glow. Murmurs echoed through the cave. Galwain turned this way and that but saw nothing except the shadowy walls of the tunnel. Even the soft bed of ferns and the rocking chairs were gone.

There was only one path to take, one direction in which to walk. As he started through the tunnel, horse reins in his hand, his arms began to ache. He held one hand up in front of his face. His fingers were more gnarled than they'd ever been, his wrists swollen. It seemed to him that just being inside the mountain made his hands worse, not better. Perhaps Iseult had been wrong. Perhaps he should have stayed home. But now he had to go on. No matter where this path took him, he had to follow it.

The stone lit the passage that twisted and turned on through the mountain. At each turn, Galwain glanced behind him. Always there was solid stone, as if the wall followed him.

Then, as he rounded yet another turn, he saw shafts of light coming from the stone ceiling. He approached the first column with caution, noticing the stone in his hand had become a black lump again. The shafts provided enough light for him to see now. He looked up to see a sun shining in a blue sky through the holes in the rock.

Suddenly something fell from the farthest column of daylight. The one giant eye of a Balor gleamed in front of him. The ogre was even uglier than he'd imagined ogres to be. Spittle spilled out from between huge lips. The skin of his cheeks sagged in wrinkled folds. He growled and shuffled toward Galwain.

The horse snorted loudly and tossed his head, pulling

the reins out of Galwain's hand, causing him to stumble and drop the stone as he reached for his sword. He knew the only way to kill a Balor was to stab his giant eye. But his gnarled hand refused to grasp his weapon. The constant murmuring and scuffling grew louder. Galwain looked to see what caused the sounds. A bow and arrow lay on the rock floor. Wondering if the weapons had once been Maeldun's enchanted stone, Galwain reached for them. But he could no more lift that than he could his sword. The Balor edged toward him, nearly tripping over his own giant feet.

Two squat humans appeared before Galwain, both wearing long green coats, tiny green caps, and long green stockings – Lu Chorpan! They were nothing but misfortune. He wondered what they were going to do.

The Lu Chorpan worked together, one taking the bow and one the arrow. Galwain knew Lu Chorpan were solitary creatures, appearing to humans one at a time. To show themselves before him like this must mean they worked together against a common enemy. But Galwain didn't know whether he or the Balor was the enemy.

The Balor hobbled closer, grunting and grasping at the air. The muttering and scuttling like a thousand rodents grew louder. The two Lu Chorpan in front of Galwain strung the arrow onto the bow then aimed for him. He clawed at his sword again, the ache in his hands shooting up his arms. The weapon clattered to the floor.

"No, turn around. Turn the other way. Shoot the Balor, oaf, not the human!" shouted one wee body to the other.

The little men swung around, pulled the arrow back and let it fly. The arrow, skilfully shot by the tiny archers, hit its mark. The Balor groaned and dropped to the ground with a resounding thud.

"The ogres'll not come back to our mountain," said one Lu Chorpan, proudly.

"Aye," agreed the second.

Then both of them flitted away and the murmuring waned again. Galwain fell to his knees. The Lu Chorpan had first tried to kill him with a rock, then they'd saved his life. Wasn't that just like a wee body? But of course, they'd been protecting themselves as well, this time. The Balor was a bigger threat than the foul human that Galwain was. He fumbled for the sword and managed to slip it back into its sheath on his back. His arms burned like fire at his sides. He stood up and although he couldn't grip the reins, the horse followed obediently when he clucked.

They moved through the shafts of light until they came to an entrance glowing with soft orange light. Just outside this entrance, sat a bard, reciting poetry. As Galwain approached, the bard looked up at him. "And who might ye be?"

"I am Galwain of Cork. Son of Mark of Cork, brother of Ronan. . ."

"Yes, yes," said the Bard, as though remembering someone from long ago. "And why might you be here in the mountain?"

"I wish to seek help so I may become a Finn MacCool warrior."

The Bard nodded. "Ah yes. Then you must answer a few questions."

"And they might be?"

"Tell me lad, who are the children of Erin's Land?"

Another gate, thought Galwain. But this one was easier than fighting unicorns or ogres. "The children of Erin's Land all have the same mother."

"Aye," said the Bard. "Her name, young squire."

"Dana. Her offspring, the children of Ireland, are Tuatha De Danann."

"Very good," said the Bard calmly from his stone stool. "Now tell me how Finn MacCool obtained his knowledge."

"The old druid Finnegan gave him the Salmon of Knowledge to eat."

The Bard nodded again. "Now me lad, you must answer a riddle.

"Tis the gift of life
"Which comes from a mother, a doe, a wife
"Twas given to you
"And feeds all offspring too."

No wonder the questions were so simple. The Bard was playing with his mind, making him think this test was easy.

"You think about that, me lad," said the Bard, getting up and disappearing into the glowing entrance beside him. Galwain didn't know when he would be back. It could be minutes or days.

'Tis the gift of life. Water was the element of life, but water came from the ground not people or animals. *'Twas given to you.* Maeldun had given him an enchanted stone, but stones, magical or not, certainly didn't feed offspring. Galwain turned to his horse and tried to grasp his mane. His gnarled fingers just slid across the horse's neck and through the hair. "What is it, Charger? What's the answer?

Where are the fairies and wee bodies now?"

He wished the fairies were here, with their stone cups and soft beds. He could use rest and drink now. But he dare not rest, lest the Bard come back and find him asleep, without an answer to the riddle. Galwain started to reach into one of the satchels on the horse. He could surely eat and think, couldn't he? But as he stretched forth his hands, he realized he couldn't grab a piece of bread or a wineskin, even if he wanted to. How had he made it this far with only the porridge and water Iseult had made for him on that morning that felt so long ago. He'd had nothing more, except…

"Milk," he whispered into the horse's neck. "The fairies gave me milk. 'Tis what she meant by remember it. She gave me the gift of life. Mother's milk, doe's milk. 'Tis how offspring are fed."

"How wise you are, Galwain of Cork."

Galwain spun around to see the Bard sitting once again on the stone. "Is the test done?"

The Bard laughed. "What makes you think 'tis a test?"

"'Tis it not a gate I must pass through to get the help I seek?"

"You are wise indeed, Galwain of Cork. But there is one more thing you must do before you go on."

"What is it?"

"A poem. You must recite a poem. All of Finn MacCool's warriors must do this. Surely you knew that before you came."

Galwain nodded. He did indeed know. There was very little he didn't know about Finn MacCool and his band. He'd been prepared to study the required poetry and prose to be a MacCool warrior. He was even prepared to leave his family to live like a minstrel for the rest of his life.

"You may begin now."

Now? He was expected to recite on demand? "Am I to be given no time to think?"

The Bard stood up and stepped toward Galwain. "No. Finn's men must be able to recite upon demand. Your wit must not be dull in Finn's band."

Galwain swallowed dryly and began to stutter out a poem:

"There was a young man named Galwain
"With hands that were wrenched in pain
"He passed all his tests
"Now he just wants his rest
"Then with MacCool's band he'll reign."

The Bard backed off with a smile on his face. Galwain wanted to slap himself. Why had he been so presumptuous and said he passed all his tests? Why had he said reign? He should have said train; with MacCool's band, he'll train, not reign. Had he come this far only to fail?

"Very well, me lad. You may go on to seek the help you need." The Bard bowed slightly towards him, then disappeared into the glow.

Galwain shouted with joy. "I passed the test. I shall go past this gate." His words echoed in the darkness but Galwain didn't care. He was closer to finding what he needed. He hooked his curled fingers around the horse's reins and led him into the orange glow. But, stepping through, he found himself facing the same moor as he'd ridden through before. Except, now he looked at it from high up in the clouds. But he knew it was the same one. He recognized every bog and every shrub with its branches stretching out as if to reach up and pull him down.

The wind whistled furiously, blowing Galwain's hair into his eyes. The hood of his cloak shuddered on his shoulders. Galwain knocked the hair away from his face, to search for the path, if indeed one existed.

He saw a narrow dirt path twisting around the mountain. He'd about need to become a part of the mountain to travel it. One wrong step meant tumbling to his death in the heath below. Putting one leather-clad foot onto the path, he forced his gaze away from the green death below. A hag stood where no one had been before. Galwain leapt back toward the mountain, away from the hideous creature.

"You must follow me," she cackled, showing broken, black teeth. "The path is sometimes narrow and most times treacherous. Do you wish to go on or turn back?"

She stared at him with narrow eyes, awaiting his response. Her long white hair lay on her shoulders as though no wind whistled around the rocky wall. She pulled her cloak tighter around her with wrinkled hands.

"I will follow," answered Galwain. He did not fear her ugliness nor her magic.

Behind the hag he trod carefully, pressing against the mountainside and praying the horse could hold his own. Often the path took sharp turns, squeezing through columns of rock or going almost straight up. Galwain closed his eyes and continued his steps.

At last, the path threaded through two tall, stone pillars. Atop these pillars lay a slab of rock, causing the formation to look like a doorway. Upon passing between them, the hag became a beautiful maiden, a wreath of flowers upon her flowing golden hair. Behind her lay a rippling blue-green pond.

"My name is Morrigan." She spoke in a voice as sweet as honey. "The water in this pond will cure your affliction. But you must swim in it for three days, unclothed." With this command, the maiden became a raven and with a screech, flew away.

"Of course," Galwain mumbled to himself. "The legendary Morrigan. The shape-changer that offers both trickery and aid."

But Morrigan's command seemed to contain no trickery, so Galwain began to take off his clothing. In his exhausted state, even the simple task of undressing fatigued him. How would he manage to keep his head above water for three days? Especially with hands like his.

Galwain pawed at the buttons on his long underwear but his fingers could no longer work them open. Exhaustion and frustration ripped through him and he kicked at his cloak lying on the ground. He threw his arms around the horse's neck and screamed, "What am I supposed to do, Charger? I will never be a knight, never!"

The horse reared up, pulling Galwain's arms apart and knocking him down. Pain shot up his back as he fell on a sharp stone. Galwain flung his clawed hands over his face. Knights were not supposed to act in this infuriated manner, but most knights didn't have claws for fingers. Hot tears ran down his face, but they only made him more furious. He was a man, not an infant.

A loud cry caused him to look up. Morrigan had returned and was sitting upon Charger's back. The horse, now calm, sniffed at the water's edge. Morrigan shrieked again and hopped up and down, flapping her wings. Galwain pushed himself to his feet and went to her. She leaned toward him to tug at the buttons with her strong black beak. She dropped each one to the ground, and when the last had fallen, she looked up at him. Galwain wiped at the wetness still on his cheeks.

"Passions flow hot in the mountains." The black bird spoke in a human voice. "You are a man, not a stone. And a man you must be to become a knight." Then she flew away once more.

Galwain watched her flying high in the sky. Everything in the mountain seemed to be nothing but riddles. But he had no time to figure this one out. He had to splash about in the water in an attempt to swim out his aches and pains, for if the pond didn't work, he'd not even be able to go back to the King's Service as a squire.

The pain flowed up into his elbows now; he could feel it pushing on up, even to his shoulders. He rushed into the tarn, flailing his arms, struggling to keep his head above water.

By the end of the day, his arms felt like lumps of thrumming dead flesh. The wound in his leg throbbed and his back felt tied in knots. He gulped in great breaths of air, pushing himself on, sinking below the surface, then bobbing above it. Sinking and bobbing, sinking and bobbing, he went until the break of dawn.

As the sun marked the beginning of the second day, his leg stopped its constant pounding, his back untied each and every knot and his arms began to feel lighter until he floated, his muscles resting.

By nightfall he had fallen asleep, and in his dreams he saw himself in battle, no pain in his hands, his body, his fingers. He saw himself being chosen for the best duties rather than the paltry ones. He saw himself weeping over many deaths and Merlin, the old knight who'd trained him, beside him, tears shining on his face. Perhaps it was acceptable for a gallant knight to weep.

Galwain saw princesses being tortured by dragons and more knights in battle. He saw himself a victorious knight.

The morning of the third day dawned bright and warm. Galwain felt the water streaming over long, straight fingers and hands that had become strong and free of pain. For a moment he felt as nimble as a fish, but his arms grew heavy again. This time, no matter how he struggled, he couldn't push himself onward and upward. His head sank below the surface. Down, down, down into the deepest recesses of the mountain lake. Now, he would drown alone and unknown.

Up, up, up out of the water Galwain rose, lifted by black swans. Then the swans became ravens that carried him through the air to the shore where they laid him beside a blazing fire. An old man, wearing a hooded cloak knelt beside him and offered him a skin of water. "There be meat as well, me lad, when ye be ready for it," the old man said, his voice grating, like leaves crumpled under foot.

Galwain sat up and tried to stop the shivers that racked his body. Without a word, the old man wrapped a heavy woollen blanket around Galwain's shoulders while he drank from the skin. Then he gave him meat in a wooden bowl. With the first mouthful, Galwain realized how hungry he was and greedily devoured all that was given. There seemed to be no end to the food.

When Galwain's hunger was sated, the old man pushed his hood down and smiled. His teeth seemed too big for his mouth. Although his grey hair was long and shaggy, he wore no whiskers and his eyes looked as young as Galwain's. "Me name is Finn MacCool, laddie, and who might ye be?"

Galwain stared at him. Could this indeed be Finn MacCool? Paladin of Erin's Land? Surely it could not. But how many shaggy-haired, big-toothed old men might live in the mountains? Galwain dared not insult the old knight by questioning him. "I am Galwain of Cork, sir."

The old man nodded. "'Tis the water that kept me alive for more years than I should be. Perhaps a little magic from the fairies as well. What might ye be wantin' a way up here in me mountain, lad."

Galwain held up his hands. "They once were painfully misshapen, sir, keeping me from proving my use as a MacCool warrior. But the water has healed them now."

MacCool reached over and touched Galwain's leg. "Fixed ye leg as well, me lad."

Galwain looked down at his leg where the unicorn had pierced him. The dressing the fairies had wrapped around it was now gone, leaving a faint green trace. Only a small round scar remained. "Yes," he agreed.

"The unicorns were your first test, me lad. Now ye have passed all but one."

Galwain didn't understand. His hands were healed. He could join the ranks of knights that had become Finn MacCool warriors. He'd survived all that the mountain had put before him. What test had he failed?

"Dress yeself, lad. Then fetch me your magical stone," commanded MacCool, as though he'd read the younger man's mind. He turned his back on Galwain.

Galwain found his clothes folded upon a stone and he put them on straightaway. Then he went to his horse and slid his hands into a satchel. Long, straight fingers slipped across the leather. No knots, no pain... and no food. At once he realized there was nothing in his satchels. No skins of water and none of the bread and cheese Iseult had sent with him. Worst of all there was no small, black, enchanted stone. Where had it gone? Had it fallen out of the satchel? Had someone stolen it when he'd been in the lake?

Then he remembered he'd dropped the stone in the cave. Even if the enchanted stone hadn't turned into the weapon the wee bodies had used against the Balor, they certainly would have kept it if they found it. If there might be a chance they had not, how could he find it? What kind of knight allowed his things to be stolen? Was this the test MacCool meant? Had he failed to prove his worthiness to be a Finn MacCool warrior? If he couldn't even protect what belonged to him, how could he protect the people?

"Ye be young, lad. Ye might have another chance to prove yourself worthy of being a warrior in my service."

"What would I have to do?" asked Galwain.

"Pass back through the mountain."

"That's all? Just go back?" asked Galwain and the ancient MacCool nodded, a smile on his lips and a twinkle in his eyes.

Galwain curled his fingers around his steed's reins and stepped toward the entrance to the mountain's heart. A scream from within the mountain, sudden and piercing, told him what the old warrior's smile had tried to. He only had to go back to prove his worth, but going back would have its own trials.

Inside the dark tunnel, the screaming continued but Galwain could see nothing. All forms of light were gone.

He would have to depend on his ears to lead him to the sound. He stumbled toward the sound and soon came upon the shafts of light, where the Balor had tumbled in from above. Another Balor now stood near the deceased one, holding none other than Galwain's own half-sister, Iseult. "Help me, Galwain," she cried. "Mark has sent me to fetch you. Ronan is. . ." The Balor clapped his big fleshy hand over her mouth, cutting off her words.

Ronan was what? Here? Marrying? Dead? And why had Mark sent his message with a young woman?

Galwain reached for his sword and clenched it in his new strong fingers. Wielding the weapon above his head, he dashed toward the Balor. But apparently, he wasn't as witless as he looked. He ducked his one ugly eye behind Iseult as though she were his shield.

As Iseult struggled to be free of the Balor's grip, Galwain stopped and fixed his feet fast upon the ground. Gripping his sword with both hands, he held it above his head, waiting for the perfect opportunity. With the eye covered, the Balor was blind to whatever Galwain chose to do. Keeping the blade ready, high above his head, he shambled to the left of the Balor. The ogre grunted and groaned, spittle soaking into Iseult's dress. Although she wriggled fiercely, she watched her half-brother silently.

As Galwain approached the Balor from the left, the ogre lowered Iseult, his giant eye roving the cave, no doubt searching for Galwain. The squire leapt toward the monstrous Balor, as quickly as a wild cat upon prey, and stabbed the sword deep into the big black eye. As the ogre toppled, Iseult fell from his arms. Then her form became a raven, swooping up toward the light. Had it really been his sister, wondered Galwain, watching the black speck grow smaller as it flew higher, or had it been Morrigan?

Scuttling and laughter drew his attention away from the bird and back to the dark cave. He needed to fetch back what once had been his, but how would he find the wee bodies? "Lu Chorpan, Lu Chorpan, where be ye?" he called out, not expecting to hear a response as he replaced his sword.

"Is this what ye be lookin' for, laddie?" came a voice from the shadows, startling Galwain.

Galwain turned around and saw a wee body holding up the enchanted stone. It glowed green in the little man's hand. Galwain held out his own hand to take, it but the wee body snatched it back. "What'll ye be givin' me in return for yer magical stone?"

"I have nothing, but the stone is mine," said Galwain.

"'Tis in my hand, 'tis mine now," argued the wee body.

Galwain stared down at him, afraid all the tales he'd heard were true. "I shall give you the side of my blade if you don't give me the stone."

The wee body laughed.

"You helped me before. Why will you not help me now?"

"Now I have yer magic. And it was such easy takin' too."

That reminded Galwain of how he'd lost it in the first place and he almost took his eyes off the wee body to make sure no more ogres tumbled in from the columns of light. "You'll not get away from me this time, Lu Chorpan."

The wee body wriggled uneasily as Galwain continued staring at him. The scuttling and murmuring resounded behind him, but this time there was no food to be had from his satchels.

The little man twitched and took off his green cap. Sweat gleamed on his bald head.

The murmurs grew louder. Thuds and knocks came and went but still Galwain stared at the little man, who began trembling.

"There's a Balor behind ye," claimed the wee body. "Don't ye feel his hot breath? Can ye not smell his stink?"

"I'll not be tricked by you again. Come over here and give me the stone, little man," demanded Galwain, pulling his sword from the scabbard on his back.

The wee body shivered so badly now, the tails of his little green coat shuddered behind him. He used both hands to wipe away the sweat from his eyes and as he did, Galwain's stone dropped to the ground. The squire lunged toward the troublemaker.

With the tip of the sword at the wee body's neck and his eyes boring into the wee one's, he felt around for his stone. Only when he had it in his fingers, did he pull the blade away from the little man's flesh.

"Aye, I'm no good as a wee body anymore, I'm not. Ye beat me at me own game, laddie. What shall I do now?"

"Aye yourself, wee one. You'll not trick me with your words. Find another dullard to play your games with."

"Ye needn't look at me anymore. Please turn yer eyes away."

"The sack, little man. I need the stone's sack."

The wee body slumped as he reached into the pocket of his coat. "What will ye give me for it?"

Galwain pressed his sword harder against the wee body.

"Aye, ye can have it, Sir Knight." The wee body took the sack from the pocket of his coat and Galwain snatched it away. He placed the stone carefully inside, hung the bag around his neck, tucking it inside all of his clothes until it lay soft and warm against his chest. He sheathed his sword and turned away from the Lu Chorpan.

Finn MacCool stood before him. Galwain glanced back into the shadows. The wee body was gone.

"Finn MacCool, sir," he said, looking at the fabled warrior.

"Ye have passed your final test. Ye have learned a valuable lesson here, me lad. Never forget it. Ye will be a good addition to the MacCool band."

"Thank you, sir."

"Now ride, Galwain of Cork, ride like the wind on your warrior's steed."

Galwain turned to Charger. The horse now wore armour with a shamrock-shaped pendant dangling from the breast collar. The new knight turned back to MacCool, but like the wee body, he was gone.

Unicorns no longer guarded the entrance to the cave. The horse with its rider shot out into the blinding sunlight, through the moor and along the dirt path to the barge. Charger had just begun to breathe heavy as they stopped at the river's edge.

Looking at the wide, blue river winding between green banks and Maeldun pushing his barge across it, Galwain heard a cry from above. Lifting his gaze toward the sky, he saw the raven, circling over him. Iseult or Morrigan, he wondered once more.

Though the old ferrier eyed Galwain, he did not speak until they reached the other bank. "Are you on your way home, young squire?"

"Ah, a squire I no longer am, Maeldun."

Maeldun nodded as if those words alone told him all he needed to know. "You'd best avoid Mark's house, lest his anger destroy you."

Galwain got off the barge in silence. He knew he'd never see his family again, and yet the battles he'd fight would be for them. The rights they'd earn would be, in part, because of him. Tears dampened his cheeks as he kicked Charger's flanks. Wind whipped his hair as he rode. Twin ravens, from out of nowhere, flew on either side of him. His strong fingers gripped Charger's reins.

To protect his country's populace, even against his father's wishes was, for Galwain, the greatest honour in all of Erin's Land.

Emily S. Dodge

Born in Massachusetts and currently residing in Nova Scotia, Dodge has been turning heads with her early entries into fiction. She has won the *Nova Writes Joyce Barkhouse Writing for Young Adults Award*; was longlisted for the *Voyage 2020 First Chapters Contest*; and took third place in the April 2020 Kit Sora Flash Fiction Contest.

She brings with her her story, 'Counting Gold,' her first published work.

Counting Gold

She saw the ache in him as he counted, a gnawing hunger that chewed him away piece by piece. It was present in him as long as she could remember, and like her, only grew. It was at its worst in this room and she rarely came, though others scrabbled to see it.

She peered into the room, her hand above her eyes to soften the harsh glare before her; a glare made from gold and jewels. The steady clacking sound of metal on stone was accompanied by her father's counts. *One, two, three.* Every piece, over and over, until each bit of treasure was coated in a fine mist of his breath.

She placed a foot in the room and then drew it back, but it was enough. The light touch echoed in her father's ears and the counting stopped. He turned his head slightly to the side. She could not see his eyes, but she knew he saw her all the same. He said nothing, and why would he? She was the one who had disturbed his sacred time.

"Father," her voice crept up from her throat like a shy rose on the vine that had yet to feel the sun's warmth. "There is a man at the gate."

Still, he said nothing. Her words hung in the air so fully she felt she might reach out and pluck them back.

Then the sharp screech of his chair pushing against the marble floor cut the silence and he strode past. He did not bother to look at her, did not notice that she blinked back tears perpetually suspended in the corners of her eyes.

Philomena trailed her father down the vast hallway, under the gaze of royals long dead. They scolded her with every step. Did she not know how hard each of them had worked to accumulate that fortune? Even her mother's painted eyes shone with disapproval, and Philomena touched her ruddy brown tresses, so unlike the painted crowns of gold that adorned every portrait.

Guards parted as they reached the gate. Their metal breastplates flashed under the glow of freshly lit lamps as the sun fell out of sight, releasing its blinding grip on the day. Her father halted and Philomena felt his anger reach back to her. The figure at the gate was no noble, but ragged in all respects, from his clothes to the fetid stench that even the rose garden failed to conceal.

The stranger threw himself at her father's feet, begging for scraps and a safe place to sleep. She felt her father ready to throw him out, but then he finally looked at her. Their amber eyes met and for a moment he saw her. It was enough. He ordered his men to show the stranger to a room, to give him fresh clothes and food. Philomena allowed herself a smile but as her father marched past, he whispered, "His keep will come from your dowry." And then he was gone, and the steady clacking echoed through the palace once again.

The stranger departed before a tally had been drawn up, and her father was left to continue his counting. Weeks later, when he had taxed back the difference and then some, another appeared on his doorstep, though this one did not need an introduction.

The god of wild things did not often come to the homes of men, instead lingering in the untamed parts of the world. It was the first time Philomena had seen a god in true form and not as a passing flower or bird, and her heart hammered against her ribs. She counted her breaths to steady herself as she watched their new visitor. Here in the palace, he walked on polished marble, and held onto the finest silver, but still he brought the wildness with him. The heady intoxicating scent of a rich summer's day laden with heat and haze and all manner of green things preceded his every step. Ivy draped from his body like exotic silken threads, and a crown of twigs and moss perched on his head. Philomena watched as the people at court ate up that wildness, drank it in heavy draughts until the floor grew slick with wine and sweat, and manic laughter drowned out all other sounds.

The night and festivities wore down until all good things were at rest, and it was just Philomena, her father, and the wild god who sighed out the wine and finally addressed the king.

"My good King Midas. You have helped my dear friend. In gratitude, I offer you payment in the form of a wish," Dionysus said. Philomena watched as her father stroked his chin. She could see him calculating the amount of gold and riches that he should ask for, but she knew that figure could never add to enough. Her father looked down at his other hand, laden with gold rings and a spark lit in his eye.

"I wish for everything I touch to turn to gold," Midas told the god. Philomena's voice caught in her throat, and she was frozen like a statue, unable to speak or even breathe.

"Are you sure?" Dionysus cautioned, but the king was

resolute. The god sighed, his mind once again aching for the release of wine.

"When you wake tomorrow, all that you touch shall turn to gold," he told the king, and then like a shadow, he was gone, stolen back to the woods and wilder things. Air rushed into Philomena's lungs and she found her words.

"Father, what have you done?"

The king waved his hand at her. "I have ensured you will be left with the greatest of legacies," he answered. "Be thankful." He retired and Philomena was left with the silence and a debris field of golden cups and platters, the aftermath of all their excess.

She did not sleep after she left the banquet hall. Every time she closed her eyes, a golden light shone back at her, crept its way into her head, and she gasped awake. When the sun finally rose, it was so bright that Philomena had to shield her eyes to open them. Before she was fully awake, loud shouting echoed through the palace, followed by the clattering of heavy metal things. Then she remembered. The god, her father, and the wish.

She followed the trail of golden wreckage until she came upon him in the garden. The sweet musk scent was gone, and in its place a monolith of golden roses that reeked of metal. Her father hunched there, tears spilling through his fingers, each golden piece clanging to the ground. *One, two, three.*

"Father," she started. His eyes rose to hers, glassed over with tears. He reached out in a desperate gentle embrace and Philomena raised her arm. His hand brushed hers, and the horror of what was done set in. Her legs changed first, welding together, followed by her arm still extended like a magnificent shield. Then it crept up her chest, and her faint breaths echoed in her lungs as they turned to metal. Finally it stole up her face, and the last thing she saw were golden spiderwebs that feathered out in her vision, cracking the world into a thousand gilded fragments, and then there was nothing.

There was no one left to hear his howls, and even if there had been, Midas would have no longer cared. The perfectly composed king was filled with despair and his rage overflowed. He screamed and tore at the earth, kicking up golden dust. Every clink of dirt turned metal echoed through his mind, taunting him with their clattering. He yanked on the roses, once his daughter's favourite, but they were now permanently embedded in the ground, their golden roots too heavy and burdensome for him to wrench from the earth. The metal thorns sliced through his tender skin, and crimson blood emerged, only to pool at his feet in golden puddles, but he did not notice. He strained and he pulled as the wind whispered through the metallic petals of the roses. He screamed louder to drown them out until he collapsed from exhaustion.

Midas woke at his daughter's golden feet, the nightmare sprung back to life. He knew what he had to do. He had spent his life lifting gold pieces and now he hoisted the statute onto his back and struggled towards the woods.

By the time the wayward god appeared, Midas' throat was raw. He had no water to ease it and even if he did, he would only choke up gold.

Dionysus appeared silently as if he had melted out from the trees. All the wild things quieted when he spoke, straining towards his words as if they were a cool breeze. "Good king, why do you disturb the woods with your cries?"

Midas' words spilled out like sand, the begging rough against his lips. Dionysus studied him, a famished king starved from all the things that made gold worthless, and sighed. Lifetimes of the same story were beginning to weary him.

"There is a river that rises from a mountain in Lydia, its name Pactolus. Carry your daughter there and throw yourselves into its water. The river cannot be marred by magic, and so it will cleanse the curse."

Midas thanked him, and hurried off to make the journey, leaving a pile of golden stones where he had cried. Dionysus picked them up, and as they fell through his hand, they changed to water, and the earth drank them up.

Midas hauled his daughter for miles, leaving a shimmering path of golden dust, the sweat transformed from his brow as he trekked the long journey. After many days he stood at the river's edge. It had crept up on him, its muddy brown waters blending into the landscape so well that from a distance it appeared as if there were no river at all. For a moment he despaired at the god. What foul water was this, so turmoiled and murky that could wash away a curse as glittering as his?

But he had travelled so far, and so he dipped his hands in and held his breath, waiting for the water to seal his hands in a golden tomb. But it didn't. The water rushed through his hands, taking the dirt of his journey with it. The king howled with laughter and dragged his daughter out into the water, until the current swept them up in its fold. But even the river could not hold the weight of his child and as he clutched her, they sunk to its depths, wrapped in the water's icy chill.

They sunk down until even the sun could not reach them, but still he held fast. The golden sheen of his daughter turned black, but still he did not let her go. His body tingled, then turned to fire as it demanded air in the watery depths.

His chest throbbed, as if the air would burst through all on its own, but he would not leave her. Midas pulled at his daughter, but she was lodged firm in the riverbed. He tugged until his hand slipped and the current pulled him up.

He could swim back down, but instead he reached for the sunlight that sat shimmering on the water. The sun lit the water with a thousand specks of golden dust. He smiled and water rushed in. For a moment he felt relief; the water stayed water and didn't turn into molten gold. The relief turned to fear when it didn't stop; didn't stop until it filled the whole of his lungs. His body heaved, one final time, and then it was quiet.

Years ambled on and the water and all its creatures ate away at the king until even his bones turned to rock and mud. The river peeled flakes of gold from his daughter's form, piece by piece, carrying them downstream, alighting the river with its sheen. Finally, one day, the soft glow of flesh appeared and Philomena shook free, kicking up towards the muted sunlight that sat on the river's surface. She broke through and pulled air into the soft pith of her lungs. Air thick with the sweet scent of grass and summer. She dragged herself to shore and stood, shaking the last fragments of gold from her body, counting as they landed. *One, two, three.*

Corinne Lewandowski

Corinne is an award-winning poet from Halifax, Nova Scotia whose previous credits include poetry published in Loose Connections and poetry that won the Joyce Marshall Hsia Memorial Poetry Prize.

She currently lives in Lower Sackville with her wife and two cats.

Her first published prose story was 'Family Business' in *Dystopia from the Rock,* followed by 'The Final Invasion' in *Pulp Science-Fiction from the Rock.*

She brings with her her story 'Only Deities Need Apply.'

Only Deities Need Apply

The Scotia Square Mall food court was crammed on payday Thursday. Add happy students on a PD day, IT techs, government workers, and international sports teams trouping around in matching tracksuits and it was chaos.

Chaos and no payday for the unemployed.

Mimi checked her favorite watch from her great-grandfather. A Wittnauer wristwatch, the leather strap, embossed with the letter K for his first name, Kairos, was worn soft from generations. Real numbers stood out on the dial, easy to read in a hurry. Mimi liked to wear it loose. It was anachronistic compared to her interview outfit of a modern black dress jacket, purple collared shirt, and black pants.

Trains had set their timetables by Wittnauer timepieces. She would be late unless she hustled. Mimi athletically weaved between people, dodging the lotto booth line up, and headed to the Barrington Tower elevators.

Luck. A little luck, please.

Another failed interview was not going to appease her oddball landlady.

The thrumming hum noise, waving between sharp and dull pain, undulated from the crowds, leaving it hard to have a decent conversation.

The three deities sitting in the food court close to the lotto booth couldn't be noticed within their protections warding against nosey eavesdroppers and gawkers.

Freyr, the Norse god of sacral kingship, virility, and prosperity slugged his second hazelnut latte. Horus, the Egyptian sky god eyed up his next piece of sushi with his one good eye. Kali, Hindu goddess of time, creation, destruction, and power crunched shortbread cookies and sipped cardamom chai tea.

The deities watched Mimi as she ran for the open elevators and miss them.

"That's the one!" Kali decreed, nodding towards Mimi. A large man had cut in front of Mimi to take the last space in the left car. "She's the one we must help! That's the fifth interview she's blown."

"Yes," Horus said around a mouthful of unagi. "Mimi's landlady is nasty, and it doesn't help she's late on..."

Freyr interpreted with snorting out hazelnut latte.

"And why not him?"

An elderly Indian man, in line for some of the best Indian food in the city, glanced towards Kali. The moment of seeing her luscious dark skin, flowing black hair, and red eyes were not imagined. Kali's image was in his heart and mind from decades of prayers. He cast his eyes down when she looked at him.

"Thought he would've mustered up the courage to speak to you. Every Thursday. Glance, shuffle, glance, shuffle, collect his green bean veggie curry with two poppadums, and glance again. I would've had him at the second glance. We could help him," Freyr snickered.

Kali's lips smiled enigmatically, but her red eyes glowed.

"I help him. He's mine. Aadarsh speaks to me in his daily prayers to the Mother of the Whole Universe. True devotion does not come from being enamoured." Kali punched Freyr's leg hard. "Keep your charms away from him."

"Freyr meant he thought Aadarsh could be chosen and get the courage to be vocal about his devotion, right? Touch arrogant, Mother?" Horus snapped up some sashimi and daikon radish with his fingers as if they were chopsticks.

Kali shrugged. "I don't choose the titles my devotees give me, oh god of the sky, sun and moon."

"Don't talk about my Moon." Horus touched his left eye socket, bereft of his Moon. "We need to get moving. I need to get outside and . . ."

"Spread your wings and fly away little bird!" Freyr pounded the table so hard in laughter, he spilled the rest of his hazelnut latte.

"Hush!"

Freyr stretched out his arms and boomed his voice across the food court. "We are deities in a CONE OF SILENCE! No one can HEAR US!" His deep voice bounced off the tiles and reverberated across the food court. "And they're NOT EVEN LOOKING!"

One person, out of hundreds, paused, looked around as if they should notice something while they slowed briefly in their race to get back to work. In a blink, amnesia removed their curiosity thanks to Horus. Except for

Aadarsh, who gave one more lingering look to Kali before scooping his last bite of curry with a poppadum and leaving.

Kali touched Freyr's leg. "Yes, darling! You're a big, strong presence and handsome and loud." She pierced her nails into the same spot she'd hit earlier. Freyr struggled to muffle a yelp and retain his sense of strength.

"Bloodstains in my designer jeans!"

"Focus! We've work to do." Horus dropped three paper straws he'd been clutching onto the table. One was half the length of the other. "Straws."

"Awwww," Freyr whined.

"No more dice. Everybody skews the results. You both skew the results," said Kali. "Let's see who gets to help Mimi first."

Freyr fist-pumped the air. "Yessssss. I win!"

"Not a contest. We stick together in the New World to help these lost humans. Humans need our help more than ever. Our methods differ, but the destination is the same," Horus finished eating a plate of sashimi.

"Oh darling, our destinations are vastly different too." Kali reached out to stroke Horus' arms. He yanked away his hands and folded them under his arms.

"No touching! I am a king!"

Freyr ran his hands through his golden mane then pulled out a lock of hair to dangle by his eyes. His tight shirt showcased his muscles. He straightened the seam of his new jeans just so. Soft and form-fitting. Much better than wet wool pants on a freezing winter's night in Norway. The current era had some perks over Ancient times.

Everyone waiting for one of three elevator cars to the Cogswell Towers was sneaking looks at him. One young lady with hot pink hair giggled. A man, in a tight white shirt and black suit, felt a surge of heat and took off his jacket and stared at him.

To be seen in his full glory by Mimi, Freyr needed to lower the illusion masking his presence and energy. A few extra folks were going to benefit from his charms today. Ah, there she was.

Mimi briskly came around the hall's tight curve to the elevators and didn't check the corner. She stopped short of running into Freyr.

"Sorry." Mimi didn't look at him. She verified the up button was pressed, checked her watch, and tapped her foot. She groused in her head about the back to lunch crowd, slow elevators, and the one elevator that, she swore, never worked.

Hmmm. Freyr looked around. No one else had a problem seeing him. He could feel the familiar sweet wash of all the energy fueling their love and lust for him and ignored it this time.

How would *she* not see him? A clever thought occurred.

"Mimi!"

She ignored him.

"Mimi!" This time he added a gentle touch to her shoulder.

Mimi flinched her shoulder out of the way, spun to face Freyr, took a short step back, and raised a hand defensively.

"Can I help you?" Her voice was void of helpfulness.

"Don't you remember me?" Freyr powered more

charm through his intentions and smile. Someone behind Mimi sighed.

"No."

The first up elevator dinged. People lingered in loading. The claxon triggered when a gawker, mesmerized at Freyr, held it open too long. The claxon broke everyone *else's* fixation on Freyr.

Mimi backed herself into the last space. It was the last two days of her contract work and she was going to not be late for it.

"We met at that party."

Mimi snorted and stabbed her button, wishing the safety triggered slow closing door would slam closed.

"I don't think so." All that and a bag of chips. Not even for British Paprika Pringles would she have gone out with him back in her teenage years of dating guys.

The doors closed in Freyr's face.

Freyr's lips stuck out, sullen as a rejected junior high kid. The sting wasn't just foreign. It made no sense. Freyr always had the power to draw the attention of anyone of any orientation. You didn't get to be a god bestowing eons of pleasure and prosperity on mortals by not getting their attention. Icky weird. No one had rejected his offers in any millennia. Ever.

"I'm sure I met you at a Tower Road SMU party," Pink Hair had stayed in the hall and stood inches from him. Tight White Shirt sat on the bench, coat in his lap, playing cool while his face glistened desire.

"Oh hello," his face lit up, showing off his dimples. "Yes, I'm sure we did meet. Angie? Wasn't it?

"Yes," Pink Hair said, forgetting her real name. "It's Angie. Fred, wasn't it?"

"Sure." Freyr walked toward the Food Court, waving Tight White Shirt to come along and join them.

"Let's get drinks at the hotel resto just around the corner."

Mimi could wait. Or Horus or Kali could give it a go.

We hired someone more qualified. You're overqualified. You're not the best fit. You don't have the education to match your experience. You don't have the experience to match your education. Your resume is weird. Your contract is not extended.

Mimi's head rattled with the heaping rejections. Every tweak on her resume based on feedback garnered the polar opposite effect.

Bad, bad, bad luck. Something had to give. If she got ahead just a little it would help. Two of the part-time jobs were a half-hour bus ride away from each other if she was lucky with traffic. Lately, she wasn't. Usually, two hours on buses daily. Her third job was a contract ending soon. She just had to hold out for a renewal or a new job.

Even with the construction and massive crane on Barrington Street congesting up the pedways with extra walkers, it was faster to walk to her next job from her last interview. She'd already eaten her packed lunch and couldn't afford to eat in the Square today. Besides, there were too many strange people milling about. Like that weird dude hitting on her by the elevators. There were *rules* about that kind of behaviour.

Mimi just wanted one good full-time job. She and Kitty Midnight could live in a place without her invasive landlady. One without roommates opening her bedroom door. The last present dropped on her bed had been still moving. Its substantially bloody death left a stain on her favorite quilt. Midnight looked as if he were innocent, but it was similar to his "I never got treats, really" look.

Checking her watch, she had some time to kill.

Her great-grandfather's voice floated into her head. *A little luck today is all you'll need.*

Hmmmm.

Mimi stood in the open area by the lotto booth, the noisiest part of the food court behind her. She thumbed the last forty dollars in her pocket for the next two weeks. Nahhh. Tickets were too random.

Roulette though. She could work twenty dollars for an hour at the table and mostly come out ahead. It was more skill and knowing when to stop. And maybe three hands of blackjack from the pretty electronic dealer. Just a little go at it, then a hop-skip to her next job.

Mimi nodded to herself and headed the pedway route to the casino. Just pay attention and don't be greedy for bigger wins. Great-grandfather's gift of a little luck never hurt.

At least the casino was quieter than the food court this time of day.

Freyr tapped Horus on the arm and pointed. "There! Told you she's hard to see."

Horus glared at Freyr then looked at Mimi. She was standing by herself in the open area by the lotto booth. Horus stared at Mimi. He had as much trouble seeing her as Freyr did, despite his vision, and had to work to keep seeing her.

Kali could see Mimi. Nothingness surrounded Mimi as if she was in her own protection. Could this oblivious lady even generate this kind of . . . no, no, no. The woman clearly needed their powers to succeed. Humans always needed their help. Kali settled things in her mind and her observations drifted away.

Freyr was blithering on about how he'd tried to help Mimi, but Horus and Kali knew he had distracted himself with Pink Hair and Tight White Shirt.

Horus kept his keen protective eyes on Mimi. Freyr was distracting Kali. Mimi started walking fast towards the pedway.

Horus' view of Mimi was as if he was standing right next to her. A black cat as tall as a human was sitting at the other end of the pedway. The cat went unnoticed except by Horus. The cat cleaned off a toenail with a snap and stared right back at Horus. She stuck her tongue out at him.

"Hello, little bird!"

Horus walked as if he flew, passing in front of an oblivious Mimi.

"You have no business here. I'm King. I protect her," Horus declared.

"Oh, but I do and it's none of your business." Bastet flexed her cat neck and twisted backways to look behind herself.

Death, cloaked in black and scythe in hand, stood behind Bastet.

Horus spread his hands, now turned falcon wings, the tips sweeping the pedway's windows as he flew straight at Bastet and Death to protect Mimi.

Bastet ran down the escalators and Horus dove after

her.

Mimi crossed the pedway. Its air was cold today despite the warm sun and the noise from the construction below on Barrington Street echoed in the space

Blink. Blink. Something large with black fur looked like it had been sitting by the corner of Citadel Coins' shop and the escalator.

Everything odd seemed focused on her lately. She'd had enough of weird men, dark shadows, and bad luck.

Mimi channeled her intent on getting to the casino in time to relax. She decided things in the universe were going to head her way. Starting now.

Mimi stopped in her tracks when Death spoke to her from the same spot by the coin shop.

"Nice to meet you, Mimi."

A dark, round shadow filled the pedway. Metallic snapping and a shout were muffled outside the pedway.

Fresh air blasted over Mimi's head as if fanned by wings.

This way.

A forward direction would walk right into Death.

Kali swept past Mimi and Death, her gorgeous, flowing robes marking out a path beyond to the escalators around to the left of the pedway.

She didn't want to lose the opportunity created by the lady as it filled with other people who seemed extra rushed today. Mimi focused on nothing in front of her and only on the lovely lady beyond and her own swifter pattern emerged from the people. Mimi pushed through and passed the nothingness made of Death.

Death would have gaped his mouth open more if he could have. He was pissed.

Mimi's new course was so efficient and safe that she was already beyond the next set of pedways and escalators. She stepped into the noisy slots area of the casino in record time. She didn't hear a thing that happened on the pedway.

The massive round shadow was partnered with twisting, snapping metal, yelling construction workers, and people in the pedway screaming and scattering.

The giant steel ball crashed through the plate glass windows.

The wrecking ball stuck the landing where Death planned Mimi to be standing. That girl was special. Mimi must be acquired.

Any possible bonus collateral souls had been warned or whisked away by those meddling deities. Except one. The wrong soul, but Death never refused a gift.

The oblivious man listening to his music, texting, and walking was the only one shocked by his own death.

"Dude, nice costume. Halloween isn't here yet."

"I'd say nice to meet you, Reggie, but I'm 'fraid you're not the one I wanted." Death looked to his handy work. Reggie's body was pasted under the wrecking ball, with only his bright orange feet sticking out. It was not as satisfying as it should have been.

Reggie stood next to Death, looking down at the crushed body. The bloody pulp had the same special edition basketball shoes he'd received yesterday. Reggie looked over at Death then back at his own body.

"Man, I got blood on my new . . . Shit."

"I'll take you anyway. Dude, anyone ever tell you texting kills?" Death laughed at his own lame joke and Reggie's soul vanished.

The emergency responders, police, and firefighters were in a fury of activity around the destroyed pedway linking Scotia Square to The Barrington Hotel.

A ring of blue tarps circled the wrecking ball trying to cover the pieces of Reggie's body sticking out from underneath. Barely a dozen people had been injured by the debris thanks to the efforts of Horus, Kali, and Freyr.

Death was so consumed with thoughts of Mimi that he didn't notice Freyr standing beside him.

Freyr lifted a piece of Death's hood and leaned in close trying to see Death's face.

"Odin, is that you messing about again? This is outside the rules and subject to fines. And not funny!"

Death slapped away Freyr's hand with exasperation. "I am Death. I am here for Mimi."

"You could not possssssibly be Death. Death knows it is against the rules to actively come after humans. Like this hot mess you've created!"

Kali was at one end of the pedway helping paramedics treat wounds and Horus was at the other end gracefully guiding people away from adding to the chaos to gawk.

"Clear up your mess and leave Mimi alone. The Authority will do it for you if you don't. They're very fussy. I just got fined for buying drinks for two humans who approached *me*!"

"I don't care. My headhunters confirmed Mimi would be an asset to the team." Death turned away and headed to the casino and snorted. "You still don't have your sword or any other weapons that can hurt me."

"Your arrogance is greater than my vanity," Freyr whistled loud. "Gullinbursti!"

Slipping in from between then and now, his massive, shining boar appeared. A dwarf made gift, Gullinbursti's withers were almost as tall as Freyr.

On Freyr's signal, Gullinbursti charged, hitting Death in the back and knocking him to the ground.

The energy of the slam disrupted the presence of the masking preventing humans from seeing and hearing deities who, at the moment, were side by side them in this plane. People started looking around trying to find the source of the noise.

Horus flew overhead and the protective silence and invisibility returned. Kali redirected emergency personal to ignore their senses and refocus on the wounded.

Death stood, spotted his scythe, then reached for it. Gullinbursti charged again, knocking him down.

"That's not hurting." Death got up again.

"I know," Freyr raised his hand a third time to signal Gullinbursti. He could keep Death busy for a while and maybe The Authority would show soon.

Death cocked his ear to one side. "Alrighty already," he said to the air and vanished.

Freyr rubbed Gullinbursti mane. "Good boy!"

Mimi was in danger from Death. Death was breaking all the rules. It was the New World but there were limits on interfering with humans and Death had crossed the line.

Time for his coffee break club to step things up a notch.

Mimi's fingers rubbed the last casino chip in her pocket. The rest had been cashed yesterday, but she liked to hang onto one a little longer. Its weight was a warm security blanket marking her return of a little luck at the right moment.

On her way out of the casino, she'd gotten a job offer and her new job started today. Mimi's new employer was a large international firm. She did so well in the interview that her starting responsibilities and salary were larger than expected.

It was a very successful end of the week, despite the strangeness.

The roulette table's rewards would keep her landlady mollified and there was a bit extra. The extra winnings were going towards a lunch platter for her and the new team she was leading. Food rewards helped staff diffuse the stresses of being compliance officials with antagonistic clients.

The deli between the pedways had great sandwiches and side dishes in addition to the scrumptious buffet-by-weight offerings. Mimi had already called in the team's sandwich choices.

Mimi was so immersed in enjoying the comfort of security, thoughts of the exciting work ahead and the fresh roast turkey smells from the buffet that she nearly ran into Death.

Death blocked her path between the scattering of tables in the hall and the buffet bar to the cashier.

"You're special, Mimi. The skills and abilities you have should be thoroughly compensated for with meaningful work. We have an excellent health plan, great vision coverage, and instant travel available to staff for their holidays. I need you on my team."

Mimi stood still.

"Oh, the turkey here is the best. And the perogies. Might get some for supper," Mimi faced the buffet.

Death stepped in front of her.

"You hear and see me." Death blocked her way again as Mimi tried to walk around him. "Took a bit, but I figured you out. Dodging the crane, even with their help – it should have clipped you. And seeing me. And Bastet."

"Sir, you're blocking the containers," a man complained.

"Harumph." Death never let his gaze leave Mimi as he tipped his scythe towards a buffet client behind him and commanded him, "Extra gravy and add ribs to go with your turkey." Someone's heart would stop sooner than later and join him.

Mimi pulled a card out of her wallet and held it an inch from Death's head.

"Ah, see! You do see me, see?" No one ever confronted Death about his terrible banter.

"Lovely company. I work here now."

Mimi reversed the card and moved it closer to him.

Death stepped back from the glowing letters.

"Do I need to have a non-compliance form served to your boss from mine? The infractions from today alone. Tsk. Tsk."

Death hemmed and hawed. Then he glowered at the

people filling their buffet containers and yelled at them. "Eat a dozen perogies!"

The people scrambled to load perogies, fried onions, and sour cream into their containers and rushed to the cashier to get their food weighed. The ribs and gravy man shoved two perogies in his mouth. The clerk happily rang up person after person, box after box priced over twenty dollars for the weight. Two lost perogies were nothing to the hundreds of dollars she'd just rang in.

"Ack! You're not worth the hassle." Death vanished in a puff, leaving the chaos of people nearly attack the poor clerk who loaded more steam trays of perogies.

Mimi eased out the breath she'd been clenching, as she picked up her pre-paid order.

She hustled back to work going the proscribed detours to avoid the pedway Death had destroyed. Hopefully, it wouldn't look too awkward that she'd be filing another incident after a half day's work.

It was best she ignored seeing Kali, Freyr, and Horus arriving to rescue her. She didn't want to have to add that paperwork on top of Death's on day one of her new job. Pffft. Deities. Rescue this, attack that, show up late. All they'd remember would be their own heroics. So many had trouble adapting to the New World.

Not everyone needed rescuing.

Mimi sighed and called a different deli to order sweet treats for the afternoon. The paperwork on Death alone was a killer. The treats might detract from the pile up of fines to process. Mimi couldn't afford it long if the team got used to this spoiling.

"Uggggh! How can you eat after all that?" Freyr sipped his enormously oversized quadruple sweetened frappa-cappa.

Horus devoured a skewer of rare lamb kabab. "Big Deity talk for someone with whipped cream on his lapel."

Freyr set his drink down, sloshing out precious sweet foam and whipped cream to crane his neck checking for spots.

"Where?"

Kali snorted golden chai tea and Horus squealed with such energy that several people in food line-ups looked around for the source of noise breaking through their cone of protection.

"Good one! You made him look! Worth the spice up my nose." Kali crooned at Freyr and flattened and caressed his collar and shirt. "Don't worry, darling, your very soft black silk shirt has nothing on it."

Freyr's face coloured redder than the pickled turnip on Horus' plate. "Ummmm. Anyway. We saved Mimi just in time and drove Death away. He won't be bothering her."

"I heard he was fined by The Authority." Horus yanked more kebab meat off the skewer, pushing the turnips away so they wouldn't touch the meat.

"If it weren't for us, she'd have been lost. My sword went right through Death's head in a brilliant overhead back-handed shot, I might add. I heard Mimi's got a new job and doing well." Kali nodded towards Mama Gratti's Deli.

Mimi was heading to the elevators with two carafes of coffee and a tray of baked sweets.

"Ohhh, now that things are good, maybe she'll . . ."

Freyr started to stand and felt sharp nails pierce his leg. "Owww, Kali! Not again!" Freyr turned and saw Horus' eyes gleaming with tears as he dug his talons in harder.

"Things would have gone smoother if you didn't leap into things, Freyr."

Whining, Freyr sat.

Kali wiped the tears from her eyes and daubed the second round of chai spray from her face.

"I see that's mine."

No one else had been waiting for the elevator.

Mimi turned slowly, not wanting to tip the balance of an overload of treats and two coffee carafes.

A portly woman with short black hair reached for the old school paper cheque sticking out of Mimi's breast pocket.

"Ah, yes. I was coming to your floor later. Thanks for your patience on the rent. A little luck and just the right timing of the job were perfect."

"No worries. You always pay in the end." Bastet swiftly moved to hold open the elevator door and they got on. "Top level, please." Bastet made Mimi press the button with a free pinkie.

Mimi decided time crawled slower the heavier the carafes. "Are you going to tell me why you were helping Death, Bastet?"

"No."

"Or why you were in the pedway?"

A deep, low purr filled the elevator, followed by chattering. "Not a fan of falcons. I prefer them raw and not squawking and flying in hallways. Anytime I can piss off

Horus is a good day. Never you mind about that."

Salvation arrived as Mimi reached her floor. "See you tonight when you get home," she eased out the doors.

"Stop at the fish truck for halibut cheeks and scallops. To make up for the late rent, you can score me t-shirts from your new work at The Authority. I like to line my baskets with their products."

"You're a mean landlady. I just started. I don't have any pay yet. You have all my money."

"You'll find a way. The great-grandchild of Kairos, the god of opportunity and luck, shouldn't be complaining. You always find a way without anyone's help."

"I do alright."

The following Thursday, Freyr, Kali, and Horus sat at the same table, this time talking about "helping" a thirty-year-old child refusing to move out of his parent's place.

Death was hovering behind people using an electronic ordering board whispering, "Upsize your fries!" and "Screw the diet pop!"

Mimi tucked in one of the chairs behind the fireplace area and took out her book. She pulled out her bookmark and settled down low in the comfy seat so no one could see her. Then she fired off a text to one of her staff to investigate a deity infraction.

It was the first proper lunch break she had had in ages.

The return to anonymity was blissful and she was enjoying a good read of fluffy science fiction. As if aliens were real. Pffft.

Lisa Timpf

From Simcoe Ontario, Timpf is a storied author and poet with over thirty speculative fiction stories published to her credit in a variety of venues, including "Roxy," "Roxy's Rule," and "Gone" in *New Myths*; "The Disconnect" in Third Flatiron's *Brain Games* anthology; "The Caller" in the anthology *Future Days*, and "It's All Good," published in the anthology *Enter the Rebirth*. She has two novelettes coming in 2021 from JMS Books.

Her speculative poem "No Fairy Tale World" was included in the *2020 Rhysling Anthology*, which included all nominees for the Rhysling Award. She was also one of ten finalists in the 2015 Rhyme Zone contest, with the poem "His Hands, and a Question."

She brings with her her story, 'The *Messenger*'s Mission.'

The *Messenger's* Mission

"There you are!" Herm yelled triumphantly as the door to the space station's east side gym hissed open. In a fenced-in area just to his left, his shipmate and half-brother Percy, muscular and sweating, held the pose of his follow-through, watching the discus he'd just released hit the netting in front of him.

The netting flexed to slow the projectile's momentum, then rebounded, sending the discus sliding across the floor until it rested against the toes of Percy's neon blue training boots.

"Based on my calculations of speed and angle, that, sir, would be a record throw at the Interstellar Games," Blue, Percy's Oracle XXX android, intoned.

"Thank you, Blue," Percy said. "I'm hoping to get back into Grandfather's good favour with a strong showing at the Games," he explained to Herm. "He's been giving me the cold shoulder ever since his Oracle warned that I'd be the death of him."

"An Oracle IX, right?" Blue could manage a disdainful tone when he wanted, and never overlooked an opportunity to remind anyone who would listen how much more advanced he was than earlier versions. "Olympus Inc. removed the fortune telling programming from the Number Ten model onward, and I must say I agree with that decision completely."

"That will be all, Blue, thanks. You can go back to the ship now," Percy dismissed the android with a wave of his hand. "I presume you didn't hunt me up to talk about the Games?" Percy arched his eyebrows as he looked over at his half-brother.

"We've just landed an assignment," Herm said, then paused for a moment before adding, "On Seripha."

Percy's handsome face was suddenly guarded. "What kind of assignment?"

"We should likely talk about it back on the ship," Herm inclined his head slightly, and Percy understood. They didn't, after all, have the gym to themselves. To the right, an eight-legged horse galloped on a giant treadmill under the supervision of a massive, broad-shouldered blond man with long braids. To Percy's left, a furred humanoid with two sets of arms performed an aggressive set of bicep curls. Though he seemed intent on his workout, one of the fur-man's long, donkey-like ears seemed inclined in their direction.

Percy nodded and headed for the door.

"Thena's setting the course right now," Herm said briskly as they moved down the corridor toward the exterior ring of the space station.

"I'll miss the station," Percy said, sighing. "The *Messenger's* a good ship—fastest one out there—but she'll seem like cramped quarters after this."

"Better shower up and get going," Herm replied flatly. "You know how Thena hates to be kept waiting."

"It's the usual job. Someone needs a monster issue resolved." Herm ran a hand through his silver hair as he briefed his two half-siblings. The trio were perched on yellow plastaform chairs around the table in the *Messenger's* mess hall, which doubled as a meeting room.

Thena turned to Percy. "Didn't you live on Seripha for awhile?"

"Yeah, we ended up there after Gramps set Ma and I afloat in orbit in an old cargo barge." Percy shuddered. "If we hadn't been picked up by that scrap hunter Dicky, I don't want to imagine what might have happened."

"Well, the king of Seripha, Polidect, has hired us to get rid of the Gorgon, Medusa." Herm's silver eyes flashed with annoyance. "Apparently they are expanding their crops into a new area and this Medusa is causing problems."

"Let me guess. Turning people into stone?" Percy asked.

"Yes. That's it," Thena replied.

"Does she *really* have snakes attached to her head?" Herm repressed a shudder.

Thena nodded. "Apparently the whole thing is the result of a hair implant gone wrong. Gene splicing technology. Rumour has it she crossed the Poseidon cartel and that was their repayment."

The other two nodded. The Poseidon cartel was notorious, both for their trade in endangered sea creatures and their harsh treatment of anyone who got in their way.

"Well, the job will pay enough to cover our ship fees for a year," Herm said. "But to collect, we need to show evidence."

Percy scowled. "What kind?"

"Polidect wants to see Medusa's head."

"A little extreme, isn't it?" Percy protested. "Usually we're asked to resolve monster issues. That doesn't always mean dispatching the monster."

"Like the example of the Horta, Sir, in 'Devil in the Dark'," Blue intoned.

Percy let his head drop, just for a moment. At one point, the inclusion of old Earth books, TV shows, and movies in the ship library had seemed a good idea. But since Blue had become obsessed with *Star Trek*, dropping a reference to that particular show at least once a day, Percy had started to question the wisdom of that decision.

Thena, though, conveyed more empathy. "Precisely, Blue," the tall woman said, favoring the robot with a kindly gaze.

"Oh, and there's one more thing," Herm paused. "He insists it be you, and only you, Percy, confronting the monster."

Percy shrugged. "Isn't that always the way?" he asked. "You're the engineer, and Thena's the brains. That leaves me to do the dirty work."

"The attack needs to be at night," Herm sounded confident of that, at least. "I can engineer a persona distort that will make you invisible. During daytime, they might be able to notice objects behind you appearing fuzzy, but at night, it should work."

"What about the method of dispatch?" Percy asked.

"There's the laser gun I nicked during our last mission. That thing would cut through titanium," Herm said.

"How can I kill Medusa without looking at her? I don't

fancy becoming a statue."

The three half-siblings sat in silence for a moment.

Blue cleared his throat. "What about a vision shield?" With uncharacteristic restraint, he refrained from mentioning where he'd first seen the idea in action.

"There might be something to that," Thena said slowly. "I could rig up a pair of mirrored eyeglasses. That way you wouldn't be looking right *at* her, but you'd still be able to see. It'll be a little tricky because objects will appear backwards, but with your physical coordination you should be able to pull it off. I can even make them look normal—like sunglasses."

"It's all set, then," Percy said, keeping his voice upbeat.

Yeah, the little voice of doubt that he found himself unable to quell sometimes whispered as he walked away from the informal conference. *What could possibly go wrong?*

Sweat beaded Percy' brow and trickled behind his reflective goggles as he backed up, step by reluctant step.

The black eyes of the snakes wreathing Medusa's head glittered and the serpents' sinuous bodies writhed in a mesmerizing manner. Had it not been for Thena's special reflective eyewear, Percy would have fallen victim to the monster by now—he felt certain of that. Still, the goggles didn't completely shield him from the intensity of the Gorgon's gaze. He couldn't so much as blink, and as for raising the laser cutter at his side—impossible. His muscular arms hung immobile, as though paralyzed.

How confident he'd felt as he stood at her bedside

moments ago, brandishing the cutter, ready to sever the monster's head! The greenish light from the largest of Seripha's three moons had cast enough light into the room for him to see the bland expression on Medusa's face as she snored, the snakes quiescent. He'd almost had the cutter in position on the Gorgon's neck when her eyes had flown open.

To make matters worse, the distort aura that Herm had rigged hadn't fooled the monster for a nanosecond. She'd *seen* him clearly. Percy ardently wished his half-brother was here in his place, experiencing the effects of that particular piece of non-functioning gadgetry. He sighed as he took another crab-wise step in retreat.

Focus, he told himself. As if *that* came easy, with the whirl of chaotic thoughts inspired by the snakes, whose rhythmic gyrations were now making him sleepy—

Percy stumbled. His shoulder encountered something solid behind him. *A wall.*

Medusa smirked. Tongues flicking, the serpents' heads moved higher until their pitiless black eyes peered down at the Gorgon's intended prey.

Those myths about an alternate universe where Herm and Thena are gods and I'm a hero, he thought. *What wouldn't I give to be there now.*

But no. He lived in *this* universe, where fellow monster-hunters Thena and Herm waited aboard the *Messenger* for him to come back with his intended bounty.

As the monster advanced, Percy glanced left and right, frantically seeking an escape route. What was it Thena was so fond of saying? *When all else fails, cause a distraction.*

Striving to regain control of his muscles, Percy managed to slap his open palm against the wall. This gesture produced a sound so weak even Percy could barely hear it. Nonetheless, Percy sensed the monster's concentration sagging. Medusa's "hair" fell limply. The snakes' eyelids snapped shut, and the hissing halted.

I can move! Percy thought as he flexed his arms. Before he could take advantage of his returning strength and take aim with the laser cutter, his keen ears detected a scuffing sound from the dimly lit hallway.

Another monster, perhaps? *Better hurry, then.* He took a step toward Medusa.

But the noise he'd heard hadn't sounded like the rasp of talons, or the inexorable padding of paws. More like human footfalls—humanesque, anyway.

Percy craned his neck to see around Medusa's bulk and blinked in surprise. There in the doorway stood a bleary-eyed child in a pink nightgown patterned with white centaurs. The girl's fine features bore the promise of future beauty, if you overlooked the tiny snakes wreathing her head.

"Mommy, I'm thirsty," the child whispered.

"Oh, sweetie," Medusa sighed. "I'll get you a glass of water. But then you have to go right back to bed, okay?"

The child nodded, and Medusa slipped away down the hall.

Sensing the child's attention turning to him, Percy hid the weapon behind his back and plastered an innocent smile across his handsome face.

Medusa returned with a tumbler of water, which the girl gulped down.

"Thanks, Mommy," the child whispered, handing the glass back to her mother.

"Back to your room now," Medusa said in that fond-but-firm voice peculiar to parents.

"But what about the monsters under the bed?"

"We checked already," Medusa replied. "They're all fine. Remember?"

"I remember." The girl sighed. "Goodnight. And goodnight, mister—whatever your name is."

"Percy," the monster hunter replied, bowing graciously. "My name is Percy."

"Goodnight, Mr. Percy."

After the girl padded away down the hall, man and Gorgon regarded one another solemnly.

This makes no difference, Percy told himself firmly. *A monster is a monster is a monster, even if—*

"Where were we?" he asked the monster, arching his right eyebrow.

"As I recall," Medusa said, her voice grating. "I had you backed against the wall."

"Ah yes," he replied, flourishing the laser weapon. "But you're the one responsible for the distraction. I say we pick it up from here."

"Very well," Medusa replied, taking a step forward.

Damn! Percy felt his right arm moving slowly, slowly downward, as though weighed down by the cutter. "We've had complaints that you've been harassing the population, turning them to stone," Percy said, trying to keep the desperation out of his voice.

Medusa laughed, a sound with a bitter edge. "King Polidect's people, at his urging, broke the treaty. They encroached on our lands. So, yes, we have turned some—the ones who ignored the warnings—into stone." Her eyes narrowed.

Percy recalled the numerous billboard signs, with increasingly threatening messages, that he'd passed on the way to the Gorgons' lair—"Go back now!" "Danger! Gorgon residence ahead!" and so on. *Medusa has a point; I have to admit. There were plenty of warnings along the way.* "Fair enough," he said. "But that doesn't justify killing."

"Killing?" Medusa's shock seemed genuine. "Who said anything about killing?"

"Seriously?" Percy couldn't believe she'd deny the obvious. "You turned people to stone!"

"They're simply in suspended animation," Medusa's voice betrayed, of all things, hurt feelings. "It's a way of protecting them from the shock. But they can be restored to health."

Percy thought for a moment, sifting through this new information. "Here's the problem," he confided. "King Polidect has hired us to bring him your head. I sympathize with your position. Still, a deal is a deal. Bad for business if we don't come through."

"I understand," Medusa said. "But you need to know that I'm not the monster here. Besides, I have an idea."

"No guarantees," Percy said. "But I'll listen."

A shame it has to be this way, Percy thought as he shifted on the marble bench he'd been led to by the castle's gatekeeper. *Maybe I'm too soft, like Thena says. Maybe—*

A voice interrupted his reverie. "King Polidect will see you now." A uniformed attendant peered around the corner, gesturing down the long, echoing hallway which Percy knew from past visits to be the way to the throne room.

Percy swung to his feet, making an effort to project a confident aura. "My business with the King is...personal." He hoped the attendant hadn't noticed how much his palms were sweating. Then again, the gatekeeper's practice of leading all visitors the long way past the dungeons probably had a similar effect on most of the King's guests. The reaching hands, the moaning—he'd almost preferred the Gorgons' lair.

Percy stood quietly. The success of his mission depended on being alone with the tyrannical King, who now seemed to Percy as dangerous a monster as Medusa.

"A private audience. As you wish, milord." The attendant inclined his head in a gesture of respect and strode away, his chain mail clanking. Percy breathed a sigh of relief and proceeded alone, his corded muscles barely registering any strain as he toted the grey pack in his left hand. Although Herm had initially been reluctant to lay out the extra money for the anti-grey assist on the all-purpose carry-bag, Percy had come to appreciate it.

Three steps into the throne room, Percy paused. He'd noted a flicker of disappointment on Polidect's chiseled features as the king watched him approach. *If I'm not mistaken,* Percy thought, *he'd have been equally happy if my mission had failed.* Which would mean, he, Percy, had been killed or turned to stone. He scowled.

"Started wearing glasses, have you?" Polidect offered stiffly by way of a greeting.

"I had a late night," Percy countered, not offering to remove his mirrored eyewear. He cleared his throat, then barked, in his most authoritative tone, "You have the payment?"

"Show me the evidence, first," Polidect replied, leaning forward.

"You didn't think it worth trying some other measures before killing the monster?" Percy asked.

The King tipped his head back and let out a bark of laughter. "You're just like your father, Big Zee," he sneered, staring at the youth standing in front of him. "Arrogant. Self-righteous. No, of course I have no regrets."

"What about the treaty?" Percy took a step forward.

"Only a fool would honor a treaty with a monster."

"Indeed," Percy replied.

The King's hand landed on the hilt of his weapon. "Step aside," he snarled. "I'll take what's mine."

Percy placed the pack on the marble floor in front of him, raised his hands, and stepped back three strides, watching as the king fumbled with the catches. As Polidect flipped the pack open, Percy noted the eagerness in the king's expression starting to morph to something else as Medusa, who had been patiently crouching in the dark confines, poked her head out. Since Percy had positioned the pack with Medusa facing in the Polidect' direction, the king immediately turned to stone.

I didn't break the contract, Percy told himself nervously. *I brought Medusa's head. It just happened to still be attached to her body.*

When the King's retainers rushed in, the Gorgon crouched back into the bag. Percy stepped forward to flip the top of the pack shut, then froze, his expression wary.

The group's leader, a bald man with slightly bowed legs, walked around the statue that once had been Polidect, examining the expression on the stone face with interest. The look on the king's face was, Percy had to admit, worthy of study, falling as it did somewhere between gloating and turn-and-run terror.

After a pause, the man turned to Percy with an outstretched hand. "You've done us all a favour," he said. "The king is—was—a piece of work. Thank you."

Relieved, Percy nodded as he shook the older man's hand. This could have gone very badly. He was glad he didn't have to call on Medusa's services again. Witnessing that once had been quite enough for him.

Thena used a red kerchief to mop her brow as she stepped out of the makeshift operating room.

"Did everything go—well?" Percy winced, afraid to hear the answer. She'd been in there a long time.

Thena flashed her brilliantly white teeth in a dazzling smile. "I removed all the snakes, from both Medusa and her daughter." She paused. "A long process. Detaching them without causing harm proved tricky."

"Without doing harm?" Herm asked.

"The daughter insisted," Thena said, shuddering slightly. "They're to be released in the garden."

"I hear they crowned Richard, Polidect's brother, as the new King. Do you think he will keep up his end of the bargain?" Percy turned to Herm, who leaned lazily against a pillar, resembling coiled quicksilver despite his outward calm.

"He's agreed to honour the treaty," Herm said. "Since Medusa restored everyone who'd been turned to stone back to life, he had little choice."

"And I used my modest debating skills to convince their lawyers the contract had been less than definitive about *how* exactly Medusa's head should be presented," Thena said, flashing her teeth in a predatory grin. "They'll pay us the full bounty with no questions asked."

Percy grunted. As he understood it, Thena had argued their case before the planetary high court. The Seriphans hadn't stood a chance against her logic.

"So, ah, with the bounty, we've got operating expenses for a year, huh?" Percy asked.

Herm nodded. "Your point?"

"The Interstellar Games." Percy couldn't help bouncing with anticipation. "Who knows, maybe Grandfather will come to see me throw." Though he struggled to maintain an even tone, he couldn't keep the yearning from his expression.

"Be careful what you wish for," Thena said.

"Somebody should have told Polidect that."

"What's next for Medusa and her sisters?" Herm asked.

"They decided to form a rock band. I heard they're calling the group 'No Stone Unturned'," Thena said.

Herm's silver eyes sparkled with amusement. "You know," he said, nodding sagely. "It wouldn't surprise me if they had some monster hits."

"Don't give up your day job," Percy said, clapping his half-brother on the back.

"What? I'm here all week," Herm replied.

"And next week. And the next." Percy rolled his eyes. Still, he couldn't help feeling a sense of anticipation. Another successful mission, and the Games ahead. He could put up with a few bad jokes.

Interstellar Games, here we come.

Shannon K Green

A gifted author with a talent for the strange, Green has been recognized in both the genre community and the contemporary literary community for his pursuits. In the past, he has been shortlisted for the 1996 Arts and Letters Award, and later won the 2015 Audience Choice Steampunk Newfoundland Showcase.

Green's short fiction has appeared in *Fantasy from the Rock, The Hamthology, Jibbernocky* and the bestselling collections *Chillers from the Rock, Dystopia from the Rock, Flights from the Rock, Pulp Science-Fiction from the Rock,* and *From the Rock Stars.*

In 2021 Engen Books released Green's first novella, *The Snows of Aetalus,* as a part of the Slipstreamers series.

Cats' Cradle of Civilization

In the beginning there was a cat. A striped cat of all colours and the cat was pleased. It strolled about with the curiosity and pride that all cats possess until it felt an itch behind its ear. This was the first person.

Cleaning itself to dislodge the itch behind her ear, the cat took in enough fur to create the first hairball: it was all of black fur. This became a second cat. The two cats and the being frolicked in the void until the cats grew bored and turned on each other. The fury of their fighting ended with an ear torn from one and the tip of a tail from the other. These became the sun and the world sitting in the emptiness of the space which the cats and the newly formed person inhabited.

The cats forgot their quarrel, as cats often do, and the cat of all colours now with a tattered ear began playing with the hairball and set the planet spinning into orbit. As it spun, the planet picked up the shed fur of the cats, the dropped whiskers, the crumbs of void the cats had dropped as they ate, and gathered them onto its surface where they became plants and trees and rocks. It also collected the person that had sprung from the ear of the all-colours cat. The black cat with the tattered tail simply dozed beside the newly formed sun.

The person called to the cat from the spinning hairball, saying, "Oh great being, it is lonely here for just me."

The cat responded by batting the new planet about, terrifying the person with dread earthquakes and falling paws; while the other cat took the opportunity to search for food and mark territory as its own. Between them, the cats had created the land and waters of the planet and the dirt deposited from their paws became the beasts of the field and birds of the sky and fish of the waters. And the person felt less alone, though they still desired companionship in their own form.

After a scuffle between the cats, the person, still lonely, waited for one of the cats to fall asleep, then scaled its paw. The journey was arduous, their grip on the cat's smooth fur was tenuous at best, but eventually the top of the head was reached, and more people were found sheltered in the great shadow cast by the tattered ear of the cat.

"Come to the hairball with me: all we need to live is in the sunshine; it can be found there. There are fruits and the beasts of the land, birds of the sky, and fish of the waters which the cats have shown me are safe to eat; and plants from which to make our own fur," they said.

"The cat provides for us here," the people replied. "It gives us fur and warmth and only dislodges some of us in its cleaning," they said. "We are happy here."

The first person did not respond to them directly, instead pulling clumps of hair from inside the cat's ear. The cat yowled, scratching furiously at what remained of the tattered ear. This dislodged many of the surviving people who followed the urging of the first person and moved to the tip of the tail.

The first person next waited for the other cat to fall asleep, thinking that if there were people on one cat there must be more on the other; after all, that is where they came from. Repeating the process, the person climbed through the much coarser fur of the partially tailless cat. On the head of this cat, they found more people. They repeated their pleas, as they had done to the other people. Receiving the same response as before, the first person tickling the inside of the cat's ear with a stray whisker and returned to the earth. The cat, predictably, set about twitching the ear that had been so offended, knocking the people there to the earth in the process.

Many of the people attempted to return to their places among the fur of the cats; some succeeded, some failed, some died in the attempt. Others decided to follow the lead of the first person and began living on the new land, harvesting the plants of the fields, the fish of the waters, the birds of the air, and the beasts of the land.

The winter came and the people were cold. The first person went to the cats with the intention of begging them to provide shelter and warmth to the people. Instead the first person found the cats asleep near the sun, blocking its rays from reaching the earth. The person decided to take a piece of the sun home instead.

As the person crept past the cats, the one with the tattered tail lazily opened its eye and purred, "What are you doing here? Why have you come to trouble our slumber?"

The person replied, "You look so warm and comfortable here, I came to share your sunbeam."

The tatter eared cat growled low, "Then be quiet about it, both of you. Some of us have important sleep to be about."

"I could be ever so much quieter if I had some of the sunshine for myself," the first person said. "I would never have to disturb your sleep again."

At this both cats gave low growls. "What need have you for the sun?" the tatter eared cat said. While the cat with the tattered tail told the being to, "Be happy with our leftovers; this world is ours."

The person simply stroked the fur of both of the cats until they both fell asleep. Then as quietly as they could manage, the first person made their way as close to the sun as they could, then reached into the ball of flame, took hold of a piece of it, and returned to the people.

When they awoke, the cats saw that the people had all built small boxes in which to live. Each box glowed on the ground like stars in the night sky. As the cats approached the boxes, they saw that the people had made holes in the boxes so they could look outside, but it let the cats look in as well.

The cats saw piles of leaves and grasses and discarded fur, which looked soft and welcoming. They saw foods warmed over the pieces of sun which smelled delicious. And the cats saw the people, bowing before crude carvings made to resemble the cats themselves.

It was then that the cats birthed their first litters. The tatter eared cat of all colours birthed seven, one for each of the colours in its fur. The black cat birthed only three: one black, one white, and the last was grey. The first cats, their litters delivered, returned to the stars to rest.

The new litters, cold in their new fur and hungry their first time outside the womb, cried shrilly in the night air. The first person heard the cries; recognizing the hunger of all newborns in the piteous, angry wailing, they took the kittens into the boxes, which the people called huts. The kittens grew strong, and big, and over time began to repay the people by killing rodents and other vermin which stole the stored foods of the people.

And ever after cats have dwelt among the people, worshipped for their ancestry while earning their keep.

Nott's Library

"It's so dark in here, Grandmother," Wilhelmina said with panic in her voice. "Are you sure we'll be okay in here tonight?"

The old woman crouched before the fireplace, her gnarled and arthritic-looking fingers scratching steel over flint with a surprising nimbleness. "Gather around and I will tell you about true darkness, children," she said. Hearing the sounds of bare feet scuttle over the floor, she continued working flint and steel.

"In the before time," she began, pausing to clear what sounded like a full lung from her throat. "In the time before, before there were people, I mean," she continued in a voice slightly husky but still loud and strong, "the gods and goddesses roamed the earth in such shapes as they saw fit. One day they might be animals, the next plants, on another they might be stars or clouds. Any shape at all, for it was often their whim to appear as whatever had caught their attention.

"Later, after people began to appear on the land, the gods and goddesses began to take on shapes like those people. Which makes complete sense if you consider that people who could move about and do things had to be more interesting than a tree that stood still all day. Yes, even more fascinating than the clouds in the sky or the wild dogs you all seem to love following about in the fields instead of doing your work."

At this she managed to get some sparks into the tinder and began blowing short puffs onto the glowing coals. Soon she had a small fire burning, and as she added twigs and sticks, the light filled the room. It was a small room that seemed crowded with the seven children who had followed her in, but it was a snug place where they could all stretch out to sleep when the story was done.

"Gather in closer. Once you're all warmed up, we'll have to move out a bit," she said simply, pouring water from a large bottle into a small pot she had brought with her. "Slice those potatoes while I tell the tale, Seamus. Slice them thin, mind; it's late and bedtime comes soon for all of us."

She paused, taking a sip of water from the smaller bottle she carried at her belt. "Now, where was I? Oh yes, people.

"The gods had seen the people going about their days in the manner of people at the time; which is to say not at all like we do today. People in those times wandered the land you see. They went from place to place. Following the animals, they hunted and gathered whatever fruits and vegetables they found which they could eat.

"And the gods and goddesses were fascinated by this strange new ape, for that is what they thought we were. Apes who hadn't grown enough fur and had been chased off by our hairier brethren as some animals will abandon the weaker members of the herd. But the people were smart. They took the fur from the animals they killed for meat that they cooked over fires. They learned to harvest not just the plants themselves but also the means of making new plants from the older ones. The gods and goddesses watched the people hunting and farming and just going about their daily business, amazed at the new hairless apes and engrossed with their actions.

"Agriculus was enthralled by the growing crops and men who worked the field. So, he took the form of an ox first to work closer with those who tilled the earth. Later he took the form of a man to work alongside those toiled on the land. Then, one day he sewed wheat in the morning, harvested in the evening, and served fresh loaves to those in field that night; revealing himself as divine.

"Wata, who had spent much of her time as water before she had seen people, followed those who fished the seas and rivers. She would sing as she stood in the waves, catching fish with spear and net with the fisher folk who never seemed to have dry feet. The day the fish followed her onto land as the sun dipped low all the fisher folk knelt and prayed to her.

"And on with all the divine troupe, each finding those they could adore and be adored by. You know them all by name I've no doubt and have probably dedicated yourself to one of them in your secret heart already. But do any of you remember the god Nott, the one most of us no longer speak off?"

As if summoned by the name, a loud boom echoed through the night air. As one, all the children turned toward the door. "Hugo, be a good boy and make sure the windows are covered up, will you?" the old woman said. "We'll be safe and warm in here as long as we keep all that nonsense outside.

"Now Nott, as you probably don't know because we never speak off him, was an honest sort. He didn't really like people because he found them too fidgety. He preferred to muck about in places where things moved slower as a rule; but the place he loved best of all was the library he had built for himself where the desert met the sea. Carved into a cliff face at the water's edge, the library was accessible only by a thin strip of sandy beach, and only when the tides were low; for the rising tides would drown the beach and much of the stairs which led to his doors. It was there that he stored the volumes where he had recorded not just his observations of the world around him but also the plays and poetry the people produced. He would visit his sibling gods from time to time, to see the people perform their arts, but he preferred the more sedate life of a country scholar, studying things away from the bustle of people. At least he did until the first time he saw Luse.

"Now Luse, as you all know, enjoyed her time with people. She would sit and listen to music for hours on end. She delighted in spending her time watching people tend the fields or perform plays, and when she grew tired of their company, she would wander the fields and forests making the wild flowers bloom, for she loved plants more than she loved the invented delights of people. It was during one of her wanderings that she stumbled into Nott's realm.

"Luse, having spent most of her time among growing

things, had never been to where the desert met the sea. Part of her was appalled at this land where nothing grew, but more of her was curious about the seaweed and other plants that grew in tidal zone. She spent the whole of a day there, glorying in her new discovery like a babe given their first taste of candy. It wasn't until her feet began to feel wet that she realized the sea was coming to meet her. The water had risen almost to her knees before she decided to seek someplace dryer. Searching about her, she saw the nearby stairs leading to the library doors. It was there she went."

The old woman paused in her recitation, taking the potatoes from Seamus and dumping them into the now boiling water as the booming noises continued outside.

"Nott had been watching Luse as she explored the tide line in front of his library home, and found himself drawn to her studious manner. So, when he saw she would be trapped, he rushed to the door. Opening the portal for her, he called to her, 'The tide leaves you the choice of waiting here or swimming to shore. Please come in and explore my library.' Luse looked from the sea to the doorway and entered the library.

"As her eyes adjusted to the gloom, she was dismayed to find herself surrounded by so many books. More so when she realized what they were and what they contained, for nobody who had not been to the library had seen a book before. Nott had hoarded them all for himself until now.

"Now though, Nott brought out volume after volume hoping to entertain and impress the goddess. First, he showed her the works of his favorite engineers, but Luse had no interest in engineering. Then he showed her volumes of poetry from those considered great, but she cared little for the flowery language. He read to her transcriptions of the great orators and the most beloved speeches, but she yawned as he grew more passionate. When Nott brought out the plant guides, showing her the illustrations, she finally grew interested.

"Three turnings of the tide Nott kept her entertained with the botanical texts. Until finally, hungry for the kiss of sun on her cheeks and the caress of wind through her hair, she stepped through the doorway and found the sea had retreated from the beach once more. She made a polite farewell to the librarian, thanking him for his hospitality and assuring him she would return soon.

"And so Luse went out into the world, searching for the plants she had seen in the wonderful books Nott had shown her. She would return many times in the next year, bringing with her little souvenirs of her travels. A feather fallen from a bird, a curious stone with what looked like a bug inside it, and flowers, always flowers. Nott would sometimes press the flowers, sometimes sketch them, or simply store their seeds for later growth.

"On one such visit, Luse asked if she could take one of the volumes with her, a new invention of Nott's, a storybook. He flatly refused, telling her that he feared what damage might come to the books if they went into the outside world where the sun shone and the rain fell."

She paused in her telling, facing the children. "We all know what can happen to paper if we take it outside and aren't careful, don't we?" the old woman asked as she tested the potatoes. "They need a few more minutes, so...

"Luse respected his wishes, staying until she had finished the volume she had wished to borrow. After that, she began to stay longer when she visited, sometimes remaining with the scholarly god for months, only taking short breaks to sit on the stairs which led to the beach or explore the beach itself, before returning to her entertainment among the books. Eventually though, she would always grow bored and return to her explorations and life outside the library where the cliffs met the sea.

"After one such journey, Luse returned to Nott's library with a fellow goddess. Luse explained to Nott that this goddess, Doeth she was called, was mainly interested in hunting. Upon hearing of the library, she had asked Luse to take her there so she might pattern her travels to mimic those Luse had taken; though while the latter had sought out plants, Doeth would be seeking animals. Nott welcomed the pair into his home, bringing them volume after volume so they might study and plan their journeys. At the end of a fortnight, the pair set back out into the world."

The old woman reached into her bag and brought out plates, serving the potatoes to her enraptured audience. She rose from her place near the fire, going to the windows to look out at the storm she knew would be out there. Though the booms continued, she could see no sign of their source. Glad that it must still be quite distant, she resumed her story.

"After the two goddesses had left, Nott began returning the books to their places on the shelves, for while he had brought the goddess many books, he had returned very few to the shelves as long as they were there, in case they wished to consult them again. It was then that he discovered a book was missing, specifically the newest storybook about creatures who roamed the sea on floating pieces of land."

"You mean a book about pirates?" Hugo asked excitedly.

"Yes, it was a pirate story that had gone missing," the old lady responded with a wink as the thunderous sounds outside began getting louder. "The story is almost done, hopefully I'll be finished before that noise outside is overhead.

"Nott went through the piles of books, hoping he had simply mislaid the book but couldn't find it. He checked under the tables and chairs. He searched the area near the doors. He even searched the privies. The book was no longer inside the building. Furious, he stormed outside to follow the pair only to find that the tide had risen since the goddesses had left.

"He paced the steps outside his door. As the water receded, he would pace closer and closer to the beach until finally he could walk the land and he went in search of the goddesses. In the branches of a nearby forest, he found Doeth. She denied having seen the book, even allowing Nott to search the small bag she travelled with when Nott was not satisfied with her promises that she had taken nothing from the library.

"Next, he set off in search for Luse, but her travels were wider and he was unsure of which direction she had gone. After searching for a year and a day without setting an eye on her, he returned to the library. Frustrated with the fruitless nature of his search, he again searched the library for the missing volume. He was nearing the end of his search when Luse appeared at the door. Furiously he turned on her, his normally cheerful greetings replaced with angry accusations of thievery.

"Before the goddess could respond, he forced her from the library and locked the doors forever."

The children all sat quietly as the booming grew closer. The sounds of engines could now be heard between the explosions outside. As Wilhelmina began collecting the plates from the other children, she asked, "Grandmother, you said this story was about true darkness. How is a closed library true darkness?"

The old woman smiled slightly "Can any of you answer her question?" After a brief pause to study the puzzled faces of her charges, she spoke again: "Because knowledge is the true light, and in taking away all that knowledge, Nott let true darkness fall over the land."

Teresita E. Dziadura

Dziadura has steadily been making her voice heard in the Newfoundland writing scene more and more over the last two years, making her presence known at NaNoWriMo writing events and seminars as a force to be reckoned with, bringing wit and insight to every conversation she's a part of.

She made her first mark in the world of published fiction with her short story 'Beyond No Man's Land' in *Chillers from the Rock,* a chilling tale that cemented her as one of the fresh new talents in the industry.

Dziadura describes herself as a sci-fi and horror nut, but is also a longtime fan of British comedy. She has studied Marine Biology and has four children with her husband of twenty-five years.

Her first novel, *Corporate Invasion,* is set for a 2021 release.

The Call of The Morrigan

The red wolf followed the scent through the woods, as it had for the past four days. The strength of the scent waxed and waned, but it was always there, a stink of rot, decay and death that occluded the fresh earthy scents of the green wood. She growled at the foul stench. She would know what creatures had the temerity to disturb her home.

Her prey had been wreaking havoc on the countryside for weeks. Wherever they travelled, disaster and death followed. A family killing each other without any cause, riots, and crops rotting in the fields. One entire town's power grid went down after the generator exploded, killing a dozen workers and injuring more. Another town's water supply was poisoned, but investigators had no culprit or known toxin, just hundreds sick or dead.

Then, two days before, the scent had brought her through a village where a friend of hers, a Selkie, lived amongst the humans. The village was in ruins. Not a single house had been untouched by the conflagration that had consumed the town of nearly a thousand families. The skeletal remains of the houses jutted up from the earth like the desiccated corpses of some unknown beasts.

She'd stopped here and transformed into her human form to search the debris. She pulled a cell phone from her jeans pocket and dialed her friend's phone. It went straight to voicemail. She swore, stuffing the phone back into her pocket without leaving a message. She strode through the ashes, her black boots crunching. She sniffed the air and sneezed.

Celene, her husband, and their children were not to be seen. Nor were their remains in the ashes of their home. Her keen nose would have caught the distinct scent of charred remains. They were just gone. Vanished.

The woman turned, taking in the ruined town, her mouth drawn down in a frown. Her long black hair fluttered in the thermals, looking more like feathers than human hair. She pulled her leather jacket in tight against the flames that still flickered from some of the posts. A black smoke swirled around her, but not from the fires. She was The Morrigan. Goddess of war and death. And she was hunting.

Morrigan shook the memory from her mind as she spotted a footprint in the mud. Next to it were a few drops of blood. Her hackles rose. She was nearing her prey. Once sporadic and faint, the scent was now steady and growing stronger to a point that it was nearly overwhelming. No longer could she smell the earthiness of the woods; her nose was filled with their stink.

She was used to the smell of death, but those had been honest deaths; though often gruesome and bloody, they'd been honourable. Men and women had died in their own time, their destinies complete. This was different. This was corruption. This was evil and The Morrigan would have no part of another meddling in her domain.

She slipped through the trees, silent and wary. Following the trail of the ones who had wrecked so much damage to her home, who had taken her kith and kin.

The girl huddled in the back of the cave. It was cold and dark and smelled of waste. Only a single torch, hung high on a wall just outside their holding pen, provided any light. She felt alone, though her family and friends surrounded her. Though that had often been the case, long before these creatures had come in the night to steal her and her people away. She was used to it.

She looked around. Just a few feet away, her mother and father sat, with her younger brother and sister. Ros was still just a baby and Calum was a toddler. They were scared and needed their parents more. She wasn't really theirs anyway. They'd taken her in with her real parents who had died when she was only a little girl. She didn't remember her father at all and only remembered her mother's hair, the same colour as her own, and a lullaby her mother would sing about a mockingbird bringing her baby shiny things. She'd lived with Celene and Aemon now for ten years. Tomorrow would be her thirteenth birthday, if she lived to see it.

She sighed and leaned back, trying to ignore her growling stomach. She pulled out her cell phone. She and a few others had tried to call for help, but one by one the creatures had caught them. The offenders had been beaten, and the phones destroyed. Only her phone remained, and it was dead. She'd tried to call for help, but you can't make a call when there's no signal. And then it died. So, she used it as a mirror. As always, her hair disappeared in the black glass, leaving her looking at a mask. Her pale skin was paler than usual, making the dark circles around her eyes stand out. Her cheeks were sunken from four days of no food and little water.

"I look like a zombie," she muttered.

"Mira, did you say something?" Celene said, looking up from nursing the baby.

"No, Mama."

Celene looked at the phone. "Put that away before they see it," she whispered, looking from Mira to their captors. "You don't want to end up like the others, do you?"

"No, Mama." She slipped the phone back into her hoodie pocket and leaned back against the cave wall.

"Mama?"

"Yes, sweeting?"

"Do you thin-" She never got to finish her sentence. The largest of the creatures, Dain, lumbered in, a dead deer hanging from under his arm. He tossed it to the ground.

Mira looked at the three captors; the boss was Dain. He was large, well over six feet, with massive muscles. His face looked like someone who'd gone fifty rounds with a boxer. His nose had been smashed and set a dozen times, and his face was a web of scars. While Dother, the one feeding on the deer, was smaller. Not just shorter, but thin. He was handsome in comparison but there was something off-putting about Dother. He was all sharp angles, and while Dain's eyes were filled with fire, a rage barely kept at bay, Dother's were empty. Soulless. Dain was an active volcano to Dother's glacier. The third brother almost never left the shadows. When he did, he was still impossible to see, your eyes would slide over him.

"Brother, I thank you for this meal," Dother said.

"Eat well, brother, the time is soon."

A voice came from the shadows, "Tomorrow is the solstice, is it not?"

"Aye, Dub, it is." Dain looked over his shoulder at the humans huddled in the cage. He looked over their faces, seeking, until his eyes came upon the raven-haired child. A chill ran down her spine. "Tomorrow took a very long time to arrive."

"Brother?" The creature was hunched over, feasting on the deer.

"Yes, Dother?"

Dain looked at the captives and licked his lips. "May I have just one?"

Dother looked down at his brother. "No."

"Please, brother? I'm still so hungry."

"We need every last one for the morrow." He looked down at his brother and the girl could swear his face softened and he smiled. "I promise you, when we are done, you can feast."

Dain's grin was gruesome as he bobbed his head.

"Dub?"

"Yes?" the shadow said.

"Do you have everything you need?"

The shadow moved, what the girl assumed was a nod.

"Then we are ready. We will start at midnight."

Morrigan had settled down outside the cave, her head on her paws. She knew this place. The valley had not changed in the thousand years since her last visit. The clearing was in a hollow, surrounded by elder trees with an expansive cave set on one side. It oozed of evil. In all the years since that battle, no humans had ever settled here. Not even near it. Even they felt the dark power of the place.

The last time she was here, she'd been a companion to the goddess Danu, more commonly known as Gaia or Earth Mother. Danu had been at her peak then, her green gown of living ivy glowing with power. She was there to lend that power to her followers, the priestesses of the Tuatha de Danann who had come to kill a witch who had been plaguing the people of Ireland, the Carman, and her three evil offspring. Their purpose was noble and pure.

The Morrigan, dressed in her ebony feathered armour, stood behind the Danu, waiting and watching for the battle. Her feathered children were perched in the trees behind her. They were here for the carrion feast that would follow the battle.

The battle was fierce and bloody. The valley was alight with magic. The greens of the Tuatha's nature magic, the orange of the Carman, the silvers and reds and blacks of her sons. Many of the Tuatha had fallen at the hands of the witch's brood, while the Carman and her boys stood their ground. Danu looked to Morrigan, held out her hand and cried, "Help us. Please!"

Morrigan looked at the battle. Danu's gown had dimmed, the ivy hung wilted. Her energy was being drained by the mag-

ics of the Carman. The Tuatha were losing.

"Danu, it is not my way to interfere. Just observe." She shrugged and stepped further into the shadows. Then Dub slipped from the shadows. With a sweep of his hands, the ravens and crows that surrounded Morrigan fell from the tree without a sound. Their feathered bodies littered the ground around her feet. Morrigan's blood ran cold and she screamed.

The valley shook with the rage and anguish of that cry, and with her heart in her throat, Morrigan took Danu's hand, offering her strength. Their magic combined, turning Danu's soft green emerald with black veins. It cut through the Carman's defenses like a laser, striking her down. The crone collapsed to the ground.

The Tuatha advanced and the three sons fled with the priestesses tight on their heels. Morrigan walked up to where the Carman lay dying and looked down. Her shriveled face sneered back from beneath an unkempt mane of red and silver hair.

The crone coughed, "Ha! The Morrigan. I should have known. You overstep." Another cough wracked her body and she winced in pain. "This was not your battle."

"Your son murdered my children."

"They are naught but birds."

"They were my *children. Each one of them. Your beast of a son escaped my wrath, but you shall not."*

Morrigan held out her hand and the shadows swirled to form a spear; she lifted it above her head and drove the point home. The witch grabbed the haft, holding it tight. Rust coloured tendrils of magic dug into Morrigan, following the spear up and burrowing themselves into her hand. She gasped but could not pull it away. Morrigan locked eyes with the Carmen. Amber eyes filled with vengeance locked with grey eyes filled with spite.

The Carmen spat, "With my last breath I curse thee, Mor-Riogain."

"Curse away, old woman. I fear you not." Morrigan's teeth were bared against the pain of the tendrils digging into her hands.

"You will carry a bairn."

"Me? A child?" Morrigan laughed. "I think not, old crone."

"It will be your doom."

Carman's hands slid from the spear and the tendrils of her magic dissipated.

Danu stepped forward and looked down. "It is over." She laid her hands over Morrigan's and when she removed them, Morrigan's wounds had healed.

"Thank you."

"We would not have won without you." She waved her hand over the body of the Carmen, the earth folded over her, drawing her down. "What did she say to you?"

Morrigan snorted and turned her back on the grave. "Nothing of importance."

In the centuries since that day, this valley had lain here, unchanged, like an insect trapped in amber, but the rest of the world had moved on. Including Morrigan, who'd forgotten about the witch's final words. Until now.

Old gods had fallen into legend, replaced by the gods of the digital era. Danu's powers had waned. The earth was ailing; too few cared. The last time Morrigan had seen Danu, she was living in a cottage just outside Dublin on the River Leth with her prize winning garden and twelve cats.

Morrigan? Well, she'd grown stronger. As long as humans breathe, there would be wars and death. Her power would never wane.

The sun set and Morrigan transformed into her human form, crouching down behind a fallen log.

"I can still feel the magic from that battle. Even after all this time," she said to a raven that had perched near her head. It turned to look one beady eye at her. "I'd have thought it would have faded a little, but it still radiates." She held out her hand and the rainbow of energy rippled over her fingers. She felt the tingle of energy up her arm.

Morrigan closed her hand into a fist, snuffing out the sparks. "I might be able to use this."

Mira grabbed Aemon's hand as Dother herded her family out of the cave. It was pitch black outside and a full moon lit the glade in a soft white light.

They were the last. One by one, people of her village had disappeared with Dain. None returned.

"Pappa, I'm scared."

"Me too, sweeting."

Celene walked behind with the babies held close. "Stay near us, Mira." She and Aemon shared a look, one of parents who are trying to stay calm only for their children.

Dother lead them to a clearing. Dain stood over a dark patch in the grass, and opposite him was the shadow Mira assumed was Dub.

"Where is everyone?"

"They're here," Dain said with a laugh, sweeping his hand before them.

"Hush, Mira." Aeomon said, squeezing her hand. She shot her father a sideways glance but said nothing else.

A flick of movement on the tree line drew her attention. She thought she saw two amber eyes looked out but when she blinked, they were gone. She looked back at the dark splotch on the ground. She had a suspicion of what it was, but she, once again, chose to keep that to herself.

Dother brought them to the edge; the air was tinged with the smell of copper and it made her gag. "Aemon-" Celene began, but was cut short when Dain grabbed Mira and pulled her away.

"No!" Celene and Aemon yelled in unison. The babies began to cry.

Mira glowered at Dain but did not resist.

"You have been chosen," he began.

"Chosen for what?" Mira asked. She should have been afraid, but she wasn't. She was angry.

"A very long time ago, your mother killed ours. Now you will help us bring her back."

"Please no!" Celene cried out, reaching a hand for Mira. Dother grabbed her arm. She broke his grasp and pulled away, but in doing so, she lost her grip on Colm.

Dother scooped him up, grinning. "Stop," was all he said and Celene did.

Aemon made a dive for his daughter. A black tendril shot out and hit him. He fell, unmoving, to the ground.

Celene looked at Mira. "I'm sorry…" her voice broke.

Mira looked from Dain to her father and then to her baby brother and finally her mother. "It's okay, Mama."

Celene pulled Ros in close and buried her face in the baby's hair.

"What are you going to do to me?" Mira looked back up at Dain. His fingers were biting into her arm.

"We are going to kill you, little one. And when you are empty, well, you will become our mother."

"I don't think I want to do that," she said.

"I don't think you have a choice," Dain said with a sneer.

"But I do."

From her hiding place, Morrigan watched Dain wet the soil of the Carman's grave. It was easily identifiable. It was the only spot in the glade where grass would not grow. With a shudder she knew what the brothers were planning and when they dragged out her friend's family and Aemon fell, she knew it was time. She stood and for a brief moment she'd caught the dark-haired girl's eye. She could only hope the girl would remain silent.

Wreathed in darkness, she moved along the tree line until she was behind Dub, the one she considered the most dangerous. This close she could hear him chanting. The words were in a long dead language that would one day become Gaelic. She recognized them; Dub was summoning. She could feel the power of it thrumming through the ground. It was close.

Morrigan felt the tingle of her magic. It would not be enough. She looked at her friends, their children and the girl who looked like a smaller version of herself.

"Mira," she whispered.

She saw the defiance in Mira's eyes and knew she had to act soon. Mira would not give in as easy as the brothers hoped.

Morrigan drew on the dark forces that permeated the area, letting it fill her. Beneath the shadow, her body sparkled with reds, greens, and golds.

Energy shot from her extended hands, catching Dain full in the chest. He dropped to the ground opposite Aemon. Mira broke free and ran at Dother.

Morrigan had changed her target at the last second. Her instincts redirect the blast, freeing her child. She spun next to Dother, a ball of energy held in one hand ready to throw, but he was already wreathed in violet fire with Mira holding his arm. The energy radiated from her hands and he jerked like a trout on a hook. Morrigan's mouth fell open and her magic faded. Mira had magic. Morrigan had not known. She looked at Celene who looked equally dumbfounded.

Mira was screaming. No words, just a scream of rage. Her scream sounded like the cry of a raven.

They'd forgotten about Dub who'd continued his summoning. A bright ball of light flew up from the grave and hit Mira between her shoulders, throwing her forward. Dother dropped to the ground, twitching. Celene and the children screamed.

Morrigan cursed herself and drew dark magic and hit Dub where she suspected his heart to be. He cried out. She hit him again and again. He'd stood no chance. Exhausted from the summoning, he could not defend himself and Morrigan drove the attack home.

The shadows dissipated, leaving a pale young man lying on the ground. He looked no more than sixteen. His upper body was shirtless and covered in heavy tattoos.

"Wizard," she muttered, turning her attention from him to the orange umbilical of energy that had attached itself to Mira. Mira's eyes were wide and sightless, her arms outstretched. Celene was pulling on her arm. Mira did not respond.

Morrigan looked at the area. Aemon was down, maybe dead. Dub was dead, she hoped. Dain and Dother were unconscious. Celene was trying to save their child. The child Morrigan had begged her to take. The child she had abandoned. The child of Morrigan, goddess of war and Lir, god of the sea. The Selikies' god. Celene's god. She'd been eager to raise the child of her friend and her god and now she fought to save her.

Morrigan watched as a lifetime of missed opportunities flashed before her eyes. She took a step, drawing on the dark magic. She watched as her daughter's hair turned from raven to red to silver. She took another step, holding the energy in her fists. She watched as her daughter's beautiful violet magic turned to a rusty orange. Another step. She felt as if she were going to explode. Every cell of her being vibrated with the magic she held.

"Celene?"

The Selkie looked up. "Morrigan?"

Morrigan's head bobbed a yes. "When I break the connection, grab her and run."

"Morrigian, what are you doing?"

Morrigan looked at Celene and smiled. "I'm being her mother."

Celene's mouth opened, but she never said whatever it was in her mind. Morrigan stepped between Mira and the grave. The force of the umbilical took her breath away.

She staggered forward but stayed standing.

Mira collapsed. Celene pulled her to her feet and wrapped her arm around her. Colm held onto his mother's shirttail as she led what was left of her family away. She looked over her shoulder at Morrigan. Saw her friend turning to white. "Tell her of me," Morrigan called and Celene nodded.

Celene and the children barely made it past the clearing when the shockwave hit them, driving them all to the ground. Celene rolled onto her side, protecting her baby. St. Elmo's fire danced harmlessly along their limbs.

"Mama? What happened?" Mira said, her voice barely a whisper. She was shaking, but okay. As soon as the tether had been broken by Morrigan, her hair had begun to turn black again. All but a single stripe of red and white on each temple. Celene choked back a sob. They'd survived.

"I'll tell you everything soon, sweeting."

The red and silver wolf ran through the forest. Its violet eyes taking in every movement, every flicker; its keen nose catching every scent.

She was hunting.

Jeff Slade

A resident of Salmon Cove, Slade is a prize-winning author and avid reader who enjoys both making and hearing puns, playing the guitar, and cats.

Slade has previously been featured in 2018's *Chillers from the Rock* with his short story 'The Culling,' in 2019's *Dystopia from the Rock* with his story 'Anchored,' in *Flights from the Rock* with his story 'Flight of the Puffin,' and in 2020's Pulp Science-Fiction from the Rock with his story 'The Daring Mid-Flight Heist on the Moonbeam Express.'

His award-winning story, *Extinguished,* was featured in *Kit Sora: The Artobiography.*

Prey

The hunter said a silent prayer to the gods for his good fortune, pulling his wagon over to the side of the dirt path before hopping off. Anson tangled the reins into a nearby tree branch, swiftly tying a knot to keep his horse from running off, then reached into the back of the cart for his bow and quiver.

From his high vantage point, he'd spied a deer darting into the bushes just ahead. While he'd already caught one earlier in the morning – more than enough to feed his family for the next few weeks – and had caught more game in the days prior, he couldn't pass up an opportunity to catch even more. Besides, it wouldn't delay him long.

Anson's wife, Matilde, had cautioned him that he shouldn't overhunt the area, that he would be sorry. He laughed at the thought now; when he offered his extra game to the mayor, who would be sorry then? Perhaps such an offering would grant him a position on the council next spring or would increase their social status in the community.

He stayed low and tread carefully along an old dusty path, following the deer's tracks. The woods grew more and more quiet the further he ventured, a good omen to

Anson that meant no one knew he was coming. He prayed again that the gods would allow him to sneak up on his prey, and it appeared that they were listening.

Once he made his way through the bushes, Anson found himself in a small clearing. There, not more than a stone's throw away, stood the deer. It was munching on the long grass that dotted the clearing, interspersed with purple and yellow flowers that perfumed the late morning air. He took in the scent, taking that as yet another blessing from the divine.

Anson knelt in place to steady himself, nocked an arrow from his quiver, and took aim. The deer remained blissfully unaware of his presence, and he let the taut bowstring go, watching the arrow as it whizzed noiselessly through the air at his target.

The deer flinched at the last second, and the bolt pierced its hindquarter, setting the animal into motion. It darted out of the opposite end of the clearing and further into the dark tangle of trees beyond.

Cursing, Anson sprung to his feet and headed in the same direction. A dark red puddle where the deer had been standing confirmed his strike, and small splotches highlighted its retreat. He mouthed another silent prayer to the gods for his ability to track his quarry, thankful that he'd been graced with such pursuit.

The trees on the opposite side were much closer together than the bushes he'd pushed through earlier, and Anson found himself constrained to a narrow path. The branches bore keen thistles that cut and scraped him, warding off potential trespassers, but he persevered. It was meant to be, he told both himself and the scolding memory of his wife's warnings.

It took no small amount of blood, sweat, and tears – both of his clothing and from his eyes alike due to the sharp sting of the thistles – but he fought his way through. His reward awaited him on the other side in another clearing. This one was darker than the last, due to the canopy of trees whose heavy leaves overlapped and blocked out most of the natural light.

The deer laid on all fours on a short hill at the other end of the field. It stared at the hunter, pleading with its eyes for him to retreat and leave it be.

Anson's response was to reach back into his quiver to retrieve another arrow. He grinned as he closed in on the deer, seeing how large it was. He didn't care how difficult it would be to extract his kill; even if he had to carve off pieces and leave the rest behind, he still could take more than enough to present as a gift to the mayor. He truly was blessed.

Before he could nock the arrow, a sound to the left drew his attention. Emerging from the thick copse of trees was a wolf, its fangs bared and eyes locked onto Anson.

He took a step back, then stopped as another wolf appeared to his right, followed by two more, one alongside each of the first pair, then finally a third from behind. He was surrounded.

Panic set in as the wolves marched towards him in unison. "Gods save me!" Anson cried.

Funny, came a voice inside his head, *that humans believe they are the only ones who have gods to hear their pleas.*

He searched for the source of the voice, his eyes finally resting on the deer above him. He could've sworn he heard a light chuckle as his gaze met the deer's.

The wolves of the forest descended upon him as one.

Ali House

Ali House is an award-winning, bestselling author, originally from Newfoundland. She is a graduate of the Fine Arts program at Sir Wilfred Grenfell College (MUN), and currently resides in Halifax where she works in arts administration and spends more time than a person should in and around theaters. She is a master storyteller whose work has helped define the landscapes of science-fiction, fantasy, and horror writing in Atlantic Canada.

To date, House's short fiction has appeared in every volume of the From the Rock anthology series, as well as *Bluenose Paradox, Kit Sora Artobiography,* and *Terror Nova.* Her short fiction was collected in 2020 in *The Lightbulb Forest*.

Previous novels include *The Six Elemental* and *The Fifth Queen,* both a part of her creator-owned Segment Delta Archives series. Other works include the fantasy series *Choose Your Own Adventurer, The Santa Claus Protection Program, The Island Adventure* as a part of the Slipstreamers series of novellas, and *Variety Show* as a part of the Engen Universe.

Trust

Orpheus and Eurydice married young, in a time when everything was simple and it seemed like all you needed to survive was love. And for a while it was pure bliss. For a while.

After their marriage, they moved into a small house on the outskirts of town, away from the rest of the world. During the long summer days, they would sit on the soft, green grass and Orpheus would serenade her with songs of love. At night they would lie on their backs and Eurydice would name all the twinkling stars in the sky, creating constellations just for them. They would spend all day together, eating wild foods that grew near their home, freshly picked at the height of ripeness. Often Orpheus would be summoned to play his music for the rich folk in town, and while he was gone Eurydice would feel as if her heart was torn in two, and when he came back it would be whole again.

Months passed, summer faded into autumn, and a cold reality began to set in for Eurydice, pulling back the gauzy veil of newlywed life she'd surrounded herself in. Winters around these parts were harsh and food could be hard to find. If a person didn't prepare for the cold months, then they could quickly find themselves in trouble. Before her marriage, Eurydice lived with her parents on the other side of the village and had fond memories of gathering and preserving food for the winter together. Realizing that she was already late in this matter, she hurried to Orpheus.

"We have to start gathering food for the winter," she told him. "The cold months will be upon us soon, and we don't want to be caught unprepared."

He frowned at her. "But I have to work on my music. I don't have time for that kind of thing."

"But the cold months..."

He turned back to his guitar. "I have survived winters before without this nonsense. I am sure I will survive again."

She left him, confused about his confident attitude. She wondered if she had overreacted. But the thought of harsh, frigid winds, and opening the pantry to find nothing inside haunted her. She knew she had to do something.

After informing Orpheus that she was going for a walk, she grabbed a large basket and went out to gather food. She didn't want to take the food around their home, as they still needed it, so she went to an old trade path that wound through the forest. It wasn't used often and had slightly overgrown with grass, but it felt safer than going deep into the forest, where no paths existed.

After an hour, Eurydice had filled almost half of her basket. There weren't very many trees or vegetables close to the path, so she wasn't as successful as she'd hoped, but it was better than nothing. She returned to the house and began the preserving process, felling good about having achieved something.

The next day she asked Orpheus again if he would accompany her.

"Didn't you find enough yesterday?" he said.

"Not for the two of us, for the whole winter," she replied.

"Can't you stay with me and listen to my music. It's so much better when you're around."

Eurydice felt a tug on her heartstrings. She wanted to stay with him and be his muse, but the image of their almost empty pantry danced in her mind, and she had to decline.

"I won't be gone lone," she said, smiling. "I'll listen to your music when I get back."

Orpheus didn't seem happy, but he nodded and turned back to his guitar.

When she left the house, she knew that she couldn't take long. Rushing along the path, she kept her eyes open for any kind of food but didn't find much. When it was time to return home, her basket wasn't as full as the day before.

Orpheus was pleased to see her return so quickly, although she did notice him looking at the basket with a confused expression on his face, as if wondering why it wasn't fuller. She wanted to explain that she'd hurried in order to be with him sooner but knew it would sound defensive if he didn't ask the question first. Instead, she said nothing and obediently listened to his music.

After another day of barely finding any food along the path, Eurydice knew that she needed a new tactic. There would be more food deeper in the forest, where plants grew wild and free. If she found one such area, then she could easily fill her basket and wouldn't have to spend so much time searching. The only problem was that she was afraid to go on her own.

"Orpheus," she said the next day, "would you go with me to gather food in the forest?"

He frowned. "I have already told you that I need to work on my music."

"But I need to go deeper into the forest, and I'm scared to go alone. There might be wild animals."

"And what would I do against wild animals?" he scoffed. "I am a musician, not a hunter."

She didn't know what to say to that.

"Why do you have to gather food anyway?" he asked. "I've already said that you don't need to worry. You're making a big deal out of nothing."

As he began to pluck the strings of his guitar, Eurydice found herself unable to enjoy his music. How could Orpheus be so confident? Then she remembered his patrons. Whenever he sang for others they would wine and dine him for hours. He brought nothing back, except for stories of how luxurious the food had been and how the people had doted on him. In summer it had not been a problem, as she was able to provide for herself, but winter was different.

She knew what it was like to be hungry, to feel a pain deep in her empty belly and watch her weak hands shake as her body tried to conserve what little energy remained. There had been a few winters when the cold refused to leave, dragging the season out longer than anyone expected. Snow piled up outside their home, making travel treacherous, and they could do nothing but watch the pantry slowly empty, hoping that they would not starve before the cold season ended.

Eurydice did not want such a thing to happen to Orpheus and her.

So, every day she continued to ask Orpheus to accompany her, and every day he declined. She continued her desperate search for food alone, and her outings grew longer as she strayed further and further along the well-picked path, but her basket became no heavier.

When she would arrive home, with the sunlight almost gone and darkness covering the land, Orpheus would look to see what she had picked. At first his suspicions went unsaid, hanging silently in the air like storm clouds over their heads, but over time he grew bold enough to give these ideas a voice. Was she doing something else in the forest aside from gathering food? Was she perhaps meeting up with another person during those long hours? How else could she be gone for so long and bring back so little?

Eurydice would protest, saying that she was trying her best to provide for both of them and that she would never be unfaithful. He did not reply, but she suspected that he didn't truly believe her, even though it was the truth. Each time she returned home, she could feel his eyes watching her, searching for signs of infidelity.

One day, after weeks of this torment, Eurydice could take no more. As she walked down the path, her empty basket in hand, a rush of cold air moved past her, and she knew that winter would be here soon. Perhaps it would be best for her to die and leave everything to Orpheus so that he might survive the winter. Although he had cast suspicion over her movements and motivations, she still loved him and wanted him to live, even if it was at the cost of her own life. Despair overcame her and she fell to the ground, the empty basket tumbling from her hands as she began to cry.

"What's the problem, my dear?" a smooth voice asked, interrupting her sobs.

She looked up and saw a tall man in dark robes standing a few feet down the path. There was a regal quality to the way he stood, and his dark hair was neatly pulled back, framing dark eyes. Although he was a stranger to her, there was something about him that felt familiar.

When she didn't reply, he gently repeated his question.

"I'm worried about the winter," she said softly, wiping the tears from her eyes. "I don't think I'll gather enough food before it comes, and I'm worried that we will starve."

The man looked around. "There's not a lot to pick around here. You'd do better further into the woods."

She shook her head. "There are beasts in there. I can't possibly go in alone and I don't have anyone to accompany me..."

The man paused to consider her predicament. "I could accompany you, if you wish. I am quite a skilled hunter. Not that many creatures would dare to attack me," he smiled proudly.

She shrank away from his offer, fear crossing her face.

"I'm sorry to frighten you. I assure you that I intend you no harm and am merely offering my company." He bowed to her, leading with his arm. "My names is Hades, God of the Underworld, so you can believe that my word is true."

Her eyes widened as she recognized him from the many pictures and statues around town. "But why would a god care about someone like me?" she asked.

Hades shrugged. "Sometimes helping mortals can be entertaining."

Still Eurydice hesitated. Gods were notoriously tricky and dealing with the Underworld was no laughing matter. "What would you ask of me in return for this favour?"

"Ah, I see you've dealt with gods before," Hades smiled. "I would ask nothing of you, but the pleasure of your company. And, if possible, no more tears. As God of the Underworld, I see far too much crying as it is."

Although she was not completely comforted, the offer was a good one and she could not afford to decline it. Eurydice picked up the basket and rose to her feet, wiping away any remaining tears. "Thank you," she said. "Your offer is a kind one."

Hades bowed his head and gestured for her to walk with him.

Eurydice didn't say much as they moved deeper into the woods, so Hades did most of the talking. He explained that many of the tales about him were falsehoods crafted by his brothers, but that he dared not correct them because they enhanced his reputation. Every now and then he liked to come up to the living world and do something good for a change, but usually it was done in secret, so he'd greatly appreciate if she kept this knowledge to herself.

They were not approached by any wild animals on their journey, which was perhaps one advantage to walking with a god. Eventually they reached a small clearing filled with trees and bushes heavy with produce, and patches of tall offshoots poking out from the ground. Hades remarked to her that he had located it on one of his walks. Most of his walks were in the deepest parts of the forest, as that was where he felt most comfortable.

Eurydice's eyes lit up as she took in the abundance of food, and she quickly set about filling her basket.

"If I may ask," Hades said as she worked, "you mentioned that 'we' will starve. Of whom do you speak?"

Eurydice paused for a moment, her outstretched hand clasped around an apple. "My husband," she replied, plucking the apple from the tree.

"And where is he today?"

"He is busy with his music," she said as if reciting a well-known fact. Hades was silent for a moment, and she felt relief that his curiosity had been sated, but then he spoke again.

"Orpheus, yes? I remember hearing of your marriage. He is quite talented."

"Yes, he is," she replied.

"You'd think that his music would bring enough coin for the two of you to live comfortably forever."

Eurydice put a smile on her face and turned to Hades. "He does not believe in taking money for his gift. It is quite noble of him."

A half-smile crossed Hades' face. "If only nobility could fill one's stomach."

Tears began to gather in Eurydice's eyes. "I love my husband," she said, her voice wavering.

His half-smile disappeared, and Hades crossed over to her. "I know, my dear," he said seriously. "I'm sorry. I can see how much you love him and how much pain you are in. I am sorry if I caused you any distress."

She nodded but said nothing.

He gently picked up her hands, leaving his grip open so that she could pull away if she desired. "If you wish to tell me your troubles, I promise to listen."

Suddenly it all spilled out of her, her worries that she was not doing enough, her frustration that Orpheus did not take her worries seriously, and her fears that she would die hungry and alone. Hades continued to hold her hands as she talked, but she wasn't able to look him in the eyes, keeping her gaze downcast and focused on the ground. She felt as if she was betraying her husband by speaking of such personal things, but the words would not stop. Only now, with the God of the Underworld standing next to her, did she realize how much she needed a friend.

From the moment she had met Orpheus, it had only been he and she. All of her friends and family seemed to melt in his brilliance until there was nothing but him. It hadn't been apparent before, but now it was so obvious. She had given up almost everything for him, but he had given up nothing for her.

"My dear, you seem to be under tremendous pressure," Hades said softly. "I offer no judgement, but if you require my help—even if it is for finding food—please come to the forest and say my name. If I am able, I will come to you."

"Thank you," she said, blinking back the tears in her eyes.

He helped her finish filling her basket and then they headed back to the path. The walk was silent, and Eurydice was thankful for it. She felt as if she'd said all the things she could ever need to say. When they reached the edge of the forest, she thanked Hades again for all of his help. He wished her luck and then disappeared into the forest.

Although her basket was full, her spirit quickly began to deflate. Despite having met and befriended a god, she was suddenly worried about having said so much to him. He seemed trustworthy, but one should always be careful of words. What if this came back to Orpheus? Would he be furious that she'd talked to someone about their relationship and voiced doubts about his ability to provide for his family?

She wondered if she should hide this from him. The thought of keeping secrets from her husband made her feel ill, but he already suspected her of being unfaithful. What would he think of her wandering through the forest with a god?

When she arrived home, she tried to pretend that nothing was out of the ordinary, but Orpheus quickly noticed her laden basket.

"You had a successful day," he said, his voice tinged with a strange tone she didn't recognize.

"There was a grove," she replied. "I was lucky to find it."

Orpheus' eyes narrowed, but he said nothing and turned back to his guitar. The music that he played, however, wasn't the sweet and melodious song of before. Now the notes were sour and incompatible.

"Orpheus, my dear," she said gently. "Is something wrong?"

"Why would anything be wrong?" he replied, plucking a sharp note. "Especially when your new lover has been of so much help."

"There is no one else!" she cried. "I..." Eurydice

paused. Should she tell him of Hades?

Her pause, however, spoke volumes. Before she could say another word, Orpheus growled and grabbed his guitar, storming out of the house.

Tears pricked at her eyes again. She wanted to run after him, but was frozen in place, regret holding her back. Why had she not told him of Hades? Would it have made any difference if she did? Perhaps he would have stormed away no matter what. Why could he not see how much she loved him?

When she was able to move again, she focused on preserving the food she'd gathered. Working into the late hours of the night, she'd pause at every sound, wondering if it was Orpheus coming back. Eventually she went to bed alone.

When she awoke in the morning, Orpheus was still nowhere to be seen. Instead of going out to gather, she stayed home and hoped for his return.

She didn't know where he had gone, but it was likely the village. With his guitar in hand, someone would surely recognize him and offer food and lodging in return for his music. It was her worst fears realized—he would always have someone to take care of him, but she would be left alone, having to fend for herself.

After two days without him, she knew that something needed to be done. She couldn't wander the streets, asking where he was. If she caused a scene, it would only make Orpheus angrier. She needed help.

Walking to the forest, she called out Hades' name and waited. For the first few seconds, she wondered if he'd lied to her. Then she wondered if he was too busy to come to her. Gods had more important things to do than help silly mortals.

"How are you, my dear?" his rich voice asked, and relief filled her as she spun around to see him. He looked just as regal as before, but when he saw the look of despair on her face, his expression turned to concern. "Eurydice, what is wrong?"

"Orpheus has left me," she cried. "I am sorry to bother you, but I didn't know where else to go."

"It's okay. Tell me everything."

Her words spilled from her just as easily as before, but she managed to tell the tale without crying. Too many tears had already been shed.

"How do I make him realize that I love him and would never betray him?" she asked helplessly.

Hades paused to think. "My dear, I do not think you need to prove your love to him. For him to turn his back on you in this way, let jealousy corrupt his feelings, and fail to think about the future of your lives together is a grave mistake. He should be asking for *your* forgiveness."

"But what if he does not see it that way?" She felt a pain in her chest as she realized that Orpheus likely saw no wrongdoing in his behaviour. He never doubted anything he did, but he'd allowed himself plenty of doubts about her. His refusal to acknowledge the future and any possible hardships they might face had driven a wedge between them, but instead of looking at it from her point of view, all he could see was suspicion. And yet still she loved him with all of her heart.

"If you trust me," Hades said, "then I will devise a test. It will not be a simple one, and there will be many factors that must go right in order for it to succeed. But I assure you that no matter what happens I will take care of you. Do you trust me?"

She looked into his eyes and at first it was difficult to make out the expression she saw, but then she recognized it as concern for her wellbeing.

"Yes, I trust you."

He smiled and began to tell her his plan.

As Orpheus drew near to the home he shared with Eurydice, he paused to look at the letter in his hand. It had been delivered to the house of one of his patrons, where he'd been staying for the past few days, and it was only two lines long: *Orpheus, I love you. Please come home.* Although jealousy still coursed throughout his veins, he was tired of people constantly wanting his attention and longed for the peace of home.

He wondered if Eurydice was ready to apologize. Even if she did, he wasn't sure if he could forgive her. Just the thought of her being with someone else made his stomach turn. Still, he owed her the chance to confess her sins.

Bracing himself, he opened the door and entered the house, but instead of being greeted by a weeping and regretful wife, he was presented with silence. Placing his guitar against the wall, he looked around for Eurydice. He'd expected to find her in the front room, nervously awaiting his return, but the room was empty. Maybe she had left. Maybe she'd realized that she couldn't face him and ran away to be with her new lover.

Sighing, he let the letter fall from his hand and walked further into the silent house, but as he approached the kitchen his eyes widened in shock.

Eurydice was crumpled on the kitchen floor, unmoving. He rushed over to her, searching for a pulse, but she was cold and dead. As he tried to figure out what might have happened, he noticed two bloody puncture marks near her ankle. Orpheus let out a cry of pain and agony. If only he had been here, he might have seen the snake and driven it away, but he'd left. He'd rushed off in a fit of anger, with no thought or concern for her well-being. He had been selfish and now his wife was dead.

"Better today than a month from now, eh?" a voice behind him said.

He spun around to see a beautiful woman sitting in his front room. Her curly hair was piled elaborately on top of her head so that a few strands cascaded along her face, framing her dark eyes.

She sighed wistfully. "I know it sounds coarse, but there was no way she'd have survived the winter with the meagre amount of food you have. She'd have died a little at a time, day after day, until the hunger finally became too much. Honestly, it's better to have it all over and done with in one swift moment."

Anger rose up inside of Orpheus. "I never would have let her die."

The woman raised an eyebrow. "What would you have done? You never once invited her to those parties you're constantly attending, nor helped her gather food, like she'd asked you to do so many times. My dear Orpheus... By the time you'd gotten your head out of the sand, it would have been far too late."

"And who are you to talk of things you know nothing about?" he angrily rose to his feet.

The woman stood up, smoothed her deep purple dress, and extended a hand. "Persephone, Goddess of

Springtime and the Underworld. Pleased to meet you."

Orpheus' eyes widened and he bowed low. "I am sorry for what I said, Goddess. Please forgive me."

Persephone smiled, lowering her unshaken hand. "I should be asking your forgiveness for interrupting your grief. I simply wanted you to know that this was a better way."

"It's all my fault," he said, glancing back at Eurydice. "I should have helped her. I should have thought of her more."

She regarded him thoughtfully. "What if you were given a second chance? Would you do things differently?"

He stared at her, confused.

"Persephone, remember?" she said. "Goddess of the Underworld. I could get you an audience with Hades."

There was a moment of hesitation, where Orpheus' mind thought of every possible danger involved in speaking with the Lord of the Underworld and wondered if it would be wise for him to risk his life in such a way. But then he remembered those summer days spent with Eurydice and how happy they had been. He would make every day that wonderful if only he could get her back. After all, wasn't this the kind of stuff that legends were made of? Yes, they'd had problems, but if he could rescue her from the Underworld then everything would be great once again. He'd be famous. Stories would be told of his adventure.

"Please," he said. "I must get her back."

Persephone smiled and gave him instructions on how to safely enter the Underworld and where to find Hades. Before he could ask, she said that she could not accompany him and disappeared.

Orpheus prepared himself mentally for the journey. Persephone had assured him that he would be safe, but that he could only attempt this one time. If he turned and ran away before reaching Hades' throne room, there would be no second chance.

Taking his guitar with him, he walked into the forest, to the entrance of the Underworld. He had to go deep into the forest, but no animals bothered him as he approached the cave. It looked unassuming, but as he drew closer to the entrance, a strange uneasy feeling filled him.

Taking a deep breath to strengthen his resolve, Orpheus entered the Underworld. The darkness inside was thick and heavy, and smelled of stale air. Soft blue lights lit his path, guiding him to the stairs down, which hugged the cave on one side while the other side remained open to the darkness. As he walked down, the empty void beside him seemed to contain his worst fears, so he stayed close to the wall, softly humming to himself, finding comfort in his music.

Keeping his eyes focused on the path, he tried to assuage his fears by writing the epic song that would tell of how he rescued his one true love. He'd have to leave out a few details, but the snake bite and his descent into the Underworld would be dramatic enough.

Finally he reached the bottom of the staircase, and as his feet touched solid ground he saw that Persephone was waiting for him, wearing a dark red dress that matched the colour of her smiling lips.

"I'm glad you made it," she said. "He's expecting you."

Orpheus followed her along a wide hallway, to two

large black doors carved with intricate designs of death and suffering. Opening one of the doors, she ushered him inside.

The throne room was somehow more and less elaborate than he'd been expecting. The room was almost empty, and the colours were limited to black and red, but the dais and throne were horrifying—seemingly crafted from blackened bones and skulls. Orpheus tried not to focus on where such items had come from and instead kept his eyes on the god sitting on the throne.

Hades held himself not just like a god, but like a King. His dark eyes were eager and aware, and although his posture was tall and rigid, it was obvious that he was comfortable sitting on a throne.

"God of the Underworld," Orpheus said as he neared the dais, lowering himself to one knee and bowing his head. "I come to seek your mercy."

"Well, that is something that does not happen every day," Hades said with a hint of humour. "What do you request, human?"

Orpheus raised his head and looked at the god. "My wife, Eurydice, was taken too soon. She was bitten by a snake and died alone. I have come to ask you for her life, for a chance for her to live again and be reunited with her one true love."

Hades regarded him coolly. "I am aware of your situation, young Orpheus," he said. "I am also aware that she never would have survived this winter. Why do you wish her alive who would be dead in a matter of months?"

Orpheus steeled himself. "I was unaware of many things. Since she was taken from me, I have learned and know the importance of my decisions. With my help, we will both survive the winter and live many long years together."

A smile crossed Hades' face. "So you have forgiven her?"

His question startled Orpheus. "Forgiven? For what?"

"For her wrongly assumed unfaithfulness."

Orpheus opened his mouth to deny such a thing, but Hades interrupted him.

"There is no purpose in trying to deceive. We gods see all; we know the truth."

Hanging his head low, Orpheus sighed. "I have learned many terrible lessons."

"So you have forgiven her?" he repeated.

"If I could go back in time and correct all of my mistakes I would."

There was silence, and when Orpheus looked up, he saw that Hades was lost in thought. Had he said the wrong thing? Should he say more?

Hades turned to Persephone, who had appeared next to the throne, and she gave him a knowing look. A smile crossed his face and he reached out, taking Persephone's hand in his and giving it a kiss before turning back to Orpheus.

"While I am not entirely convinced, I will give you the chance to prove that you trust your wife completely," Hades said. "However, if you fail this test, then she will be trapped in the Underworld forever and you will never see her again. Do you agree to this test?"

Orpheus paused, wondering what kind of test it would be. If he failed, Eurydice would be trapped here forever and his epic story would turn into a tragedy. But if he did nothing, she'd be trapped here anyway. He nodded. No matter the risk, he had already come this far.

"The test is this," Hades said, rising from his throne. "You shall guide Eurydice out of the Underworld, back the way you came. However, you will not be able to turn around to see if she is following you. You must keep your eyes ahead at all times. If you make it out of the Underworld without having turned back, then she will be restored to life. If you turn back to look at her even once, you will fail and lose her forever. Do you agree to this test?"

He almost laughed at this inferior trial. "Yes, I agree."

Hades smiled and walked over to him, extending his hand. "Then we have a deal."

"We do."

After they shook hands to seal the deal, Hades turned back to Persephone. He gave a nod and she disappeared into the darkness behind the throne.

"Good luck," Hades said before returning to the dais and sitting down. While they waited, he stared past Orpheus, as if he was no longer in the room.

Soon Persephone reappeared. Behind her was Eurydice, and it felt as though it had been years since Orpheus had seen her last. When she saw him, a wide smile lit up her face, bringing back to him the memory of how beautiful she'd looked on their wedding day.

"You came for me," she said softly as she drew near him.

"Of course I did," he replied.

"I'm sorry."

"It's all in the past and the past is nothing. All that matters now is our future together."

Relief filled her face and she wrapped him up in a hug, holding him tightly as if she was afraid he wasn't real.

"It's time," Hades' voice filled the room. "Orpheus, please face the entrance. Remember, you may not turn around during your ascent. You must trust that she will be behind you at all times."

Orpheus nodded and gave one last look to his wife before turning to the door. Taking a deep breath, he awaited Hades' next instruction. When the order to leave was given, he confidently walked out of the throne room with his head held high.

As he started to ascend the staircase, he realized that he hadn't heard Eurydice's footsteps behind him. Had she been wearing shoes? Perhaps she was barefoot and walking so softly that he couldn't hear her. There was no reason for Hades to trick him and keep Eurydice from leaving the room, but Hades hadn't ordered Eurydice to follow. Had she been made aware of the deal? Was she truly behind him?

Giving his head a small shake, Orpheus told himself to be calm. Doubts would serve nothing—he simply had to make it out of the Underworld and then life would go back to normal.

But would it? What was normal before this? Was it spending all day gathering food in the woods? Was it neglecting his music? Was it not trusting his wife? Hades had said that her unfaithfulness was wrongly assumed, but if that were the case, why did he have to forgive her? Had the god secretly been trying to tell him something? Had she been unfaithful after all?

While Orpheus' mind worked a mile a minute, his feet continued walking, taking one step at a time. Turmoil hung over him like a cloud. All around him were the sounds of wind whistling through the passage, his own footsteps on the stone, and haunting whispers coming from the darkness. Through all of this he still could not hear Eurydice—not her footsteps nor her breath. How could he trust that she was behind him? What if he made it to the top of the steps and discovered that she wasn't there? What if she'd refused to follow because her heart now belonged to another?

The exit was near, but the small doubts in his mind had spun into giant webs of uncertainty. He couldn't trust his wife before her death, so what had changed? Had he been so swept up in the idea of a heroic adventure that he'd forgotten reality? He'd already been blessed by the gods once with his talent for music, so was it foolishness to think he'd be blessed again with love? Was he rescuing his wife only for her to leave him for another?

Orpheus stopped walking and listened for any signs of life behind him. There was no bump from Eurydice at the unexpected halting or question from her about why he'd stopped. His breathing and heartbeat were the only sound of life around him. He was all alone in the passage.

Gritting his teeth, Orpheus realized that he'd been a fool. He'd created an idealized version of his wife in his head, but that wasn't who he was rescuing. He was rescuing a woman who had hidden secrets from him and made him feel guilty. Hades had tricked him. Eurydice wasn't following him; she was back in the great room, laughing with Hades and Persephone about how gullible he was.

The way out was only a few steps away, but Orpheus refused to be made a fool of. He spun around, defiantly glaring at the empty space behind him. Only, it wasn't empty—Eurydice was there.

As her eyes met his, her expression fell. "Your trust in me has gone," she said sadly, "and there is no way for me to win it back." She turned and descended the staircase, her dress flowing behind her.

Instead of trying to run after her, Orpheus stayed still, shocked at how wrong he'd been. She had been there the entire time: it hadn't been a trick. When Eurydice disappeared into the darkness below, he turned and headed out of the Underworld, his head hung low and his steps heavy with loss.

At the exit, Persephone was waiting for him. "She never cheated on you," she informed him. "She was more true to you than you could ever be to her. More fool her, in my opinion."

Orpheus didn't know what to say. With heavy steps, he began the journey home.

The mood in the throne room was subdued, but not unexpected.

"I am sorry, my dear," Hades said, "but at least now you know for certain."

Eurydice nodded. She was heartbroken by the outcome, but enough tears had been spent on her former life. It was time to be strong and move onward.

"As we agreed, you are free to leave and start anew." He gave her an encouraging smile. "And remember, if you ever need any help or simply wish to talk, call out for me."

She looked at her new friend and a smile appeared on her face. "I promise I will."

Jennifer Shelby

Jennifer Shelby hunts for stories in the beetled undergrowth of New Brunswick's fairy-infested forests. She fishes for them in the dark space between the stars. These stories, and many others, are made available through her catch-and-release program. You can learn more at jennifershelby.ca or on twitter @jenniferdshelby.

In 2020 she released her first novella, *Plague of the Dreamless: A Slipstreamers Adventure.*

The Moths of Luness

The witch laid down in despair at the end of the world, worn thin and brittle and waiting for the next crushing blow in an endless series of setbacks. The apocalypse had yet to mar the meadow she lay in, though dark smoke curdled the sky. Bees still buzzed, crickets still chirruped, beetles still wandered through the undergrowth, and these things brought her comfort.

A large, green Luna moth clung to a stalk of grass beside her, its tissue-paper-thin wings held still, its fuzzy white body just visible around the stalk it clung to with six pink legs. At the base of two feathery antennae sat dark eyes which observed the witch with a secretive intensity.

"You're a pretty, fae thing, aren't you?" said the witch. The wildflowers bent towards her in a breeze carrying acrid smells of the destruction in the distance. "Distract me from my doom, winged one. Tell me the story of your species." The witch sighed. "Soothe my ragged heart."

The moth did not answer, and the witch's anger was quick to flare until she realized the creature had no mouth. "By my will and my magic, I give you the gift of temporary speech," she said, casting a spell.

The moth trembled its wings, warming them, debating escape, but there were too many birds lurking in the daylight, ready to make a meal of its flesh. 'Twas safer to stay and give the angry witch what she wanted and besides, stories were meant to be shared.

"The story of moths begins in a world on the far side of the stars," spoke the moth, testing its new voice. It didn't like the sound, too coarse and human, but a moth can't choose its wings, after all, yet is happy to have them.

"Trees covered the world of our birth: an emerald planet swirling around a star the colour of Earth's setting sun. In the time before moths, solar flares reached out from this star and broke free, propelling themselves into the universe on vast wings of flame and gas. Some burned out and disappeared, but others flourished, becoming goddesses of fire. One of these fire goddesses made her home in the sky of our world.

"Her body was long, fat, and blessed with a hundred grasping legs. Her gaseous wings shimmered with blue flames that faded to orange at her wingtips and her name was Luness.

"She fluttered many years in the vast skies of our green world alone. When at last she grew lonely, she plucked a leaf from the trees, rolled it between her many legs, and breathed life inside of it. The leaf filled with silk thread and flesh, woven with hunger and possibility: the first caterpillar."

The witch fiddled with a sheath of grass, tearing it down its middle. "Just one caterpillar? Human myths always start with two."

"There is never just one caterpillar," answered the

moth, its tone offended. "Luness made many 'pillars this way, giggling with delight as she showed us how to walk along the long limbs of the trees, which leaves were the tastiest to eat, and which ones we should avoid. We gorged ourselves on the delicious foliage until our bodies could not hold us anymore and we grew through our instars. We thought the trees' bounty would never end."

The witch snorted, tossing away the ruined greenery. "You consumed too much and killed the trees, didn't you? How very human of you." She sighed, wondering if she could pull the meadow over herself like a comforting blanket and fall into oblivion.

"We did eat too much," said the moth. "And our trees suffered for it. Sunlight fell upon bare branches and what few leaves remained struggled to feed their trees. Our bellies ached with hunger, driving us to feed even as we recoiled in horror at what we'd done.

"We turned to Luness for help. 'We need to change,' we told her, 'but we're so afraid.'

"Luness was quiet a long moment before she answered us. 'When we first left our star, many of my sisters were lost. They clung to their lost star-lives and it made them brittle as obsidian, so brittle they shattered in the pressure of open space. Change can hurt us if we're too rigid, my loves. 'Tis better to let go of who you think you are and allow the change to reshape yourself.'"

The witch pursed her lips. She'd felt brittle and bitter for years, though she supposed she hadn't shattered. Or had she? She never used to fantasize about oblivion.

"Luness showed us how to spin cocoons from the silk she'd stuffed into our bellies when she made us. We wove hidden beds on our beloved trees and willed ourselves to sleep through our relentless hunger. Luness promised to awaken us when the trees recovered and our lives could resume. Our skin stiffened into the hard shell of our pupa but inside we were fluid and we let go of who we thought we were."

"And how long did it take to heal your ecosystem?" The witch swallowed, her mouth suddenly dry as she pondered the possibility of a post-destruction world. It had been so long since she felt hope the sensation set her magic tingling.

"I cannot say how long we slept, for time was not something we measured in those days. Our goddess awakened us to a sharp, green foliage healed of our mistakes and as we struggled from our cocoons, we discovered she had given us a gift: she had remade us in her image. 'I have given you flight in return for your selflessness,' she told us, but she had also taken away our mouths, for we had eaten enough.

"Our wings slowly unfurled, and we flew our first flights in Luness' embrace. The sky filled with her laughter and tales of how she'd missed us.

"Those first moths spent their lives with her in the sky or mating in the trees, laying precious eggs among the leaves they liked best when they were new. Another generation took their place, cocooned, and change became a constant in our lives. For thousands of generations we lived in our beautiful green world. We called it Luna, in honour of Luness. The trees grew hardy, the waters rich with minerals, and the soils dark with nutrients.

"But while our trees were healthy, our sun-star was

not. We watched her slow change in the sky above us all. Her light grew dim and our trees struggled to survive on what light remained."

The witch shook her head. "Change again, huh? Sometimes I think change must be humanity's nemesis. We fight against it till our very souls are bloody."

The moth paused, thinking this over. "Do you win this fight?"

The witch cocked an eyebrow. "Let's just stick to your story, mothling."

"As our sun dimmed, we saw fear crease the face of our goddess for the first time. These were lean years, our caterpillar seasons short, our food thin, and the air cold. Many of the oldest and the youngest trees died while others dropped limbs grown weak and light-starved.

"Finally, our sun-star exploded in a final, brutal pulse of light. Pieces of the star flew like comets into every direction. Luness gathered us into her wingspan and held us inside the cool flames of her wings. She carried us away from our green world and into the star space of the goddesses and gods. From there we watched the supernova of our star wash over our home. The trees did not survive, pulverized to dust, our waters evaporated, and our world broke into barren rocks." The moth, now used to its voice, spoke the words softly, echoing a whisper of its species' ancient sadness through countless generations.

"You're lucky your species survived," said the witch.

"Indeed. We wept within Luness' wings for our lost home, but we knew our goddess would protect us.

"There was nowhere to cocoon ourselves in her wings, but the cold kept us in a dreamy, half-aware state that stilled our hungers. We remember the journey as Luness moved through the galaxies, seeking new worlds where we might safely live.

"By journey's end, we moths of Luness were spread across the universe, tucked into corners where we might be safe, where we fit, and where we are careful to do no harm. Earth's native butterflies were gracious enough to give us the night while they kept the day, a kindness we will never forget.

"At first your world frightened us, but we've become accustomed to your predators and the excitement of danger. We delight in our butterfly cousins, and the stars of your night sky remind us of the journey we took in our goddess' wings.

"Long ago, Luness delivered to us one of the remaining pieces of our beautiful, lost home, worn round from our star's debris, a piece you call the Moon. It rests in the sky as a beacon to remind us of our story.

"Luness still watches over us, but she cannot always be with us now that we're stretched across the universe. Instead, we are content to know she will protect us when we need her."

The witch squinted in the direction of a fresh plume of black smoke rising in the distance. "It's too bad your Luness isn't here to save you now."

"She would be," said the moth, "if we needed saving. Perhaps this particular apocalypse isn't the ending of all things. Perhaps it is only the upheaval that brings change."

The witch laughed a loud, clear laugh that scattered birds to wing. "I was looking for a quiet ending to my fight, not a pep talk from a moth."

The witch pulled back the spell of speech from the creature, already regretting the loss of company. The moth swayed in the breeze with the leaf that it clung to, unconcerned. The sky above boiled with smoke, the air electric with human anxieties, the meadow yet green and inviting, the ground cool. It might be nice to give up and allow herself to shatter, but the witch's magic still clung to the hope the moth had offered and something in the brittle edges of her thoughts had softened, melted, and let itself go.

She got to her feet. Her magic shimmered as she walked away from the moth, creating an illusion of moth wings on her back. They waved, softly, and the moth waved back.

Heather Reilly

Heather Reilly is the author of the Binding of the Almatraek medieval fantasy series, and has written and illustrated several books for children.

Reilly is the proud recipient of the Noble Artist's Author of the Month award for February 2015 for her short story that appeared in *Fantasy from the Rock*, 'In the Moonlight.'

Reilly currently teaches music in Newfoundland, where she lives with her husband and three beautiful children.

Origin of the Sphinx

The boat moved steadily up the Nile as the uneasy lioness roared her displeasure. The sound reverberated through the chests of the men guarding her, making their hearts race and their blood run cold. Hating the water, she would swipe at anyone foolish enough to come close to the bars of her wooden cage. Some of the men had learned that the hard way and were doing their best to tend to their wounds while still pressing onward. The men on duty couldn't wait for this detail to be over; they didn't trust the solidity of the cage to protect them for long, and they feared that it was only a matter of time before the angry lion figured that out as well. Luckily, they were almost at their destination and they would be rid of the foul beast that watched their every move.

In the desert palace in the dead of the night, the almost silent padding of little feet and glowing green eyes could easily be detected following the skittering of rodents. Cats had always been revered in Egypt as fierce protectors of the home. The invaluable felines not only prevented the rodents from ruining large quantities of grain, but also kept each family safe from venomous snakes and scorpions which might wander into a household left unguarded. Almost every home could boast having at least one cat and the palace was no exception. Pharaoh Khufu's extensive family was defended by a plethora of felines that languished and hunted throughout the palace. Each of Khufu's twenty-four children possessed one as a pet, and while most were content with a kitty that could hunt vermin where they might lurk in small spaces, the biggest of the lot was about to be an unnamed lion meant for his eldest son, Kawab the crown prince.

The lioness finally arrived by boat that morning – one that promised the unbearable heat of the unshaded desert sand. The pharaoh oversaw his precious cargo unloaded, and commanded the servants to take the lioness in its cage to the room in the palace used to worship Bast. They struggled to carry the weight of the giant cat through the palace and into the room which sported the great alabaster likeness of the lion-headed goddess. At her feet shone jewels, perfumes, and other offerings that had been laid to ensure that she would watch over their home and protect the palace's inhabitants. Perhaps she would calm the fierce beast.

Pharaoh Khufu planned to present the lioness to Kawab at that evening's feast for the summer festival. His eldest son was grown and married and the pharaoh wanted to honour him at the birth of his third son. However, as the king sat on his throne conferring with his vizier about how the trade had gone with Nubia, a guard rushed in with the news that his son, Kawab, had met an untimely death and had been discovered only moments before.

Khufu felt as though his heart had cracked in two, but it was imperative that he show no weakness while on his throne. He broke off his conversation with the vizier, and could only bring himself to nod that he had received the news, not trusting his voice to be steady. He waved the messenger away as he tried to process the news. This sudden loss tainted Khufu's ability to continue with the meeting and he went to seek out the queen to share with her the news.

Sure enough, she was devastated. She had thought the sun rose and fell with her first son. The king was stunned by the timing, but not overly by what had happened. There was a reason that pharaohs had many children. Next in line for the throne was a dangerous thing to be -- death lurked behind every corner of the palace, and often at the hands of another possible successor. Kawab's life had been cut short, and rumours among the slaves suggested that his own wife, along with his brother Djedefre, had been among the possible culprits. This news vexed Khufu greatly, and even though Djedefre was now the new heir apparent, Khufu's suspicions about the murder prevented him from wanting to hand over the prized feline he had just acquired to the questionable new heir. But something had to be done with it; it had cost a small fortune.

Despite the death of the prince, the preparations had already been made and the hour for celebration was upon them, so the feast was to go ahead while the lion was to remain caged until a suitable decision about its fate could be made. Remaining in their chambers in grief, the pharaoh sent Djedefre to oversee the launch of the celebration. The pharaoh and his wife were distraught, but seen as godlike himself, Khufu knew that he was expected to at least make an appearance. He dried his wife's tears and swallowed his own disappointment as he turned to go. The queen was too despondent to see to her own duties, so she sent the younger prince, Khafre, to their temple-like room of Bast in order to pay tribute to the goddess and ask her to watch over those that were joining their home for the revelries.

Still only a boy, but now technically the second in line for the throne, Khafre nervously made his way through the expansive corridors toward the room of Bast. The heady scent of the perfumes he carried would normally put him in a soothing, calm frame of mind, but right now all he could concentrate on was that every slap of his bare feet against the marble floor sounded magnified. Terrified of who might lurk behind any of the pillars, statues, or alcoves that lined the walls, his walk bordered on a skittish run as he tried to look in all directions at once. Since the death of his eldest brother only hours before, Khafre was now completely on edge. His life had been carefree with two possible heirs before him, but now he feared that he may be seen as a real contender for the throne, and therefore might also become a target. If he could only get to her room, he could ask Bast – the goddess of protection for the home, children, and royalty – to shield him from evildoers. Feeling relief at the warm glow of the torches that greeted him from Bast's room just ahead, he raced up the three steps expecting to see only the black, towering statue carved in the form of a woman with the head of a cat. Almost at a run now, he flew between the pillars at the entrance but stopped short when he saw the wooden lion's cage in the middle of the floor, and the sleeping creature within.

Fear and surprise at the unexpected sight almost caused him to drop the tray of offerings he had brought for the shrine. Khafre's heart pounded in his chest, and he swallowed hard. The giant feline appeared to be stretched out in a deep slumber, and the boy found himself ensnared by curiosity. Khafre took a shaky deep breath and crept quietly closer. He could almost reach out to touch her soft, course fur, and as he transferred the tray to one arm to do just that, the bowls and bottles of perfume slid into one another and they faintly clinked together. The boy managed to retract his hand and right the tray before the contents spilled, but the lioness' great ear had turned toward the sound and her piercing golden eyes had snapped open and now held him in their gaze. Khafre hastily backed away in fright, but not across the room to the base of the statue, only out of paw's reach. The two of them regarded each other for a long moment, silently sizing each other up. The young prince backed up a couple of paces more, quickly turned to the statue, and reverently placed the perfume bottles and bowls he carried at the idol's feet.

"Have you come to protect me?" he whispered to the smooth alabaster carving. As if in answer from behind him came a deep, rumbling roar that made the boy jump. The prince quickly rose and turned back to the caged animal on legs so shaky that he wasn't sure if they would hold him. He looked at the lion for a long time, trying to pluck up the courage to draw near it again.

"I'm Khafre," he introduced himself as he tentatively reached out toward the large cat once more. Even if this was not Bast herself, he knew she was watching over him, and he had faith that no feline would harm him under her watch. The lioness turned her head toward him and her nostrils flared in pulses as if to sniff the proffered digits. Immediately the lioness found her feet, her interest having been peaked. Her great, pink tongue licked her lips as she regarded the boy.

"Are you hungry?" Khafre asked. The lion only stared back steadily.

He turned back to the offering he had just laid at the statue's feet among all the others. Along with the perfume were a large pottery bowl of milk and another of mutton. He reclaimed the bowl of meat and regarded it as his own mouth began to water. He supposed that he could venture to the kitchen and make up another offering, but he wasn't ready to share the secret of what he had found yet – right now it was all his.

After several long minutes of debating how Bast would react if he took back something he had already given her, he asked her for a sign to guide him. Again the lion released a roar that made Khafre's knees grow weak. He turned to it and saw that the lion was now pacing and agitated inside her cage, perhaps from having been interrupted from her slumber, or possibly bolstered by the wonderful smells coming from the meat. He looked at the myriad of offerings already given to Bast and decided that if she had come to him in the form of the lion, feeding her would still be making the offering anyway. If not, he knew the lion was at least sent by the god and sustaining her would be important to Bast.

There was no way that the bowl would fit between the bars of the cage so Khafre plunked himself down with the bowl between them. He had the lion's full attention now and once again she licked her lips in anticipation. Khafre was a smart boy, and though he trusted that Bast would watch over him, he had no intention of putting his hand in with a hungry lion. So he picked up a handful of the savoury meat and tossed it between the bars. The lion immediately scooped it up with her teeth, tossed her head back, and swallowed it whole. That handful was followed by another and another until the bowl was empty. The lion looked at him expectantly for the next bite, so he placed his empty hand next to the bars to let her see there was nothing left.

"It's all gone," he told her. The lion's tongue snaked out between the bars and licked at his palm, removing all the spice and grease coating it from the feeding. The tongue felt smooth at the edges and like his hand was being pelted by sand in a sandstorm in the middle, but he endured it, feeling that he was bonding with the animal. The lioness soon lost interest in his clean digits and set about to licking the smooth marble where the meat bits had landed to make sure she hadn't missed any morsels. The sound was a thick half-wet, half-sticky sound that made Khafre laugh. She was clearly still hungry and Khafre understood that. The bowl hadn't contained all that much for a lion. When the cat realized there was no more food coming, she extended her two front paws before her to display her sharp retractable claws and stretch out her back. Finally, she let her back end drop neatly between her hind legs to rest on her belly. She was one of the most proud and regal looking creatures Khafre had ever seen.

The prince knew he was late for the feast but he dreaded leaving. He had already begun to think of the lion as his and he was worried that if he left she might be gone when he came back. On the other hand, if he didn't show up at the feast, he knew his parents would send a servant looking for him. If someone found him here, they would also find the lion and he didn't want that. This had to stay his secret. That made up his mind. He said goodbye to his new friend and promised Bast that he would return with another offering to replace the one he had fed to the lioness.

Now that he knew Bast was watching over him, he didn't feel the need to constantly look over his shoulders anymore. He took the empty bowl to the kitchen with a bounce in his step. He spoke to one of the servants there, using his young age to his advantage and taking on the guise of a sheepish, chided child. "I'm afraid I tried to carry too much and spilled the offering. It has already been cleaned up, but I need another. He lowered his voice and affected a fearful expression as he spoke conspiratorially with the servant, "I must please the great Bast; I don't want what happened to Kawab to happen to me for my error, so maybe you could make me two."

The servant took pity on him. "Don't worry, I will make you an offering fit for a king."

"Thank you. I will come to fetch it right after I have my supper."

The servant nodded and Khafre went to go sit to dine with his parents. He could tell his mother was distraught as she barely touched her food. Khafre tried to appear tired though he was brimming with energy from the excitement of his secret discovery. The mutton and hippo tasted divine, like they could almost melt on his tongue. Before him people danced, music played, and women sang. It was one of the biggest turnouts to the festival that he had ever seen. Part of him wanted to join them, but the lion tugged constantly at the back of his mind. So he made a great show of yawning multiple times throughout the course of the meal, and declared how exhausted he felt from the trials of the day. Finally, he rubbed his eyes and asked to be excused. His despondent mother only nodded, and his father excused him with an understanding, "of course."

Khafre had to remind himself to walk as his feet seemed to want to dance to the rhythm of the music coming from the other room. The joyous melodies moved him as people lifted up their voices in appreciation to the gods. He returned to the kitchen and saw two bowls larger than the last bearing a mixture of meats from the feast. Mutton, hippo, crane, and gazelle filled both in a heaping mound. It certainly was a sacrifice fit for a king. Khafre wrapped one arm around each and hefted them together. He would have to walk smoothly to avoid them slipping out of his grasp for real.

As he headed back to the silent room where the proud statue of Bast watched over all, the music faded behind him with the distance he put between them. Although the revelries would carry on long into the night, he finally began to feel fatigued from his exertions and the heavy meal digesting in his stomach. Panting and almost dropping the slipping bowl on the left, he made it to his destination to find the lion stretched out on her side with her massive head down. He didn't know whether or not to wake her for the meal. He knew his brothers could be cranky if woken from a deep slumber, and he didn't think making the lion mad would be a wise choice. He decided to quietly lower one bowl to the ground and then with much relieved arms, carried the second to the base of the statue. He said a whispered prayer and smiled up at the maternal goddess.

The sound of a deep yawn behind him alerted him to the fact that either from the scent of the food or the soft tones of his voice, the lion had been revived. He padded over to the cage with the bowl meant for what he already thought of as his cat, and offered her a piece of crane to see if she would want it. The lion greedily snatched it up and swallowed it down. When the supply of meat finally came to an end, the creature cleaned her face and paws, then continued down her body until she had reached the tip of her tail. Khafre sat and talked to her in calm tones until she had finished her bath and stretched out beside him while she regarded him with her eyes. He told the lion about his life, the loss of one brother and the fear of another, his favourite sister and his favourite place to sit and think on a set of the palace steps by the edge of a sunken garden and indoor pond.

By and by his lids began to droop, but he couldn't seem to bring himself to leave the magnificent cat and take himself to bed. He was half afraid that if he did, it would be the last time he would see her; that she would be gone the next day as if he had never been there. He stretched out beside the lion and felt the cool marble cause goosebumps to rise on his otherwise warm skin. The lion stretched her legs out stiffly before relaxing into a curled-up U. She extended her paw through the bars, and when the boy tentatively stroked the thick fur there, she didn't pull away. She only yawned again and both of them contentedly closed their eyes.

Khafre awoke in the dark to the sound of echoing,

whispered voices. He felt disoriented and his neck was stiff from sleeping without a head rest. The warm fur under his fingertips reminded him of where he had fallen asleep. He sat up groggily and the whispered conversation in the hall outside the room that had woken him continued.

"No, it wasn't easy, but it is done."

"You ran a great risk choosing today to complete the task. You could have been easily caught with all of the people gathering here for the festival." This was a disapproving female voice interposed between two men's.

"It was the distraction I needed to get him alone. Everyone's minds were somewhere else, focused on other tasks. Things worked out exactly as I had planned."

"Very well, then." The sound of a clinking sack of coins changing hands met Khafre's ears and as he watched, shadows cast on the wall of the opposite side of the hall told the same story. He shivered though he wasn't cold. He had recognized one of the voices as that of his brother.

"And what of the other ones?"

"Are you sure that is necessary? No one else stands in your way."

"True, but what is to stop them from attempting to do as we have done tonight?"

"As you wish."

"Only the oldest one, mind you." This was the female again. She too sounded strangely familiar, but Khafre couldn't quite put his finger on who it was. "The others are much too young to be a hindrance, and by the time they would be old enough, there will be a new pharaoh."

Khafre nervously bit his lip. He could hardly believe

his ears. He had to get away from here. He had to hide, but the statue and the lion cage were the only things of any size here. He was out in the open with nowhere to go. He tried to get to his feet and his heel hit the bowl he had left aside. It moved only slightly on the floor, but it still made a sound.

"What was that?" the strange voice from the hall was insistent and nervous.

"We can't be seen together. Take your leave to plot your move. We will investigate. It sounded like it came from in there."

Fear made Khafre's stomach leap into his throat. He glanced around quickly. There was nowhere to go. The braziers in here had not been rekindled and the ones in the hallway were the only source of dim light now. Perhaps he could hide in the shadows. He held his breath and moved silently to the back of the lion's cage where he tried to find a suitable place to go. Nothing. The dim light made the pattern of the bars on the floor. The only solid shape was the lion herself. Footfalls were coming, he had to think, quick! He had no time to run across the open area to the statue. Using the last second before they would round the corner and enter the room, he did the only thing he could think of. He unbolted the door of the lion's cage, grabbed the bowl, and crawled inside.

The big cat was awake now, and her eyes glowed as they reflected the dim light. Khafre knew he was risking his life, but it was already in just as much danger out there. *Please don't eat me*! he thought the silent prayer to the lion, hoping Bast would hear and protect him. He crawled toward the cat and curled up with his back against her soft belly. The lion brought her muscular paw down on him, sniffed him, and rested her great head above his own. With each puff of her warm breath that wafted over him, Khafre smelled the rich meats that might have made up his last meal on Earth.

Two sets of footsteps came to the bottom of the stairs just outside the room. Khafre could imagine them peering inside the temple-like room. They should only be able to see the lion's back if he stayed low enough. He held his breath as he lay curled up against the warmth of the big cat. He waited while his brother and the woman scanned the room. Khafre kept his head down, though the span of silence and curiosity almost got the better of him and made him move too soon.

"Well, well. Look what we have here." Khafre's mouth went dry with the words. He knew he had been found out. He began to panic. He didn't know what to do. He was contemplating coming out and giving himself over to whatever evil was meant to befall him when the voice went on. "It must have been meant for my brother. Now, like the throne, it will be mine. I wonder when it got here."

"It must have arrived today. Is it dead? Why isn't it moving?" There was something about the on-edge quality of the voice that made it even more familiar to Khafre, but he still couldn't quite make the connection as to whom it belonged.

"I don't know, why don't you go ask it." His brother's voice was patronizing this time. The lion adjusted her hind leg and knocked the bowl. The ceramic made a faint scraping sound as it moved against the marble floor. "There you have it. It's not dead and the mystery of what we heard is solved."

There was another brief pause and then the woman

spoke again. "Come, we've tarried away from the feast long enough. We must return before they miss us."

As the two sets of echoing footsteps receded, Khafre made to sit up, but the large lion paw pressed down and held him fast. After the hallway had been empty for a long while, Khafre once again tried to wriggle away. This time the lion's large mouth opened to bear its sharp teeth.

A servant nervously alerted the feasting pharaoh to the fact that the boy's bed was empty. Tears welled up in the queen's eyes. "Oh, Khufu, not another one! My heart will break into a million pieces if I am to lose two sons in one day."

"I will find him myself; I swear it," replied the pharaoh stalwartly. She placed a hand on his arm in thanks as he rose. "Show me," he commanded the servant who had come to tell him the news.

"There were no signs of a struggle, great one," the servant informed him. "Everything is in its place; his bed has been untouched."

Sure enough, there wasn't a hint that the boy had ever gotten to his room when he had excused himself from the celebration. The shendyt and jewelry the boy had been wearing were still missing. His senet game rested peacefully, with all the pieces still standing tall on their coloured squares, ready to be played. Nothing seemed amiss here, which made Khufu believe that Khafre had never made it this far. The pharaoh began to send servants looking for his son. The news among them spread as swiftly as a sandstorm. When word got to the kitchen, the servant who had provided the platters of meat for the child's offering came forward and prostrated himself before the pharaoh.

"Your majesty, I saw the boy as he left the feast. He had me prepare two offerings for him to take to Bast."

The pharaoh's copper skin paled with the realization that his favourite son had gone to the room which housed the lion, and the pharaoh mentally noted how flimsy the cage had looked when it had arrived. What if Khafre had gotten too close and had been horribly injured or killed?

Khufu took off down the hall, leaving all reserve behind. His bare feet slapped the marble in a pounding rhythm as his knees rose and fell, outpacing his wildly beating heart. Seeing only a single dimly lit brazier left outside the room of Bast ahead on the left, his eyes searched the white marble for any signs of shimmering pools of his son's lifeblood. He saw nothing as he got closer, and part of him felt relief. Still another part filled his belly with dread at the thought that the only lead as to his son's whereabouts may have been wrong.

"Quickly, relight the braziers!" Khufu ordered as the servants caught up. Within moments, the hall was bathed in light and the servants began to work on the ones in the room.

The pharaoh took the steps in a single bound and came to a halt at the sight within the room. There was his most precious child in the cage with the ferocious beast, both fast asleep. The boy's side knot was wet, and his skin was pinker than its usual tan. Evidently the lion had given him a bath as if he had been one of her own cubs. The empty bowl with remnants of spices clinging to the sides within reaching distance of his unconscious son's hand told the pharaoh all he needed to know. Now the only question was how was he going to get his son out?

Khufu went around to the door and found it unlocked, only pulled shut. He began to swing open the barred, wooden door when the lion snapped awake and partially rose on high alert. Khufu paused and spoke calmly to the lion: "This is my boy and I need him back." He slowly reached a hand into the cage towards his son and the lion bared her teeth and let out a warning snarl which woke the boy.

"Father?" the boy asked as he came to.

"Yes, Khafre, you had us all worried sick. Please, come out."

The memory of what he had endured came flooding back to Khafre. He told his father all he had heard the voices say and the pharaoh's face darkened as he listened. "Bast herself must have sent her, she saved my life." Khafre ended his tale and hugged the lioness tightly around her furry neck. Amazingly, the lion endured it without much fuss. When the boy pulled back, the lion gave him a quick swipe of her tongue. The boy giggled and it did much to lift the pharaoh's heart.

"Then she must be yours," the pharaoh decreed. "Come now, we shall bring her to your room where you must finally get some real sleep."

He commanded the servants that were there to call off the search and alert the queen that the boy had been found safe and sound. He sent for more servants to carry the lion's cage to his son's room. Only then would the boy come out. The pharaoh ordered two sentries to remain posted outside his son's room and told them to stay with him at all times. The rest of that night passed uneventfully and Khafre slept deeply into the morning undisturbed.

The young prince woke in the late morning and immediately went to the lion to greet her with the new day. Throwing caution to the wind, he reached through the bars and began to scratch her beneath the chin. The lion lifted her head and closed her eyes in pleasure and Khafre would swear he could see the edges of her mouth turn up at the corners. She began to make a talkative sound somewhere between a meow and a roar.

"I'll go get you some breakfast," he told her as he pulled back his hand. She made a happy chuffing that sounded to Khafre like someone making a succession of breathy Fahs. She rubbed the side of her face across the bars as Khafre rose.

Due to the revelries and copious drinking that flowed throughout the night, most of the rest of the family were late risers as well. Khafre went to the dining room with his sentries walking a few steps behind him. He was hoping to sit near his father, whom his mother always told him he was so much like, but other brothers and sisters had beaten him to the coveted seats and he was forced to take another where the empty chairs began. Then he heard the sound of conversation coming toward the dining hall and his heart almost stopped. They were the same two voices from the night before that had threatened his life. He looked quickly to his father so he could alert the pharaoh but he was already deeply in conversation with Khafre's mother. It was unwise to interrupt, Khafre knew that. So he busied himself by taking generous portions of food as his dangerous brother entered the room with the mystery woman.

Khafre's stomach sank as his brother Djedefre sat beside him with none other than Kawab's new widow at his side. Her clothes were torn and her eye makeup had sufficiently run as befitting a woman in mourning, however the tone of her voice was warm and coy. She laughed privately at something Djedefre had said. Khafre felt sick.

Djedefre leaned toward his younger brother and quietly said, "I heard you disappeared last night, and almost scared father to death."

"Yes, we wouldn't want that now, would we – for you both to disappear?" his sister-in-law chuckled beside him.

Khafre couldn't believe what he was hearing! He looked down at his plate but he had lost his appetite. He clenched his hands together under the table to stop them from shaking. He wondered if they had tormented Kawab before he had met his untimely end. Khafre stood so forcefully that the chair skittered backward with a sharp screech against the floor. "Father, may I be excused to feed my lion?"

It was meant partially as a warning to his brother not to mess with him, and maybe also to rub it in a little that the lion had been granted to him. Despite the very real danger of doing so, he couldn't help but take the jab at the expense of his last remaining older brother. Khafre felt that he and Kawab deserved at least that bit of vengeance.

His father looked down the table at his sons. He saw the plate of untouched food in front of Khafre and the pharaoh's new heir glowering menacingly next to him. Khufu didn't know what insults had passed between them, but he thought it would be wise to remove Khafre from what was undoubtedly a terrifying experience. He was proud of his son's show of strength in the face of what he had both witnessed and endured the night before.

"Yes, my son, go tend to your new pet," the pharaoh pointedly allowed. Khafre picked up his plate and left with the sentries in tow while his brother gaped like a fish behind him. The young prince made his way to the kitchen, remembering the conversation from the night before he had had with his father about the upkeep of the lion. The boy made a standing declaration to the kitchen staff that there should be uncooked red meat and water as a provision each day for his feline. For now he just brought a bowl of fresh water for it, saving the heavy meal for later in the day.

Khafre hummed one of the songs from the night before that had become stuck in his head as he walked the corridors to his room. The music died on his lips though as he entered and saw how agitated his cat was. He went to it and pulled the bolt as it dawned on him that his room smelled wrong. He had a moment to recognize the scent of sweat before a quiet shuffling sound behind him caused him to rise and turn in alarm.

A cloaked man came at him bearing a blade and sliced the air before him as Khafre dodged out of the way. The attacker was ready though and grabbed the prince's shoulder and spun him around to hold the curved knife at his throat. The intruder lobbed a hissing sack at the guards that were now running in from the hall. The sack landed and venomous snakes emerged, striking at the approaching men.

Inside the cage, the feline roared ferociously and threw herself against the door which sprung open. She immediately ran at the hired man and leapt into the air with her claws extended. The man raised the knife toward the cat and Khafre saw his chance to drop to the floor and quickly back away. The lioness swiped with her paws and bit the knife-wielding arm as her momentum knocked them both the ground. The lioness dispatched the man and turned to a snake hissing at the boy from within striking distance of his arm.

The lion moved cautiously and clawed at the snake, dragging it backward away from the boy. Khafre jumped up on his bed to put some distance between him and the snakes, though he knew they could climb that distance with very little trouble. One of the guards distracted one of the snakes with his spear as the other threw the bag over it. The lion finished the other she was contending with, and turned to the boy on the bed. The big cat jumped up on the bed and loomed over Khafre. But the boy was not afraid, and he reached up to stroke the side of the cat's face in gratitude.

"Your majesty," one of the guards called as he approached with his spear at the ready to save the boy. The lion turned on the guard, snarling viciously and standing between the man and the boy in a protective stance.

"Get my father," the boy ordered. "We are fine."

One guard stayed in the room on high alert until the other had returned with the pharaoh and reinforcements – only then did the sentry relax. The king rushed in to find both the boy sitting and the lion lying on the bed amicably near each other. The room was a disaster which would require a cleaning crew to scrub down the walls and floor. The guard explained what had happened and the prince corroborated the truth.

The pharaoh eyed the cage and told the boy, "I think we can dispense with that. Your lion has more than earned her freedom."

Djedefre had gotten almost everything he wanted. Not only did he rise to the throne upon the death of Khufu, but he married Kawab's widow to boot. The only thing that evaded him was the life of his next younger brother which he had so badly wanted to take. Luckily for Khafre, Djedefre's reign was a relatively short one. The murder of Kawab had never been proven, yet between Khufu and Khafre, they were able to keep Djedefre from erecting a burial temple with the rest of the family. Upon the evil brother's death, Khafre eventually ascended to the throne himself with the old cat still at his side and a wife and children of his own.

Khafre sat on the stairs by the garden's pond and stroked Mekal's head between the ears, eliciting a deep sigh of contentment from his sand-coloured friend. The lioness had been given the name which meant fierce devourer after the one and only deliberate attempt on the boy's life. Khafre, now a man, was saddened by the perpetual fatigue and stiffness with which his aged feline protector always moved. He knew in his heart that the end was near for the cat that had ended up saving him so many times.

In her honour, Khafre had ordered a giant monument to be made in Mekal's image close to the site for his own pyramid, next to his father's. It would have the body of his lion and one of the human faces of Bast, the protector of families and children, who had seen fit to send the cat to protect him. So too would the pair be able to watch over the new pharaoh and his family for eternity in the afterlife.

Lisa M Daly

A native Newfoundlander, Lisa M Daly is an archaeologist, historian, professional ballroom dance instructor, crafter, and avid baker.

Previous non-fiction writing credits include essays *Sacrifice in Second World War Gander* and *An Empty Graveyard: The Victims of the 1946 AOA DC-4 Crash, Their Final Resting Place*, and *Dark Tourism*.

She made her fiction writing debut with 'The Island Outside the War' in *Dystopia from the Rock*.

Lisa acted as the guest editor for the Summer 2019 *Flights from the Rock* collection.

In 2021 she released her first novella, *Navigating Stories*.

Songs of the Deep

In times long past, the oceans, skies, and lands were full of creatures who no longer roam the world. Of these creatures, three were maidens of the sea: long-lived women who cared for the creatures of the waters and ensured the monsters of the deep stayed in their dreamless sleeps. These mermaids once kept watch over the oceans from the warm salty waters of the Dead Sea to the cold currents of the Emerald Isle. Throughout the centuries they would swim together along the coasts and waterways, keeping balance between the species and singing to the titans of the ocean, keeping them asleep.

Amaya, the youngest of the sisters, had hair the colour of kelp that would dry into soft curls when she sunned herself, skin the light turquoise of clear water in sun, and a tail red like coral. Cherith, the middle sister, had eyes of blues and purples that changed with the light. While her eyes were like the inside of mussel shells, her hair was dark and coarse, like the outside of the shell, and gave her a dark corona whether in the water or out. Her skin was a soft pink like the inside of a conch, and her tail dark like the ocean just before a storm. Kelby, the eldest, had fine hair the colour of sand that moved with every ebb and flow of the water. Her eyes were the colour of rain clouds, her skin like dark granite, and her tail the bight blue of a parrot fish. They did not know if their ages were actually different, but it helped to think of each other in such terms. They could not remember being young or having parents, only taking care of the ocean as they always had.

The trio would swim and play, dance with the fish, and seek out the monsters of the deep. Sometimes they would come across a monster who was no longer sleeping, but dead in its crevice or cave. The sisters would weep for the death, but rejoice knowing that the creature could never harm their world. After eons, very few monsters remained, but the three dutifully visited each one over the millennia and sang a lullaby. On their journeys, which would take hundreds of years, they would explore all the waters of the world.

The oceans always changed. New species of fish and crustaceans would appear, and the mermaids would crowd around new plants, picking flowers and leaves to carry with them. They would weave discarded shells into their hair, only to drop them some time and some place later, and would find more. They would mimic the songs and sounds of dolphins and whales, and though neither creature would understand each other, they all appreciated the company. The three would breach the surface and float, watching the birds and clouds in the sky. Sometimes, they would find themselves a rock and climb up, drying their hair and sunning their long tails. If they happened to find a storm, they would always surface, allowing the waves to lash them about. They would make high pitched noises from deep in their bellies, thoroughly enjoying the tumult. Sometimes, they would find a rock and let the rains wash the salt from their skin until they would dive deep, immersed in the salt water once more.

They had few dealings with the creatures of the land. They would see some on the shorelines and the beaches, and in later centuries, some creatures would come to the water, splashing in the shallows or floating in vessels on the surface. The creatures could not swim in the depths like the mermaids. In storms, they found their bodies. Even when they brought them to the surface, the creatures would not wake up and swim. In rare occasions, they would find the creatures floundering, and return them to their vessels to float on the water once again.

They did not do everything together. They were sisters after all. Sometimes they would fight, angrily, whipping one another with their tails. They would go their separate ways, sometimes for full seasons, but they would always come together again when it was time to sing to the monsters. They had a duty, a responsibility, and no matter what, they would always sing together.

This time, it was Amaya who had angered both Cherith and Kelby. She had stolen a shell from Kelby and weaved it into Cherith's hair, hoping to spend time alone with Kelby without Cherith. It had worked many times before, though sometimes the other two realised what she was doing and she was turned away. This was one of those times. Cherith convinced Kelby that Amaya had woven the shell into her hair, and quickly undid the plat and gave back the shell. The two sisters then turned on Amaya, pulling at her hair and striking her with their tails. Amaya left, angry and disappointed that her trick had not worked. She left for her favourite rocks, to sit and wail at the skies.

Kelby and Cherith continued on, also angry and sad about their sister. They knew it would not last, and knew they would be together again at the ocean canyon where the Kraken slept. They swam their way, allowing Amaya to go her own way for a while. They explored the waters, and followed the vessels full of creatures. They were big like whales, but never went under the water. And the creatures on these shared some features of the mermaids, like hair at the top of their heads and long appendages that could reach and grasp and work and weave. The sisters were amazed by these creatures, and would follow them on the surface of the water, spy on them, and disappear back under the waves. They were just another ocean creature to play with.

The only creature they had conflicts with, besides each other, were the sirens. The flying creatures seemed so like themselves, including wanting to sit on the rocks in the sun and sing. The sirens were known to fly at the mermaids, claws out, forcing the mermaids to flee into the water. They would swim away, and glare back at the sirens who would cackle songs of triumph. The mermaids didn't know what the songs of sirens did to the creatures on the boats. When the mermaid sang, they would often splash away before the ships came too close to the shoals. The sirens would keep singing until the vessels wrecked and the creatures on them would be thrown into the water to drown.

Kelby and Cherith found a favourite singing rock. The

sun was bright and warm, and the two dried themselves in the heat, lines of salt running down their bodies where their hair had dripped. They sang and used their fingers and claws to comb each other's hair. It was a beautiful and peaceful day. Birds flew overhead, and a school of dolphins passed them. A boat could be seen in the distance. The mermaids sang and hoped maybe it would come closer and they could watch the creatures on board. Cherith stopped weaving Kelby's hair and watched something leave the vessel. It was a small black dot against the sky. Moments later, another and another joined the first. Kelby followed Cherith's gaze and they watched as the things grew closer. The first one hit the rock and landed in front of them. Kelby reached out and picked it up. It was long and narrow with a cold, sharp, triangle on the end. A second later, the next one pieced Cherith's tail, going through her fin. Cherith pulled, but the point was imbedded in the rock and moving tore at her flesh. Another one grazed Kelby's shoulder, drawing dark blood. More of them flew from the boat to their rock, cutting, scratching, pinning. The mermaids were trapped and terrified. They grabbed on to each other, hugging as they were bombarded. Once the arrows stopped, the two were still; covered in blood, still hugging each other.

Amaya was only a little way behind her sisters. She knew enough to stay far enough away that they would never see her, but close enough to join them when it was time to sing the lullaby. She was floating on rough waters when she noticed a gathering of birds. A few at a time was common, but this was a flock, circling something. Curious, Amaya swam to see what had the birds so excited.

She hauled herself up on the rocks, and was confronted with her sisters. The two were in each other's arms, but their skin was broken and being plucked away by the birds, but she could see it was her sisters. She knew of no other creatures like themselves, and while the colours of their scales, skin, and hair were dull, they belonged to the only creatures in all of the oceans that she cared for.

Screaming, she clawed at the birds, chasing them away. She tried to pull Cherith toward her, and realised Cherith was stuck. She found the pointed sticks and pulled them out of her sisters, releasing them from the rock. As she started to pull Cherith to the ocean, she heard a noise above her and saw the sirens flying toward her. They landed and flapped their wings aggressively at Amaya. She responded with hisses and scratched her claws towards the invaders. The sirens scratched at the rocks, scratching grooves and sending small rocks flying at Amaya. One siren turned around and kicked at a large boulder. It dislodged and fell on Amaya's tail, trapping her like her sister had been trapped. Amaya screamed and flailed at the creatures who took to the air and flew at her, claws out, ripping at her. She fought back, but they could easily fly out of reach. Cackling, they flew away.

Amaya understood that she was trapped with the bodies of her sisters. She struggled and tried to move the boulder, but it was too big, and she could not angle herself in such a way to give it a big push. Every time she tried to move it, she would crush the bones in her tail, stopping when the agony would become too much. Eventually, she gave in and cried out, wailing her anguish. She clung to the corpses of her sisters, and cried out her sorrows, and her guilt for playing childish games with them, causing them to turn her away. The sun beat down on her, and dried her scales, her skin, her throat. Her wails became hoarse and scratching, dried and strained. She would not die, and her cries kept all other living creatures away. The sirens never returned, not able to stomach the cries. The men on the floating vessels thought the shoal haunted and gave it a wide berth.

Amaya screamed and cried and mourned her sisters and herself for years, a corpse still alive enough to feel. Finally, she cried for the loss of the world, as now no one would sing to the monsters who slept under the sea.

Chantal Boudreau

A Toronto native currently living in Sambro, Nova Scotia, Chantal Boudreau is an avid and prolific author with over sixty credits to her name. She is the author of the Fervor series of novels, as well as the *Masters & Renegades* series and *The Snowy Barrens* trilogy.

Boudreau is likely best known for her work in short fiction, and the anthologies she has appeared in have been shortlisted for both the Bram Stoker award and the Aurora award.

Her extensive short-fiction bibliography includes fantasy, dark fantasy, and horror. To date she has over seventy published short story credits.

Mythology from the Rock will be her fifth time being featured in a From the Rock anthology.

Stitches in Time

Glynnis Rhiordan's nimble fingers painted a picture with needle and floss. What emerged upon the cloth was not your ordinary embroidery pattern. Glynnis' gift had been passed from mother to daughter in her family for centuries. She didn't just stitch out pretty designs for beauty's sake. Each little dash or x was a means of predicting the future, the finished product of her handiwork a scene from an event that would occur weeks or months from the day she completed it.

"You really do have the Blood of the Norns," her mother observed, watching her efforts. "It sometimes skips a generation, but it didn't skip you. We weave a small part of the tapestry of life when we sew. It's our special magic."

Glynnis smiled. Her mother was the only person she would allow to watch her work.

"Is that a coffee shop?" the older woman asked.

Glynnis wrinkled her nose and shrugged. "You've seen mine. Fair's fair. Let me see your current project."

Her mother tensed, the lines in her face deepening, her eyes pained. Glynnis had never encountered reluctance from her mother before. Her stomach knotted.

"What? What's wrong? What did you see?"

Her mother sighed, lowering her gaze. "I promised I would never hide anything from you…including this."

Glynnis saw too much black on her mother's embroidery piece for her liking. After searching the work for details, she raised her piercing green eyes to meet her mother's. "A funeral? Whose?"

"Mine, love."

The knots in Glynnis's stomach tightened, causing her to retch.

"No, Mom, no. You can change it. Change it." She knew that while it was something that was rarely done, her kind could do it.

The older woman shook her head. "It's not that it's difficult, Glynnie," her mother explained. "We can easily influence time because of our birthright – we can manipulate the future whenever we choose to. I could pull the threads and rework the scene, forcing them to show something else to save myself, but there are consequences to those actions. If it is done for selfish purposes, the repercussions are harsh and we are blinded to time for a spell, until we pay for our choice. If I save myself, I could end up losing you instead, and not see it coming."

Glynnis felt tears springing to her eyes. Her mother continued, "No, there is nothing cruel or evil being done here, daughter. Death is a natural part of the cycle of life. I won't suffer the hardships that result from changing the future to forsake nature and preserve myself. If the Goddess has deemed it my time to leave this Earth, so be it. Promise me you will never play with time out of selfishness or whimsy. If you change a scene, do it only to right a real wrong. That way the repercussions will not be as severe."

Glynnis gritted her teeth and swallowed back her tears. She wished her mother would change her mind. She wasn't ready to be an orphan.

But she knew that would never happen.

"I promise..."

The college counsellor pursed her lips, her gaze searching the air for solutions that just couldn't be found.

"You have no family? Nobody that can help you out?"

Glynnis shook her head, frowning.

"What about student loans?"

"I could apply but it will take weeks to get an answer. I'm homeless – sleeping on friends' couches for the moment so I can't provide a permanent address. Eventually, I'm going to run out of hospitality and patience. I have to get my own place."

A gentle face palm told Glynnis plenty – the counsellor had nothing more to offer.

"Didn't your mother leave you anything?"

Glynnis groaned inwardly. It wasn't like her single mother had ever had any money to spare. The majority of her meagre estate went to cover her funeral expenses. Thanks to living off of charity and ramen, Glynnis had enough left to put down a deposit on a cheap apartment but if she wanted to pay her rent and feed herself, with her limited experience and skills, she would need to work full-time. She knew she couldn't juggle full-time school, full-time work, and the demands of her gift.

And like it or not, she was beholden to her gift.

"I'm practically penniless. I need to find a job. I need to sort things out. I'm just asking for time."

Glynnis noted the fatigue in the woman's face as she rubbed her eyes and glanced at her computer screen.

"I can offer a year's hiatus due to special circumstances. If you aren't ready to come back by that point, I'd advise you to drop-out of your program. Go get your life back in order, Glynnis. You may be able to find something on the job posting board and the 'for rent' listings that can meet your needs. And I'm very sorry for your loss."

Feeling quite hollow, Glynnis left the counsellor's office and headed straight towards the job posting board. She searched the posted cards for something she felt she could handle that didn't ask for "previous experience." Her eyes settled upon a listing for an employer called "The Green Bean." A co-op seller of fair trade, organic coffee, they claimed to support local artists as well.

"A coffee shop," she sighed. She knew that was the one.

The stitches had offered her up a picture of her future, one tied, in a way, to the image in her mother's work. At the time, however, she hadn't been able to understand what it was saying.

"Have you worked in the service industry?"

Glynnis bit her lip. The man in front of her, scanning her scant resume, bore the standard hipster combination of man-bun, beard and non-descript glasses. His shoes were cruelty-free and the flannel shirt he wore screamed "lumberjack".

"I'm a college student, taking a year off for personal reasons. I've never had a full-time job. Does helping out at my junior high cafeteria count?"

"Of course – anything like that. Volunteer experience?"

"With the scouts," Glynnis offered.

"Okay, we like people in touch with nature. And artists – we support local artists. Are you an artist?"

"Embroidery..."

"Sure, sure – folksy stuff. We like that. We encourage our employees to display their work in the shop. You can even put it up for sale. All we ask is for a small commission, 5%, if a piece sells."

Glynnis wasn't sure if her work could ever sell. The images ran from mundane to puzzlingly cryptic. People did admire her talent but were put off by the strange scenes she had captured in the cloth. Somebody eccentric might see some value in them, more as curious novelty items rather than prized artwork. They didn't understand the significance or Delphic power behind those scenes.

"As long as you are willing to learn, we are willing to give people a chance. If you are comfortable working with the ability-challenged and ex-cons, we can offer you a place here."

Glynnis didn't feel like she had the option to say no. She needed this, and according to the Blood of the Norns, it was foretold.

"I can... I will."

Her new manager smiled, offering her a hand, which she took and shook.

"Welcome to the Green Bean family, Glynnis. I'll add you to tomorrow's shift."

"Hi, I'm Selma. Richard said you'll be shadowing me."

The girl stood almost a foot shorter than Glynnis, with what would be normally described as a mousy or bookish appearance.

"I'll run you through the way we work all of the equipment and where everything is kept. You'll pick it up quickly enough. Just follow my lead," Selma said with a grin.

At first Selma went through the motions with confident care, clearly comfortable with the layout behind the counter and how the various devices worked. About an hour into the morning, her demeanor changed. She suddenly tensed up and her gestures became clumsier as a result.

"What's wrong?"

Selma nodded her head towards the professional-looking woman with tightly bound dark hair who stood at the back of the line-up to the counter.

"That's June Hart. She's part of our newest clientele. The Green Bean is known for being green and socially aware. That's trending with the corporate crowd – shallow businessmen and women who have traded off their luxury lattes at the fancy coffee franchises to try to suggest they have a conscience."

Glynnis knew it was all for show simply by the way this woman treated Selma when she reached the front of the line. "Curt" was an understatement, as if having to even speak to such a lesser being was a matter of disdain. This June Hart offered nothing in the way of common courtesy – no "please" or "thank you". From what Glynnis could see, rather than just failing to be polite, this customer went out of her way to be downright rude.

"Wrong again," she snapped at Selma with a sneer, after tasting the coffee handed to her. "This must be the tenth time this has happened; I ought to slap you silly if you screw up my order again. Give me another of those customer service complaint cards; I can't believe they haven't fired you yet."

Selma flinched, her eyes tearing up. She handed the ornery woman a complaint card and set about making her a fresh coffee.

June Hart tried the same tactic with Glynnis her first time serving her at the counter. Unlike Selma, Glynnis never flinched or backed down in the face of June's bullying. Glynnis knew the truth – that all bullies were cowards at heart and preyed on others because of a sense of insecurity and self-loathing.

"I'm sorry, I must have misheard you. Can you repeat the order and I will write it down to ensure I prepare it correctly."

June never targeted Glynnis directly as a result, preferring a weaker, less resistant victim. The callous businesswoman did occasionally throw an insult Glynnis' way, however, by maligning whatever pieces of embroidery happened to be hanging on the coffee shop wall at the time.

Despite fatigue from long days worked at The Green Bean, Glynnis could not ignore their demands when the needles, floss and her cloth canvas called to her. She would sometimes work late into the night, more and more of her pieces now centered around her place of employment. Sometimes they foretold happy incidents – an engagement announcement or the celebration of a birth or graduation, but Glynnis soon noticed that any of the scenes that spilled out of her fingers where June was present were overcast with a dark and heavy misery. The woman had no bliss in her own life, and if she couldn't find happiness for herself, she was prepared to steal it away from others.

"You'd think she could be civil at least some of the time," Selma sighed.

Glynnis shot her a half-smile. "She has her good days. You know, the ones with minor incidents – a sour word, a harsh look or a petty complaint. It's the days she throws tantrums or goes on tirades that ruin it for everyone else. Those are the days I would wish away with a magic wand if I could."

As much as Glynnis wished she had an excuse to pull the threads from any of her embroidery containing June, she would not break her word to her mother. June presented no serious wrong to right and therefore her occasional misdemeanor did not merit changing the future. Any threats she had uttered had been idle ones so far, and any insults flung, while hurtful in the moment, would not damage any of the people in the cafe for life.

Glynnis also had no idea what consequences reworking her embroidery would bring. If they had warranted a warning from her mother, though, she knew they wouldn't be something of little concern. The punishment for meddling with time and fate for frivolous reasons would no doubt be grave. Glynnis did not look forward to a day she would discover just how terrible that might be.

After her third dark piece containing an image of June went up on the coffee shop wall for display and potential sale, June finally noticed the fact that Glynnis was including her in her needlework.

June was already highly frustrated because her cell phone charge had run out while she was in mid-conversation, waiting in line for her coffee. Her expression of anger and dissatisfaction when her connection dropped was sharp enough to disrupt everyone in the cafe.

"Jesus! This thing is worthless!"

She made to toss her phone across the shop but thought better of it and dropped it in her purse instead. Without her phone to keep her occupied, June stood impatiently in line, her arms crossed and a vicious scowl on her carefully made-up face. She tapped one high-heeled foot on the hardwood floor, gazing about at her rustic surroundings with haughty disinterest. By the time she had reached Glynnis at the counter, however, her eyes had already settled upon the young woman's latest piece of needlework. Her lips tightened and her dark eyes grew cold and hard.

"You're the one responsible for those gaudy, stitched monstrosities?" June said, eying Glynnis up and down.

"The embroidery-work is my creation," Glynnis acknowledged, ignoring the businesswoman's insult.

"Well, I want you to take that one down." June pointed at Glynnis's latest piece. "I never gave you permission to include me in your picture and I don't want it up on the wall for the whole world to see. That waste of space is gross and makes me look awful. If I were interested in getting some kind of portrait done, I'd go to a professional. You have some nerve thinking you could profit off of me by putting that mess up there. Did you think I'd insist on buying your junk, so you could scam me for far more than it's worth?"

Glynnis kept her cool, well aware that June was looking for an excuse to amplify her indignation to outrage. The younger woman wasn't going to play that game.

"An artist is inspired by the things that surround her. I didn't purposefully include you in the design. I was working from memories and those memories happened to be influenced by your presence. My pieces often contain images of people who look similar to those I see on a regular basis. I draw from my life, as a proper artist does." She wasn't about to admit to June that the memories she sourced were of things to come and not things that had already happened. Glynnis didn't need June denouncing her as crazy along with her other accusations.

"Well, nobody invited you to draw me – or whatever you did there. I want that taken down – or better yet, destroyed. I'll speak to your manager if necessary." June scooped up her coffee and the scattering of change that nicer people would have just left as a tip, and then stomped out.

June was true to her word. The next day, Richard, the cafe's manager, approached Glynnis with the offending piece in hand.

"You know I think your work is beautiful, Glynnis, but I can't have a piece on display that threatens to alienate one of our regular customers. I also know you'd never mean any harm, but to put it bluntly, I can see why Ms. Hart objects to this. It does seem disrespectful because it makes her look so...harsh," he said.

Glynnis sighed internally but nodded and took the needlepoint piece from him. "If that's how you feel, I understand. She was only reflected as the people here see her, based on her own actions. She is harsh. She mistreats the servers – she bullies Selma in particular."

"We're going to have difficult customers. That's just life. You and Selma are adults, you can handle it. And I don't have a problem with you seeing Ms. Hart in a negative light. I just don't want you using the cafe walls as a means of silent protest to exhibit your discontent. You can still put up your work, but just keep her out of it. Sometimes we have to acquiesce a little to the belligerent ones, to keep them happy and retain their business. She has friends here who will walk with her when she goes, and we can't afford to lose their patronage."

While disappointed by his decision, Glynnis could at least appreciate the fact that Richard hadn't minced words and was willing to discuss the situation with her in an honest and mature way. Unfortunately, Richard didn't have the foresight Glynnis had and therefore he couldn't see the problem June posed. He might be concerned about the loss of profits if the nasty woman chose to boycott the cafe but bowing to her demands would prove to be a trade-off – money for trouble.

Glynnis had particular insight into what could happen because she had begun working on a very large piece of needlework, an elaborate work composed of multiple scenes that was going to take her many days to complete. The first panel, nearly finished, gave Glynnis a good picture of initiating events. That image showed poor Selma accidentally spilling coffee on June, which didn't bode well for the scenes that were going to come next.

Just picking up a threaded needle in the face of that embroidery endeavour gave Glynnis the chills. If she hadn't been so obsessively compelled to continue work on the piece, she wouldn't have finished it.

In the days that followed, Glynnis found herself warning Selma to be more careful, even though she knew her warnings would have no bearing on what was to come. Selma was the type of person who became clumsier as she grew more nervous, and June had never failed to make the young woman feel anxious.

As the needlepoint progressed, it became clear the damage extended far beyond java-sodden clothing and a disgruntled customer. The image following the incident was a scene of Selma being fired, but there were still two more events to go. Glynnis knew that giving in to June's demands to fire Selma wouldn't be sufficient retaliation for the nasty woman. June would want more than that.

June made a point of looking smugly at the vacant spot on the wall every time she was waiting in line to be served by Glynnis, that place where the disputed piece of needlework had once rested. The cruel woman had won that battle, and from what the future was telling its embroidery oracle, she was going to win at least a couple more – at Selma's expense in particular.

Knowing Selma was going to be fired over the accident. Glynnis wanted to protect the hapless girl from June's wrath, but she wasn't about to reweave the threads stitched into her canvas just yet. She wasn't sure if changing what was to come would be considered righting a grievous wrong. Perhaps they would reveal something positive. For example, maybe Selma would be better off finding work elsewhere, in a less frenzied atmosphere.

Not that the cafe was always that busy, but during rushes, having unsteady nerves could prove to be a problem. Glynnis at least felt obliged to finish the remaining two panels before passing judgement. Only then would she make her decision, if the incidents to come would actually merit special treatment.

She had, after all, made a promise.

The next panel came slowly, Glynnis fretting over what she should or shouldn't do as the image emerged. She wished she could be as sensible and as brave as her mother, trusting in the Goddess and the Norns instead of resisting their guidance when times looked rough. Her mother hadn't struggled while stitching her death scene. She had shed a few tears, but had mostly been smiling as she had worked, once she had finished grieving over what she would be leaving behind, accepting her fate.

As much as Glynnis had wanted to share in that acceptance and believe that things were meant to be the way they were going to be, she and her mother had been of two different hearts and two different minds. Although it might be a natural occurrence, Glynnis had never felt it was fair for her mother to die so young, especially after having given so much of her life to her craft with little in the way of gratitude. Her mother had said she would be going to a better place, and her only pain was that it would mean being separated from her daughter until the future dictated their reunion.

"Blood of the Norns," Glynnis sighed as she finished up the third panel. "As much of a curse as a gift."

When she finally finished that particular image, she could only sit and stare, stunned. The scene was set within a courtroom; June having decided that Selma's firing wasn't enough to compensate her for the minor accident. She would choose to sue the cafe for her troubles...her pain and suffering...and apparently the judgement would fall in her favour.

The Green Bean had never functioned with much of a profit margin, with the intent to supply ethical products, a handful of jobs for locals who might not find work elsewhere, community support for the artists in the area, and a place where the like-minded could meet. While it had managed to survive a bad economy, thanks to the latest trends, it didn't have the ability to absorb damages from a frivolous lawsuit or the hefty court costs that would likely be involved. By losing the case, Glynnis expected the cafe would end up facing bankruptcy, June's actions robbing the community of a benevolent business and an artistic hub. Selma's mistake would escalate into a full-fledged disaster.

Glynnis, paralyzed to act on what she had witnessed in her needlework, went about her daily routine for the next couple of days like a zombie. She was sure now there was a legitimate wrong to be expected in things to come, and she was greatly tempted to pull out the threads and rework the panels. But this meant changing the future, and she found herself fearing the consequences such drastic measures would bring with them – her mother's warnings echoing in her mind. She also still had one last panel to complete before coming to any decisive conclusions.

In the end, she conceded to a combination of reluctance and curiosity, vowing she would finish that final image as quickly as possible, so she could face everything the unpleasant future had to throw at her.

Her fingers flew across the tight-weave cloth that night and she worked steadily through to dawn. A knot of anguish and terror rested within Glynnis' belly, one that had seeded itself there as soon as the scene started taking shape. Selma would apparently blame herself for the calamity that would befall the cafe and all its employees and patrons. Since it was her clumsy act that would cause the lawsuit, she would feel wholly responsible for the outcome. She wouldn't be able to live with the guilt and the last panel showed the girl in a dingy bathroom, taking her life in a moment of complete despair.

Once finished the full four pieces, Glynnis's eyes scanned them, contemplating the future she could expect because of anxious, young Selma and mean-spirited and vengeful June. The last image especially chilled her to the bone, and Glynnis knew what it meant she had to do.

"There is a wrong here to right, Mother," Glynnis said, hoping her words would reach her mother's spirit. "And to make matters worse, that wrong will lead to a death. It's not just the natural ebb and flow of life. It's cruelty. It's malice. I can't allow this to happen. Whatever the consequences, I'm going to stop it."

And with that declaration, Glynnis began pulling threads.

Glynnis waited with bated breath, watching for the moment when she would have to act. She knew today was the day it was meant to happen because June was dressed in a new outfit, one with brighter colours than she would normally wear, and Glynnis recognized the clothing from the first panel.

As Selma turned to carry June's coffee over to her, Glynnis purposefully intercepted the girl and in the collision that ensued, Selma lost her tenuous grip on the cup. The coffee fell to the floor, a puddle of hot brown that splashed back a little onto Glynnis' calves and ankles. She felt the sting of a mild scalding and knew the spots where she had been splashed would be red and sore to the touch for a couple of days, but she had averted disaster.

"Oh gosh, Glynnis, I'm so sorry. I'm such a klutz sometimes," Selma said, her expression apologetic. "Let me go get a mop and clean this up." With that, the skittish girl disappeared into the back.

"I saw that," June growled.

Glynnis turned to look at the bitter-sounding woman. She wore a glare that threatened murder.

"I don't have time to wait for someone to get me another. I have an important meeting to get to, with or without my coffee. I won't be able to use *this* as an excuse for being late. You ran into her on purpose, you little witch. There's not a doubt in my mind. You probably just did this because you're still being pissy over the fact that I had your ugly artwork taken down. I'm leaving now, without my coffee, but believe me, your manager will hear about this." Sneering at Glynnis, June swiveled on her high heel and stomped out of the cafe.

Watching Selma return with the mop, Glynnis sagged against the counter and sighed with relief. She had reworked the threads after completely disassembling her work from all four panels, but once she had changed the first scene, embroidering herself into the picture as a barrier between Selma and June, the foresight had stopped there.

For the first time in her life, Glynnis didn't know what would come of it. The three panels that had originally followed the first remained blank – blinded to the future for a time as her mother had told her she would be. Glynnis might be fired for what had happened, once Richard got word of the incident, but June would not have an excuse to sue the coffee shop this time.

Come what may, Glynnis would manage. Because she lived so frugally, she had some savings that would carry her until she found a new job, if necessary. Whatever the consequences for the change, they couldn't be any worse than what had been fated to be.

Selma gave Glynnis a hopeful smile as she cleared away the last of the spilled coffee, oblivious of the sacrifice her cohort had just made to spare her life.

No matter what might happen, Glynnis was certain she had made the right choice. She now understood the purpose of her gift. She now understood the lessons her mother had tried so hard to teach her.

And she would never consider the Blood of the Norns a curse ever again.

Dani West

From Lorneville, Saint John, New Brunswick, Dani West was molded by the mudflats while listening intently to the whimsical gales from her childhood home.

She brings with her her first published story, 'Home Is Where the Heart Is.'

Home Is Where the Heart Is

Odin, ensconced at the head of his table resting upon the mountaintop, regarded the festivities around him and pondered his cumbersome dilemma.

Out of reach for any mortal man sat the celebrated structure of the Gods, Valhalla. The Great Hall was a dimly lit homestead. Every evening, it housed the background ambiance of triumphant tales and fallen heroes. Their shields hung from the ceiling while they stuck their dulled spears anywhere they could find room on the walls. In the welcoming hall, the smell of the finest meads stuck to the clothes of patrons and the aroma of cooked boar were endless. Stepping out from the cold Asgardian night, Róta took to Odin's side.

"Allfather, you wished to see me," the Valkyrie said with an accompanying bow. Her hair intertwined with her headdress that was draped in moonlight. Her wolf skin coat covered up most of her golden amour. As she stood, the buttons off her coat tapped against her breastplate. Odin's focus homed in on a patron in the back of the feasting hall. He was truly hard to miss being surrounded by men and women twice his height; aged like a man yet wore a face of youth.

"Róta," Odin's voice rumbled. "What do you think of our new hero?"

Róta looked out into the crowd to where the Allfather was pointing. Among the crowds, people hung off of every word that slipped from the storyteller's mouth. The crowd listened to tales of his home, with its strange customs and objects. How powerful emotions could be distilled into funny little faces, or how a portal of communication could stretch out around the world and into the stars. The day he walked into Valhalla, he became the hot new topic.

"I mean look at him," the Allfather grumped. "He's just a boy. Not a warrior. He lacks any combat skills. How am I to expect him to survive Ragnarok?" Odin groaned. He grasped his drinking horn and washed his mouth out with mead, flicking the few drops that fell into his beard.

"Then why did you pick him, Allfather?" Róta asked.

"I didn't," he grumbled. "He was recommended by Heimdallr and from what I can see here, I think the White God's Sight is fading."

"So, what are we to do about it?"

Odin with an unamused glare that his Valkyrie was surrendering more questions than answers, dismissed her presence. He scratched his chin as he continued to ponder on how he could undo his wrongdoings on his choice for a poor excuse of a hero.

The crowd cheered as they hungered for more stories. Noah sat crossed legged in a plumb scarlet chair, twirling the rose quartz in his fingers that laid on a string around his neck. A playful grin danced on his lips as he soaked in the newfound attention he enjoyed so much.

It wasn't just his stories that made him unique. Most who arrive at Valhalla have lost a mortal limb, so Odin's greatest dwarves craft the hero a stone or gem replacement as a thank you for their service. Noah came intact for the most part; only a couple of broken bones that realigned once he stepped into Asgard. Instead, he was given his trinket; the gem would carry his voice into the crowds or let him whisper into the ear of a target of his choosing. He was particularly fond of causing torment in the older population, pretending he was a ghost from their past looking to pick up debt in the Afterlife. It was something he wished he had on his person during his youth. High school would have become a lot more interesting if that was the case.

"Alright, alright." Noah raised his hands for silence. "What story should I tell next?" The flickering flame from a nearby fire danced excitement in Noah's eyes as the crowd tossed out names of stories they wished for him to retell.

"Tell of the one that took your life," a cold voice answered from the back.

The crowd collectively turned their gaze to the Allfather. As he crossed the Hall of Heroes, the joyous celebration paused. They bowed their eyes in his presence, while Noah tried his best to push down his nerves into the knot his stomach began to form. With a shaky hand, he took a couple mouthfuls of drink, but no such liquid could keep his throat moist or push down his fears. He couldn't tell which was louder in his ears: his racing heart or Odin's heavy boots zoning in on his location. It was as if all the sound and life was sucked out of the Hall by the time Odin took a seat beside the plush velvet chair. Noah tried to face the god staring down at him, but with Odin's shadow blocking out the flames from the fire, so too did Noah feel his flame of confidence extinguish.

"Well, go on, storyteller," prompted Odin. "Tell us how you lost your life." Odin's one eye was fixated on Noah in a skeptical state, while the other patrons shuffled in closer, interested in hearing a new tale from the well-spoken, baby-faced man.

"You wanna know how I died?" Noah started off slowly, taking another shaky slip of honey water. The crowd unanimously nodded for continuation.

"Well, it was a fire that took my life." Noah paused to swipe over the crowd. They eagerly waited quietly.

"I was taking nursing in college, and one summer I took a job at an old folks home to sharpen my skills. One day, a fire broke out downstairs in the kitchen. Everyone was able to leave but one woman couldn't. She got scared and hid somewhere in the faculty. The fire department wasn't gonna make it in time, so I ran back in. Miraculously, I was able to find her balled up in the corner. However, her fear restricted her movements and she just sobbed into my shoulder as I prayed someone would get us in time. But I wouldn't be here if that was the case."

"May they celebrate you on Midgard as we celebrate you here, my friend!" someone cheered.

Everyone joined with a toast and guzzled down their mead. Yet Odin continued to stare down the storyteller.

Noah for a split second thought his heart stopped completely when he remembered he was dead. Could you die a second time? Well, if it was at the hands of Odin.... most definitely.

"Noah."

"Yes, Mr. Odin Allfather sir," Noah squeaked like he forgot he went through puberty.

Odin leaned into the lad so close he could smell the stale stench of mead, take note of the day-old boar meat he had stuck in his teeth and the endless wrinkles that coursed around his face like a winding road map.

"Do you wish to know if they celebrate you in Midgard?"

Noah crumbled in on himself. "No, I'm perfectly fine leaving my past in the past, thank you."

Odin laughed as he slapped Noah on the back. The impact almost tossed him out of his chair. "Nonsense! Of course you do!"

This was the first time Noah had seen the giant smile since he got here. Smiles bring joy but why did Odin's have to look murderous?

"I do?" Noah answered back in surprise.

Odin rose from his seat and returned to his throne. He turned back to Noah with two very large cloaks. He draped his massive shoulders in one fair swoop with one. He tossed one to Noah, who fell to the floor by its weight. Odin tossed his head towards the door with a grunt and began to make his exit.

Noah struggled to throw the weighted clothing over his shoulders. Meanwhile, Róta had returned to the main dining hall with her supper. She found Noah wrestling with the cloak and was not at all surprised to see him losing the fight. Róta put her plate down at the bar with a sigh and an eyeroll. She walked over to help Noah and picked up his cloak with one hand. She glanced down at him as his cheeks became rosy. Noah looked up with a guilty smile. He rose quickly and dusted himself off.

"Róta," he said in his most manly voice. "I was asked to follow the Allfather when this beast attacked me."

"The cloak attacked you?" Róta's voice was flat with a tint of questioning.

Noah's proud demeanor extinguished back into his simple human form. "Well, I wish it did. That's a bit more heroic than what actually happened."

Róta hummed her response quietly as she began draping the cloak over Noah's shoulders. The collar practically swallowed him up.

"Róta, you don't understand, you know what that means? He's taking me somewhere to see how they 'celebrate' me in Midgard. He's gonna find out I'm not a-"

"Listen," she snapped his doubting fears with her razor tongue. "He's taking you to Heimdallr, the White God. He can see the future. Heimdallr himself chose you. So, you have nothing to fear!" She spun him to the door and shoved him forward. Noah stumbled around like a toddler, briefly knocking into chairs and tables before he got used to his newfound weight. "Now get out there before the Allfather wonders what is taking you so long."

After finally reaching the exit, he turned back to Róta, who was starting to eat her supper. "Thanks again, Róta." He smiled. She brushed off his appreciation and shooed him out the door.

Noah pulled up the collar to his cloak. He melted into the heat of the cloak. The comfort reminded him of the same feeling when Róta plucked him out of the frigid snow and into his forever home. He was happy to have a kick-ass guardian angel like her. But the way it looked now, forever was getting an expiry date. Noah stumbled down the path in the Asgardian winter and caught up to the Allfather.

Odin and Noah started their journey to the outreaches of Asgard. Odin caught wind of Noah's amusing childlike wonder at the sights he encountered on their travels to see the White God. He rolled his eye at him. Noah had been living in the heavenly pasture for six months and he had yet to tire of the beautiful imagery of this Afterlife. Each picturesque scene reminded him of his favorite backdrops at his high school theatre, but these weren't visionaries' thoughts put to canvas. This was Noah's new reality.

Never had he seen seasons change before his eyes. The trees bloomed with apple blossoms to then form into the fruits from the tree's mothering care. They shifted into leaves of fiery reds, brilliant yellows and cautionary oranges before they fell to the heels of their Mother Tree. The night and day melted into each other so seamlessly, like the moon, sun, and stars were just drifting aimlessly in a river that encapsulated this heaven. When it rained, the expansive willows braided into an intricate lattice that provided refuge from storms. If someone was caught in a blizzard, the snowdrifts would move aside for them in mountainous clumps. A path would illuminate in a soft purple hull and brighten with every step until they arrive at the safe location. This place housed things people only dreamed of and yet he felt a ping of guilt over whether he was fitting to be living there.

A bitter wind glided off their backs and Noah's nose picked up on the scent that emulated off their cloaks. The scent of deep smoke from a pipe and sharp spices of ginger and liquorice. Noah rubbed his nose along the woolly collar with a smile.

"The cloaks are enchanted," Odin gruffed over his shoulder.

"I'm sorry?" Noah asked, removing his nose from the outerwear.

"My wife, Frigg, crafted these cloaks and enchanted them for me. It was to keep me company on long journeys across the nine realms. The cloak will give the person wearing it any memory scent they desire. What do you smell?"

"I smell my grandfather's pipe and my grandmother's baking. Every Sunday after dinner, Nan would reheat the desert she made that afternoon while Papa and I watched American's Funniest Videos. He smoked on a pipe his father-in-law gave him on their wedding day." He gave it another sniffle and cleared his throat. "I can almost smell the shampoo used in the chesterfield."

"They raised you?"

"Yes," he said, bundling himself closer to the fabric. The wool brushed away any homesick tears.

Odin shuffled his cloak to shield the wind but also dug his nose in the scents of childhood he grew to love. The two walked in silence, separated in their own bubble of memories.

They found themselves with their journey leading them to the ends of Asgard's earthly bonds.

Here laid a rainbow bridge that looked to be made out of a sheet of glass. The closer they got to it, the louder whispers from the past echoed into their ears. It was the portal of all portals, the Bifrost. Sitting at his post was a man happy in his own company while gazing out across the stars.

As they approached him, Noah picked up on a tweeting tune the old man was whistling as he drummed his fingers in tune against a thin long instrument. In the distance, he looked like a white ball of light like a lighthouse's beacon on the end of the Asgardian shore. His long white hair and robes melted together and cascaded over the clouds that encompassed the bridge. The man took notice of the newcomers with a smile. His teeth became an unsettling sight the first time Noah laid eyes on them. His mouth was filled with gold and his smile could blind a man if they stood too close.

"What do you seek, Allfather?" Heimdallr rose to meet Odin's scowl.

"You gave me a defected hero," he grumbled.

"Did I now?" Heimdallr said in high spirits. "And what proof do you have?"

"He told his death story, and it was complete rubbish. This boy wouldn't enter a burning building. He's the type to run and hide." Odin's voice became colder with every word. The Allfather pushed Noah in front of the White God.

"We'll see about that," Heimdallr said as he turned his gaze to Noah, who uncomfortably squirmed under the Norse god's sight. Heimdallr bent down to Noah's height and Noah made the mistake of regaining eye contact with him. He gazed into his shimmering golden pupils in perturbed interest. Heimdallr gave Noah a quick once over and returned to meet Odin's height.

"No, Noah Parish is deemed a hero in Midgard. He deserves a place at your table, Odin."

"Like Hel he does!" Odin spat. "He makes a mockery of the real men we port back in Valhalla."

'Ouch. Still standing right here,' Noah thought to himself as if to lick his own mental wounds.

"Odin," Heimdallr hushed the Allfather. "I give you my word young Noah is worthy to sit at your table. He just hasn't completed his hero's journey yet."

Odin crossed his arms over his war treasures and trinkets. The huff of breath he exhaled pushed passed his whiskers. Noah mentally began saying goodbye to this Afterlife and welcoming his upcoming second death. Thankfully, Heimdallr stepped back into the conversation with a resolution.

"Noah has some deliveries to make."

Both Odin and Noah crinkled their brows in confusion. They went so far as to share glances with each other for an answer and when it became evident that no one, but Heimdallr, knew what they were talking about, they shifted their glance back to him.

"It's simple really. Noah's body has made the deliveries, but his spirit has yet to do so. Hence why you, Odin, feel such a disconnect to his heroism."

Noah was dumbfounded over the Allfather stumbling on his thoughts over Heimdallr's logic. Odin was a man so sure of himself that he could lead men into countless battles and victories and shouldn't be stumped by an old man's wisdom. Odin ran his fingers through his beard for what felt like an entirety. He finally shook his head with an exhausted sigh.

"Alright, Heimdallr, I'll play your game. Finish up with the lad and if he doesn't meet my requirements, he is no longer welcome to my table." Although his statement was directed at Heimdallr, Odin's eye never left Noah, staring him down farther with each sentence.

"As you wish, Allfather." Heimdallr spoke with a gentle bow.

Odin grunted his approval and shot Noah one last icy glare before taking his leave up the mountain to the ancient stronghold.

"Well, that went a lot smoother than I expected. I thought I was going to have to do a lot more convincing to have 'The Great Allfather' see my way of things," he said with a lighthearted chuckle.

"Right, so you know the truth, huh?" Noah chuckled nervously.

"But of course. I know all because I see all."

"Then there's still one thing I truly don't understand?"

Heimdallr rested back in his seat. He waved his hand in circles to silently ask Noah to continue what he was going to say.

"How do you think I'm a hero? I died in a snowbank!"

"Did you now?" Heimdallr spoke to Noah as if he were a child and not an adult. Noah wondered if it was worth asking Heimdallr what was in his future because right now all Noah could see in his future was his skull becoming an angry god's new drinking cup.

"Yes." He gritted his teeth through the painful memory. "I took an embankment too sharply and my snowmobile crushed me. I went alone so I died alone. I was probably out there for hours before I succumbed to my fate."

"Actually, you died in three minutes and Róta retrieved you in five. You bled out from your femoral artery when your legs were snapped in the accident," Heimdallr added factually.

Dumbfound for a moment. Noah scowled at the old man and his truths. "Thank you for being so lighthearted when analyzing my death. You must be great at parties," he remarked sarcastically.

Heimdallr chuckled as he rose back to his feet and patted the unimpressed Noah on the shoulder as he passed him. "Come along, hero. It's time to finish your journey."

Noah, wanting answers more than Odin, caught up in pace with the White God who sported a lopsided grin. "Yeah, mind telling me when you're going to fill me in on those details? Seeing as this is my journey to make."

"In due time, you will understand and so will Odin. Don't worry, you won't have to give up your seat that easily."

Noah heaved a heavy breath of shaky confidence. "Whatever you say, Heimdallr."

The pair stood at the edge of the bridge. It stretched off into the stars and branched out into worlds unknown.

The whispering voices now blended and mixed into a low angelic hum. Shimmering lights fanned out on the bridge like the sun glitter off a reflective pool. Heimdallr walked on it with hesitation. Yet Noah looked at the structure with fear and uncertainty.

Heimdallr turned back to face him. "Are you coming?"

"You're kidding, right?" Noah looked straight down. Past the soft colors of mist and stardust, there was only a soulless unforgiving black void.

"Have faith, Noah. You can do it," he called back and continued on his journey.

"Have faith," Noah whispered to himself in a mocking tone. He huffed in a deep breath as he took a couple steps back from the edge of the bridge. He shook the nerves off his hands, gearing himself up into a runner's start. "Can't die twice, right?" he asked his fears.

When no one responded, Noah jolted forward and took a leap of faith onto the bridge. The transparent structure came crashing hard into his jaw as he made impact with it. The audible thud and groans of pain set in the reality that the misty mythical bridge was solid to all who stood on it. Heimdallr helped Noah to his feet with a couple of snickers.

"I guess I should have mentioned that the Bifrost becomes solid when I step upon it."

"Yeah, that would have been nice," Noah said with a groan as he dusted himself off. "But I get it. You're probably lonely out here on your rock with your horn and crave a bit of entertainment."

"Clever hero too." He patted Noah on the back and

started back on the path. Noah, with a bruised ego and jaw, followed quietly behind.

Once Noah stepped off the Bifrost, he was greeted with a scene of familiarity. No longer was he on the cliffs of some glorious palace of gold. He stood on the street of his youth on a warm summer's evening.

"Summer? Like summer of this year?" Noah spoke with a touch of curiosity.

"Yes, it's August of the year you died."

Noah let go of a heavy sigh. "Don't remind me." He grazed the location. The properties were complete with white picket fences, recently cut lawns, and identical bungalows doused in pale pastels. Noah set his sights on a home with a blooming garden of lavender and daisies. Yet the old ruby red Cadillac that usually sat in the yard was absent and struck a nerve of worry in

Noah's heart.

"Hey, Heimdallr, mind if we take a detour?" Noah asked with his eyes still glued to his beloved childhood home. Noah stepped closer to the home in hopes to see his family one last time. However, a million questions shot through his mind with every painstakingly slow step. How was he going to present himself? Could he simply walk through the front door? If he did, he'd probably give his grandparents a heart attack.

"Not yet. You need to make your deliveries first," Heimdallr tugged Noah to the opposite side of the street. He tried to fight out of the god's hold but when Heimdallr easily tightened his grip as a warning, Noah thought it best not to challenge the Asgardian. He walked alongside with a frown as if he was a child who was tugged away from the candy aisle.

"You still haven't filled me in on what the delivery is. Don't you think this would be a good time?" Noah asked as he was dragged out into the middle of someone's front lawn.

"You'll see," Heimdallr said with a smile. He looked up at the house before them.

"You Asgardians really love playing vague, don't you?" Noah commented.

Heimdallr chuckled. "Noah, please enlighten me on who lives in this home."

"This place?" Noah hiked a thumb up to the home that had chalk drawings on the driveway's blacktop, a beat-up old mini van and countless princess stickers in the windows.

Heimdallr nodded.

"This is Katie Leone's house."

"And what can you tell me about Katie?"

Noah's eyebrow twitched up in skepticism. "Why?"

"Because this helps in your journey and you are such a great storyteller." Heimdallr spoke with enthusiasm in attempts to flaunt Noah's ego.

Noah snickered and looked back to the house.

"She moved in here just before I started high school. Katie used to be my high school theatre teacher. I ran lines in her home for upcoming shows and we had the best cast parties." Noah ran his hand over his chin and touched a dull scar, he'd gained after falling off a picnic table Katie had in her backyard. It was a poor attempt to recite the barrack scene from Les Miserable.

"My nan babysat her daughter, Emily, while Katie and John were out of town. John has pancreatic cancer and can only receive his treatments in the city. Katie missed most of my senior year because of the travel. We held a benefit concert to help with the bills but the last I heard, he still had a long road ahead of him." Talking his memories out loud, Noah remembered a key part to the story that dribbled tears in his eyes.

"Katie's sick too. I can't believe I forgot about that." He wiped away his premature tears.

Heimdallr stood there quietly and listened to what memories were coming back to Noah. But Noah stopped at the sound of the front door opening. He dashed across the yard and dove into the Leone's family's hydrangea bush. In his mind, he thought it was a perfect hiding spot, while Heimdallr opted to stay stationary.

"For the senior celebration for theater, Katie came back for a short time," Noah continued his tale from his bushy hideout. "It was tradition for all the graduating seniors to put on a show of their favorite scenes from past shows. Katie always stepped up to play a part. But at the party, she couldn't do it. She looked over the script time and time again. With glasses. Without glasses.

Finally, she jokingly said she would adlib, but then she knocked herself into a couple of settings and props. She broke down. She told me in her office that her worst fears had come true." Noah looked up to Heimdallr with blurry vision. "She has an eye disease that was never going to get better unless she got a special surgery." Noah wiped away sweat off his brow with the cloak and then brushed away some tears.

Katie walked out of the home. Noah looked at her with endearment. She looked completely different since the last time he saw her. Due to all the stress, she had lost a lot of weight. Her blonde hair was flattened and brittle, and her sparkling eyes were always tired and dulled. But now, it seemed her spark had returned. Her blonde, bold hair was wrapped up in a red handkerchief. Her blue eyes danced with excitement and her body had regained some weight – especially in her midsection as evident by the swollen belly. The new Katie was complete with her award winning smile as she helped a scarecrow of a man step out of the house. His rosy complexion and thinning hairline echoed volumes into Noah's heart.

"John, are you sure you're not hurting?" Katie asked kindly with a tone of worry.

"Kate, I'm fine." John patted his belly. "The scar doesn't hurt as much as you think. Now how are you feeling?"

"Baby and Mama are A-1." The couple shared a laugh and locked eyes on each other longingly. Katie kissed her husband's cheek. "It's so great to finally be home."

"John's starting to look healthy and Katie's pregnant again!" Noah cheered. "But how?" Noah looked to Heimdallr only to notice he hadn't been by his side the whole time. Heimdallr remained in the middle of the front lawn.

"Will you get over here?" Noah whispered harshly to Heimdallr. "They're going to see you."

"Emily! Come out, sweetheart. Gerald and Millie will be home soon," Noah heard Katie yell back into the house.

A tiny girl erupted into the front lawn in a fit of giggles. Heimdallr couldn't suppress a laugh over the sight of her youthful enjoyment.

She ran underneath an old oak tree and straight through Heimdallr. When she emerged from the other side, strains of gold lingered with her for a moment. She stopped her fun and inspected herself, wondering if she somehow got caught on a stray spider's web. When she appeared to be fine, she trotted over to her mother and hugged her tightly.

Noah came out of the bushes slowly when he felt a sudden wave of fatigue blow into him. Like he just ran all the way here from the Asgard. He leaned against Heimdallr, who happily bore the extra weight. They continued to watch the family as they parted from their home and crossed over to his old domain. The young family smiled brightly and waved as a Cadillac pulled into the driveway. Or that's what Noah thought he saw, but he couldn't be too sure. His tears drowned his vision and no amount of wiping the tears and sweat away would dry his brow. That's when reality crushed him harder than his snowmobile did.

"Heimdallr?" He spoke with shaky breath. He looked up at him and only saw wavey tones of white and gold like looking at oil sitting in water.

"I can see you've completed two of your deliveries. Congrats to you, Noah," Heimdallr proudly stated.

"Yeah, thanks, but I'm not doing so hot right now." Noah's voice raised in panicked octaves. "Is this what you meant by deliveries? Did I get Katie's eye disease?"

"Yes, because you gave her your corneas."

"Come again?" Noah was having a hard time processing this knowledge. His mind was spinning, making it difficult to keep on track with his situation. It felt as if his body was shutting down on itself. Decreased sight, painful back aches, and fatigue weighed him down like rocks.

"Your corneas brought back sight to a woman who eagerly awaits being a mother again and your pancreas and kidneys gave a father a chance to watch his children grow up."

Noah was quiet for a moment. "So, this is what you meant when you told Odin I was a hero?"

"Yes, you've improved the lives of three individuals. Their lives will branch out and touch so many more."

"Three? Wait, who else do I have to help? I thought we were done?" Noah's voice dragged on as Heimdallr slowly gripped Noah's shoulder and coaxed him forward.

"Come along Noah. We still have more to see."

Noah didn't argue as Heimdallr slipped them away from Katie's front lawn. Noah started stumbling around while trying to use the Heimdallr as a crutch. In a blink of an eye, Noah's feet touched the carpet but in his mind, it felt as if he stepped out on a blanket of memories. Memories of strolling in for supper, or cruising through to get to a living room, or shuffling in quietly after curfew. Noah's pain seemed to melt over his tired bones and sink into the carpet.

"Heimdallr," Noah said with a gasp. "I know where this is."

"Where are we, Noah?" Noah could hear the smile in his voice.

"You brought me home," he croaked.

Noah started to pull away from Heimdallr as his fingertips guided him through a blur of a thousands of memories he had of this place, but something seemed off. The years of old pipe smoke that leaked into the furniture and discolored the wall was absent. Even his grandmother's baking was nonexistent. It was just the smell of dust and cold, stale air.

'*Has no one been here*?' Noah thought to himself as he looked at the lace curtains that hung in the dining room window. He could make out the shapes of people embracing and could hear their upbeat tones. He decided to continue forward in his relaxed environment and found his favorite place in the living room. Someone in this house was taking something from him. It was best to sit down for it. He was able to anchor himself to the old chesterfield, but yelped when his backside hit the old discolored blue carpet floor.

"What the Hel? Where's the chesterfield?" he cursed. A strong arm looped around Noah's and hoisted him up. He gritted his teeth through the pain.

"Things have changed since you left."

"Changed how?" His voice sounded defensive.

Heimdallr guided Noah to the edge of the dining room and pulled him a chair. Thankfully the same wood furnished touch still linger through the change. That's when the front door opened.

Noah tried to focus on the figures, but it was proven difficult when the lights in the dining blinded everything around him. He had to rely on his ears for the time being. His empty heart started to swell at the sounds of his grandparents' voices but it fell into the pit of his stomach when he could make out the shape of his grandfather in a wheelchair being pushed around by his grandmother.

"So, it's my grandfather." Noah's voice broke with thought of the news. "I always believed nothing could take out my grandfather. So, what did he take?"

"Watch and you'll find out soon enough."

Noah turned back to the happy interaction among neighbors.

"Is it good to be home, Gerald?" John asked.

"Very much so." Gerald chuckled but his face turned sour at the sight of the living room. "Oh, Millie, you took the chesterfield away."

"We had to. We would have never gotten this wheelchair in here without it being removed. It's only temporary until you're fit enough to walk on your own." She set the wheelchair next to Gerald's favorite old navy-blue corduroy chair. Millie was preparing herself to help lift her husband into his chair, but John and Katie stepped in.

"We got him, Millie." Katie smiled.

"Thank you, Katie." Millie kissed Gerald's cheek once he was settled back into his preferred comfort and Noah could almost picture the bright red lipstick she wore. It would stain any cheek she came in contact with.

"We're all home," Millie sighed. Noah sat up at the sound of the sudden sink in his grandmother's tone as he could hear her softly weeping.

"Nan?" Noah questioned his grandmother's distress. He tried to stand but was held down by Heimdallr with a simple touch on the shoulder.

"Oh mama, it's okay." Gerald said softly. His voice

was like rolling thunder in the distance. His callus palm rubbed down her cashmere sweater. "You're right. We're all here now."

Noah hugged himself in replace of the absent hug he yearned for. "Heimdallr, please." He begged but his grandmother's words took him back into their conversation.

"I can hear him," Millie said softly through the tears.

"And I can feel him too." Gerald imputed with a contented smile, pushing past the crack in his voice.

"I wanna hear!"

"Emily, no sweetheart. Not now."

"Oh Katie, it's not a bother." Gerald patted his knee and Emily, with the help from her father, sat with Gerald. She lowered her ear to Gerald's chest. A puzzling look formed on her tiny face.

"Are you sure it's Noah, Mommy?" Her innocent question shortened Noah's breath. His chest felt tight and no amount of hungry breaths would expand his lungs.

"Yes, sweetie." Katie's cracked tone set the emotions high in the room. Katie held her husband tight as Millie cried silently in the crook of her husband's neck. The little girl couldn't understand the mood shift. So, she took it upon herself to change it for the better.

"Mommy got news today!" she cheered, still on the pedestal of the old man's knee. The adults started to come out of their depression to press on what the little girl was so happy about.

"What news did you get?" Millie asked, smiling through her tears.

"Oh yes, it's news about the baby. We're having a boy

and we're calling him-" Katie's emotions wouldn't let her continue. She cut her sentence short and crumbled into her husband. He kissed her forehead and rubbed her back.

Emily couldn't hold back her excitement at the news. "My baby brother is going to be named Noah!"

Noah closed his eyes and leaned forward. He tried to not reflect on the gripping pain he felt all over and let his ear pick up on the tunes of celebration, but it was becoming increasingly hard. He felt like his heart would implode along with all of the other malfunctions his body was dealing with.

"It seemed as though years of smoking had taken a toll on your grandfather's heart and hearing the news of your death was enough of a push to cause a heart attack. They were going to lose two members of the family, but you didn't let that happen."

"Heimdallr! Please make it stop!" he wheezed as he gripped his chest.

"No, Noah, it's all going according to plan," the White God said, but Noah felt like he was frozen in a time frame of gut-wrenching pain. It caused him to fall off his chair and to the floor.

Yet instead of carpet, he was swallowed by a pit into the unknown. He nosedived into nothingness, leaving his family and friend's happy reunion behind.

"Congratulations, Noah Parish," Heimdallr's voice echoed off the noir barrier. "You can now reap the benefits and join us in Valhalla, hero."

"No!" Noah clawed at the blackness. "No, I don't want to be a hero. I want to stay. I want to go home!" he cried out. Noah's body came to a halt and stopped in front of Heimdallr. Through terrible vision, he could make out Heimdallr's honey soft expression tense up into an icy stare.

"If you return, Noah, you will never feel love or warmth again. You are a soul who is no longer bound to Midgard. You'll only be hurting yourself and the ones you love."

"But--" Noah fought past the fatigue as the tears ran down his face like a river. The pain still anchored him to this desolate limbo. "I never got to say goodbye."

Heimdallr softened his tone. "You don't have to, Noah, because you will now never leave them in a physical sense and your friend will pass down your name. That babe's mother will tell tales of you and all your sacrifices. So, you will never have to say goodbye because you will always be on their minds." Heimdallr put his hands on Noah's shoulders. "It becomes easier over time, trust me. Your Midgard memories will always be the cornerstone of what makes you Noah Parish, but now, you are reborn a soul of Valhalla."

"Will I return to Valhalla as swiss cheese?" Noah tried to joke with a small smile.

"No," Heimdallr chuckled, happy to see Noah understood his message.

"No?" Noah questioned.

While he wondered where Heimdallr was going with this, Heimdallr simply smiled. The dark abyss where they stood bled into a sudden sharp white light. Noah shielded his eyes, not knowing what became of Heimdallr nor what would happen to him. That's when he could feel his body become full again. His chest pain became absent, his sweats dried, his back no longer ached, and the fatigue became a distant memory. He was even hungry. Hungrier than he could ever imagine. The White God formed before his eyes in blurry doubles for a moment, before reforming into one god standing at the bottom of his bed back on Valhalla. There were others in his room. Odin rested on the doorframe with crossed arms and Róta sat on his bedside with a warm smile.

Noah groaned. "Okay, are you telling me this was all a dream?" His question was aimed at the smirking White God.

"Oh no, you just passed out shortly after we arrived back in Valhalla. Good thing too because it made for quick work on your replacements."

"How do you feel?" Róta asked.

"Great actually. Hungry and confused but feeling like my old self again." He looked back to Heimdallr. "You said replacements. Is that why I can see you all so clearly right now?"

Heimdallr nodded. "Icelandic Spears. A clear crystal from our brothers to the north."

"And my pancreas and kidneys?" Noah said as he touched his back. He was relieved to feel no pain.

"They gave you charcoal for your inners," Odin gruffed. "It will cleanse your body.".

"Cool, but who are they exactly? Who did you let play Surgeon Simulator on my body?"

"The dwarves," Odin answered in an exacerbated tone. "I had enough of this. The boy proved himself and I have things to attend to." Odin left shortly after, causing much commotion as he walked down the hall.

"I came back to Valhalla like I was attacked by a hole puncher and he still doesn't respect me?"

"Oh, the Allfather respects you. He just hates being wrong," Heimdallr chuckled. "Now, why don't we check how your heart is doing?" Both Heimdallr and Róta leaned in to see the dwarves hardy work but Noah became shy under these peering eyes.

"Guys, can't I get a bit of privacy first?"

"Oh, come on, Noah." Róta impatiently grabbed Noah's shirt and yanked it over his head. She tossed the garment across the room and gazed at the young man.

"Róta!" he squeaked and tried desperately to cover up.

That was until his hand clanged against something hard and colder than any other part of his body. He looked down to see his chest was now a port hole filled with a shimmering thick glass. A window into his chest cavity revealed a solid rose quartz heart.

"They took your necklace and turned it into a heart for you," Róta said softly. Her warm fingers pressed against the cool glass. She watched as the organ skipped a beat while Noah tried to keep the blush from spreading on his face.

"That's amazing." Noah gazed down at his new feature. "Is it still enchanted?"

"Something you'll have to find out for yourself," Heimdallr answered as he returned Noah his shirt.

"You bet!" Noah smiled, with his new Icelandic Spear eyes shining brightly. "I can't wait to share this story with everyone!"

AJ Ryan

AJ Ryan is a freelance fiction editor, writer, and artist based in Mount Pearl, Newfoundland. She holds a BA in English from Memorial University of Newfoundland and Labrador.

Ryan is passionate about conveying stories with clarity and creativity. She also works to expand diverse representation in the industry by supporting 2SLGBTQIA+ writers and stories. This includes her work as a lesbian writer creating diverse romance novels. As part of her work to help others bring their stories and skills into the industry, AJ has spoken at conventions and association panels for writers and editors since 2016.

Ryan is currently one of four editors selecting stories for the as-yet unnamed 2SLGBTQIA+ collaboration collection between Engen Books and Quadrangle. In 2021 Engen Books will also release from Ryan *Secret of the Ohks*, a novella in the ongoing Slipstreamers series.

Olympic Dynasty

Business ebbs and flows, but a dynasty company, that has its own special strength. Such was the quote that Hestia read from the magazine left in her office. The article did a short chronicle of the company, tag-lining what was practically their family motto. They had spoken the words back when Olympus Enterprises first took the world by storm and it was a rallying cry ever since.

Gazing past the bobbing foot of her crossed leg, she spied the photograph on the wall. The original six who had built the company: herself, her sister Demeter, and their brothers Poseidon, Hades, and Zeus, along with his wife Hera.

Then she remembered she had been asked a question. Demeter was pestering her again. Something about whether she was sure about the move to step down from her active position at Olympus.

"It's time to take a step back. I'd like to enjoy some free time, take actual breakfast at my home once in a while."

"Let me know what that's like. Maybe I can dream about it while I taxi my teenage daughter around." Demeter grinned, taking the magazine off the table. She flipped through it before she tossed it back on the glass-top surface.

"I'll try to soak it up for you," Hestia promised.

"Then let's go get this over with. You've got new horizons for me to live vicariously through." She bopped her shoulder off Hestia's, then took the lead out to the front of the building where cameras and microphones were set up at a podium.

The crowd grew as employees and media personnel joined the space, and then it was time. Zeus arrived with Hera. He took to the podium while she stood back in support.

"You all have heard or read the news, that as of today my eldest sister, a founding member of this company, will be taking a step back. Hestia, you have brought warmth to our colleagues and clients. Your strength brought a unique approach to how we do business. You are the heart of Olympus Enterprises, and this family." He paused for applause. "Family is important here at Olympus. We pride ourselves on working together and teaching the next generation as well. It is with that in mind that I am pleased to introduce into the role, my son, Dion."

There was a moment, not entirely noticeable, a hesitation just before the applause came again. Hestia caught an unusual expression from Hera, but when she looked again, she wasn't sure it had been there at all.

Dion stepped up to the front. He had only been in university for a year or two. She hadn't heard anything about his coursework though.

"Thanks, everyone. I'll be sure to bring the best to this company."

That was all the young man had to say. Hestia glanced to Demeter, who simply shrugged off any perplexed wonder they had. Her brother, Poseidon, who was across the crowd showed a little more concern, but no one said anything while Zeus clued up the conference and took questions from the crowd. They dispersed quickly after that. She had to wonder if no one wanted the job of bringing up the obvious. They all had excuses for her, work they had to do, appointments to get to. So, Hestia stuffed her phone back in her pocket and waited for Zeus by his private elevator. Naturally, it was up to her to ask the tough questions.

"Need more paperwork?" he asked as the door opened, and they entered with Hera in tow.

"No, Zeus. I uh...got a spark of inspiration." She waited as the elevator jerked to a halt and they exited into his office.

"Let's hear it," he said, going straight to the coffee station and pouring a mug out for each of them. He plunked down next to Hera on the leather couch and eyed his sister expectantly.

"You brought Dion into operations awfully early," she began.

"It was better than wasting time and money on that school."

Her brow raised, but she forced a neutral gaze by the time she looked back at him. She could read between the lines. By the sounds of it, they either had to pull him out or he'd be kicked out, which would have been bad for the family's reputation, especially when they were in talks to purchase Titan Industries.

"He can learn on the job," Zeus declared.

While she could recognize the merits of learning while on the job, the plan was an awfully big leap. "Don't you think throwing him into such an important role is harsh?"

"What are you trying to say?"

"At least pull back on his responsibilities," she tried again.

"Don't worry about that. He's up to the task," he insisted. "Already looking at completing the negotiations with Titan."

She almost choked on her coffee. Was her brother completely out of his mind? Sure, he was beginning to show shocks of gray in his dark hair and beard—the women in the family had begun to tease him that he was looking like the model from a popular comb-in dye box—but he was historically a sound businessman.

"What do you have in mind, Hestia?" Hera prompted before the siblings brought their tempers into a raging inferno. She tended to step in and influence clarity between the siblings.

"Oh, uh..." She scrambled for an answer. "I can mentor him," she spit out faster than she could think it through.

"With your all-girls classes?" Zeus became incredulous, if not insulted.

"No, of course not," Hera soothed, looking to her sister-in-law with beady desperate eyes. She could only cover the flames for so long.

"Ahem. No, no. I meant privately." She waved her hand and laughed a little to diffuse the tension, although she felt it taking refuge in her shoulders instead.

Zeus pondered this prospect, then nodded his head from side to side. "Alright. We'll give it a shot. Just don't take the steering wheel from him. I don't want him to get lazy about it."

"Of course. I'll schedule some meetings and after-hours study with him."

Hera looked so relieved, Hestia was surprised she didn't jump up and hug her on the way out.

When Dion missed the first meeting, she shrugged it off. Not a big deal; she could use the time to enjoy a book or maybe even try a new roasted chicken recipe. However, the second and third time, that was too much. Now she was having brunch with Zeus and Hera at their home but didn't want to drop the news until after the meal. Sadly, table conversation had its way of needling out the truths into the atmosphere.

"How is Dion managing everything?" Hera asked as she tapped a spoonful of pomegranate onto her plate.

"We don't have to talk about that now," Hestia murmured, slicing through her Eggs Benedict.

Zeus looked up from his bacon, "why not?"

"There's so much more to talk about." Hestia pushed the conversation quickly, "Did the pomegranate come from your new orchard?"

Zeus' knife struck the plate hard. "Hestia."

She could see the flash in his eyes. "Fine then. I think you should pull back on Dion's responsibilities."

"Whatever for?"

"He is clearly unprepared," she replied, but then noticed the flash in his eyes igniting toward rage. She laid down her fork and knife and continued before lightning could strike, "He's missed every appointment I've made. When I call, if I do track him down, he's been out gallivanting around town, or flown off to go skiing."

"He's working with investors. You know there's a certain amount of wooing into these corporate buyouts." His voice shook with the force he withheld, though his face reddened under the pressure.

"I think it's too risky to leave the Titan deal with him any longer." She finally came out and said it.

"Really?" Zeus demanded.

She glanced to Hera and realized that maybe she could get through to one of them by rewording the issue. "Is it really fair to him?"

"He can handle it. He was born for this," Zeus declared. "It's in his blood."

"Are you serious? This doesn't just come from the air." Hestia waved around at everything that the family had gained through their business. "Don't you remember all the work we had to do to get this?" she cried, incredulous of what she was hearing from him.

"Don't overreact," Zeus said. "What I mean is exactly that," he assured her. "He's got all of that knowledge right here." He waved around the table to each of them. "He can save all that time we wasted looking for others to learn from. Just give him a chance to settle in."

"If you're sure…" Hestia backed off, feeling she was unlikely to get any further with him. His eyes were already sparking for a fight. This was his son after all. Zeus had high hopes and long-built dreams invested in the boy. Many parents put all those expectations on their kid, but never once stopped to realize they were focused on a moving target. This was about Zeus' expectations, his dreams. But he hung on hopes that Dion didn't appear to have any interest in thus far. The boy wasn't interested in building the company. He was more concerned with what the business did for him.

Her attempts to leave the problem of Dion at the office and in Zeus' hands did not last. When she made it home from her morning walk, Hestia spotted a red sedan parked in her driveway. She spied Athena sitting on the little brick wall beside her front door, reading the daily paper.

"Good morning," Hestia called as she trotted down the drive. "What brings you by?"

"Good morning." Athena smiled over the newspaper. "Tech stocks are trending down this month." She sighed. "Too bad," she concluded, folding up the paper.

"Those numbers are within reasonable margins," Hestia replied while she unlocked the door and led the way inside.

"Indeed." Athena nodded, fixing her circular lenses back up the bridge of her nose. "I heard you spoke to Dad a couple days ago," she began.

"I did." Hestia busied herself, boiling the kettle and setting out teacups.

Athena perched at the table. The knees of her chinos were scuffed, as were the sides of her loafers. She must have been crawling around wiring computers at one of the offices earlier. She didn't speak until Hestia served the tea and they were both seated at the table. "Dion is putting us into a scramble."

"How so?"

"Well, you know how before, we were complaining that he wasn't using our calendar program?"

Hestia nodded. She had the job of showing him how to use it once they realized he had been scheduling activities and meetings without record.

"Now I wish I could block his access," she grumbled.

Hestia couldn't help but chuckle, "oh dear, it can't be that bad."

"It is. I spent my entire evening rewriting half his tags. He couldn't be bothered to double check his choices in the drop-down. So, anyone from the tech department to accounting has been scheduled for things that have nothing to do with them. It's a damn circus." She sipped her tea sharply.

Hestia's expression dropped. "Oh, that boy." She shook her head, wishing she felt disbelief.

The cup clinked upon the saucer with purpose. "It's like he's been given a new Lamborghini without a single day's experience actually driving. He doesn't need to know the cost of buying the car, or the cost to repair, or anything else regarding the vehicle for that matter. Dad just shrugs it off as a learning curve," she complained.

"I know," Hestia murmured. Dion had no appreciation for the life's work of their entire family.

"Someone needs to do something before he crashes it into a bridge."

"I'll try to keep a better eye on him. I may yet be able

to sway Dion toward better business practice."

"Thanks," Athena said as she finished her tea and got up from the table. "Will you be coming into the office later?"

"Not today," Hestia said with a hint of apology. "I have my mentorship course today."

"I remember those days," she said wistfully. "I learned so much from your mentorship. If only he was half the student as your young women." Athena gave her a quick hug and left.

If only.

By the next week she was invited out to dine with her brother, Hades. Arriving at the restaurant, she was shown to a private room where he was waiting with drinks already poured for her and another.

"Good evening," she greeted the two at the table. "I didn't know you would be here." She nodded to Poseidon.

"We were catching up and Hades invited me last minute."

"Good." She leaned over and gave him a kiss on his bearded cheek. "I didn't think you'd be staying in town, Hadey," she said, looking to their younger brother.

"I wasn't, but everything got thrown into the air."

"Ah." She slumped a little, fairly certain she could guess what was coming next.

"I had a meeting over lunch."

"With the bright new hire," Poseidon filled in, his voice slowly unfurled with sarcasm.

"That boy had the audacity to question my work. Somehow, he doesn't see the importance of buying and building satellite offices."

"He even wants call centers," Poseidon choked out the words through his teeth, then took a swig of his cocktail.

"Did Zeus correct him?" she asked, hesitating because she was no longer sure she wanted to know the truth.

"Absolutely not!" Hades cried. "He actually suggested reviewing the divisions."

Poseidon drew in a long breath and let it out slowly, which his siblings mimicked. "Have you spoken to him?"

"More than once," Hestia muttered. "But he's begun to make it clear that my voice no longer holds weight.

"No," Hades breathed in disbelief.

Poseidon's eyes were stormy as he gazed at his sister apologetically. "I was actually on the last conference call. He called it…what was it? A courtesy."

She recalled the meeting. Hades hadn't called to join in because he was mid-flight. Hestia had questioned, if not outright challenged, the random directions Zeus was beginning to take. After all, he was seemingly happy to follow along with his son's meandering course.

"You're only here as a courtesy," Zeus declared before she went too far in her line of questioning.

Appalled, she shot back quickly, "Do you want me to sue you?"

Yet he didn't waiver under that threat. "Do you really believe that will work out in your interest?" His voice rolled like thunder, a warning of what might come.

"It's fine," she sighed, preferring not to stir the embers.

"It's an insult. A slap in the face!" Hades hissed, "how could he show such utter disrespect for someone so important in the building of our company."

"I'm beginning to think he's attempting to...come along with the times? Or that could be what he believes it is."

Hades shook his head in disbelief as their soup was served.

Poseidon stirred his bowl quietly, gaze drowning in the steaming pool.

Meanwhile Hades was practically blowing smoke out of his nose. "We should vote no-confidence. Remove him altogether."

"Excuse me?" she gasped. The very suggestion left her cold, despite the soup that was supposed to warm her stomach.

"Now hang on a moment!" Poseidon cut in.

"Come on, we can take over." Hades' voice lowered, his eyes darkening with the seriousness of what he was suggesting.

"I don't think so." Hestia put her spoon down. "Zeus and Hera's shares are equal to the three of us combined. And now Dion holds shares too."

"Well, we'd have Demeter," Hades insisted.

"You can't be sure of that," she declared. Demeter had lost a lot in her divorce after all. She had been making decisions differently ever since.

"I was going to try and speak to him again, maybe spend time with Hera at the club," Hestia offered.

"I don't think that would be a good idea at this point,"

Poseidon admitted. The stormy look in his eyes seemed to be clearing. "Maybe there are other options."

"How so?" Hades leaned forward, arms resting on the table.

"Think about it, Hades," he prompted. "You've been telling me about the flood of start-ups you've seen on the road. They like talking to you, and some even ask you to be an advisor."

"Which I never do."

"He's not questioning your loyalty, Hadey," she told him with a sear only an older sister could serve up in her voice.

"Try to reflect on the ones that impressed you the most," their brother instructed.

"What are you plotting?" Hades cocked his head to the side. He looked more interested than worried about deception, but Hestia didn't feel the same.

"I don't think this is a constructive line of thought," she said, picking up her spoon again, signaling that they eat in silence for a bit. Surely, jumping ship at the sign of discord was not the answer they truly wanted.

Apparently, her brothers felt it was, though. As she arrived at the coffee shop two days later, she found Poseidon had brought friends.

"I wasn't expecting this to be a party," she said as she approached the table with her latte, eyes burning into her older brother. Yet her stare evaporated into steam, rolling off his back easily. He smiled, looking chill as ever. It must be nice to be able to go with the flow so effortlessly, she thought to herself.

"I wanted you to meet the Faust brothers." He nodded to the two young men sitting opposite him. "Romulus and Remus, this is my sister, Hestia."

They shook hands with Hestia in turn. Remus had long hair in a ponytail while the other, Romulus, was scruffy with his hair slicked back. Both were handsome, and possibly the same age, but not identical in the least.

"We can't thank you enough for the opportunity to speak with you," Romulus said.

"And what is it that we're here to talk about?" Hestia slid into a chair next to her own brother.

"We have a business."

"You do?"

"Well, we're a start-up," Remus chimed in, winning a knowing nod from Hestia.

They told her of their goals and their values. She would glance to her brother from time to time, wondering if he had coached them beforehand. She couldn't be sure, but they felt genuine. They felt familiar. She didn't realize until the end, why that was.

"Well, I am intrigued by your work," she told them after, sitting forward and folding her hands together. "More than that, I am interested. But I won't invest on just words." Before their eyes could light up too brightly, she brought down the staff of judgment. "There's a company looking to sell, you might have heard, Titan Industries." The brothers calmed down but did not deflate. That was promising. "I want you to pitch them. Make an offer."

"Really?"

"I'll make the introduction." She then picked up their

business card from beside her coffee cup and tapped it on the table. "I'll call you soon with the details."

"Thank you!"

"Thanks."

They smiled and shook hands as she and her brother said goodbye and headed toward their cars.

"You've surprised me," Poseidon said as they walked side by side.

"You started it," she joked, bumping her shoulder into his.

"You usually take time to think about it."

"I do," she agreed, feeling the flutter in her chest, excitement and anticipation. "But they've got something. Something going for them that I hardly ever see."

"Oh? What's that?"

"They remind me of us."

Then came the day. Rumours had already begun throughout the office. Titan was going to back out. They weren't going to sell to Olympus. Hestia sat in her office watching the boardroom across the hall. Many of the staff were watching from afar or making excuses the pass by as well. Dion, Hera, and Zeus were arguing back and forth. Hera eventually had to step out. Poseidon sat with his arms crossed over his chest, and everyone else on the board appeared to be tight-lipped and on edge. Eventually, the meeting broke up, and Zeus made his way over to her office.

"Hestia," he greeted as he poked his head in.

She waved him in to sit on one of the cushy seats in

front of her desk. "Tea?"

He shook his head and pushed both his hands through his peppered hair. "Hestia, Titan has stopped negotiations. They won't return my calls. I..."

She waited while he got himself together enough to finish his request.

"You got along with their C.E.O."

She nodded. "Mr. Kronos and I have always enjoyed our conversations," she agreed.

"Would you call him and bring them back around?"

"It's been made clear to me that anything I have to offer is no longer important," she replied.

"Come on, Hestia," he said, trying to play off his past behavior.

"I'm not making the call, Zeus. This is not my mess. Not one bit," she insisted.

He let out a frustrated grumble but marched out of her office. She watched as Demeter approached him, skittish, but assured. Hestia breathed out a long sigh and sat back to wait for the announcement of what was to come. She'd had a feeling that Demeter might crack under the heavy atmosphere. It had been a risk to ask her to join in her new business venture, but Hestia couldn't do this without telling her sister. If Demeter told him now, it didn't matter. There was nothing they could do to stop what was coming, anyway.

She was called to Zeus' office shortly after. The television was on, but muted. The Faust brothers, Romulus and Remus were on replay while Zeus paced behind his desk, stiff in his movements.

"You purposely refused to help me. You refused to help this company because you were out scheming toward its ruin!"

"Don't be so dramatic, Zeus. You're not ruined." She would have rolled her eyes if they weren't filled with fire for the mission of this moment.

"How dare you!" he burst out.

"Really? Your blatant nepotism was running the family out of here in every direction. I didn't want our system to go to waste. Everything we had, what we could do…we can still be great."

"Then help us be great," he urged. "Help me find the next industry to buy up."

"No. Not here. Not with you, or Dion. As the new Chief Operating Officer of Rome Unlimited, I can do it right. The rest of us can save ourselves from the ruin you began."

"You're putting yourself in line as our competition," he sneered.

"I hope so," she declared, a smirk beginning to form upon her lips.

He took a deep breath, and closed his eyes. "Then get out. I'll have security gather your things."

"I'm not done yet."

"I am! I don't want to hear any more of your deceptions," he snapped.

"Deceptions? Zeus, you forgot the heart of this company. Or was that all platitudes? Are you so self-important—"

"Get out!" he roared.

She waited a couple of beats, and took a deep breath, sighing.

"I'm sorry. That's not really why I'm here." She faced him down with ease, hardly disturbed by his outburst. He was her little brother after all. She'd tied his shoes, and she'd worked with him to build this empire. "Here's the notice of everyone coming with me." She opened her purse and held out the file folder containing letters from Athena, Poseidon, Hades, and more.

He couldn't even speak. He merely stared her down, electricity practically running through his eyes. But it wouldn't work this time.

"I tried, Zeus. I tried to make you see what was happening, what you were doing to those around you. All for your golden boy. You lost sight of those who invested in the dream." She dropped the file onto his desk, turned around and walked out of the office, feeling taller with every step.

Demeter was waiting outside the door of his office.

"Are you sure you won't come?" Hestia asked her one last time.

"I can't." The look in her eyes, Hestia couldn't quite place it. "After the divorce…I just can't take a chance on fresh blood in business. Even if you think it's a safe deal… they're unpredictable."

Hestia nodded. "I'll try and keep the door open for you."

"I just hope you know what you're doing..."

Hestia spotted Athena down the hall with a box of her belongings in hand. She walked onward to join her with Demeter's words in tow: "Or you just destroyed the family for nothing."

Stacey Oakley

Stacey Oakley is an author originally from Moncton, New Brunswick who became a vibrant part of the local Newfoundland writing scene after the publication of 'The Sorrows of War' in the 2016 edition of *Sci-Fi from the Rock*.

She has since gone on to independently publish her own novel, *Hunter's Soul*, it's followup *The Necromancer*, and in 2018 was crowned the winner of the 48 Hour Novel-Writing Marathon.

Tangled Web

"Any more creepy messages?" Jet asked as they sorted through the boxes of new books, putting them onto carts to make shelving easier. Somehow the words sounded more dramatic with his Celtic accent.

"I changed my number," Rose replied, a slight shudder going through her. "And I blocked his. Again."

Jet gave her a sympathetic look that seemed a little out of place on an elf. But over the last two months of working at *Tangled Web Books* she'd learned a lot about the beings she'd once believed to be fiction. "Do you think that'll stop him?"

She shook her head, feeling a little sick. "No, it won't. But it will give me a week or two while he tries to find my new number." She wished he would just leave her alone, but that didn't seem to be in her cards. "I don't know what to do. I moved fourteen hours away, started a new job, got new phone numbers, new emails, everything. But he keeps finding me." The old anxiety started to grip her and turn toward panic.

"If you talk to Arachne, she'll find something that can help you," Jet said, gently taking the book she was holding before her overly tight grip could damage it. "Magic hasn't quite caught up to what technology can do, but I'm sure there are non-lethal options, if that's what you'd rather choose."

His tone didn't really make her feel better, the implication in it. "I don't want him to die." She knew how far down humans ranked in terms of powerful beings: it was written in myth, legend, and folklore. Never trust the fae, be careful what you wish for. Humans were often just playthings and food. Her position at the bookstore protected her from harm; the mysterious owner of the chain saw to it that humans under employ were safe from the beings they dealt with.

"Why not? He's already tried to kill you."

"Just... I don't know! I don't want to be the reason someone else dies." And because she was working with people who wouldn't blink at a human's death, she had to be careful with her words. "I just want him to leave me alone." Desperate to get away from the topic of her stalker, she changed the subject. "Why haven't you asked Arachne out yet? You two flirt often enough."

Jet hesitated. "You're familiar with mythology, so would I be correct in assuming you know her story?"

Rose nodded as she cut open another box. She'd wondered how Arachne returned to human form.

"Well, half of it anyway. About three centuries ago, she went to Zeus to be returned to human form. She had been beautiful as a mortal, so he agreed, for a price. And part of that was she was forbidden from weaving ever again, because he didn't want to anger Athena."

"Oh." That was... not what she'd expected. Part of her had hoped it would be a happy ending, but when did Greek myths ever end well? She knew enough about Zeus that she didn't have to ask about the other part of the price. "I thought it might have something to do with you turning into a spider at night." A very large spider, who enjoyed giving the newbie at work a heart attack the first time she worked with him past sunset.

"No. Well, not entirely." He sighed and started on another pile of books. "I was cursed by another faerie, not punished by a god, so what happened to me can be fixed without 'divine' intervention."

"Like with iron or salt water?"

"Iron would kill me, and I'm not human, so cures don't work the same for me."

Rose nodded, filing the information away in her mind. She'd been learning all she could since starting. Caleb and Jack, the other human employees, had been helpful in pointing out good resources.

"So, what will it take?"

To her surprise, he grimaced. "True love's kiss."

"Seriously?" Of all the clichés…

"True love's kiss is the only thing that'll do it, because the bastard figured that if he turned me into a giant spider half the time, no one would want me. Which was true enough of the faerie we were both pursuing at the time. He managed to frame me for a crime and convince the Queen of Underhill to let him punish me. He was a favourite, so it wasn't that difficult."

"Oh."

"Yeah. I believe the human phrase would be 'sucks to be me'."

She didn't comment on that. "Is Arachne your true love?" She couldn't quite keep the scepticism out of her voice. While it turned out that a lot of what she'd thought was fiction was true, the whole 'true love' thing still crossed too many lines. Or maybe she just really didn't want it to be true. She didn't want to have just one 'true love' that she was supposed to hope would show up at some point in her life.

"Yes."

"But I'm guessing you haven't told her."

"No."

"Can I ask why not?"

Jet shuffled a few more books around before replying. "Because I know she would kiss me to free me of the curse, but then we would lose everything else between us, and it would be unfair to her. I hope that one day I'll figure out how to get rid of the ban the gods put on her weaving."

Rose was starting to feel like a character in a fairy tale. Caleb had warned her that it would happen sooner or later. "How do you know she's your true love?"

"Perhaps because I saw a dozen seers and they all gave me hints pointing in her direction. Or perhaps I saw her reflection by the full light of the Beltane moon," he drawled. For someone who couldn't lie, he had sarcasm down to an art.

"Don't be an ass. I just mean… how do you know it's *true love*? Is it the whole 'soulmate' thing? Is that really true?"

Jet turned serious again. "Scholars both human and fae have debated whether my kind have souls or not for centuries, so I can't say much about 'soulmates', but there are many kinds of love in this world, and all of them can be just as true as romantic love. Take familial love, or the love between friends. It may not be romantic, but it is just as strong." He shrugged. "But I'm merely a very talented tailor, not a philosopher or scholar. Still, the idea of only having *one* 'true love' is terribly boring."

She nodded in agreement, trying not to think of Mark's last messages proclaiming his love. She suppressed a shiver. "What's your plan so far?"

"Well, I've been working out how to communicate directly with Athena herself. Zeus may have placed the ban on Arachne's weaving this time, but it was on the goddess' behalf. And let's face it, I think Arachne would lose some respect for me if I allowed myself to be manipulated by the same god. I am, after all, quite beautiful."

"And not at all vain," Rose muttered. "You can really find Athena and just talk to her?"

Jet snorted. "I'm a faerie. We're all beautiful, terrible creatures in our own ways. Anyway, no, *I* can't contact Athena. A Greek Goddess would never stoop to speak to a Celtic faerie. My hope is that by the time I figure out the summoning ritual and find an active temple that is hopefully closer than Greece, I will have found a human willing to help me. One who I can offer something equivalent in return."

Now she definitely felt like a character in a fairy tale. "Why not Caleb or Jack? They know a lot about magic and gods." Both had been working at the bookstore for over a decade.

"They also have each other," Jet pointed out. "They don't need my help finding true love when they have it in spades. I also can't directly offer to make a deal, as per my contract." He'd mentioned that before, that the owner of the bookstore had been wary of hiring a faerie due to their reputation for deals and trickery. Jet had deemed it a wise decision on the owner's part.

Rose looked away. "But… I'm not Greek. And I'm not really ready to start dating again. I don't think I will be for a while, true love or not." Not with everything happening with Mark over the last six months.

"Plenty of people in Greece weren't Greek even at the height of the pantheon's power," he pointed out gently. "And like I said, true love doesn't have to be romantic. I wouldn't push you into finding another lover before you were ready."

She glanced at him, and she was seriously considering it. Maybe it would be nice to have something good happen, to be a hero in someone's story when she felt so helpless in her own. It wasn't like she had much else to do. Her friends and family were all several hours away now.

"Alright. I'll make you a deal. I'll help you get Arachne's weaving back, and in return, you'll help me find true love," she said, her voice shaking a little.

"Deal," Jet said, holding out his hand and grinning. Rose shook it, jumping when she felt a tingle go up her arm and through her body as Jet's eyes glowed for a moment before he pulled away.

"When do we start?"

"On the full moon in two weeks. I found a summoning ritual that should work. Of course, I'll be a spider, so you'll have to follow very careful… what's with that expression?" He trailed off as he looked up, frowning at her.

"You're not going to just email her or contact her online?"

Jet just blinked at her, and it was hard not to laugh. "What?"

"The Greek gods have a whole website set up; I heard Thor telling Loki to stop spamming them with porn the other day because some of them were getting really annoyed."

"Are you serious?"

She nodded. "I don't think it'd be that hard to find. You really never thought of checking online?"

"Look, I've been around for centuries and the internet has only taken off in the last twenty years," he grumbled. "Besides, I don't own a computer."

"Why don't you come back to my place after work and I'll show you the kind of magic humans can do with technology?" she offered, grinning.

Jet rolled his eyes. "Fine, impress me with your skills."

This late in the year, sunset came early. By the time Arachne and Jack arrived to replace them for the night shift, Jet was a very large, very fuzzy spider. But he could still talk. Rose still hadn't decided if that made him more or less creepy as they left.

"Did you see that old lady's face?" he cackled.

"Just be glad I convinced her you're a decoration," Rose replied in a dry tone. "Otherwise I'm pretty sure she was going to throw that stack of books on top of you. Or have a heart attack."

"That wouldn't have killed me. I think."

"This is a nice place," he said once they were in her apartment a short drive later. It had one bedroom, bigger than she'd expected for the rent she was paying, which was nice. It even had a small balcony. What she really liked was the fact that there was a camera at the front door, so she could see who was pressing the buzzer without using the intercom.

"Thanks." It was still a little sparsely furnished and the closet hid boxes that hadn't been unpacked, but it was a home, and she felt at least marginally safer than she had in a long time. "Shall we start our quest?" She waved at her desk, her laptop already sitting open.

"Yes." Jet made his way to the desk and waited as she started it and got into a search engine. Surprisingly, it didn't take much to find the site, though she did dig around to see if she could verify it. The domain seemed to be owned by a company she knew was associated with the Greek Gods; she'd seen it in their client files at the store while filling orders to be shipped. "Who knew humans could come up with such a marvel?" For once she couldn't hear sarcasm in his voice.

"Don't underestimate us," she said with a grin as she looked for anything connected to Athena. "Well, the good news is that she seems to be one of the more active gods on this site. There's a whole thread of people helping her find errors about Greek myths on other websites."

"Well, she is the Goddess of Wisdom," he replied. "How do you contact her?"

"It looks like I can just send her a message... hang on, I might have to create a profile..." She hesitated. "Would I be dedicating myself to their worship or something if I did?"

"I... don't know..." Jet replied. "This is entirely outside of my realm of expertise. Can you look that up on another website?"

"Maybe? Hang on, I found the terms and conditions,"

she said. Of course, it was just a huge, dense legal document she would normally never read. "Do you get this legal stuff? It just gives me a headache."

"Yes, give me a moment." Rose moved back a little so he could get in front of the screen. It was strange to watch a spider operate a laptop, but he managed to figure out how to scroll with the mouse. "It looks like it's more a waiver of liability than making users sell their souls. They aren't responsible for the terms, conditions, and punishments the users agree to, users are responsible for the consequences of their actions…" he was silent for a few more moments as he kept reading. "No mention of dedicating yourself to the worship of the Greek Gods here. There is a way to have your account removed from the site, if that's of any use to you. I suspect at this point they're just desperate for whatever attention they can get." There was more than a little amusement in his tone as he moved away. "The last fifteen hundred years haven't exactly been kind to pantheons."

"Right." She moved back into place and made the account, reluctantly using her real information, since Athena likely wouldn't be pleased to find out she'd been lied to. Stories like that never ended well for the humans. "What should the message say?"

"I would just be direct about it," he replied. "I don't know if any of them have kept tabs on Arachne since she left Greece, but she'll know who you're talking about."

"Including mentioning you?"

"Yes, it'll be a source of intrigue that could get her to talk to us if nothing else," he replied. She nodded and typed up the most polite and straightforward message she could.

"How's that?"

"You can tell you've been in university," he replied. She glared at him. "In this case it's not a bad thing, though. Send the message. Perhaps the fact that you're interested in learning will gain us favour."

Rose nodded and sent the message. "Has she ever been in the bookstore?" She thought back and couldn't recall seeing any of the Greek Gods there, though she'd seen plenty of other deities.

"They aren't allowed," he replied. "Not in our store, anyway. The owner gave that assurance to Arachne when we came to Canada. I believe they go to the branch in Paris for the most part."

Rose nodded and leaned back in her chair, stretching. "Now we just need to wait for a reply. I don't know how long that'll take." As she finished speaking, she got a notification that she had a new message. "Nevermind. She must have been online." She went to the message and found a request for a video call in half an hour. "Okay. We can do this, right?"

"Right."

She wrote back accepting it. "So, what's the plan now?"

Jet paced across her desk. "I didn't really plan this far. I thought it would be far more difficult to contact her, and by then I would have thought of something."

"Okay, well, we have less than thirty minutes now."

"Damn…" She'd never seen the elf nervous before. It would have been entertaining under other circumstances. "Well, I have to tell the truth, so it's not as though we'll be able to hide anything."

"Do you want tea or something?" It was the only calming thing she could think of, and it was something to do that wasn't panicking.

"No, thank you," he replied. She got up to make some for herself, trying to keep her hands from shaking too badly.

"Maybe this'll all work out, and it'll all be fine, and you and Arachne will get together and she'll break your curse."

"Maybe."

It felt like both no time and an eternity had passed when she heard the sound of a video call coming through. Rose quickly accepted it and found herself face to face with a goddess. Athena was, of course, flawlessly beautiful, with gold skin and dark brown eyes. Even through the computer screen she had a very intimidating presence.

"So, you wish to discuss Arachne." Her heavily accented voice was just as beautiful and intimidating.

"Yes." She almost pulled off the confident tone she wanted.

"You know, I always wondered how she turned back into a human," Athena remarked. "And what she was willing to pay." She seemed to look past Rose. "Who else is there with you?"

"That would be me." Rose didn't dare look away from the goddess as Jet moved up to her shoulder.

"You must be Jet," she said, apparently unsurprised.

"Yes."

"And what interest have you in our little weaver?"

"I love her." He did not sound intimidated at all by Athena. Of course, he was a centuries old faerie. And probably had more power than she did right now, if gods truly derived power from worship. "Your father is the one who returned her to human form but would never let her weave again out of deference to your… tantrum." Rose barely held back a gasp, but she could feel all the warmth drain from her body. She'd already been afraid of angering a goddess. Jet had insulted her without hesitation.

Athena narrowed her eyes at him. "Yes, I can see why she would like you." She sighed. "I was young then, though she should have known better than to mock the gods. Still, she must have been desperate to go to my father for aid." Rose was certain she saw something akin to sympathy in the goddess's eyes and decided to take a risk.

"Would you allow her to start weaving again?" She kept her tone as polite as she could.

Athena glanced at her, then back at Jet. "Are you hoping to win Arachne's love by doing this and free yourself of your own curse?" That hadn't been in the message, but then, she'd likely heard from elsewhere, since so many beings went through the bookstore.

"No, I am not some knight to slay a dragon to win a maiden," he replied. "I would still do this even if I were certain she would refuse me as a lover. She is still a dear friend."

Athena fell silent for a long moment, clearly thinking. "I think Arachne has served her punishment long enough. But I do not have the power to change that currently." She turned her attention back to Rose. "You are dealing with a problem of your own, I hear. A lover who will not leave you alone."

"Ex," she corrected out of reflex, then tensed. But Athena didn't seem offended. "Yes, he's been a problem."

"I am the goddess of heroic deeds as well as wisdom,"

she said. "And being capable of saving one's self rather than relying on another is still heroic. Slay your tormentor with my sword and that will give me the power to free Arachne." She glanced at a phone Rose could just see off screen and typed something into it.

Wait, did she intend for Rose to *kill* Mark?

"Now, I must go. Dionysus and Hermes are arguing over who will become the God of Memes and I do not wish to miss the debate." A phone notification went off on her side. "And according to The Fates, you will have the opportunity to complete your task in less than half an hour. I will have one of my servants watching." The screen went black as she signed off.

"Did she just text the Fates?" There was just so much to sort through. "Does she expect me to kill Mark?" She wasn't a violent person, let alone a murderer.

"Yes, to both of those questions." Jet moved back down to the desk. "You have to remember; the Gods see mortal lives differently. You're fleeting interests or annoyances at best. Like insects. But don't do this. We can find another way."

"But won't she be angry that I failed?"

"She just won't give Arachne back her weaving. That's all. I'm not willing to make you commit murder for that. And I really don't think Arachne would consider it either. We can go to the Norse Gods. There's enough of a rivalry that one of them would do it for spite." He was pacing now. She wanted to, but she felt frozen in place.

"What about the sword?"

"Behind you." He waved one of his many legs. She turned, and sure enough, there was a sword on her coffee table. There definitely hadn't been one there a few minutes ago. It wasn't long or elegant, but the blade and heavy pommel gleamed with a near ethereal light.

"But he's coming here. He knows where I live..." It was hard to decide what to panic about first.

"I can call Arachne; she'll send someone over."

"Won't you have to explain how we know? She'll find out about everything!"

"Rose, there are more important things. She'll be angry about it because she gave up hope long ago, but this is too much to ask. My ability to use magic is almost nonexistent in this form, so I can't do much to protect you. We need to call someone."

It felt like she couldn't get enough air. She stood and rushed out onto her small balcony, gasping in deep breaths of frigid air. Then she spotted the snowy owl on the roof of the building across the street. "Jet... Athena's symbol is an owl, right?" She couldn't repress her shudder as he crawled up her back and onto her shoulder.

"That would be one of her owls," he replied. She stepped back into her apartment and shut the balcony door before leaning with her back against it and sliding to the floor, hugging her knees. "I'm so sorry I dragged you into this," he said, gently squeezing her shoulder in something akin to a hug before moving back to the floor. "Where's your phone?"

"There's no point. Anyone we call will take too long to get here." She looked up at the sword on her table. Somehow it seemed the only way out.

"No, Rose. Think of the human laws. If you have a body in here and you have a bloody ancient Greek sword it's not going to look good for a number of reasons," he pointed out. The edges of her vision seemed to go funny. She couldn't tell if it was because of tears or lack of oxygen.

Someone knocked on the door. Rose's head snapped up. She didn't want to answer it. But maybe it wasn't him. Maybe her neighbour just needed sugar or something. It was a foolish enough thought that she didn't voice it out loud. There was another knock, louder. She pressed back against the glass. Something moved out of the corner of her eye and she almost jumped, but it was Jet bringing over her phone.

"Call. For. Help. I don't know your password."

Her lock clicked open. She looked up and barely kept from screaming. She'd forgotten to put the chain in place. The door opened and Mark stepped in.

"Rose?" He looked around and spotted her. "Rose, you know it's polite to answer the door when someone knocks." He shook his head at her. "I know you've been having a hard time lately, but I decided to come over and we can figure out this misunderstanding." He took another step in. She lunged for the sword and held it up so it was between them.

"Leave," she said, one hand covering the scar she had from the last time he'd found her.

Mark held up his hands. "Now, Rose, please be reasonable. We've been over this. You need to calm down."

"Actually, you need to leave," Jet said with silky menace.

Mark looked around, his expression twisting to one of rage. "Who's that? Are you cheating on me?" He turned to glower at Rose. "How dare you." He took a step forward, and Jet dropped down to eye level.

"Really, now, who needs to calm down?"

Mark let out a shriek and fell back, away from the overlarge spider. Jet dropped onto his chest, ignoring the other man's whimpers.

"Really, now, this is completely unnecessary."

While Mark focused on Jet, she lunged forward and smashed the pommel against his temple, where she'd been told to hit. Mark's eyes rolled back as he went unconscious and she dropped the sword, staggering back and almost stepping on her phone.

"Call for help," Jet said in a gentle tone. She nodded and called. Somehow, she managed to tell the operator what was going on. The sword vanished, and she looked out the window. The owl was gone. But she couldn't focus on what that meant.

"What about you?" she asked him as he scurried over to her.

"That's a problem…" he admitted. She held out her hands and he crawled into them.

"What if *I* kissed you?" He was her friend, and she was willing to face gods for him. That had to count for something, right?

"You picked a hell of a time to re-enact *The Princess and the Frog*."

"Would it work? You said it didn't have to be romantic love."

"You can try…" She leaned down and carefully kissed the top of his head. It felt so strange, he was so fuzzy. For a moment nothing happened, then he was suddenly standing in front of her as an elf. He stared down at his body, but they didn't have long; sirens quickly approached the building and they had to figure out what they were going to do.

"When's the trial?" Arachne asked her a few days later. She was flipping through a catalogue of looms.

"In March," she replied, sorting through books. Athena had decided to count knocking Mark unconscious and getting him arrested as 'good enough' and held up her end of the bargain. Arachne had, predictably, not been thrilled at the risks they took, but things were slowly getting back to normal. Well, a better normal.

"Alright."

"The lawyer you got me is amazing," she added.

"We take care of our own," was all her manager said, smiling slightly as the bell above the door rang. From Arachne's expression, Rose knew it was Jet. She turned to face the elf, who was holding something behind his back.

"Alright, you held up your end of the bargain, now I have to do the same," he said.

"Right. Finding me true love."

"Close your eyes and hold out your hands."

She frowned but did as he asked. Something warm, furry, and squirming was put in her arms and immediately started licking her. She opened her eyes and looked down at the black and brown puppy, its tail wagging furiously. Rose couldn't help but smile as she rubbed behind its ears.

"See? True love," Jet said smugly.

Arachne snorted. "Just don't let him chew the books."

Elaine Rigas

Elaine Rigas has published short stories in several Greek anthologies, and has also translated into Greek an anthology of French horror short stories by Maurice Level "Stories of Grand Guignol," published by Archetypo Publishing. Other anthologies that she have participated in include "Στα σύνορα του Τρόμου" (In The Borders of Terror - published by Alloste publishing), "Κόκκινος θάνατος: Ιστορίες εμπνευσμένες από το έργο του E.A.Poe (Red Death: Stories inspired by the work of EA Poe - published by Universal Pathways), "Το έπος της Φαντασίας" (The Epic of Fantasy - published by iWrite) , "Νυχτερινό Ανθολόγιο" (Nocturnal Anthology - published by Nightread) and "Metal Chapters, Vol.1" (published by Pigi), as the translator of the short story "Ex voto" by Graham Masterton.

A Montreal native currently residing in Sparti, Greece, Rigas brings that depth and knowledge to her short story, 'Erinyes.'

Erinyes

First came Alecto, for that unholy envy started it all. Then Magaera, for the injustice that prevailed enraged the gods. And last came murder, and brought Tisiphone along...

There was something in the salty air of Lagia that made every breath feel like sin. Facing the sea, its small, stone houses rose along the mountain hill, so far from the seashore, yet so close to watch over it with restless eyes. That savage village was long ago forgotten somewhere in the south of Greece, but not its stories. Those tales of undying revenge and bloodthirst vendettas were still alive in the memories of the few who still inhabited its old, mouldy stonewalls and in the sleep of the many who inhabited its deep, dark graves. You see, the most peculiar thing about that place wasn't its fading legends or its primitive burial customs; it was the fact that every house, in its backyard, had its very own little graveyard, where the bodies of the dead rested under the same soil the living walked on...

Among the decaying crosses and the marble tombstones of Lagia laid the neglected grave of Kirki, who was the daughter of its lighthouse keeper more than two centuries ago. Although her death was a merciless execution, the nightmare that followed was the reason no one would ever again bury a loved one in the village's cemetery. No one wanted to see them the way they saw Kirki the night of her funeral. No one wanted the Erinyes to wake up again.

You see, that lighthouse was built right upon the ruins where the ancient Gate of Hades was believed to once be, which made it more than just a ship guardian – it was also a guardian for the lost souls. Once Kirki fell in love with Alexios, a young captain, she would pray to its light day and night to keep her lover safe and guide him back to her arms. One night, her prayers weren't heard.

When Alexios' lifeless body arrived at the village, Kirki was accused by the other women as a witch for bringing bad luck and death to the young man. Those words were no more than pure jealousy, not a single drop of truth hidden within them, but the envy of the women for the love Alexios felt for Kirki was strong. That accusation was all the men needed to condemn the young girl to death. Despite her father's cries and pleas, right after Alexios' burial, a bonfire was lit and the young, innocent girl was led to a nightmarish death. While her skin would burn to crisp, while her eyes and face melted, while despair altered her cries, her poor father would offer his life and body to the spirits of the sea, diving from the top of the lighthouse to the rocky shore below, accompanying his daughter to her final rest. The lighthouse saw it all, and the gods lurking its grounds saw it too.

Once it was all over and the villagers, satisfied by the punishment they forced upon the 'witch', went to sleep, Kirki, or rather what was left of her, was kissed by the Erinyes, Alecto, Magaera, and Tisiphone, and rose from her inhospitable grave, searching to avenge her murder and her father's suicide. That was the first night the Erinyes tortured the villagers in their sleep, causing them to wake up violently with visions of nightmares still bright in their memory, and witness Kirki's burnt corpse walk in a gracefully eerie way as her skinless fingertips touched every grave, one by one. They didn't know what that meant, but they knew deep in their souls that the place belonged to her now.

Each night, as the Erinyes broke loose and tortured the sleeping villagers till sleep was rest no more, Kirki wandered the grounds of the cemetery, and its soil grew bitter, hostile to human flesh, which would no longer rot and melt. The miasma would unsettle the dead, exile them from their endless sleep, make them seek a way to escape their tombs. That's when the vampyri finally appeared. The villagers, terrified, sought ways to break the curse, but in terror, they would finally realize that nothing, holy blessed or unholy whispered, would work. They were condemned to live with the ghost of Kirki among their grounds, but what petrified them was the realization that, in death, they would become prisoners of her inexhaustible revenge. No one would ever bury a loved one in the cemetery again. Backyards were turned into family graveyards and the remaining graves in the cemetery were enclosed with metal fences and spikes, to prevent the dead from escaping.

Years passed, centuries passed, the lighthouse would become nothing more than an abandoned carcass and Kirki's story would fade in the sound of the waves crushing the rocks. But the unexplainable fear of even approaching the cemetery would remain, the gods of the lighthouse would remain, the Erinyes would remain and, for the unlucky ones that passed by Lagia on their way to an exciting road trip, the helpless cries and blurred apparition of Kirki would remain...

David Lynch

David Lynch was born in St. John's Newfoundland but grew up in Bellevue Beach. He is currently working on a high fantasy series titled *The Egimian Chronicles*.

In October 2020, Lynch won the third annual WANL "Nightmare on Water Street" contest.

He brings with him his story, 'Influence.'

Influence

The old man walked ahead of the younger, his frustration obvious in the way he knocked aside the bothersome alder branches that danced before his face. His hands shot out with blinding speed in an effort to simultaneously part the branches and gesticulate his absolute vexation, both of which were equally thick and snarled.

The path had not been trod in many years, he saw, and the Good Mother of Nature had seen fit to heal the scar that had been cut across her hawthorn breast. The young man kept back a respectable distance, his face still smarting from a couple of vicious licks that the snapping limbs had placed on his cheek. The old man continued to mutter as he looked to the sky, gauging the sun's descent.

"When last I came to this place," he rasped, "the path was not such a struggle."

"Are you sure we follow the correct path, old boy?" The young man wiped the blond hair from his eyes, sweat forming on his brow. He smiled. "Memory is surely enshrouded in mist in a past as vast as yours."

A grunt from the old man, who answered without turning. "Was it not for your need to take up arms and risk your cursed brainpan at every opportunity availed, your sword would still be intact, along with your head. Furthermore, I'd not have to bring you here to replace the former, nor intervene to save the latter!"

"I'd have bested him without your interference." The young man's voice was tinged with hubris, and distant as if he were still back on the field engaged with his opponent. He was used to being chastised the old man knew; had in fact spent much of his childhood allowing his skin to callus against such reproach from those who'd fostered him. The lad's eyes were on the trees around him. It was new territory for him; an area of the forest he'd not seen, which must have seemed strange indeed given the ground he'd covered in recent years. It was his land after all. His country. His narrowed eyes were trying to peer between the branches when he was struck.

The crack to the side of his head brought his attention to the moment fully. He cried out, spinning on the soft earth. His hand flew to his ear as the wound suffered in the battle four days prior began to trickle once again. His eyes found the old man.

"God's bones!" the young man cried. "Truly, is there a need?"

Myrddin Wilt – mentor, sometime guardian, and on better days, friend – stood beside the lad, the cursed willow switch held firm in his hand. Moving without sound or stir was an action that the enchanter rarely invoked, doing so only when he deemed that some sort of lesson was necessary.

"Interference, Artur?" He tilted his head, as if the lad spoke in foreign tongue. "Should it be called thus? My interference... my... my influence is what's kept you alive since you were a suckling babe, and-" He raised the willow switch slightly to point at Artur's face, causing him to pull back. "-And it would appear that the need for such influence is greater now than ere before!" He opened his mouth to continue but could see the restrained smile on the face of the young man.

"Pah!" He threw his arms in the air and stormed off through the branches. "The hope of Prydain indeed. I've seen runt pups quicker to learn. And more eager as well."

"Pups?" Artur was again pushing away thick branches. "Wolf pups, no? Tell me, old boy, were they kin, as the stories say?"

Myrddin had stopped, as if uncertain which direction was the proper course. He did not look at Artur. "The alpha and the omega," Myrddin said as he started forth again. His voice was quiet. Gentle now. "Do you recall the difference, Artur?

"The alpha leads," Artur replied. He paused. "Well... of a sort." Despite what his mentor said, the lad fell so readily into the role of pupil that Myrddin could not help but smile. "The alpha has power. It makes decisions. It doesn't give orders, as it were, but has the freedom and authority to make decisions, and the pack follows."

A nod from the old man. "And the omega?"

"An unenviable position." Artur was once more a dozen paces behind his mentor. "A low position of rank. Subject to frequent shows of dominance and superiority from others. A valued member of the pack, but it must often engage in displays of subordination, whining from its back and-"

The blow this time was not of a willow switch. Artur caught the swinging branch of the elm fully in the face and fell sprawling in the leaf strewn dirt. Myrddin, still a dozen paces away, turned and slowly walked back to Artur.

Myrddin's eyes were serious, crow's feet cutting trenches of frustration into his temples. He leaned over, hands clasped behind his back as he regarded his pupil. Artur sat up with effort, a hand on his bloodied lip. He opened his mouth, but Myrddin raised the switch and cut off the younger man's growl. Shaking his head, the enchanter tilted the thin stick sideways and another elm branch bent, seemingly of its own accord, poised to further the painful lesson.

"You were the omega, Artur." The old man's voice was not unkind. "You were the omega in that duel, and you did not recognize it – did not recognize your place." He extended his hand to the younger man, who took it in his own, albeit reluctantly, and let himself be helped to his feet. "Your place – if you are to be alpha, if you are to truly lead – must be considered wisely. The alpha's role is to make sage decisions, decisions that will benefit the entire pack. Your challenge of the Sable Knight was not done for the betterment of Prydain. It was rash. It was selfish and unnecessary."

The two regarded each other. Myrddin could see the anger slowly melt from the boy's face. The boy, he thought sardonically. The boy had passed his eighteenth year, and Myrddin still regarded him as the wayward child. Yet, however rash Artur may be, he accepted and appreciated the value of Myrddin's lessons and allowed himself to be guided. Myrddin reached out and placed a wrinkled hand on Artur's shoulder. He leaned in close when he spoke.

"What you fought those days ago was a rabid wolf. As stately and honorable as Pellinore may have looked in that sable regalia, his colours were true and clear when he was bereft of his helm. Did you not see the red in his eyes, lad? Did you not see the white froth forming at his mouth, collecting on his matted beard as he pinned you to the ground?" Myrddin sighed, and patting Artur's shoulder gently, he removed his hand. "When the wolf is rabid, greater powers may need to intervene. History has taught me such. Mind my lessons, Highness..." The old man turned, shuffling through the leaves and undergrowth as he forged his path through the quiet forest. "And mind the branches..."

The pair pushed on, through elm and hawthorn and the growing mist that swirled about their feet. As the mist thickened, the growth that hindered their movement seemed to lessen. It was only in the most troublesome areas that Myrddin called Artur forth and asked him to use his blade to cut through the thicket.

The blade. Broken now, like a dissipating dream that loses its sharpest edge, or a legend come apart too fully, its complete form lost to memory. As Myrddin watched, he recalled the morning that Artur had come to possess the blade: the chilly breeze, the cold block of marble in the empty churchyard, and the look on Artur's face as the truth was finally revealed. His notion of family had been shattered as surely as the blade he now held, as he'd learned that the blood of kings coursed through his veins.

His face had contorted then, much as it did now as he navigated the snapping limbs, but it was overwhelming emotion rather than determined branches that had stayed him on that day. His history had been revealed, and he'd struggled to come to grips with the fact that Ector was not his father. He was of the line of Uther Pendragon, and nothing would ever be the same again.

Myrddin shook his head, thinking of the boy's subsequent transformation. Artur had become more serious overnight, more sure of himself, which was ironic indeed given that he'd just learned that he was not in fact who he thought he was. His smile had taken on a sardonic tinge, though the true joy still shone through from time to time. Shadows and secrets. Lies and legends.

History, Myrddin thought, could be as insubstantial as the mist that now surrounded them, and equally as difficult to grasp.

He looked up suddenly to see Artur ahead of him. He'd fallen behind, and the boy waited for direction.

"The deeper your thought, the slower your gait," Artur said. "Be you inclined to share these thoughts?"

"I was thinking," Myrddin replied, "what an inconsistent teacher history can be."

Artur nodded, but didn't speak. Waiting.

"Just the rambling thoughts of an old man, Artur."

He nodded again. "Perhaps history would teach us more if it wasn't so readily put behind us."

"Is there any other place for it?" Myrddin grunted. "Surely not before us, boy."

Artur hesitated a moment. "No, but perhaps we could gather it back from its place behind us and set it beside us;

within us even." His brow lowered, and he studied the edge of his broken blade. "Perhaps it's not history itself, but the sharing of it that teaches us the most."

Myrddin's eyes narrowed, as he saw the path Artur now trod.

"Come, old friend. Is the time not suitable to share more with me? I'm a man grown...and your king as well. Perhaps by royal order I might have the words ripped from your tongue?" A raised eyebrow, and the smallest smile.

"Pah!" Myrddin strode past him, though his step was hardly quickened.

"What of the mists?" Artur asked.

Myrddin slowed.

"Truly, my Mage, are you content that I know so little of enchantment?"

He stopped fully now. Rare was it for the boy to use such honorifics. Old boy, old friend, enchanter. Occasionally his actual name. But to refer to Myrddin as mage was new ground for them both.

"Am I not, now and ever, under your esteemed tutelage?" Artur gestured to the path before them. "We walk into the mists, into a land that you've told me is itself shrouded in enchantment. You would lead me to the Fae, Myrddin. I know near nothing of the Fae, and what little knowledge I have comes from Morgaine, whose hatred no mist could hide. These lessons that history has provided you – speak to me of this history, Myrddin." Artur would never plead, Myrddin knew. Nor would he relent.

"Speak to me of the Fae," Artur said. And more quietly, "Speak to me of magic."

"Magic..." The word was followed by long moments of silence, as if the old man were unsure of how to continue.

"Magic, Artur, is a living thing. It must be respected, and greatly. There is magic all around us. Understand that the magic of which I now speak is different than that of the Fae. What we call magic is but a part of the very nature, the very being of the Fae. It is not something they learn and practice; it is a part of who and what they are. It has been a part of them since the Dawn, existing within the very first of the Faerae. The magic I wield, which might snap a branch at an unsuspecting young man, is a little different."

The old man saw the furrowed brow and paused for the question that invariably followed.

"This is what I have trouble understanding, Myrddin. If you were so vexed by the trees that blocked our path, why would you not use magic to move them?"

"Let me answer your question with another. Why would I use magic to move them?"

"It would have made things much easier."

"That it would have. As well, brewing a cup of tea would be much easier without having to light a fire and boil the water. Yet, I continue to cut tinder for my little hearth, a task which in itself would be much easier without the cursed chopping. And don't even get me started on the washing of my robes. But I do these things, Artur, much like everyone else. Why do I not use magic?"

"Because it is not necessary?"

"Precisely. Magic is no plaything. Nor is it to be used for fickle purposes. Much like our very bodies, it has limitations and is expendable if used without care. It is a gift, Artur, and must be treated as such."

"Where did it come from?" Artur now walked beside Myrddin. The trees continued to thin, and their path opened up to reveal small glens of grass and flower. "You say it's a part of the nature of the Fae, but how did men come to attain the power?"

Myrddin stopped and looked at the grass before him. Bending low, he parted the thick grass with his willow stick. Artur moved beside him to behold a nest of tiny rabbits in a shallow depression in the ground. After a moment, Myrddin replaced the grass gently, and with his stick gestured for Artur to give the spot a wide berth as they continued to walk.

"The life that resides in everything can be influenced. Just as you might influence another to help you with a task, or convince someone to take a particular course of action, so too can a select few do this with all aspects of nature…not just with words, and not just with people." He slowed, stroking his beard as he silently inhaled the misty air.

Artur listened.

"Many, many years ago, there lived a Faerae creature who fell in love with a common human. Rare it was indeed for this to happen, but happen it did. The girl grew into a woman, and in the years that followed, she became with child. The Faerae was very protective over the woman and the child that grew within and wished to do all he could to ensure that no harm befell either. The lands in which the woman dwelt were, in that Age, wrought with conflict, so the Faerae shifted his beloved, and took her to a world that he deemed acceptably safe."

Myrddin saw the sudden shift in Artur's posture, the narrowed eyes and half-opened mouth. He raised a hand, his index finger slightly bent. "One tale at a time, lad. That one will have to wait for another day.

"Now, for months the woman lived comfortably in her new world. She was doted upon by the Faerae, in a little cottage by a lake, and her pregnancy progressed well. Until the Darkness came. The Darkness, Artur, is a sickness of sorts. It is the affliction which may occur in one who has been shifted. In many cases, if a shift occurs whereby the individual arrives in a world that is not appropriate to their being, the Darkness comes. Some say that the Darkness can come to those who must be shifted, even from their own world... folk who've never been shifted before. It is said that the Darkness also forces an individual to be shifted if Fate requires their presence, or that of their descendants, in another world. Whatever the reason, the Darkness necessitates a shift, and this pregnant woman was brought by the Faerae once again to the fair vales of Prydain.

"Yet the Darkness remained.

"In many instances, the shift will set things right and the individual will heal in time. The condition of this woman, however, progressively worsened. The Faerae began to despair. He brought Healers and Water Fae to help the woman, but nothing worked. The woman grew weaker, frailer, and the Faerae could see that her slender body would fail.

"On a stormy midsummer night, the woman and her child together seemed to realize that the baby's chances of survival would be greatly improved if it were separated from its ailing mother. When middlenight fell, the child was born. As the infant boy squealed his first breath of life, his mother breathed her last.

"The Faerae was overcome. Grief surged up in him like a mighty wave, and he did what no Faerae had ever done to that point. He cried. He cried as a human would, for such was his bond with the mortal race. He held his baby close, and tears ran from his face, falling like sorrowful rain upon the little babe he held. So close he held that child, it being the last and only connection to his beloved. In an attempt to calm the crying baby, he began to sing. The song of the Faerae; so powerful and intense. In the face of such loss, he sang of love and of strength, of things he felt he'd never again possess."

Myrddin and Artur walked through tall grass, dense enough to slow their progress. They were crossing a meadow, and the mist around them was such that it was often difficult to see the trees. Myrddin looked up, and through the white wisps that floated by, he could see a clear blue sky directly overhead. Nearby, the sound of a gurgling stream caught his ear.

"The poor child," Artur said. "Baptized in tears of sorrow. A most unfortunate way to start out in this mad world."

"Indeed," said Myrddin. "It is said that the Fae lost his hold on sanity on that woeful night. As I've told you, the power of magic lies in its ability to influence. Tales from time immemorial tell us that the song of the Faerae is one of the greatest influencers ever known. People have been swayed by the songs of Fae: misdirected, made to walk uncertain paths for as long as Fae and humans have interacted. But the songs can be used for good as well. They can help to heal and to comfort. And this is what the Faerae attempted to do that night. He sang to comfort the babe, but as he did so, he directed the power of the song at himself also. He was torn, as though he existed as two entities, one soul singing to the other, and the child caught in the middle. It is said that he detached, irreparably."

"Madness in a Faerae? I didn't know such a thing was possible."

"My boy, in this vast world, and the worlds beyond, all things are possible."

Again, Artur seemed tempted to delve further into this notion, but he stayed with the present tale. "And what of the child?"

"He survived, and that in itself was something of a feat.

"The boy was brought to live with distant relatives of the mother – not so much brought to as disposed of, for the Faerae knew that the couple would not be welcoming of another mouth to feed, especially one that mewled as often as not. But there was little choice. He could not tend to the child, and the very sight of the boy brought naught but grief and melancholy to the creature.

"The boy grew, somewhat, and learned to fend for himself as best he could. He was beaten as often as he was fed, perhaps sometimes because of the very fact that he needed to be fed. He learned to eat little, and skip as many meals as possible. He made sure to complete the chores given him to avoid the great uncle's wrath, but when not engaged in such duties, he stayed away from the homestead. He learned to hunt and gather what was needed. So, the day came when, scarcely beyond his tenth year, he did not return to the home of his kin. He created a shelter for himself many leagues from the place he'd grown up, and would not return there for long, long years."

"A brave lad," said Artur.

"Necessity," said Myrddin. "It does not always take bravery to do what one must. Perhaps, had he been braver, he would have helped the aunt; saved her from the bruises that likely doubled in his absence. But, he was a boy. What do boys know?"

Myrddin pulled up the sleeves of his dirty brown robe, for the trees were now scarce and the air warm. He directed the boy to the stream and told him to fill their skins. As Artur did so, the old man seemed to consider the next part of his tale, his grey bushy eyebrows pulled low, as if to better determine the path of his story. Artur said nothing, waiting patiently for Myrddin to continue.

"The boy made every effort to avoid attention, to keep to his own little vale, but this could not last of course. With time, the foxes and wolves came nearer, drawn by the smell of meat and weakness." Myrddin noted the look in Artur's eye, and smiled. "Yes, wolves. For what would a story be, Artur, without the great and terrible wolf? Yet, these animals were not as terrible as one might expect. At least, most were not. The initial encounters were tense, filled with flames and pointed sticks. But despite the spindly arms of the boy, he showed an admirable resolve. This – coupled with the fact that the woodland provided ample prey for the beasts – might account for the accord between the boy and the wolves.

"And of course, there was the song."

Myrddin stopped and looked around. The mist was almost thick enough to carve with a finger now. He knew full well where he was going but acted as though he was considering the way. With his back to Artur, he smiled. He often stopped mid-story, giving Artur time to digest the words, time to reflect and consider questions and possibilities…

Ah, but who was he kidding? He did love to build a little suspense as well.

"Yes, Artur, he hummed a song," he continued finally. "It is said that the song of the Faerae on that fateful night found its way into the heart and memory of the child. Encountered by a particularly hungry wolf on a cold night, the pair had eyed each other. As the wolf took a tentative step toward the boy, the lad began to hum. A tilt of the wolf's shaggy head, and another step. The boy hummed louder, yet in the gentlest manner. Short time passed, and both went their separate ways."

"He enchanted the wolf?" Artur asked.

Myrddin shrugged his shoulders. "I'd be more inclined to say he influenced the animal.

"The boy continued to practice this newfound ability, humming his way out of some dire predicaments. Yet the day came when his gift failed to work…"

Myrddin stopped, fumbling with his belt as he-

"Oh, come on, old man! Enough with the breaks!" Artur smiled. "I know full well what you do. If you're too winded to continue, sit for a spell and finish your tale. You have my attention. Make use of it." Still smiling, he jerked his head upward a little, gesturing for Myrddin to continue.

"Ah, the impatience of youth," Myrddin shook his head, scratching at his temple. "Truly, must everything be so hurried and-"

"-and his gift failed to work, and..." Artur prompted. He held out his hand loosely, making a circular motion with his fingers.

"Pah! You've no appreciation for the art of storytelling. Yes, yes, the day came when his humming did not work, and he found himself in the gravest of danger. The boy wandered across a grassy land, rolling meadows and the occasional shallow pond. Little did he know that he was tracked the entire time. A wolf, yet one unlike any other. It came to within twenty paces of him, and the boy turned.

"The wolf was rabid. Its teeth dripped white foam, its rheumy eyes narrow and focused. It took a step toward the boy and staggered, just slightly to its left, like a very young squire sampling a very old wine.

"The boy began to hum, quickly and with great force. He looked around, searching for a means of protection. There were no trees to climb. No rocks to be thrown. Only erratic boulders and a few saplings growing beside a pond that was scarcely larger than a stagnant marsh pool. He backed up, as far as the water, and the wolf continued toward him. Stumbling into the boulders, he stopped, moving beside them to stand amongst the little trees which were not yet as tall as his shoulder. The wolf, its deranged mind undeterred by the shaky tune, crept forward.

"The boy was certain that this particular encounter would be like none he'd previously experienced, and he lowered his head. As he closed his eyes and drew upon whatever inner strength he could muster, a tear ran from his face... and he began to sing. Not hum, mind you, but sing. He sang the actual words, the song that his Faerae father had sung to him so many years ago. Words he had not heard since. As he sang, those long hidden words drifted from his subconscious mind and danced slowly upon his tongue. The intensity of the song strengthened. The boy's muscles tightened, and he felt the fear begin to fade. The words came with growing force, rising from some unknown place within him, and he opened his eyes. He felt every fiber of his being, felt his aliveness, his influence, his connection to all the life that surrounded him and he knew that he would not die on that day.

"The wolf, in its tormented state, was unaware of everything but the boy. All it saw, all it sensed was the prey that cowered within a thin patch of young trees. As the boy continued to sing, the wolf seemed further infuriated, as if offended by the audacity of the boy to sing in its savage presence. The song still had no effect on its demented mind. Vicious now, its slow, furtive walk broke into a full run, its dark red eyes narrowed as the spittle flew from its snarling mouth.

"When it was but paces away, the beast leapt to a rock and propelled itself into the air. The boy bent the smallest of the willow saplings in the direction of his attacker, pointing the feeble limb at the maw of the animal. And as he did so, the words continued to burst from him, through him, like a raging river that had been pent-up for far too long. The willow sapling shuddered in his hand, and a feeling more intense than any he'd ever felt, or would ever feel, rushed through his body, through his arm with such intensity that the willow snapped free in his hand. In that instant, the words, which had grown more potent with each utterance, exploded from his mouth, from the willow in his hand, and struck the beast that flew toward him. With a violent jerk of his hand, the boy's power pulled the beast sideways, directing it into the nearest boulder. Its neck snapped upon impact with a sickening crack, and the wolf rolled to its side, resting in a lifeless heap at the feet of the boy.

"On that day, my young friend, magic came to the hand of Man."

Myrddin stopped, and Artur came to stand beside him. Long minutes passed before either spoke. The old man turned to consider the younger, as the younger continued to consider the tale.

"So there it is lad. While the Fae have held this power in their being since the Dawn, it was only at this point that man, or at least, one not of true, pure Fae blood, could wield the power. It required the willow stick, a most simple, elemental piece of nature, but through it, power was gained. And continues to be gained. We need only learn to influence…"

Another pause before Artur spoke. "Is the tale true, old friend?"

Myrddin inclined his gaze to the sky, licking his dry lips. "There are those that say the truth lies in the telling. In the very telling, the tale becomes truth."

"More riddles." Artur sighed, and twisted his scabbard, looking at the broken sword. "Pray, tell me this then. In truth…" He looked at Myrddin and waited for his eyes to rise. "Are you the boy in the story?"

"Me?" Myrddin chuckled, his thin shoulders shaking. "Whatever would give you such notions?"

"Oh come, Myrddin! Raised in the wild? Orphaned. The wolves. The enchantment?"

Myrddin said nothing, only smiled.

"Myrddin?"

The old man sighed.

"Boy, truth to tell, if it was me, how might I be called upon to remember events so long ago? I've heard it said that memory is enshrouded in mist in a past as vast as mine."

With those words, he swept his hand through the air, and the mist parted. Enchantment, like a gentle breeze. Indeed, those who refused to believe might convince themselves that the slightest of winds had caused the gossamer curtain to part. But then, any form of enchantment could be explained away by natural occurrences, if one were so inclined. For wasn't nature in itself the greatest of all influencers. Artur took it all in. The mist, the swaying trees and the wide lake that rested beside them.

Artur turned with a start. He'd not realized how close they'd come to the water, Myrddin saw. For the water was so still that no sound rose from its gleaming face, even in the place where the stream was welcomed into its deceptive depth.

Artur made to step toward the lake, but stopped. "Is this it?"

The old man nodded.

"And if I'm deemed worthy, will the sword protect me?"

"Any sword may protect any wielder, if the wielder is able to wield…"

"God's bones," Artur muttered. "What I mean, Myrddin-" He sought the right words. "…will I be able to influence the weapon?"

"That remains to be seen, boy." He twirled the willow

stick he'd retrieved from his pocket, seemed to study it, then put it back once more. "Perhaps it is you who'll be influenced." He gestured over Artur's shoulder.

Artur turned, and beheld the Lady. Myrddin noticed the almost imperceptible bend in the lad's knees when he saw her. The Lady stood in water to her hips, the white samite of her dress clinging to the lake's surface. Yet, the waters did not stir. They held still, like the lady herself, who held before her a sword that reflected the middleday sun.

No words were spoken. Myrddin watched.

He watched the sun dance upon the blade; dance upon the engraved words that had been etched in ancient tongue. Take me up, it implored. Or cast me away. The Lady held the sword gently in her right hand. It pointed to the sky, its blinding tip shining into the unending blue that spread over all. In her left hand, she held a scabbard. Myrddin smiled. The scabbard, she held firm.

He watched Artur move forward. Tentative. Cautious. The Lady still did not move. Nor did the waters in which she stood. As he reached the lake's edge, Artur raised his head. The sun gleamed in his pale blue eyes, and cast a shadow of his body, a shadow greater than he himself, whose end could not be seen.

Myrddin watched as the young man stepped into the lake, and at last, the waters moved.

The ripples spread, and would continue to do so, through water and time, like old tales through an eternity that, like the shadow, would end where none could see.

On the shore behind the boy, the old man began to quietly hum a song.

Andrew Hawthorn

From St. John's, Newfoundland & Labrador, Andrew Hawthorn is an accomplished author best known recently for his reporting with CBC, the author has previously worked in fiction, writing comic books. His work includes 'The Man Who Knew Everything' for Benday Comics, and 'Mere Appendix,' which appeared as the feature story in issue #54 of *Tales of the Teenage Mutant Ninja Turtles*.

He brings with him his story, 'Silvern Voices.'

Silvern Voices

Listen, and this is a theory I had even before all this went down, but music is just too intense for us to handle. Maybe it always is. Like strong drink. I can't taste anything anymore either, by the way. There's something in the connection sound makes in the brain, maybe. Or the connection with the brain and something else, anything else, outside us. Like, musical instruments were always the most advanced technology, precision machines in a world of clubs and sticks. It seems like all of it was too complex for people to have just invented like that, don't you think? Imagine some caveman who first started banging rocks together and found it felt better if he did it on a rhythm, and then that it felt good to move his body this way or just tap his foot because of the song of rocks, just some frigging rocks or something, hitting off each other. How did we invent that? This here is the difference between invention and discovery.

I don't play anything; I couldn't stand practicing. It takes forever. Writing on the other hand was easy. You just say something and type it. People gripe all over about how hard it is to just sit down and write or "craft a tale" or whatever stuff they say now, but it's just saying stuff and then you type it. I could do that without practicing. Try playing a piano, even that's an effort I just don't have in me, especially now.

You won't believe me, but this was supposed to be a puff piece. People in Newfoundland, we like our folklore. The university has a whole dedicated department. Storytellers get state funerals around here. This isn't a place that is eager to give anything back to you; you've got to put something in first. And what we put in is music and stories, and a lot of that makes it on the news, especially on a slow day. And there are always slow days. So, whatever happened afterwards, my part in this started as a simple interview with a local celebrity.

Actually, I'm not sure Charlotte Chen even counted at that level. She had put out a couple albums while she was doing her degree here, mostly the regular kind of Irish-inspired... like you know, kind of sea shanty chic. That's hard to say, isn't it? That's kind of what it is though, taking an old folk song and dusting it off with some modern production, maybe rock it up a bit. Her first CD *Lake of Shadow* was all that. For a while there the trad-rock stuff was really selling, it was all you would hear about, even though, by the way, the St. John's punk scene, and the electronica too, is nothing to sniff at.

So, Charlotte. She came from an old St. John's family. Everyone in metro knew her already before the album. Used to play at the Ship all the time downtown. She had played violin since she was like six. You can really tell on that second album, *Sometimes, If at Sea,* but it didn't sell as well. She was doing a music/folklore degree. She had been writing about throat singing. They do that up in Labrador, have you ever heard much? It's a really old tradition, Inuit. Really haunting, guttural, I mean literally guttural sounding stuff. But what's interesting is it's also a game. Like two people will hold each other and throat sing at each other until they crack up laughing, just laughing at the sounds and faces they're making. I once saw a pair do it at a funeral, they just burst out laughing, the whole family over there in tears. Craziest thing.

Where was I? I can't focus like I used to. Right, the degree. Charlotte had been up to Labrador and started all this research on throat singing, then she switched out, and started working on something else she'd found. Soon after she'd just vanished for a while. When I talked to her family, they said she'd gone overseas somewhere to study. There was some story about the Greenwich museum, that's for the Royal Navy. Someone said she was there, again doing this sea shanty stuff. Working out of the University College of London. I called them at some point after and they'd never seen her. Actually, she'd never left the island.

At the time of the interview, I assumed she'd been interviewing old timers in the towns, people that live the stuff. You ever hear of Fred Emerson? He was one of the first to notice Newfoundlanders had culture, started writing down songs to preserve them, "We'll rant and we'll roar", all those songs. Back in the twenties he said he figured we'd already lost 90 percent of what songs had been written here. He died in the seventies; they bulldozed his house a while back.

So, I figured Chen to be like a modern-day Emerson,

with kind of a post-colonial edge, trying to go back a bit farther and look at a lot of the music that had been ignored by the establishment, which is to say, us whites. That's where my head was at going into the interview. But that's not what she was doing.

Here's the thing: Newfoundland is big, even if you ignore Labrador, which most people around here do, by the way. If you look at the towns, whatever makes up civilization in Newfoundland, it's just the coastline and then the single line of the highway going through it. End to end, from St. John's to Port aux Basques, it's what, 900 kilometers? And the whole island is over 100,000 square kilometers. You get just a bit away from the coast, it's all wild land. She could've gone anywhere.

I guess what struck me when we met up was how different she was. This was about a week before the concert. She had been this laid back, Doc Martin's and a t-shirt rocker before, she'd stamp around the stage when she played, looked like she was having a party. But this Charlotte was all business. Completely buttoned down, quiet. Hair completely straight and long, plain, formal clothes, sitting forward on her chair like she was nailed to a board. She looked like she'd aged a decade. Not in the Keith Richards way you think rockers age, but like she'd started as the rebellious kid in school and grew into the principal.

I was doing a piece in the leadup to the show. This was... I think it was supposed to be about her basically presenting her findings. It was like a thesis report, or a recital. I'm having trouble remembering what her degree was on at this stage. Or even if she was still with the university. The concert happened there. It was supposed to be a smaller thing than it ended up being but there was so much interest from the public. Like I said before, she was well known. There was a lot of buzz about what kind of music she was doing, a lot about a possible third album. People wanted to be there. I think that's why it was moved to the Reid Theatre; it was a much bigger space.

"We all interact with the world by making copies of it. Copies of copies," she said to me. Here I was asking about her music. We did the interview in a cafe downtown, that's why all the background noise. "Copies are the only way we can get our heads around things. Even words are just models of something, but they are imperfect. There's nothing about the words "tree" or "water" that resembles their meaning. In English we say "rock", in French, "roche" or "pierre", the Mikmaq word is "guntew". But imagine a stone on the ground, or a great mountain of shale, and what about this evokes the growl of the letter R or the fricative staccato of a hard G?

"Music is different. When we read a word, our brain has to translate it, unpack it into an image of what it represents. But music is the language of emotion, or more accurately perhaps, its sound. It stimulates the limbic system, it forces you to feel, to a degree, without giving you a choice. What is wonderful about old music is that it is letting you feel what someone felt decades, or centuries ago. It's an involuntary process. There is no barrier, no interpretation or copy between you and them. If you listen, you have to feel it, in all its primal, original power."

It wasn't just the music that she had been researching, but the way it had been played. Forgotten techniques, instruments, and found objects. A different way of thinking about produced sound. She said she'd adapted it into a new way to play, a mix of old and new which she wouldn't be demonstrating or showing to anyone until the concert. She didn't want me to see it yet either.

"This is an ancient land. There are traditions here that took root millennia ago, which can still be found. This is a very exciting time. There are tradition bearers here carrying seeds of music going back to the original inhabitants of Newfoundland and Labrador and no one has ever collected it before."

This is where my interest was piqued – you can hear it in my voice in the recording. I asked if she was talking about Beothuk music. Almost all of the culture of Newfoundland's original people had been wiped out. The discovery of such a thing would be incredible, unimaginable even. So much so I began to think it was probably too good to be true and she'd been taken in by someone, with visions of lost culture paraded around to help some white guy's claim to indigenous ancestry. But when I mentioned the Beothuk, she just laughed at me.

She said the music had been collected from all over the province, mostly on the island, she gave me a list of places. I wanted more detail, but she said she had to save it for the concert. There's this part later, yeah, I pressed her on the Beothuk thing. That would be a hell of a hook for a story, but this is when the red flags started flying.

"It is so limiting to speak this way. People talk about the Beothuk because they like binary relationships, and the Beothuk are the most convenient. *They* are the indigenous people. *We* are European. They are older, and out of touch, and so we are oh so new and modern. They are gone so we have no guilt in claiming this place. It's such an infantile, facile way to view history. That isn't what the real story of this place tells us."

I wasn't sure what I had said here, but she was getting angry. Furious, but it might not have been directed at me.

"Do you know what happened to the Beothuk? They were wiped out. By starvation and disease almost before your English ancestors came to finish the job. But then what happened to the English? Cabot, who we pretend discovered this place, was lost with all hands. The man who claimed Newfoundland for England, Humphrey Gilbert? He tried to do so by stealing earth and breaking the limbs from a tree to take back across the ocean. He was drowned for it. A thousand years earlier, the Norse were forced to abandon their own scarring, parasitic colonies. Just a century before today, poverty and war crushed what independent government we had built here into dust. We have never been allowed to recover.

"There is a common theme, like a refrain repeating again and again with every new invasion, from the Tuniit and the Beothuk to the Irish, French, and English. This is the tradition that all our culture comes from. *That* is the true voice of Newfoundland. It thinks and feels, and it has thoughts and feelings about *us* that have been given voice. We can try and drown it out, but it's still there in the waves against rock, in the trees torn in the wind, and all through the stony silence of the barrens."

What fire there had been in her voice just a moment before had died. She looked as though she'd been struck by something, like she was in pain, or maybe remembering pain from an old wound. I wondered if she hadn't been trying to convince herself as much as me with that speech.

She gave her excuses and ended the interview, actually she apologized. I remember it clearly because it was so odd. As she was leaving, she turned and grabbed my jacket sleeve and just said she was sorry. She said it three times, just like that, "I'm sorry, I'm so sorry. I'm sorry." I thought after that she might have been embarrassed by her interview answers or something, but I'm not so sure.

At this point I still had a week before the show and a few days before my deadline. I wanted to beef up the story a bit and source up some of the details she had been cagey about. Again, understand, this wasn't a sting or anything, it was still just a pure entertainment, cultural interest piece. But I was curious. I had a hunch she had been taken in by someone in some kind of hoax, or maybe joined some environmentalist group and was trying to make a statement, but even if not some details and photos of some of the places she'd been would help the piece, so I hit the road.

There was nothing near town. None of the places she had listed anyway. I had five names to check out, and most of them were in central. I spent a day in Lewisporte, which was lovely, but only helpful in that no one there had heard of Charlotte Chen. Same with Springdale and Triton. I stopped in a few libraries and archives, the usual kind of spots. No sign-outs or requests, no one remembering her, nothing. If she'd been to these places, she wasn't getting her information from the regular sources.

One place that stood out on this list was a town called

Quarry, and by stood out I mean like an echo in an empty canyon stands out to underline the emptiness you're seeing there. I'd been all over, and Quarry wasn't a place that was familiar to me. That made sense after a quick web search for the place. Quarry had been abandoned since the 50s.

The province has a history of false starts. There are hundreds of ghost towns and resettled communities all over the place. In the last century alone, thousands of people moved around trying for a do-over somewhere else, either hauling their houses along with them or just upstakes and getting out of there. Whether the fishing dried up, or the road moved, or people just kinda left, it was a common story, and part of the local fabric as it were, with whole songs and paintings dedicated to the practice of failing and abandoning home to make a go of it somewhere else. Newfoundlanders are tenacious if nothing else, we're too stubborn to learn our lessons quickly.

All that is to say that Quarry being abandoned wasn't something that had made it stand out to me, it just made it weird to be on her list. The town was settled in the 1890s, a railroad town with, if you can believe it, a quarry. They paved Water Street in St. John's with their granite once upon a time, before that got paved over too.

Quarry was near Millertown Junction, north of Buchans. You had to hike in to get there, but I had time and at the very least, photos of abandoned houses always sell a good story here, that really says "local content" in Newfoundland and Labrador, a tumbledown abandonment.

And houses there were, or what was left of them. Quarry was not one of those romantic spots where the people had mounted homes on carts or rafts to float off to their new resting places. For one, of course, it was land locked. But this was definitely not a place anyone had felt too nostalgic for. A lot of these were company buildings or shacks without much use, all based on the same design, a copy of a copy of a copy. Then the old railway station, most of this ground into the earth from decades of neglect and the heavy snowfalls Gaff Topsails region is prone to.

There were a few wrecks left standing, or partly standing. Office buildings mostly. There was a place used to hold the cut stone that was only a skeleton of girders left. The red smear of rust. A short walk away was the quarry of Quarry, like a giant slab staircase going down into the earth, only now half filled with brown, brackish water left with nowhere to go. A pond that was never supposed to be there, cut into a scar in the earth.

I spent the day picking my way over piles of rotten wood that used to be shops and houses, peeking in on the few places I felt safe enough entering into. I wasn't the first to do so of course, there were the remains of a few old fires from hikers. Any one of those could have been Charlotte Chen, if she was even telling me the truth.

A likely spot was near what seemed like an office of some type. There were a few faded ledgers which had been certainly gone over, but nothing useful to be gained from those. I took some photos anyway.

I had a lunch with me, so I sat down and thought about what I was going to write about the place, or about Charlotte Chen, that would've been worth reading.

It was getting on, and I had thought to camp out but changed my mind and started back, leaving Quarry behind. I was still walking when the sun set, one of those incredible Newfoundland sunsets, all pinks and purples, lighting up the entire sky with just the black jagged teeth of the treetops to stop it, this silver aura sharpening them all as it goes. It was the kind of sunset I would stop everything to watch while I was at home, but out there it felt off, and I sped up my pace.

There was something about the light that made me feel intrusive, the leaden *thunk* of my feet and the ragged scratch of my breath, the counter-note of these and the voice of moving air through the trees around me. I was ruining it, making it profane. The sunset was no longer a vision of red and gold, it was a wound. The sky was stillborn, it was a bruised cesarean section, crushing hope with grief and loss with each new fall of my hiking boots. This wasn't a sunset meant to be seen. This wasn't a place I was welcome.

I just banged out something for the Chen piece, I don't even remember what. I didn't use any of the photos I'd taken, barely any of the interview either. There's a point when you're trying to break a story where you can get too invested in it, in the subject or even just in the way the language is coming together, trying to get the sentence structure perfect, that kills the prose and just gives you a massive case of anxiety.

That's what happened there. I just cranked out something useless and forgot about it until the day of the concert. We all had media passes to go. I didn't even want to at that point. But there's the story you write and the story you know yourself, with all the other accompanying lines you didn't put into print, and that's the one I still didn't have an end to. That's the one I wanted to put to bed, so that's why I went. That's why I ended up there with everyone else that night.

I remember the lights flicked and we all hushed, all the talking died down like it does. But it wasn't anything, so the din kind of rose again and fell. It's one of those situations where the noise is listening to itself: if it starts to quiet, it gets quieter, to see if anything is happening. If it gets loud, it gets louder. Like the audience is one animal, or maybe like how a flock of birds knows to move in the same direction.

I didn't notice Charlotte come on stage. I don't know if anyone back of the front row did, and I wasn't front row. I was off to the side, near the fire exit. Media seating. Anyway, if they noticed, no one stopped talking, and even the tech guys didn't seem to notice because they didn't bring down the house lights till a minute later, when the people in front started applauding. Chen hadn't even made a move. She was just waiting there for us, eyes downcast. She kept waiting while the applause started and then slowly moved like a rainstorm across the auditorium until gradually dying off altogether. By then the tech guy must have woken up because he dropped the lights until there was nothing but the spot, dead centre stage, on her.

When the house lights were finally gone, that's when she looked up and out over the audience. She couldn't have been able to see much, but she took her time. Remember this was supposed to be her presentation, a part of her degree, so we were all expecting… I don't know what we were expecting. Some explanation, I guess. Here's this piece, here's where I got it, something about the person who taught it to her. That wasn't forthcoming.

Instead, she just walked over to the metal table and snapped open the clasp on the violin case. I noticed then that it was an older case, beat up. It had the brown wear around the edges, like it was splintering into fiber. And it didn't match the violin at all, when she finally took it out. It was a rich, deep golden brown colour, practically brand new. The bow was definitely new, nothing remarkable that I can remember about it. What was different is the way it had been strung.

Like I said, she didn't say anything. She just carefully, too carefully it seemed, took the instrument out of its case. She stepped forward cradling it like an infant, like she thought she might drop it, but then looking out at us with this weird expression on her face, she just held it up by the top of the neck, I think to show us the strings.

A violin usually has four strings, though sometimes five or eight. But I couldn't tell how many this one had, because it looked like it was strung by a five-year-old. The strings were tight, but they were all over the place, criss-crossing and looping around in this bizarre network. It was weirdly familiar, reminding me of something, like a cat's cradle almost. I was squinting to see, but it almost looked like some merged as well, like she had split the strings and tied them off at different places along the neck. Something else – they weren't anything like regular strings like synthetic or gut or whatever. They were all frayed and delicate looking, like cobwebs. Kind of greenish, yellow cobwebs. It was a real mess.

There was a murmur through the place, and you could tell a lot of people had figured like I had, that there was no way she was going to get a sound out of that foolishness. But she just held there to let people react, take it in, get uncomfortable. Then in one motion she put the violin under her chin and drew the bow across it to give it a voice.

The sound was… it was rich and deep. You could feel it behind your nose as she began to play, slowly and with confidence, moving her body with the movement of the bow, back and forth. Each pass would strike several strings at once, creating a mix of notes and chords, counter-notes and even intentional dissonance between notes that shouldn't mix, but suddenly did. Like salt and caramel, or hard muscle under soft skin. The whole room was filled with the rise and fall of the piece, vibrant and slow, but steadily picking up pace, as though being pulled.

Back and forth, back and forth. It was a sad piece, but with sudden stops of anger as well. It made me think back to that sunset that I wasn't supposed to see. I thought about Nonasabasut, killed and left in the dirt. I thought about what she said about Sir Humphry Gilbert splintering off branches from a defenseless tree to make a point. The snap and crack of wood seemed to punctuate the smooth lines of sound coming from those bizarre strings.

That was when I recalled where I'd seen them before. They had been strung together like a network, with trunks and offshoots, almost like Gilbert's tree branch. But that wasn't it, so much as it resembled the network of blood vessels in a wrist, veins and arteries, growing like branches beneath the skin. A tree of blood, and immune system, and DNA. The original family tree. Back and forth, she drew her bow over a small section of circulatory system. It took me a long time to realize I'd been doing the same thing.

I think I became aware that the leg of my pants was wet, and I think maybe the first thing I thought was that I had sat in something. When I looked down it was hard to see, in the dark, but through the fog of the music in my head I could smell the meat-and-copper smell of blood.

Through the dim light from the stage, I could make out my right arm and it looked wrong. It felt like it had gone to sleep. I won't tell you what I had been doing to it, it was all a mess. But it… you know, it didn't hurt and... You won't understand, it just felt like the only logical thing to do. She was playing faster now. I worked faster too.

I don't know if I'm really remembering this, or if it's just what the police told me after. Memory has a way of just copying what you hear or imagine about something you saw and messing it up. But I recall something similar to the damage I was doing was happening throughout the theatre. A woman had leaned over and stuck her teeth into her husband's shoulder without either making a sound. People tearing and banging at themselves, and the music overlaying all of it. Whatever happened in the tech booth is what started the fire.

I remember thinking about Gilbert's tree branch over and over when I jammed my arm under the chair to get enough leverage to crack the bone. I needed to. Like something had to be done to pay it back, to make right what he'd done to this place. The music was so much darker now, it just emanated disgust and you could feel it, all that self-loathing. This is what we get, I was thinking, this is what we get.

I don't know how I got out. I saw the fire coming over

the people behind me, or what was left of them. I think it was just the instinct of decades of school fire drills that made me hit the emergency exit next to me and roll into the alley. The crews got there fast; I remember hearing the sirens almost immediately and wishing they would stop, because I couldn't hear the music anymore.

After that, I passed out from loss of blood and woke up here, my understanding is four days later. That was a month ago. I doubt they'll ever open the Reid again, what's left of it. Whatever the police found in there after the fire crews were done, they would barely tell me about it when they questioned me. They would barely look at me when they questioned me either, and I get it. Like I said, I have no idea how much time had passed before I noticed what I was doing to myself in there. I think a lot of time.

I asked the constable to be sure, but Charlotte Chen didn't make it out either, didn't even seem to try. She was found in what was left of the stage, the violin was incinerated. I hope whatever notes she left were incinerated with it. I'm not really concerned with her. What I'm afraid of is, she was right, is the problem. You could hear it, Jesus, I can still hear it sometimes.

If I ever walk again, and if I was you, I'd get the hell off this island. The frigging Vikings had this figured out better than we do. We're a damn stubborn people in Newfoundland, but sometimes you've got to take the hint. I think Chen heard the true voice of this place, and it *hates* us. Just for being here. Just for daring.

Peter J Foote

Peter J. Foote is a bestselling speculative fiction writer from Nova Scotia, Canada. He runs the FictionFirst Used Books, specializing in fantasy & sci-fi titles. He also cosplays with his wife, and alternates between red wine and coffee as the mood demands.

Many of Peter's stories are a reflection of his personal life, as he is a firm believer in the adage that a writer should write what they know.

Peter's work has twice been awarded the Kit Sora Flash Fiction Prize: once in March 2018 and again in September 2018. Peter holds the distinction of being one of only a handful of authors to be featured in all the modern From the Rock collections to date.

In total, Peter has been featured in over two dozen publications, with interest in his short fiction worldwide.

As the founder of the group "Genre Writers of Atlantic Canada," Peter believes that the writing community is stronger when it works together.

He brings with him two new stories, the science-fiction flash fiction 'Goddess of the Bloom' and 'Marshmallow Bridges.'

Marshmallow Bridges

"If you have your homework done, then you can come roast some marshmallows!" Nathan's mom calls up the stairs.

His bedroom door bangs open and Nathan races down the carpeted steps, hooking his arm around the banister as he swings into the den. Or at least it used to be his family's den before his grandfather moved in.

Scuffing his feet as he crossed the hardwood floor, he glances where his grandfather's bed and nightstand occupy his former gaming corner. Gone is the beat-up leather couch where his father and he would sit and read on rainy days; now is the home of a wooden rocking chair draped with a faded wool shawl. Even the room smells different. Gone is the familiar scent of microwave popcorn and his father's aftershave, replaced by citrus and old paper.

Nathan wipes his freshly wet eyes, turns away from the room where so many happy memories were born, and shuffles into the kitchen.

"Oh honey, were you crying again? Are you sad about Dad?" Nathan's mother asks as she busies herself at the kitchen counter. There are baking supplies strung along the countertop, a dusting of flour over everything, and a cartoon of eggs precariously near the counter's edge.

"I wasn't crying! I just don't like the smell in the den. He smells like an old person. Dad wouldn't have liked it either."

Sighing, Nathan's mother drops her ladle into the mixing bowl and a fresh plume of flour rises into the air. "Nathan, we've talked about this. Your grandfather isn't here to take the place of your dad; no one could do that. He also wouldn't have wanted us to be alone, and I don't want my father to be alone."

Tucking loose strands of hair behind her ear, leaving a smear of batter along her cheek, Nathan's mother walks around the kitchen island and kneels in front of her son. "When your dad and I got married, we agreed that we would stay in Canada where his family was. I've never regretted that – he and I met in school here, and it felt right that we made our lives here. But I've missed my family too, you know. It wasn't so bad when my dad was posted to the consulate in Vancouver, but when he was recalled to China, I was sad. And after my mom died, he was all alone in China with no one to look after him. Before your dad got sick, we were already talking about bringing your grandfather here to be closer to us. This was your dad's idea."

"It was?" Nathan asks, glancing into the dark den.

"Yup. So maybe give your grandfather a chance, okay? This living arrangement is all new to him, don't forget. He's used to being alone – and please call him Waigong. It would make him happy that you're trying to learn Mandarin."

"If you say so, Mom."

Giving her son a wink, Nathan's mom stands and returns to the kitchen counter. "The firepit is lit. Why don't you run out there and keep your grandfather company for a minute? Once this mooncake is in the oven, we'll roast some marshmallows. Deal?"

"Deal!" Nathan yells with a smile and dashes for the back door.

"Nathan, I don't want you wearing your good coat, there'll be sparks. Put on my yard coat."

"Okay, Mom," Nathan yells, pulling on the faded flannel coat hanging at the back door as he dashes out. The screen door bangs twice behind Nathan as he races to the burning fire pit in the backyard.

The rich aroma of burning leaves and hardwood fills the autumn evening, the acrid yet sweet smell creating a blanket protecting those from the cooler weather coming. Sparks from the fire fly skyward and mix with the stars, appearing for their nightly visit.

Nathan stops his mad dash to the fire as he gets closer to the stone firepit. The silhouette of his grandfather stark against the flickering flames. The young boy's footsteps change their course, leading him around the small man at the edge of the flames as he keeps his eyes fixed upon the old man sitting on the lawn chair, bundled up in wool blankets. Nathan dips his head and says, "Hi, Waigong," in a weak voice before moving to sit on the far side of the firepit.

"Waisun," the old man says. His hand leaves the warmth of the blanket, grabs a wooden cane, and taps the lawn beside his chair. "Please join me, Nathan."

Sighing, Nathan gets to his feet and settles down on the damp grass beside his grandfather. His mother arrives soon afterward, a loaded tray in her arms, and a smile on her face.

"What a lovely evening. We can have our own little Autumn Festival here at home. I'm not sure how my mooncakes will taste, I haven't made them in years. Bàba, here's your tea," Nathan's mother says as she passes the old man a steaming cup. His fingers cradle it as steam rises to mix with the smoke. "This is lovely, I'm so happy the entire family is now under one roof; don't you think so, Nathan?"

"If you say so, Mom," Nathan says and glances at his grandfather. The old man is taking a sip, his eyes reflect the flames as they stare at young Nathan.

"Nathan honey, you wanted to roast marshmallows, didn't you?" his mom says, holding up a bag of jumbo marshmallows, saved for the occasion.

Nathan's tribulations about the recent addition to the family dissolve when he hears the rustle of the plastic bag. He dashes to the woodpile to retrieve the roasting stick he sharpened earlier in the day.

Returning, Nathan plops down beside his mother, away from his grandfather, and busies himself with spearing a marshmallow on his stick. With steady hands, the young boy rotates the marshmallow at the edge of the flames, the smooth white surface getting a perfect amber tan. The only sound is distant traffic, birds roosting for the night, and the snap of the burning wood.

Satisfied, the young boy pulls his trophy from the fire and holds the perfectly toasted marshmallow up for his mother, the smile on his face full of pride.

"No thank you, Nathan; perhaps your grandpa would like it?"

Sighing, Nathan rises and with tiny steps walks around his mother and holds out the stick, the marshmallow on the end shaking. "Waigong, would you like a marshmallow? I'm pretty good at making them a toasty brown."

The old man places his cup of tea on the edge of the firepit and turns to face his grandson. Grasping the roasting stick from Nathan, the old man stares at his grandson, his eyes lost in shadow.

"Nathan, I want to tell you a story, one that my Waigong told me when I was young. It's about the god Pangu and his loneliness – something I've been thinking about a lot lately." With that, he shoves the marshmallow back into the flames.

"Hey! That one was perfect!" Nathan says, the hurt plain in his voice.

His grandfather speaks to himself in Mandarin, his voice low and far away as if recalling a memory long buried.

Confused, Nathan turns away from the flames, his marshmallow forgotten, and looks to his mom. She smiles and nods and places a hand on her son's back.

The old man's voice is soft, just above the crackle of the fire. His words take on the weight of history as he switches to English.

"There was nothing. Reality was barren. Then there was the Egg.

"Willed into being or a random manifestation of the universe desiring to fill a void, it doesn't matter; one does not examine the intention of the universe. All that matters is that the Egg became part of reality where before there was nothing.

"Simple and perfect, it floated through the desolate cosmos, its pristine shell un-caressed. It may have drifted for a single second or eons, for time had not begun to flow. The Egg sailed on top of existence, mute and cold, waiting for a beginning."

Uncertain what is going on, Nathan looks between the two adults and follows their eyes to the marshmallow in the flames. The coals of the fire glow red, and the waves of heat touch Nathan's face as he watches the marshmallow darken.

"Reality started time, and the Egg swayed back and forth within its sweep.

"Seized within the river of time, the Egg bobbed and tumbled through the desolate cosmos. The friction of time caressed its strong shell, and the warmth penetrated deep to that which occupied within."

The marshmallow on the end of the stick blisters, and burnt sugar tickles Nathan's nose.

"Gentle warmth rose to scorching heat as the river grew into a torrent, tossing the Egg fiercely through its desolation. Its perfect shell became scarred and pitted from the intensity, its contents thawed, stirred, and expanded. Captured within its shell, that which had been dormant since before time was time, woke and scrutinized its prison and strove to escape.

"Cracks appeared throughout the surface of a shell, no longer adequate to encompass the being within. Its occupant roused and battered its fists against the interior of the shell.

"At long last, the Egg broke wide into two portions.

"That which had been whole, divided. It was not graceful; it was painful as creation is wont to be.

"The two pieces of the shell strayed apart. One grew into the sky, the other empty earth; Pangu was born into a world of twilight and desolation."

The marshmallow's surface bubbles and catch fire. Ruined, Nathan's grandfather pulls the sugary treat from the flames and knocks it against the stones of the fire pit where it smolders. The flames flicker and die; the black mass smokes.

Looking between the two adults, Nathan sits down on the lawn with his back to the firepit. Drawing his knees up to his chest, Nathan's eyes watch the old man leaning forward in the lawn chair.

"Naked and pure, Pangu searched the earth in which he was delivered. No breeze stirred his hair, his skin felt neither warmth nor cold; the earth was a void and he was alone in it, with not even his shadow to keep him company.

"His mighty footprints fractured the sterile earth, leaving dust in his wake. His fingers skimmed the empty sky with no cloud or star there to show their journey. No matter how far he roamed, or high he reached, he could not evade the nothingness of his world.

"Time progressed, but without obstruction to give it shape.

"It didn't touch Pangu: his consistent stride never faltered and his body never tired, even though his spirit became weary with the loneliness.

"He was alive but alone."

The roasting stick slaps down hard, the charred remains of the marshmallow crumble into black dust. Nathan jumps, pulled his knees tighter to his chest, burying himself in his mother's coat.

"When at last no inch of the barren earth was without his footstep, Pangu stopped his solitary journey and turned to despair. What is the purpose of life if one is alone?

"His tears spilled freely from his right eye and streaked down his body. Pooling at his feet, the earth became shrouded with his salty tears. A boundless ocean of Pangu's sorrow filled the world."

Nathan sees moisture in his grandfather's eyes, the tears glowing in the firelight.

"Untouched by time but doomed to a solitary existence, Pangu cast free his immortal coil and wished himself dead. His last breath became the wind, his cry thunder which rocked the clear sky and made waves ripple across the tide.

"When his body crashed into the ocean, it shattered. A flawless piece of art destroyed never to be whole again. Each piece drifting away from each other, drifting upon the unbroken ocean, striking, reforming, and settling into the landmasses of the world.

"Pangu's left eye glowed with golden light, rose from the ruined remnants of his skull, and grew into the sun. The right, scarred and eroded by tears, became the moon and stars of the heavens. His blood rivers, muscle fertile soil, hair and bone, the plants and animals of the world. Each as unique as the being from which they sprang.

"Pangu, born of the Egg. His death created a complete world, never to be alone."

The old man finishes his story and lifts himself from his chair and kneels beside Nathan. He smiles, his teeth shine in the firelight and Nathan relaxes.

With a wink, the old man fishes a fresh marshmallow out of the bag, stabs it onto the roasting stick, and hands it back to his grandson. "You know, Nathan, I've thought a lot about Pangu's loneliness in the past couple of years… maybe it's time I think about what I'm going to leave behind. Now, why don't you show me again how to roast a proper marshmallow?"

Nathan's mother smiles at her son and places a gentle hand on her father's shoulder, which old fingers squeeze.

Nathan looks between his mother and grandpa, smiles, and starts roasting the perfect marshmallow, his grandfather at his side.

Goddess of the Bloom

"Why do we have to light these fires in the orchard, Grandpa?" Saila asks as she trails along behind the elderly man. The bundles of tinder in her arms block her vision, forcing the young girl to use the towering apple trees as guideposts in the darkening night. Doing her best not to let her feet get tangled up in the long grass of the orchard, Saila almost misses her grandfather's reply:

"I knew ya' wasn't listening, lass. We need to call the Goddess Pomona to our orchard to protect the fragile apple blooms from the spring frost," her grandpa replies, his gentle voice taking the sting out of his words as he shuffles through the orchard. "The moon is full, the skies are clear, and the bite of frost is in the air. And if we don't get these smudge fires laid, the Goddess won't visit the orchard and preserve the blossoms. No blossoms mean no apples in the fall."

A wizened hand, twisted due to a lifetime of manual labour, grabs Saila's shoulder, stopping the young girl. The pair have arrived at their destination. The rising full moon shines through the laden spring branches of the apple trees, the shadows creating a patchwork quilt of light upon the ground.

Saila shivers as her grandfather helps unburden her arms of the sticks and tinder. "Da says the Goddess isn't real, that she's just a made-up story the Romans brought here a long time ago. He says it's the smoke that protects the apple blossoms from the frost."

The old man kneels down beside a bare spot in the thick grass, his trousers absorbing the dampness. The soil is scorched from previous fires, a ring of baked earth the grass can't reclaim. He stacks the tinder with care, the full moon lighting his efforts.

Motioning his granddaughter to the ground beside him, he replies, "They're connected, Saila. The smoke is her invitation to the orchard, our way of letting her know we need her aid to protect the blooms. Your Da ached to look upon the Goddess as a young man. He sneaked out here more times than I could count and never succeeded. I think that's why he left the farm. He thought he wasn't worthy of her, it made him bitter. I tried explaining to him she doesn't come when we want her to, but when we need her."

Saila looks at her grandfather, his wrinkles capturing all the shadows of the night, his eyes shining in the moonlight. "Do you think I'll see her, Grandpa?"

"There, last year's raspberries canes, trimmings of apple and cherry, bound with grapevines on a bed of wet straw, just as my grandfather taught me." The old man lights the fire with a match and the tinder catches, fragrant smoke rising into the clear sky and creating a blanket over the blooming trees.

Letting his granddaughter help him rise, he pats her arm and answers with a smile: "Maybe, Saila. How about we wait together for a while and see?"

K.A. Mielke

K.A. Mielke in an Ontario native who has a gift for melding the strange with literary sensibilities. He is best known for his short fiction, which has appeared in nearly a dozen short fiction anthologies throughout the country since 2010.

Some of his best known work includes "Old as the Sun" from A Metazen Christmas (2010), "The Disastrous Disappointment of Dictatorship" from Off Topic Publishing (2017), and, "One Breakup to Rule Them All" from The Art of Breaking Up (2020).

In 2020 he published his first novel, Victory Lap, co-authored with Riley Alexis Wood. It is an own voices novel about taking the time to find yourself, even when the rest of the world screams for you to get a move on.

He brings with him his new story 'Clay,' a modern take on the mythology surrounding golems.

Clay

Toilet water swirled around him, flooding his nose and curling his hair like soft-serve ice cream, but Elijah maintained his dignity. There was minimal struggling or screaming. And there might have been a hint of pity in the laughter of the boys who had been washing their hands as Elijah was dragged to the stall.

As the water settled, Mike said, "We gather here today to witness the swirly of Elijah Samberg."

The toilet flushed again.

Gripping his legs and restrained his arms, they dipped Elijah in and out of the toilet bowl. Coach Wyndham would have been proud of their teamwork.

"Drink it!" someone shouted.

"Take it like a man!"

They laughed, and the toilet flushed, and Elijah breathed in the water. His nasal cavity caught fire.

He dipped in and out. In and out.

"Should've coughed up the money," Mike said. Even underwater, Elijah could tell it was Mike because he was the only kid with a voice so deep and commanding. If they hadn't grown up together, Elijah might have suspected him to be one of those cops who go undercover in schools. "It's almost like the stereotypes are true."

Elijah's wallet slipped out of his back pocket. He felt one set of arms release, plunging him deeper as the remaining boy wrangled both legs on his own.

A jerk upward, and Elijah dropped to the floor like a fish, wet and gasping. Mike loomed over him, flipping through the bills in Elijah's wallet. He pocketed the money and tossed the wallet onto Elijah's chest.

Elijah coughed. Water spurted out of his lungs and into his mouth. It tasted as sour as the smell of public washroom, and he felt nausea swirl in his gut like the flush of the toilet—and he puked. His throat raw, Elijah coughed until the water was gone, his fingers gripping the edge of the toilet bowl. Mike and his friends waited politely.

"This has been a waste of my time and yours." Hands on his hips like Superman, like he was doing The People's work, Mike said, "Next time I ask for your money, just gimme your money. It's not complicated."

Elijah coughed again in response, wiping a wobbling strand of saliva from his mouth.

Mike sighed as if disappointed. He turned to go, and his friends followed. The bathroom door swung shut.

"Are they gone?" came a voice from the stall beside him.

"Thuh-thuh-they're guh-gone," Elijah croaked.

In the next stall over, a pair of feet hit the floor.

The stall door swung open. Tetsuya was small, even smaller than Elijah. He had straight black hair and a missing tooth, which Elijah could see clearly because of his out-of-place smile. He seemed to notice Elijah staring, because he said, "It fell out yesterday, they didn't punch me or anything. My dentist isn't too worried because that was my last baby tooth. I guess I'm a man now!"

Elijah got up and went to the sink. His curly hair was flattened against his head, dripping water down his face and onto his soaked shoulders. His face was red from all the dignified drowning. He turned on the faucet and cupped water in his hands, swishing it in his mouth until the taste of toilet wasn't so prevalent.

Tetsuya stood behind him. Still smiling.

"You don't talk very much," he said.

"N-n-nuh-no," Elijah said.

"That's okay. My mom says I could talk to a wall forever if it didn't get up and walk away. And even then, I'd probably follow it. There are so many things to talk about with a wall. Like, does it get annoying having people lean on you all the time? And what do they think about No Loitering signs? I bet some walls like loitering because it's probably pretty lonely being a wall. Sometimes. It's lonely being a person, too, so I just figure."

Elijah spat in the sink again. Tetsuya handed him a paper towel.

"Are you going back to class?"

Elijah shook his head. "I-I duh-don't know. I'm puh-pretty w-w-w—"

"I have some extra shirts you can borrow, and a plastic bag! Do you prefer Godzilla or King Kong? Wait here!"

Before Elijah could reply, Tetsuya was gone.

Elijah and Tetsuya were not friends. Elijah wasn't actually sure either of them had any friends, and he suspected the boy was trapping him in a friend-contract of sorts. But Elijah would rather not go home in the cold, and then have to explain why to his mom. He could probably do worse than Tetsuya, who seemed, at the very least, cleanly. A huge improvement from when the aptly nicknamed Dirtbag tried to make his acquaintance.

So Elijah waited.

Mike was a big kid.

He was taller than the teachers, as thick as a tree, and as immovable as a brick wall. He kept his blond hair short. A spattering of pimples grew in a cluster on his forehead. And when he hit you, he hit harder than a freight train barrelling through the countryside.

Elijah was essentially Mike's opposite. He was shorter than most kids in the ninth grade, and he could barely throw a dodgeball across the gym. He had a larger than average nose and curly hair his mom forced him to cut twice a year.

His grandfather had shown him Nazi propaganda posters once. The Jewish men were cloaked in black, their expressions malicious. They held whips or keys. Every one of them looked like Gargamel from *The Smurfs*. Meanwhile, Hitler was depicted as a smiling, child-loving, benevolent ruler. "This is how the world looks to kids like Michael Gunther, tataleh," Grandpa had said. "It doesn't matter how many years pass, doesn't matter how 'progressive' society thinks it is, this is what you look like to Them. And there's only one thing that changes their minds: fear."

Elijah did not think he looked like Gargamel, but ever since he'd spent plenty of time in front of the mirror trying not to see himself through the lens of Michael Gunther.

Elijah's grandfather declined to elaborate on how, exactly, to make Mike afraid of him. He simply handed Elijah an old leather-bound book and told him to hide it until the time was right. And to never tell his mother.

The leather was cracked and rough, and smelled as his grandfather smelled, of a musty library. He smiled when Elijah cracked it open—he couldn't see much at that point, his eyes sealed shut with age, but his hearing was much better than Elijah thought normal for an ancient Holocaust survivor. The book held handwritten recipes of Great-Grandma's; grainy old photographs of strange stone buildings reclaimed by nature; sketches of what looked like bulky, misshapen men; and some Hebrew phrases which Elijah had difficulty reading.

It was unclear what needed hiding from Mom. Maybe she would have been upset that her father had never shared Great-Grandma's babka recipe. The why didn't matter. Elijah did as he was asked, hiding the book beneath a loose floorboard in his bedroom. Television taught him this was the safest place possible to hide secrets.

Grandfather passed on. Elijah's mother said he'd gone peacefully in his sleep, but Elijah could not imagine a way in which death could be peaceful. To die would be a terrible, frightening experience, no matter the cause.

Mike was the first to give his condolences. "Sorry your papa's going to Hell," he'd said, some real sadness buried in his usual cruelty. He smacked Elijah's back and lowered his voice to a whisper. "Though you guys kind of deserve it after, you know"—he gestured at the room—"everything."

It was nearing the end of December, and the classroom had been covered in tinsel. Gifts in reflective wrapping paper sat on their teacher's desk. Elijah did not see any representations of Jesus, but he didn't have to—never mind that Jesus was a Jew, too.

Elijah and his mother were not very religious. They even got a Christmas tree last year. Somehow, that was still too Jewish for Mike to handle.

"Thu-thanks f-f-for your kind w-wuh-wuh-wuh—"

Pitching his voice high and squeaky, Mike mocked, "Thank you for your kind wuh-wuh-wuh-wuh. Wuh-wuh-where are your balls, Elijah?" He shoved Elijah on his way to torment Dirtbag, and Elijah went back to quietly contemplating the inevitability of death, taking what time he had left to think before Mike sat behind him and started pulling individual "jewfro" hairs from his head.

That was a year ago. Not much had changed, just as not much had been different before. This was what Elijah's life looked like, with or without Zayde.

Until he opened up the floorboards, found within the leather book the tale of the Rabbi of Prague, and understood.

The classroom was empty. The unoccupied desks were always a strange sight, abandoned to the eerie silence of a room designed to make students feel like canned fish.

Mrs. Sprinkle, the ninth-grade art teacher, believed art was the ultimate form of therapy. When class resumed after winter break, she gave Elijah a key. "Any time you feel crummy, I want you to come here and create. Just clean up the mess afterward."

Any other adult would have referred him to the school counsellor or a therapist. Some already had, though he ducked into the library instead of going to his appointments. After that, his teachers mostly left him alone. Grief was a versatile excuse.

"Super cool," Tetsuya said when Elijah told him this, locking the door behind them. "And she just lets you use whatever you want? Even pastels?"

Unsure what was so impressive about pastels, Elijah nodded.

"Whoa. Super cool," he said again, at a loss for words for perhaps the first time.

Elijah set his backpack on his favourite desk—a quality he'd determined by sitting in every desk, making something, and judging which piece of art turned out the best. (It was two columns in and three rows up, for the record.) He took out Zayde's journal.

He'd spent the last month hanging out with Tetsuya and partnering with him during class assignments. Unlike with most of his work partners, Tetsuya did not expect Elijah to do all the work himself, and this endeared him to his new friend. They often ended up huddled together at lunch, watching old black and white monster movies on Tetsuya's phone. The only time they didn't hang out was when Elijah slipped away to continue his secret project, the single art piece he'd been working on since winter break ended.

Yesterday, when Tetsuya asked for perhaps the millionth time where he went every day, Elijah relented.

Now, Tetsuya was opening every drawer and cupboard and marvelling at the sheer volume of the art supplies, the scope of the things he could create. Elijah did not know if Tetsuya was any good at art, but as he himself was decidedly bad at it, it probably didn't matter.

"Check out all the Play-Doh! We could make so many

worms. One time my cousin made me a Play-Doh burger and told me to eat it. And then when I did, she made me fries and an apple pie to go with it. I was puking rainbows for hours. My parents were so mad."

Elijah laughed. "D-do you wuh-want to see s-s-s-something?" he asked. Spitting a little, he wiped his mouth, embarrassed.

"Duh."

Elijah went to the closet at the far corner from the room's entrance, his heartbeat picking up speed and pounding in his temples, and he opened the door. He stood back, letting Tetsuya grasp the project's sheer volume and scope.

"What is it?" Tetsuya whispered, his eyes wide.

And Elijah told him.

Elijah and Tetsuya spent every break in the art room, adding Play-Doh to the hulking sculpture in the closet.

"My favourite monsters are the ones that help people," Tetsuya said. "Marrying humans doesn't count. Godzilla sequels are way cooler than the original, once he starts saving the world, you know? Less stompy-stompy, smashy-smashy. Maybe that makes them less of a monster. What is a monster, really? We just make up bad names for the things we're afraid of, to make everybody else afraid of them. Monsters might be nice or smart, but because they look weird, or because there are one or two bad apples or whatever, we think they're all evil."

Elijah nodded. "Thuh-this wuh-one isn't ee-evil. Juh-just obedient. Like a dog."

"But it does kill people."

"Dogs can k-kill puh-puh-people."

Tetsuya opened his mouth to argue. Then he shut it and added another lump of orange Play-Doh to the multicoloured monster in the closet, massaging the edges until they blended near-seamlessly into the purples and the reds and the greens of its barrel chest.

"Would you like anything else to eat?" Elijah's mother asked as she took another slice of pizza for herself. Elijah had worried that the kosher pizza place they ordered from would be strange to Tetsuya, but if he missed whatever ingredients he usually ordered, he didn't let on.

"No, thank you, Mrs. Samberg. I'm stuffed." He patted his slightly bloated stomach.

"How about a beverage? We have some soda in the fridge, and more loose-leaf tea than I know what to do with."

Smiling politely, he said, "Water is fine, thank you. Soda gives me very painful gas, so my mom says I'm not allowed. If it were up to me, I would gladly spend an hour or two doubled over and crying just for the taste of a Coke, but Mom's the boss."

Elijah's mother tossed Elijah a wide-eyed, thin-lipped look that said he wasn't wrong about Tetsuya's tendency to overshare. Or maybe that was just how Elijah, terminal under-sharer, interpreted it. He looked down at his empty plate, wiped greasy fingers on his cloth napkin, and asked, "May wuh-we be excused?"

"Is your room clean?"

"Mmhm."

"Go for it. Leave the dishes, go have fun. When is

your mother coming to pick you up, Tetsuya?"

"Eight, if that's all right, Mrs. Samberg."

"Fine by me, bucko. Have fun. No horse-wrestling."

She meant horsing around. Or rough housing. Or wrestling. It was hard to tell. Instead of explaining this, Elijah led Tetsuya upstairs.

Pausing on the top step, Tetsuya pointed at a photograph on the wall. "Aw, is this you? You're so cute. Like a small woodland creature."

Tetsuya reached out and pinched Elijah's cheek. Elijah swatted at his hand with a timid smile. "Wuh-wuh-what h-happened, right?"

He was smiling in the photo, a stupid kid with no idea how bad things could get. His dad was still here—there, rather—and his grandfather, too. His mom didn't have the dark bags and the tired, glossy look in her eyes that she had now; she looked happy in a way that was hard to fake, obvious in the crinkles and folds brought forth by her smile. They were all happy.

Things got harder after Dad left. Zayde died. Mom kept going because she had few other options. And this photo stayed the same, mocking the bad times with memories of the good ones.

"Come on," Elijah said, leading the rest of the way to his room.

It may have been a small fib to say that his room was entirely clean. Elijah hastily kicked aside a couple floor t-shirts and swept some crumpled tissues into the trash. Tetsuya immediately fluttered from bookcase to shelf to entertainment centre, looking at all the things Elijah owned (and even pulling out some things he'd forgotten he owned.) Hands in his pockets, Elijah watched him, aware of every stiff movement his body made while he stood there awkwardly. He'd never had someone who wasn't family in his room before. It was an invasion of privacy and boundaries and overall comfort.

But it was kind of nice, too.

Tetsuya set up the monster movie he'd brought over on his USB stick, *Creature from the Black Lagoon*, and flopped down on Elijah's bed, crumpling the finely flattened *Star Wars* bedspread. As stiff and lifelike as a robot, Elijah sat down at the other end of his bed. They were silent for a while. The movie opened, the scientists found the ancient fossilized arm of the Gill-Man, and Elijah watched Tetsuya watching the movie. He tried not to breathe or swallow too loud.

"I've gotta be honest with you," Tetsuya said eventually. "I kind of don't think it'll even work."

Elijah watched Tetsuya's chest rise and fall with his breathing, like a ship on the ocean. "D-do you mean—?"

"If it does, we'll obviously be big darn heroes for giving Mike a taste of his own medicine, but it feels too easy. Not that building a monster and bringing it to life actually is easy, but if there's one thing fantasy novels have taught me, it's that magic always comes with a price. And if it doesn't work… I dunno. I don't regret it. Spending all that time with you in the art room was fun. I wouldn't trade it for the world."

Elijah's heart pounded, but he wasn't sure why. Did he find Tetsuya's lack of faith upsetting? Or was it something else?

"Can I tell you a secret?" Tetsuya asked, his voice dropping to a whisper. Elijah lay down, then, leaning on his elbow, and he nodded.

"Elijah, I like you, okay?" He inched closer. "Like, I *like* like you. I have for a while now, probably since I saw you freshly swirlied and sopping wet and I've kept it inside"—he tapped his chest—"because I know you're scared easily. You don't like people very much. You don't let people in… But you let me in. I was hoping, you know, that meant something. Something more."

Elijah looked away from Tetsuya. His breath came in short bursts, like he was hiding under a blanket and using up all the oxygen. He said nothing.

"Is it okay if I kiss you? You can say no if you don't want to, I'll understand. I have a couple problems with, um, social cues, so..."

Feeling entirely incapable of words, Elijah nodded again.

And, eyes open, breath still smelling of cheese and tomato sauce, Tetsuya kissed him.

Shocked, Elijah sat as still as their sculpture in the art room. He'd never been kissed before. To be perfectly honest, he'd never even considered acquiring the skill. Warmth flared in his stomach and spread out through his limbs. His lap experienced a series of new sensations he didn't want to think about. Tetsuya's hands reached for Elijah's face, brushing his cheeks, running through his hair.

Elijah closed his eyes. He melted into the boy's kiss, and he even kissed back.

As the snow melted to reveal mud and dead grass and the days grew longer, the boys finished the project. It didn't matter much by then, because the closer Elijah and Tetsuya grew, the less the sculpture felt like work. Even

Mike's usual harassment felt more like something they could overcome together.

Something they would finally overcome today, G-d willing.

The last touch, of course, was carving the Word into the monster's head: emeth. Roughly translated from Hebrew to English, it meant Truth. Tetsuya gingerly placed the carving tool into Elijah's palm and stepped back. Elijah stood on his tiptoes and reached all the way to the monster's forehead. Its Play-Doh flesh sunk beneath his tool, the words forming trenches in its face.

He snapped Grandfather's book shut. He stepped back beside Tetsuya and held his hand.

They waited.

"Cuh-cuh-come to life," Elijah said, lowering his voice to sound more adult, more like how he imagined ancient rabbis spoke. "Arise."

They waited some more. Elijah flipped open his grandfather's notebook to see if they'd missed a step, or if it was supposed to be like how a watched pot never boils.

"We could try the shem thing?" Tetsuya offered. "Does the scroll have to be, like papyrus or something, or can we just use construction paper?"

"I duh-duh-duh—"

"Duh duh duh," mocked a voice behind them. "Dummy, more like. What are you losers doing in here?"

Even knowing Mike would come, Elijah struggled to compose himself. He and Tetsuya had done all they could to drop tantalizing hints throughout the morning, talking too loudly about their "secret project" in the art room, talking about skipping lunch, and saving their lunch money, to work on it. Leaving the door unlocked.

Mike stepped inside the room, locking the door behind him. "Holy crap, is that supposed to be me? Are you in love with me? Because that's disgusting." His eyes darted to their hands, and a smile slashed across his face. "Why don't you tell me what this thing is before I beat it out of you."

"It's a golem," Elijah said clearly. These days, the term "golem" meant dumb. A word used singularly to describe someone big, intimidating, and brainless. So, in a way, Mike was a golem, and the golem was like Mike. Two big idiots. "I-it's here to kuh-kill you."

Mike laughed. "How's your gay art project going to kill me?"

Elijah didn't have the answer to that question. He'd hoped it would have been obvious by now, but after months of work it looked like the project would culminate in the standard beat-down. His heart sunk a little as his meager muscles tensed, readying themselves to futilely defend his internal organs.

A hand squeezed his, reminding him that Tetsuya was still there. That he wasn't in this alone. "It's okay." He smiled nervously. "Maybe it's better this way. I was starting to worry about what would happen if the monster really did kill Mike."

Elijah shook his head. He'd wondered, but he didn't worry. He fantasized. He dreamed about the golem wrapping its hands around Mike's tree trunk neck and squeezing until Mike stopped struggling. Mike deserved whatever he had coming to him. It was time somebody put a stop to him entirely. Wasn't that the point? Even if the golem didn't work, wasn't Elijah still full of rage? Wasn't Mike still a bad person? Nothing would change. If anything, he'd only be angrier by the end of the day, as he nursed his swollen body back to health.

Mike made a show of punching his own palm as he approached them. "I hope you feel like a big man after threatening me. Think about this moment when you have to drink your meals through a straw."

Tetsuya cowered. Mike took one, two, three big steps, and cocked back his fist. Elijah squeezed his eyes shut and waited for the punch to land.

There was a fleshy thump. Mike screamed. Desks and chairs screeched and scattered across the linoleum floor.

Elijah opened his eyes as the floor rumbled beneath him, and the golem took its first step. His heart fluttered as fast and hard as it had when Tetsuya kissed him, filling his body with a wholly unexpected joy. He'd done it. They had done it. Thank G-d.

The golem sprayed flakes of dried Play-Doh when it moved, shedding its outer layer of skin to reveal the more fluid layer underneath. Its body was made of every colour available to them, creating a psychedelic, kaleidoscopic effect when it moved and flexed and breathed, constantly in motion. Like a person.

Alive.

It cocked back its fist and Mike scrambled to his feet and it hit him again, launching him across the room. He landed hip-first on Mrs. Sprinkle's desk and flipped over onto the floor, out of sight.

The golem pursued him.

Elijah could see now how HaShem created Man of earth, dust, and clay. Men were fragile, delicate creatures, easily crushed by the hand of something larger. It was Man's folly that he seldom imagined a hand larger than his own.

Mike, like Man, thought he was invincible.

He would regret his foolishness.

Turning to Tetsuya, Elijah expected him to share the same surprise and glee and pride roiling within himself, expected to see it all over Tetsuya's face. What he saw instead disappointed him.

"We shouldn't have done this," Tetsuya said, eyes wide with horror.

"Thuh-this is wuh-wuh-wuh-what we wuh-wanted," Elijah hissed, barely able to keep the rage out of his voice. How could Tetsuya back out once they'd finally breathed life into their creation? "We did it. We created luh-luh-life! G-d guh-granted us His power!"

The golem took Mrs. Sprinkle's desk in its meaty hands and tossed it into the wall. Mike was curled up with his knees against his chest, convulsing with fear.

The doorknob shook. Somebody banged on the door, their silhouette in the window.

But nobody was going to save Mike.

"It's going to kill him," Tetsuya muttered.

"I know!" Elijah shouted. "H-he's going to die eventually! We a-a-all are! Why not muh-make his death a-a-as painful as p-puh-possible?"

Mike screamed for help as he was lifted off his feet and forced through the ceiling, knocking the loose square ceiling tiles out of place. He looked for Elijah. For mercy.

A smile parted Elijah's lips. Warmth built up inside him. His skin tingled.

It was everything he'd imagined.

"We have to help him," Tetsuya said.

"N-nuh-no, we don't."

"How can you say that?"

"Muh-Mike is an asshole! This is justice!"

"That doesn't mean he deserves to die! Elijah, please. Do it for me." Tetsuya stepped away from Elijah, eyes welling with tears. "Even if you don't believe he should be spared. We can't be murderers."

"Thuh-this isn't murder," Elijah said. After all, the Torah did not abide by murder. But that was only one specific way to kill a man. "This is wuh-war."

"It doesn't matter what we call it. Right now, we're the monsters, not that thing. Not Mike."

"Yuh-you want to s-s-stop it? Thuh-then do it yourself."

They stood apart from each other and said nothing, only breathing, only seething, only waiting. Then, Tetsuya nodded.

He ran. His shoulder sunk into the creature's faux-flesh, but it did nothing. The golem merely whipped around and swatted Tetsuya away like a bug. The boy crumpled to the floor and did not get up.

Elijah's chest hurt. His stomach twisted into nauseated knots. He didn't care about Mike, but this stopped being about Mike the moment Tetsuya's lips touched his.

Elijah had made a mistake.

He snatched the carving tool from the desk.

"STOP!" Elijah cried, holding up his hands and rushing to the golem. With one hand, the man of Play-Doh squeezed the life out of Mike, whose face had turned blue. The other hand pulled back in anticipation of the finishing blow. "STUH-STOP, DAMMIT!"

Elijah climbed atop the desk. The golem's empty eye sockets stared into Mike's bloodshot eyes as he wheezed for mercy. A small part of Elijah couldn't believe he was about to save Mike's life.

But a larger part of him, a part now occupied by Tetsuya, urged him to hurry.

Blinking back tears, Elijah crossed out the first letter on the golem's forehead. Now, it didn't say Truth.

It said Dead.

Its fist launched toward Mike in defiance, clipping Elijah in the shoulder and whirling him around. The floor rushed toward him, the impact stealing his breath.

The golem slowed. Its motions became less fluid, less human, its great swinging arm shuddering and jerking to a hard-fought stop at the tip of Mike's running nose. A crack formed in its wrist, and its fist shattered on the floor. Its arm followed, and its leg, and the golem fell to the ground like a tower demolished, in tragic pieces and parts, collapsing under its own weight until all that remained were the scattered pieces and the dust that puffed up in clouds and made Elijah cough through burning lungs.

Mike burst from a pile of disintegrated Play-Doh hand-first, like a zombie from a grave, but Elijah ignored him. He rushed to Tetsuya's side, dropping to the floor and skidding on his knees. He put Tetsuya's head in his lap and pet his hair and prayed to G-d that he was okay.

A snap of wood gave way to brute force, a lock failing to do its job for one moment longer, and the door flung inward. Teachers flooded inside as if from a tap and asked a million questions. Elijah said nothing. He barely heard them.

"—tried to kill me—" Mike blubbered.

Students waited in the hallway, barred from entering by unspoken rules and common courtesy. Elijah lowered his lips onto Tetsuya's, neither knowing nor caring how the faculty would feel about such a flagrant disrespect for the school's intimacy policies. If monsters were real, if he could bring a golem to life, then surely he could wake Tetsuya up with a kiss.

His classmates gasped. Hands roughly grabbed him under the arms—but he wrapped his arms around Tetsuya and held his face against the boy's, and he resisted.

The hands left him alone.

Tears tickled as they dripped from the end of his nose. Elijah looked down through bleary eyes at the ashen face of the boy he probably, maybe, definitely loved. He couldn't—wouldn't—go anywhere until Tetsuya woke up.

Fingers curled around Elijah's hand and squeezed.

Tetsuya coughed, softly at first, then a deep, long smoker's cough. Hacking up the dust and the secrets kept between them. When he caught his breath, he opened his eyes and said, "You stopped it."

"I-I did. I-I didn't want to buh-be a m-m-monster if it muh-meant losing you."

Tetsuya smiled despite everything, flashing his incomplete set of teeth, and said, "Let's take a break from art for a while. Maybe take up a sport or something."

Elijah helped Tetsuya to his feet. His knees wobbled as they limped, hand in hand, to the nurse's office. The crowd parted for them, silent but for Dirtbag's slow-clapping and the terrible, frightened sobs of Michael Gunther.

Amanda Evans

Amanda Evans has a long history of writing and publishing genre fiction. Her short fiction includes *The Girl in the Summer Dress, The Polite Neighbor,* and *Fresh Baked History,* to name a few. She is one of the founders of Partridge Island Publishing, a small press devoted to publishing the viewpoints of Atlantic Canadians. In April 2020 she won the Kit Sora Flash Fiction Award with her short story 'Red, Blue, Green, and Yellow.'

She brings with her her story, 'The Feast of the Seas.'

The Feast of the Sea

"It is said that in the beginning, there was the sky and there was the sea. Eventually, the god of each wanted more. They wanted a place where the sea and the sky could meet, so they created a rock that floated on the sea and reached up to the sky.

"The two gods met on this rock and took a form most pleasing to them. The deities were happy on this land that they made. So happy were the gods with their creation that they started making more. First grass, then trees, flowers, and all forms of nature, but there was still an urge to do more, so they created animals. Creatures of the land that needed both air and water to live and so came about the animals that roam the land.

"For a long time, they were happy, surrounded by nature and the animals. But eventually, the need to create struck again. They wanted a creature that could look upon what was done and praise them for it. So together, they spent a very long time creating a being in their own image. Humanity was born. It was as they had both envisioned. But for all humanity's greatness, it was perhaps their weakest creation.

"During a warm day, one of the slow-moving humans was not able to get all the way to the edge of the rock to get water, and he died. The God of the Sea was so deeply wounded by this

human's passing, that he created pools of water on the rock so that no human would have to go too far to find water again.

"The God of the Sky did not like this deviation from their original agreement and the God of the Sky left. The Sky God knew enough now to be able to create on her own. She created other large rocks, covering them with plants and animals, and she watched them from above. It was not enough. Having lived so long with another nearby, she could not stand the quiet of the sky by herself, so she created creatures that were made only of air and earth.

"The God of the Sea became enraged at that. He took himself back to the sea and there he created his own world and his own creatures that were made of water and earth.

"Though both left the rock, both missed it. That rock was the pinnacle of happiness for them. They abandoned their children to fend for themselves. It did not take long for humans to learn that without the gods' help, they were not able to take care of themselves.

"Eventually, they realized no amount of prayer would bring the gods back, so they prayed to the animals: the gods' first children, gifted beyond what the humans were given. Through their prayers, some of the animals began to speak with them, to teach them and to share their gifts with them.

"The Gila monster taught them preservation and survival, the bear taught them courage, the raccoon taught them resourcefulness, and so on. Now every year, we have this festival in honour of the animals and the gods."

The old man told the tale to all the youths that sat around his chair. From the very youngest hearing this tale for the first time to the older children enjoying the story, it was his joy to teach them.

"Did all that really happen?" thirteen-year-old Somma asked. He was a smart lad that the entire community had great hopes for. Young as he was, he showed the owl's intelligence, and it was their hope that Somma would one day become their greatest soothsayer.

"It is the story that has been told to us, and one you will tell to your children in time," the elder said with a smile. He loved children and found that spending time with them kept his spirit young, even when they asked questions, for few adults questioned anything.

"If it is true, then why do we still pray to the Sea and the Sky?" Somma pushed. "Did they not abandon us because of their jealousy?"

"That may be true," Arikcha replied, "but it does not hurt to give credit where credit is due."

"What you say may be true, soothsayer, but I do not think that I will give thanks to those that abandoned us." The boy rose gracefully and turned to walk out of the building. A number of the youths Somma's age peeled themselves away and followed him.

Arikcha watched them walk away but could not stop them. They were getting to an age where they had to start thinking for themselves, for good or for ill. There was a pain in his head and his heart for them. To take his mind off of the unpleasantness, he turned to the rest of the room. "Who would like to hear another story?" he asked. Laughter and cheers met his words.

Somma had not gotten far from the soothsayer's building when his friends, Bidzil, Chaska, and Khickhim, caught up to him. "You did not have to follow me," Somma told his closest friends. "I do not think that I will be going back to the soothsayer's this festival."

Khickhim was the first to reply. "I think we may be getting too old for those stories as well," she replied, though in her heart, she did not feel that way. These stories were her stories, and although storytelling was a frequent occurrence, having the oldest of the soothsayers speak happened only at the festival, and he could make the stories come alive as no one else could.

"Thank you, my friends." Somma said, feeling warmth in his heart. "I just feel angry that the gods could leave us like that."

"You do have a way of looking at things as no one else does," Bidzil said with a smile. He was a burly boy, looking more like a man than a youth, and of their generation, he had the most in common with the bear.

Somma led them down along the trail towards the water's edge. The day was dying, and those that had taken part in the water contests were just packing up before it became too cold. Somma saw his father coming from the beach. His hair was wet, and he was smiling. "You missed seeing me catch the biggest fish!" he yelled.

Ziibiin was part of the water and often compared to an otter. He had yet to ever lose a contest in the sea. "I knew that you would win," Somma told his father. "I have a question for you, Father."

With these solemn words, his father stopped smiling, and Somma's friends dispersed to give space to the family. "Father, why do we give thanks and prayers to the Gods of the Sea and the Sky when they abandoned humanity?"

Ziibiin had never thought of it that way. You gave the

gods praise and respect because they were gods. Everything else paled compared to that, but his son was wise for his years and could not be given such an answer. "I don't know," he told his son. "We have always done it. I believe that it appeases the gods," he answered as best he could.

"But if they have ignored us, then why would they take notice of something we do not do?" Somma pushed.

"Gods are like us, son, they want to be praised for what they did, even if it was a long time ago. That is all that I can tell you," Ziibiin replied. "Is that enough?"

"Thank you, Father," Somma answered respectfully. It was not what he wanted to know, but it was as much as he was going to get. His father was many things, but he was not the wisest of the men.

As Somma stepped around him to go to the beach where his friends waited, Ziibiin patted his shoulder and continued on his way again as well. He did not pick up the smile he had worn previously. There were many thoughts in his head that had never occurred to him before. Why did they worship the gods that did not care? The thought was planted now, and he could not get it out of his mind. He would take it to some of the elders to see if they had an answer for him. If they did not, he did not think that he could worship the gods as fully as he once had.

"Did you get the answers you were looking for?" Khickhim asked.

"No, he does not know why we worship either." He blew out a breath of frustration. "I do not know who else to ask." He sighed. It was the soothsayers' job to soothe these questions and feelings, but they had been the ones to birth them.

"Maybe we will think better after we have eaten?" Chaska jumped in with the suggestion. It brought an amused smile to Somma's face. Chaska was a good lad, neither as smart as Somma nor as strong as Bidzil, and it was often joked that his great strength was in his appetite.

The quartet walked along the beach for many minutes while Somma thought and the others talked amongst themselves. He could hear them questioning many things, and he felt bad that he was the cause of their confusion, but it was not in his nature to not speak when he felt he had to.

They made their way towards the main festival, and they could hear the music and smell the food. Though there was food for them to eat now, the true feast would start once it was fully dark. They would give their praise and gifts when the sun touched the land and then the meat would cook while dancers showed their praise with their beautiful dances. In the main clearing, Somma again saw his father. The older man was wearing different clothes now, dry clothes. Somma could see him talking to the elders; the gestures he made towards the sea and the sky told him what his father was talking about, while around his father heads nodded.

"Your father is trying to find answers for you," Khickhim said to Somma.

"I see that. He is a good father." Somma replied with a smile.

Chaska darted towards one of the many mostly emptied platters of quick foods around them. It was cheese and bread with small bits of meat flakes rolled in it. It was filling, and if it were anyone but Chaska, there would be worried that he would ruin his appetite.

The four youths stopped when people waved at them, and to those people, they would press the question. By the time that the sun was coming level with the land, the youths had no more answers, but many in the crowd had questions.

The beating of the drums summoned people from all over the village towards the ceremony totems. They were smaller than the regular ones: these ones were dedicated to only one god, and they were painted in great and loving detail. Each new soothsayer was required to add a touch to each of these totems before they could lead their first story circle.

They were spaced well away from each other so that many people could give their offerings and prayers to the god they represented at once. Somma took himself through the forest of totems. He gave prayers and tokens to each of the animals' spirits that guided and watched over his people, but when he got to the two larger totems, he walked away, keeping the black and white stone he had been polishing for months stored in the bottom of his pouch.

He noticed, watching the crowds when he had finished, that the two Great Gods were getting a significantly less praise than the animal gods.

Somma was not pleased by this, but he was not angered by it either. People were thinking, choosing. They were not being led by tradition, and that was important to the youth.

When the last person finished going through the totems, the drums beat again. In the circle made by the totems, the dancers started stepping forward. There was a roar like the waves hitting the beaches in a squall and then a man stood in the centre. He looked like them, but not at all like them. He wore clothes of changing blue and his skin was the colour of seafoam, with blue-grey hair that rolled past his shoulders. He stood still though everything about him moved.

"I am the God of the Sea," he said with clear words that carried though he did not yell. "I created you and all the animals you worship, yet you worship me least of all!" The words were so loud they hurt. No one could reply, even the youngest of the children could not begin to bawl in the arms of their mothers. "What do you have to say for yourself?"

Somma felt his feet moving. "I have to say that we have not seen your presence or felt your touch in many generations, God of the Sea."

"You presume to tell me how a god should act?" he asked, looking at the boy before him. "You who does not know what I do for humanity!"

Somma looked at the god. The god's anger made him easier to speak with; somehow it made him more human than the wise owl or the strong bear. "How would a child that has never met their parent know what their parent does for them?" he asked calmly.

The god was fuming, and in the gloaming light, he looked at the entire gathering of the people, descendants of those he and the Sky had created. "I shall show you what it is that I do. How it is I help you," he said, and every person, no matter how near or far, could hear him clearly. "I will remove my protection from the rock, and you will be punished." With those words, He was gone and a cold, salty fog rolled out, dousing the fires.

There was a tremor through the land. Many of the people looked at each other and then ran to the beach. Somma and the others devoted to the wise Owl remained. They lit the fires, took torches, and then they followed the rest of the village to the shore.

The torches were not needed to see what caused the shaking, but they did provide heat and familiarity and made the trek to the beach less treacherous.

In the water, an hour's swim out, craggy finger-like spears reached for the sky. Ziibiin, farther down on the beach, stripped down and leaped into the water. He swam faster than anyone had ever seen a man swim before. Still, it took him many minutes to reach the dark looming obelisks. He went underwater.

Somma counted the seconds, worrying when his father took longer to resurface than he ever had before. "Will he be alright?" the boy asked with fear.

"If it were anyone but Ziibiin, I would worry," the soothsayer Arikcha replied. "But Ziibiin is the blessed of the Otter. He will be fine."

As if the words were the key, Ziibiin resurfaced much closer to the shore then when he went under. He did not look unfazed, but he did look determined. The crowd watched in silence as he swam slowly back.

He was greeted at the shore with warm blankets. In his hand was a large red-looking bramble as thick as his wrist and a thick looking vine that moved like an eel. "What are those?" Arikcha asked, walking slowly towards the wet man.

"They are at the base of the thin mountains," Ziibiin told the old soothsayer. "The grass," he said, pulling up the eel-like sample; "it grabs and wraps around anything light. Without the help of the otter god, I would have died." He dropped the eel-like plant and it wiggled on its own on the sand. Concern bloomed on faces at his words. "The red bramble is sharp and will destroy the ships that rest below the water." He dropped the piece of red bramble rather than passing it to the waiting-woman. His hand was sheeted in blood. "It is sharp and rough," he warned.

"That will prevent ships from getting in or out," Megis said. She sailed one of the boats that traveled between the islands to exchange resources.

"It will," Ziibiin agreed.

"We must discuss the situation," Asiniig, the chief, said, stepping beside his wife. Some murmurs raced through the crowd. It was a festival day. It was bad luck to do anything but celebrate and give thanks today. But this something that had never happened before, and tradition could not reign supreme.

Somma struck out first. He was the cause; he would lead the charge. The rest of the crowd followed behind him. Arikcha and Ziibiin were last: Arikcha because of his age and Ziibiin because he stopped to pick up the bramble and the plant with his hands wrapped protectively in a blanket.

The building they had used for the soothsayers' tales was back to its usual purpose, the village hall. Around the room, everyone sat; only the babe-in-arms were missing, being put to bed in the nursery, and one of the older soothsayers that was watching the children.

Asiniig took his seat when everyone else had found a spot. The room was full, and many of the children sat on the floor to give their seats to the more elderly. The chair Asiniig sat in was beside a young girl. She was pale and crying. She was also blessed by the wise owl, but she was too timid by far.

"We have heard the words of the great God of the Sea," Arikcha opened the floor. "We have seen the punishment he has set upon us. What shall we do?"

"Why must we do anything?" the scared girl beside Asiniig asked. "Can we not just keep to ourselves? Treat this as a protection, not a punishment?"

Her words were met with some nods of agreement.

"Will we have enough food?" an older woman, one of those that watched the very young children during the day, asked.

"We will have enough to stay alive," Asiniig told them, "but no access to many things we have grown accustomed to."

"I bring back metals, tools, clothes, and sweets when I sail to the other islands," Megis told them. They were not necessities, but she thought it would be good to let them know the luxuries that they would lose.

Much of the night passed with suggestions and objections flowing around the room like water. As the hours passed, some people left, too tired to stay awake after the day's activity, while some slept in their chairs unwilling to leave the discussion yet unable to stay awake.

Finally, Somma stood. He looked at everyone. "We will have to wait and see what happens. We cannot form a plan until we know more." His words were strong for one so young. Though everyone knew that it was he that had first questioned the gods, they did not pin the blame on him alone.

For the next month, every way that could be thought of to get a boat past the ring was tried. Many boats were lost both inside the ring and outside, but so far, no human had died to the trap.

The weeks rolled from spring into summer, and the work of those on the rock became hectic. Tempers flared as easy tasks became hard as equipment failed. People worked late into the night repairing what usually would have been replaced or sent to a specialist. By the harvest, they had grown even more agitated. The goods that they traded had piled up. The food was processed for the winter, but much of it would not last until next spring, and there was a chance that many people would starve.

They had gathered every man, woman, and child to the open field that housed the totems during the festival, and they threw themselves on the ground to beg the God of the Sea to forgive them. He appeared briefly refusing to help or forgive them, before leaving. That night they were lashed with the worst storm they had seen in decades. It was a storm for the legends, and it destroyed much of the crops that they had not had space to store somewhere dry.

Somma felt the guilt of everything weighing down on him. The day after the storm, he meant to slip away into the forest. He wanted to go to the mountain that brought him closest to the sky: the Wise Owl's nest. Bidzil, Chaska, and Khickhim were waiting. They each had a pack similar to his.

"You did not think that we would let you do this alone, did you?" Khickhim asked.

"How did you know that I was planning on taking this pilgrimage?" Somma asked, humbled by his friends.

"We have known you all of your life," Chaska reminded him. "You feel responsible, and you will ask the wise Owl."

Somma did not know if he was happy or annoyed that he was known so well. "This is not something that you need to help me with. I asked the questions."

"And we could not answer your questions," Bidzil told him. "We doubted too." The other two friends nodded in agreement. Somma shook his head and started leading the pack. They would stay with him. That was what friends did.

They traveled through the forests, plains, dry-lands, and marshes. Their goal ever in sight. It was the tallest of the peaks, hidden by clouds for most of the year. It was on the tip of that mountain that Sea and Sky first took form and met. Later Owl had built a nest there in the sacred space.

The walk took three days, and he found the company made the tedium bearable. Shortly after the daybreak of the third day, they arrived. It would take most of the day, or more, to climb this mountain. The group climbed the trail for all of the day and the night, and by the time the day broke on the fourth day, they had arrived. The view from the plateau was amazing. They could look over the entire rock. Chaska with his great eyes could even see the outlines of the nearest islands.

Somma stepped away from his friends and approached the nesting area alone. It surprised him that the owls nested in huts, much like the human ones. They were the same colour as the stone but seemed to be made something else entirely. The wise Owl stepped forward to meet him. Somma looked up to see all of the large Owl.

"Wise Owl, I need your help," Somma said, looking at the inhuman eyes without blinking. He dug out a gift for the great bird, three delicate feathers made out of wood and painted in brilliant colours.

"I have been waiting for you, human kin of my soul," the bird stated. "It has taken much longer than I thought it would." The large white bird could not smile, but Somma heard it in the words. It tilted its head to the side in the eerie way of the night birds. "Kyree, a gift," it called.

A tiny owlet dashed out of the nest, its feathers still looking downy and new. It came to the humans' knee. "Gift?" it asked.

Somma handed the wooden feathers to the baby bird. Each feather was as long as his forearm. The little bird took them with delight, bobbed twice and darted back to the nest.

"Come, we shall talk better where we do not keep the children awake," the Owl hooted. Together they walked towards the other humans: the wise Owl with a wobbling, bow-legged stride and the human with a much smoother one.

"Wise Owl," Bidzil, Chaska, and Khickhim said as one when he was close to them.

"We are going to talk where we are less likely to keep the owlets up," Somma told his friends with a smile.

"Where are we less likely to wake the owlets?" Khickhim asked, fearing what she knew had to be the right answer.

"Dooown," the Owl said, his beak drawing out the word.

Bidzil sighed a deep breath. It had taken them many, many hours to walk all the way up here. "I suppose we would have to go back down again at some point anyway."

The large bird clacked its beak in amusement and then lifted off with a swirling wind that buffeted them.

"Did you give him the gift you made?" Chaska asked. He had looked on the feathers made so perfectly and had coveted them.

"I did, and the Wise Owl gave them to his child," Somma said. "But I will make some for you, Chaska," he promised.

Together they made their way down the winding path that had been worn into the side of the mountain. The trial was not smooth or easy, but it could be traveled by anyone that was seeking enlightenment with a determined heart.

The walk back down took almost as long as the walk up, and by the time they arrived, there was a soreness in each of them, including the powerful Bidzil. Night was laying its blanket across the sky, and tiny diamonds twinkled in the dark cobalt.

"The gloaming hour," the great Owl stated from its perch in a thick tree. "Such an inspirational time of the day, is it not?"

"Yes," Somma panted with some pain towards his god of choice.

Again the beak clacked in amusement. "Now cousins, tell me what you seek to know." Somma grimaced; all that walking and the wise Owl did not seem to be as wise as he was thought to be. The Owl tilted his head almost all the way around, his eyes not leaving the boy and his feathers fluffed in irritation. "It is not that I do not know the situation, little cousin, but it is a show of respect to ask."

"I am sorry, Wise Owl," Somma said with a blush. "I am tired, and it has been many long months of worry."

"You are young," the Owl accepted the apology.

"The God of the Sea has chosen to punish us for not worshiping him. We have been without the ability to trade, and there are things that we need that we cannot get because of this punishment. We do not have enough food to last until the spring, and there was a storm that ruined a lot of what we had. He will not take our apologies or our prayers. We need help."

"I understand your plight," the wise Owl said. He crouched down until he was only slightly taller than the human that beseeched him. "I shall need to think on this. Stay here for two days. I will meet you at this time on the second day," the Owl instructed and then flew away.

They watched the large white Owl as it flew so easily across the barricade that kept them trapped and helpless.

"Let us set up our tents," Chaska said, putting a hand on Somma's shoulder, pulling his attention away from the white ghost. Somma nodded, and the four of them made the camp ready. During the evening, they were visited by little Kyree who took the time to give them a gift, a rabbit. It was a welcome treat after three days of travel bread and berries. They thanked the owlet before cooking the rabbit.

Sleep came easily that night; however, the next day dragged with nothing to do. Somma wondered how angry his father was with him. He had left and was not doing his share of the chores. The others would be in as much trouble for leaving during a time when every hand was needed.

The next day dragged for the four youths. Their life was one of community and of giving and take. That was how it had been since they could toddle around at their parents' sides. Right now, they were not giving, not helping. Even Bidzil's exercises could not help to pass the time or lessen the regret.

The little owlet came to visit them; he sat in the tree and watched over them. The humans spoke to the owl, it listened, but did not respond. When it got fully dark, the owlet took flight through the woods.

The second day was even worse than the first. Khickhim had managed to catch another rabbit: a gift for the wise Owl for his help.

"Good gloaming, cousins," the wise Owl welcomed at the exact moment he had said he would return. In his claws, he carried a creature that none of the humans had ever seen. Carefully he set it down.

"What is that?" Bidzil asked, looking at the strange animal. It looked like a very large dog. It was gray and shaggy, and its eyes were slitted in a way that did not look even slightly cat-like. It had long ears that flicked around.

"This is a goat," the Owl said with pride. "He comes from the bigger island."

"I don't understand," Somma said, stepping towards the goat; it had a pungent odor. "How will a goat be able to help us?"

"There is much that you do not understand, young one," the Owl admonished. "A goat has the ability to eat anything, and that will be useful. I have also brought back..."

"Are these the humans you sought me for?" asked the god newly arrived in the camp. She wore her human shape, but her colours were hard to look upon. She was mostly transparent with hair the colour of a sky at sunset and wearing a white cloud-like dress.

"They are, great God of the Sky." The Owl bobbed in reverence.

The god stepped closer to them, looking at each one with eyes the colour of the sky on a cloudless day. Her eyes lingered the longest on Khickhim, examining her outline. "You know I cannot make the God of the Sea change his mind," the god said.

"I would not ask that of you," the Owl replied, as at ease with humanity as with the great gods. "I need help creating something new." The god smiled. "Pack up your stuff, humans, we are going to the village," the Owl instructed.

Most of the camp had been broken before the Owl had arrived. Chaska offered the wise Owl and the god the rabbit they had killed for them. The Owl took it, but the god showed no interest.

"Take hold, humans," the God of the Sky commanded.

The humans rushed to obey. In moments, the god and the humans flew through the air. The Owl followed behind with the goat being carried gently in its talons. What took them three days to walk rushed below them in heartbeats. They were back home in minutes. Khickhim slapped the drum skin to get the attention of the village.

The people gathered in droves and in trickles. They met in the grand hall, the large Owl's top feathers almost brushing the ceiling. The people stared at the Owl and his companion, the great god.

"I am here, cousins, because one of you has come to me and has asked for help," the Owl spoke when all the seats were full. "I have asked the God of the Sky to help us as well. I have an idea."

Waves of murmurs washed around the room. "We have tried everything," the chief said miserably.

"You have tried everything that a human can do, not everything that a god can do," corrected the God of the Sky.

"We are going to create a creature to help you," the Owl took over; the population had quieted when the Great God spoke. "Somma," he called. The young human walked into the room; he had a hand in the tufted mane of an unusual creature. "This is a goat," the Owl continued, "He can eat anything. We are going to combine him with a fish and set him free in the sea."

"I can get you a fish," Ziibiin offered. He was up and away before anyone could say a thing.

"Your father is very energetic," the Owl clacked to the

boy leading the goat. Somma smiled. It was true, and he loved his father for it. "Let us follow Ziibiin. We will create the creature there," the Owl offered. The God of the Sky looked delighted with the prospect.

"Wise Owl," a small voice interrupted the exodus. "Won't the God of the Sea be able to command the g... goatfish?" She stumbled over the strange words.

"Not at all, young one," the Owl spoke softly, encouraging the questions of the young. "The goat's brain is a creature of the land; the God of the Sea will not have any control of him."

She smiled and rushed out to find her mother's hand to hold. The Owl watched with a pleased air about him.

The beach was getting crowded with all the people, the God of the Sky, the great Owl, the goat, and the large fish that Ziibiin pulled in behind him. By the size of it, the Owl knew that the Otter had smiled on this task.

"Somma, Ziibiin, come forward," the God of the Sky commanded. Her voice, like that of the God of the Sea, reached everyone without issue. The father and son stepped forward, each bringing with them an animal. "Step back," they were instructed when the God of the Sky took their burden. They did.

Around the gods, a screening of hazy air blocked the view of the people. Watch though they did, they could not see what was happening, and in the minds of the villagers, many new tales were being born.

It took much less time than the humans had thought it would before the haze dropped away, and two proud gods displayed their creation. "Welcome the newest of the kin," the God of the Sky said. "The Capricorn."

The creature that stood dazed and confused on the sand was half as tall again as the tallest of the men. He was wide, and he was scary looking. He had long curling horns, and the front half was that of a goat with very sharp cloven hooves. The body stayed that of a goat until it got to the hips where it turned to a fish's tail. The tail was blue with very wide fins. "Hungry," he gasped; the gills in his neck, hidden in the shaggy fur, opened and closed.

"Go," the God of the Sky commanded and then faded into nothing. The Capricorn dragged himself slowly forward. When the water licked at its hooves for the first time, elation waved over him and he reared back on his tail and then flung himself into the surf.

In more time than it took to create him, the Capricorn resurfaced. "Hungry," he said as soon as he was above the water.

"Here," Arikcha said to Ziibiin. "Feed him this." The old soothsayer passed the younger man the dried, wrapped remains that Ziibiin had first brought back with him when the barrier was erected.

"Eat," the wise Owl instructed the Capricorn. "See these and eat these and keep these waters free of them."

The Capricorn did as the god said, taking the food gently from Ziibiin's hands. "Thank you," the Capricorn said and rolled away into the water seeking more food.

"In three days, you may take your boats from here and resume your trade," the wise Owl instructed and then flew back to his nest to see his family.

The days were a flurry of activity as any damage to the hulls were scoured and fixed. Trade goods were fixed, finished, and packed. The air of the festival filled the chilly days.

On the third day, the boats headed into the water. Megis' ship was in the lead, her courage a thing of wonder. In the waves, the Capricorn danced and frolicked with the large fish. He was a giant in their midst.

When the time of crossing came, Megis took a deep breath and followed the Capricorn. Seconds ticked by as they crossed the perilous gap, and then she let out a breath and thanked the God of the Sky, the wise Owl and her own spirit-kin the Salmon god, and mostly the Capricon.

In a few days, things went back almost to normal. The boats came and went as they had before, although they took longer to make the voyage, having to angle around the stone ring. More than one boat with an inexperienced captain at the helm drove itself into the stones, but the Capricorn brought everyone back alive. On the other side of the coin, the village was seeing some advantage of having the breakwaters to stop the worst of storm-driven waves from reaching the beaches or the village.

Somma and his friends were exalted for the part that they played in the salvation of the island, and their part in the cause was forgotten. Somma was made a soothsayer and a speaker of the gods.

"The Gila monster taught them preservation and survival, the bear taught them courage, the raccoon taught them resourcefulness, and so on. Now every year, we have this festival in honour of the animals and the gods," Somma said with a smile looking out on the faces of the youths that were seated on the floor near his chair as he told the first of many stories that the soothsayers would tell this day.

This was his only one as the newest soothsayers, but

there was a pride in his heart at the way they looked at him with awed wonder.

It was a festival day, and Arikcha would take over soon when the older youths woke. Despite the celebrations, however, there was nervous energy riding under the surface, one that made everyone feel like it was their duty to live this day to its fullest with no idea what the time of gloaming would bring.

The most popular attraction of the festival was the Capricorn. He had been decorated and was being exalted. For his part, he was giving rides in the ocean. He had grown big and could easily accommodate five or six people on his back without fear they would slide off. He enjoyed the treats of the land: apples, carrots, and cabbage would earn you slobbery thanks and sometimes a kiss.

Though they fought it, the time came where the sun touched the land, and the time of praise and the forest of the totem was opened. The three totems that stood in the place of honour were the totem to the God of the Sky, the totem to the wise Owl and the totem to the Capricorn.

When the last of the villagers stepped off the grounds again, the crash of the waves sounded as the God of the Sea once again stood in the middle of the people.

"Humans, I have decided that you have paid appropriate homage at this festival," the God of the Sea said with a flourish. "I shall withdraw my punishment and offer my patronage."

The people of the village stood silently, looking to their neighbours. With the help of the Capricorn, they had forgotten it was a punishment.

"You may praise me for my generosity of spirit and

forgiving nature," the God of the Sea told them, mistaking their reservation for admiration and not the confusion it was.

Somma took a hesitant step forward. "We are grateful for your forgiveness," the youth stated respectfully, "but..."

"I know you," the God of the Sea interrupted. "You were the boy that started this at the last festival." Somma bowed but waited for the god to be ready to listen. "It is good you have learned to properly respect those that deserve your worship."

"Yes, God of the Sea, I have learned a lot about respect." Somma nodded his head in respect. "And with that in mind, I do humbly wish to ask you what will become of the Capricorn?"

"How would I know, and why should I care? He is not one of my creations," the God of the Sea told the human youth.

"Without the plants of the barrier rocks, he will starve and die. We owe him much," Somma pleaded.

"If he will die without the plants, so be it. He is getting to be too big to live in my sea," the God of the Sea stated without concern.

"Do not worry, human," another voice spoke into the clearing. A voice that was no kinder or more sympathetic, but it was a voice that was accompanied by a warm afternoon breeze. In the gloaming, it was difficult to see the God of the Sky.

"You have come to accept the accolades of these humans as well?" the God of the Sea asked the God of the Sky.

"I have come to see that no harm comes to one of my creations," the God of the Sky said to the God of the Sea contemptuously.

The wise Owl landed between the two greater gods. It bowed to the God of the Sea respectfully. "The Capricorn has proven himself helpful, courageous, trust-worthy, making him worthy of the praise that he has received this festival," the lesser god said, raising a wing when the God of the Sea opened his mouth. "We have also seen that he is growing too big living off the fruits of the sea. The God of the Sky and I have come up with a fitting reward for his services." The bird paused.

"What will you do with him?" Somma asked.

"He will be granted immortality, and he will be taken to live in the sky where he can grow as big as he wants to eat whatever he so pleases," the God of the Sky answered, growing impatient.

"But what of us; how will we be able to see him and thank him for what he has done?" Somma asked.

"You will be able to see him in the stars on clear nights. He will watch over you as he has already," the wise Owl said. Then the Owl launched into the sky, followed closely by the God of the Sky. Together they grabbed the mighty Capricorn and took him into the up, up, up.

By the time anyone looked around the earth again, the God of the Sea had vanished as well. As the Owl had promised, it was easy to see the stars of Capricorn shimmer into existence, and though the human-kin could not see it, the Capricorn continued to eat all the debris in the sky, keeping the nights clear.

Afterword

In Newfoundland and Labrador, you will often hear the phrase "who knit you" used to ask who a person's family is. We hope you have come to the end of this collection with a different sense of this, for the storytellers of mythology play a part in knitting us, too.

We hope you will continue seeking out the myths and legends that have contributed to the lives of the people around you. As writers, we carry with us the centuries of cultural imagination that came before us. We invite you, the reader, to enter those worlds. Continue seeking them out past the covers of this volume. Honour the storytellers who came before us, and help amplify the stories of those who have historically been silenced.

You'll find new stories all around you if you remember to stay open to them.

Ellen Curtis and Erin Vance
Editors

ON THE COVER

The cover image to this year's anthology was was created by Kit Sora of Kit Sora Photography, with model Mae Dalton-Summers.

The photo was part of a series taken in February 2018 and has been reproduced with permission.

Both Dalton-Summers and Sora have used visual art and photograpghy to push forward the boundaries artistic expression and genre fiction in Newfoundland and Labrador.

Kit Sora:
The Artobiography

Available now from Engen.

MYTHOLOGY FROM THE ROCK

EDITED BY ELLEN CURTIS & ERIN VANCE

For thousands of years, myths and legends have shaped the stories that humanity tells about themselves and the world around them. Now, twenty-six incredible Canadian authors offer new spins and fresh takes on those pieces of our shared cultural touchstones.

This collection honours that legacy with twenty-nine short stories highlighting the best of the modern interpretations of mythology, from minds like Ali House (*The Segment Delta Archives*), AJ Ryan (*The Secret of the Ohks*), and Jennifer Shelby (*Plague of the Dreamless*)! With introduction from Dr. Christopher Lockett!

Edited by Erin Vance and Ellen Curtis, this collection showcases the wonder and astonishment that fuelled the first stories and continues to ignite the passions of storytellers to this day!

www.ingramcontent.com/pod-product-compliance
Lightning Source LLC
Chambersburg PA
CBHW020414030726
47495CB00006B/1506

9781774780305